Sebastian leaned toward her, placing one hand on her waist and drawing her against his chest. His other hand cradled the back of her head, forcing her chin up. Gazing into his eyes, she realized he was going to kiss her.

A torrent of conflicting emotions surged through Eleanor. Being in Sebastian's arms made her feel like someone she wasn't—daring, almost wicked.

And she liked it.

A half smile played on Sebastian's full, sensual lips. "I'm going to kiss you now, Eleanor."

She felt her body tighten, her gaze roving over his face. His expression told her the truth   he was indeed about to kiss her. Her heart skipped in anticipation, certain that his kiss would be as possessive and hungry as the intense gleam darkening his eyes . . .

Books by Adrienne Basso

HIS WICKED EMBRACE

HIS NOBLE PROMISE

TO WED A VISCOUNT

TO PROTECT AN HEIRESS

TO TEMPT A ROGUE

THE WEDDING DECEPTION

THE CHRISTMAS HEIRESS

HIGHLAND VAMPIRE

HOW TO ENJOY A SCANDAL

NATURE OF THE BEAST

THE CHRISTMAS COUNTESS

HOW TO SEDUCE A SINNER

A LITTLE BIT SINFUL

Published by Kensington Publishing Corporation

A Little Bit
SINFUL

ADRIENNE BASSO

ZEBRA BOOKS
KENSINGTON PUBLISHING CORP.
http://www.kensingtonbooks.com

ZEBRA BOOKS are published by

Kensington Publishing Corp.
119 West 40th Street
New York, NY 10018

All Kensington titles, imprints, and distributed lines are available at special quantity discounts for bulk purchases for sales promotion, premiums, fund-raising, educational, or institutional use.

Special book excerpts or customized printings can also be created to fit specific needs. For details, write or phone the office of the Kensington Special Sales Manager: Attn. Special Sales Department. Kensington Publishing Corp., 119 West 40th Street, New York, NY 10018. Phone: 1-800-221-2647.

ISBN-13: 978-1-4201-1190-3
ISBN-10: 1-4201-1190-6

First Printing: January 2011

10 9 8 7 6 5 4 3 2 1

Printed in the United States of America

Dedicated with love to Ann White Braun

From the girls we were,
to the women we have become,
our friendship has not only endured,
but grown stronger.
I will always treasure the years of memories,
Annie—the joys, sorrows, laughter, and tears—
and look forward to many, many more.

Chapter 1

"Everyone, please gather closer."

The minister's voice, deep and solemn, echoed among the well-dressed group, shattering the stillness. Jaw clenched, eyes dry, Sebastian Dodd, Viscount Benton, took a step forward, swaying slightly as the bright sunshine momentarily blinded him. Following his lead, the sparse crowd of mourners standing behind him also moved, yet kept a respectful distance.

How very wrong it all feels, Sebastian thought, shifting his stance to block the sun's rays from his eyes. The weather should be chilly and damp and gray, with raindrops pelting their faces, the ground beneath their feet soaked and muddy. Instead there was warmth and sunshine, with a sky as blue as a robin's egg, solid, thick green grass, and a profusion of exuberant spring wildflowers.

Though he stood alone, Sebastian was mindful of the people gathered behind him. A few distant relatives, whom he wished had not bothered to make the journey, and an even smaller group of friends, whose presence made him feel a profound sense of gratitude.

"The Countess of Marchdale was a noble woman, possessing a strong character and a charitable heart. She was a pillar of the community, a shining example of a fine and genteel female," the minister proclaimed. "Heaven will most assuredly welcome this good lady with open arms."

Sebastian could not hold back his smile. His grandmother had been a feisty, opinionated woman who had ruffled more than her share of feathers, especially in the later years of her life. She would have laughed out loud upon hearing the minister's words, and then rapped his knuckles sharply before scolding him for exaggerating. The countess was never one to suffer false praise. Even at her own funeral.

As for her heavenly ascent, well, if such a place did exist, the countess's admittance was hardly guaranteed. She had not led an angelic life, nor a particularly pious one. She had enjoyed fully the excesses and privileges of her rank and wealth as well as—Sebastian always suspected—the delights of the flesh. After all, she had buried three husbands, each younger than her.

If, by some divine miracle, his grandmother did pass through the gates of St. Peter, Sebastian was confident that within minutes of arriving she would be expressing her opinion on how things could be improved in that world. And this one, too.

"Let us pray," the minister commanded.

Behind him, a soft chorus of voices blended together. The familiar words sprang from Sebastian's lips as he joined in, marveling at the power of memory, for it had been a very long time since he had spoken any words of prayer. At the conclusion, Sebastian lifted his bowed head and for the first time looked into the deep, dark hole that had been dug in the ground.

A shudder rippled through him. It seemed impossible to imagine his grandmother spending eternity in that darkness, cut off from everything she had once loved.

At the minister's command, four burly workmen took up their positions and began lowering the casket. *Farewell.* Sebastian voiced his final good-bye silently, yet the moment the thought solidified, a wave of sorrow rose from deep within his chest, catching him unawares. He had never been a man who allowed sincere emotions to easily flow. The tragedies of his life had taught him that true feelings were meant to be private. It was best to hold them close and keep them hidden.

The countess's death had not been unexpected. She was an elderly woman whose normally robust health had been compromised by a persistent winter illness. The day before she died she had told him that she was weary of feeling unwell and melancholy over the loss of her active, buoyant lifestyle. She confessed she was at last ready to leave this earth and begin her final adventure.

Sebastian took a deep breath. She might have been ready to depart, but he wasn't prepared to see her go. She had pestered and plagued him all of his adult life, attempting to dictate everything from the meals he ate to the clothes he wore, from the items on which he spent his money to the company he kept. She was quick to find fault and even quicker to express her displeasure.

But the countess had also protected her only grandchild with a maternal tenacity that had no equal. Her loyalty was unmatched, her love always given lavishly. Accepting the finality of her death was difficult and thus Sebastian forced himself to stare at the casket as it was slowly lowered into the ground.

It seemed to take forever.

Sebastian heard a sob, then a loud sniffle. One of the female mourners was crying, most likely his grandmother's cousin Sarah. She was a self-proclaimed delicate woman who never missed an opportunity to showcase her sensitive nature. He wondered idly if she attended many funerals, since clearly that would be the best venue to demonstrate her frail constitution.

The sobbing grew louder. Though he dismissed it in his mind as pure artifice, the mournful sound struck a chord. Sebastian felt the tightening in his chest increase. A combination of grief, coupled with the need to suppress it, he decided. He scowled, wanting desperately to turn and walk away, but that would be unpardonably rude. He owed it to his grandmother's memory to act as she would have wished, with dignity and decorum. Two qualities she often lamented he lacked in sufficient quantity.

As he fought to capture and tame his rioting emotions, Sebastian became aware of someone standing very near. Apparently one of the mourners had broken ranks and approached him. Who would dare to be so brave?

Please, dear Lord, let it not be cousin Sarah.

Sebastian inhaled and gritted his teeth. Yet before he could turn and face this unknown individual, he felt the gentle brush of feminine fingertips against his gloved hand, then caught a whiff of fresh lemons. *Emma.* The tightness twisting in his chest eased.

Dearest Emma. She was such a compassionate girl. He imagined she had spent the entire service with her eyes trained upon him, waiting for the precise moment when he faltered, ever at the ready to come to his aid when he needed her most. Heedless of the proprieties, Sebastian accepted Emma's comfort, intimately entwining his fingers with hers.

Strange how such a small, dainty hand could instill such strength inside him, letting him know that he was not entirely alone. At least not for the moment.

Cousin Sarah's lusty sobs abruptly ceased, her sniffles replaced by an indignant gasp. Apparently the scandal of holding a woman's hand—an unmarried woman, to whom he was not engaged—was enough to shock the sorrow from Sarah's breast and replace it with horror. Sebastian felt Emma sway slightly and realized she too had heard that gasp of disapproval.

Fearing Emma might pull away, he squeezed her fingers. Without hesitation she returned the gesture. His breathing once again grew steady and he felt a profound sense of relief that Emma was not easily intimidated by the rigid rules of society.

Under the minister's direction, they recited one

final prayer and then it was over. In a daze, Sebastian turned swiftly, facing the group of mourners, his hand still tightly clutching Emma's.

"Thank you all for coming this morning. Though it is more modest to say that the countess would have been humbled by this show of respect and affection, those of us who knew and loved her know the truth of the matter." He halted, swallowing back the lump of grief that had risen up in his throat. "Cook has prepared an enormous luncheon. Please, let us all retire to the manor and partake of this hearty fare."

The majority of mourners obediently turned and headed toward the carriages. The family plot where the countess had been laid to rest was in a picturesque spot bordering the estate's great woods. Though Sebastian would have preferred walking the mile to the manor house, it was unthinkable to expect his older relations to do the same.

"Would you like to ride in my coach, Benton? There's plenty of room."

Sebastian paused, then shook his head at the man who had spoken. Carter Grayson, Marquess of Atwood, was one of only two men on this earth he respected utterly, trusted completely, and genuinely liked. They had attended Eaton and later Oxford together, forging a friendship as boys that had deepened and strengthened as they became men.

They shared similar viewpoints on most matters and enjoyed a vigorous debate when their opinions clashed. Atwood's marriage last year to Dorothea Ellingham had done little to diminish this male bond, though he was starting to develop what Sebastian regarded as an unhealthy obsession with propriety. Alas, marriage and respectability could do that to even the most hedonistic of men.

The marquess was also Emma's brother-in-law.

"If you'd rather not go with Atwood and Lady Dorothea, you can ride with me," Peter Dawson suggested.

Dawson had also been a classmate and was the only other man Sebastian considered a true friend. Possessing a quiet, cerebral personality, Dawson was the levelheaded, thoughtful balance in the trio of friends, the one who had kept them all from total disgrace. Yet he still knew how to have fun.

"My coachman has instructions to return for me after he has delivered my relations safely to the manor's front door," Sebastian replied. "I'll wait for him."

"I'll wait too," Emma quickly volunteered.

"Really, Emma, you should come with us," Lady Dorothea admonished in a soft voice. "I'm sure the viscount would appreciate a few minutes of privacy."

"Oh, goodness. I hadn't realized," Emma replied.

Sebastian felt her stiffen and he panicked, thinking she would pull away. "I would prefer that Emma stay with me. If you don't object?"

Sebastian looked directly at Lady Dorothea as he spoke, but the question was obviously intended for both her and her husband. Emma might be Dorothea's younger sister, but it was the marquess who protected her. Still, if Lady Dorothea disapproved, Sebastian knew Emma would be gone in the blink of an eye.

Lady Dorothea took a deep breath as if striving for patience and understanding. She was a kind woman and he knew she cared about him, knew she was sincerely sympathetic over the death of his grandmother. Yet his roguish reputation and scandalous deeds made her leery about leaving her seventeen-year-old sister alone with him in so isolated a location. *Smart woman.*

Lady Dorothea turned toward her husband. Atwood grimaced, then deliberately glanced down at the hand in which Sebastian held Emma's. Tightening his grip, Sebastian tucked it closer to his chest. Atwood's brow rose in a disapproving manner, but he said nothing.

"We will see you both shortly?" Atwood finally asked.

It was more of a command than a question. Sebastian nodded.

It was quiet after they left. Hand in hand, Sebastian and Emma walked through the small cemetery, passing his ancestors' well-tended graves.

"'Tis a pretty spot," Emma remarked.

"Yes, all things considered." Sebastian gazed into the distance, taking note of the sea of blue wildflowers dotting the landscape, their vibrant color a sharp foil to the rich, green grass. Funny, his grandmother had always had a particular fondness for any shade of blue.

"You know, Sebastian, you might feel better if you cried," Emma said. "There is no shame in feeling such deep sorrow at your loss. I vow, I sobbed for weeks when my parents died."

"You were five years old."

Emma grunted. For the first time that day, Sebastian laughed. He knew she wanted to argue with him, to press her point, but her kind heart would not allow her to challenge him on such a sad day.

He swung their clasped hands up to his face, pressing her gloved knuckles against his cheek. Then he lowered his arm and tucked her hand in the crook of his elbow, making it all proper and correct between them. Well, except for the lack of a chaperone.

"Did you know that I saw the countess the day before she died?" Emma asked.

Sebastian nodded. "She spoke briefly of your visit. It was kind of you to think of her. Not many bothered to call on a sick old woman."

"In addition to my visit, I delivered something. Since you haven't said anything about it, I assume your grandmother didn't speak of it."

"She only told me that you had called."

Emma's brows knit together with uncertainty. "I know she wanted to show it to you, but I imagine she lacked the strength." Emma paused. "I brought her your portrait."

"You finished it?"

"Yes. The main portion had been completed for several weeks. I was worried about rushing the finishing touches, but I knew the countess did not have much longer to live. Thankfully, having a shortened deadline did not hinder my work. I believe she was very pleased with the final result," Emma concluded modestly.

Sebastian felt a tug of wistfulness. He was glad that the countess had seen the work finished, yet felt sorry that they had not had the chance to view the portrait together, especially since it had been his grandmother's idea.

Though she was young, and a female, Emma's artistic talent had impressed the countess. Without hesitation, and over Sebastian's protests, his grandmother had commissioned the portrait. But his initial grumbling quickly faded. Emma was not a giggling, spoiled debutante who dabbled with her brushes and colors. She was a serious artist with a phenomenal talent.

Spending time sitting for the painting had given Sebastian a rare gift. A friendship with Emma, his first with a member of the opposite sex. It was something he valued greatly.

"Tell me, do I look impossibly handsome in my portrait?" he asked.

"I am an artist, Sebastian, not a magician."

"You are a cheeky brat," he stated emphatically.

Emma tugged insistently on his arm. "And you are far too vain. Impossibly handsome, indeed. I painted you as you are, though the countess thought I might have embellished the width of your shoulders and the firmness of your jaw."

"Ah, so the women will be impressed?"

"Yes, they shall be swooning in alarming numbers when they gaze upon the splendor of your male beauty."

"Rendered speechless, perhaps?"

"Struck dumb," Emma insisted.

"Alas, that is hardly difficult for many a young lady in society."

Emma's brow arched the tiniest fraction. 'Twas far too worldly a gesture for such an innocent young woman. "Your opinion of the gentler sex is alarmingly insulting. We are not all a bunch of ninnies."

"I can count on one hand the number of women who possess more brains than God gave a goose."

Emma shook her head. "Have you ever considered that the reason there are so many foolish, empty-headed young women littered throughout society is because they are deliberately kept ignorant by the men who seek to control them?"

"Protect them," he countered.

"Rubbish." Emma sighed loudly. "You don't believe that any more than I do."

Sebastian admired the way her chin angled up when she grew perturbed. She was a very pretty girl. A few years of maturity on her face and figure and Emma would become a truly stunning woman.

"Though you are loath to acknowledge it, we both know there are females in society who do indeed require male protection, mostly to save them from themselves," he said. "I daresay you've already met one or two of these types this Season. Trust me, there will be others."

"Honestly, Sebastian, you are such an old curmudgeon at times. I don't understand how you can possibly have such a dashing reputation."

"I confess to working rather hard at it." Sebastian smiled. This was just the kind of distracting conversation he needed right now. In a few minutes he would have to face his relatives and then later the reading of the will. Knowing his grandmother, there were bound to be some surprises.

They reached the end of the short row of graves and turned to walk up the next. Sebastian glanced idly to his left, where his eyes set upon a tall, marble headstone. Evangeline Katherine Maria Dodd, fifth Countess of Benton. *Mother.*

The lightness of the moment vanished. For a fraction of a second Sebastian felt a bolt of fear so intense it nearly knocked him off his feet. Coldness seeped into his chest, spreading rapidly across his skin.

The rhythmic, creaking sound of a swaying rope echoed inside his brain and he shut his eyes tightly trying to keep at bay what was sure to follow. Yet the image materialized. Every inch as horrific as it had been on that fateful afternoon nearly eighteen years ago.

He had been home from school on holiday, happy to once again be at Chaswick Manor. He was happiest of all, however, to be reunited with his mother. It was a secret he kept from even his closest schoolmates, knowing they would tease him mercilessly about how dearly he loved her.

Sebastian's father had died when he was very young, leaving no lasting memories. Though there were moments when he felt the loss of a father, they never lasted, thanks to his mother.

The countess had been a beautiful woman. She had not remarried, but instead devoted herself to her only child, taking an active interest in everything he did. She had cried copious tears when he left for school, wrote faithfully to him every week, and made it seem like a special holiday whenever he came home.

Yet on this particular visit there was something very different about the viscountess. She was distant and preoccupied, at times quick to anger, at others melting into puddles of tears without cause or provocation. She spared hardly a glance at her son, keeping to her rooms, taking her meals alone, never venturing far from the manor house.

There were no special hugs, no affectionate ruffling of his hair, no twinges of pride in her voice when she spoke to him. His numerous attempts to coax a smile from her lips were unsuccessful. Worried that the reports of his less than perfect behavior and his average grades were the cause of this unwelcome change, Sebastian set out one afternoon to gather the largest bouquet of wildflowers he could find.

It had taken him nearly an hour, but the result was spectacular. Hoping the gesture would lift her spirits and return to her face the smile he so treasured, Sebastian knocked on his mother's bedchamber door.

There was no answer. He knocked harder and still no response. He should have left, but no, his stubborn nature would not allow him to be so easily defeated. Pushing the door open, he entered the room and beheld a sight that made his blood run cold.

Sebastian shuddered, unable to control his emotions, for in that instant he was once again a twelve-year-old boy, frightened and horrified at his gruesome discovery.

The creaking of the swaying rope was a mesmerizing noise. It had held him motionless as he stared at the incomprehensible sight. A rope had been tied to the sturdy drapery rod positioned across the long bank of windows. Dangling from it was the still, limp body of a woman. His mother.

She was dressed in a silver evening gown. One of her slippers had fallen off and the white silk of her stocking was visible from toe to heel. Her normally neat, coiffured hair was in wild disarray, her long, slender, white neck bruised and stretched where the rope was tightly pressed against it. Her lips were blue and swollen, her eyes wide open and staring sightless into the abyss.

Sebastian had no idea how long he stood there. He might have made a sound, or perhaps he had remained silent. The next clear memory he had of himself was that of sitting with his grandmother in the drawing room, her face taut with sadness and fear as she repeated over and over that he must never speak of this to anyone. No one must ever know that the Viscountess of Benton had taken her own life.

"Sebastian?"

The sound of Emma's voice pulled him from the past into the present. He lifted his lashes and met a pair of concerned blue eyes.

"I'm fine." He nodded, a weak attempt to convince himself of that untruth, then glanced away to regain his composure. Emma had an artist's eye, the ability to see right down to a person's soul. He did not want the darkness inside him to touch her, to taint her in any way.

The silence stretched between them. Sebastian squinted toward the road. Was that the carriage? Yes, he could see it clearly. He practically pulled Emma away from the graveyard, a desperate attempt to escape from his memories.

If only it were so easy.

Emma raised her eyebrows but said nothing until they were alone in the coach.

"You seem rather upset, Sebastian. Would it help to talk about it?"

He met her concerned eyes. It was tempting, so very tempting to unburden himself. Yet he could not. In his heart he knew that Emma would listen, would sympathize, would not judge. But old habits are hard to break and he had given his word to his grandmother. No one must ever know the truth.

For years he had suffered nightmares, desperate to know what had driven his mother to such a hideous act. Clearly her anguish had been unbearable, beyond desperation. His grandmother had refused to discuss anything pertaining to the death of her daughter-in-law, but when Sebastian reached his twenty-first birthday he confronted his grandmother, refusing to be denied.

"It does no good to speak ill of the dead," the countess had insisted.

Sebastian could still feel the rage and hurt that had risen up from deep inside him. "God damn it! She was my mother. I think the very least I am owed is an explanation."

"Her life was an utter shambles," the countess had finally confessed, "because of a man."

"A man? What man?"

"George Collins, the Earl of Hetfield." The sigh the countess expelled had been filled with sadness. "She met him earlier that year at a house party. He was very recently widowed and she understood that kind of loss. They grew close very quickly."

"How close?"

"Close enough for her to become pregnant with his child." The countess had blurted that out, seeming to shock herself with the admission. "Evangeline was my daughter through marriage, yet I loved her as if she were my own flesh and blood. I was grateful she came to me when she found herself in trouble and the earl refused to answer her letters, refused even to see her. But he saw me."

"You went to him?"

"I did. He tried to tarnish your mother in my eyes, telling me shocking, scandalous lies, but I wouldn't hear of it. I demanded he do the right thing and marry her. He refused. He was such an odious man, lacking in feeling and honor. I would have pressed the matter more strongly but soon realized she was better off without him."

"Apparently not."

The countess's eyes had welled with tears. "I had no notion of how distressed she was, how disgraced she felt. I offered alternatives, suggested we go abroad together so she could have the baby in private. I vowed to find a good home for the child with loving parents to raise it. Perhaps she could even visit them, giving her a chance to form some connection with the child. She told me she would think upon it, yet two days later . . ."

"She hung herself." Sebastian remembered how calmly he had spoken those words, saying them aloud for the first time.

"I blame myself for not doing more to help her, to comfort her," the countess had said, weeping softly.

"I blame Hetfield. He murdered my mother as assuredly as if he placed the noose around her neck with his own hands. For that he must be made to pay."

"Sebastian, no." The countess had risen from her chair. Her voice rasping and slow, she fought back tears. "You must put those thoughts out of your mind this instant. I beg of you, for my sake. I too clamor for revenge, but it will be a hollow victory indeed if you are injured or worse. You must promise me that you will leave it alone. Promise me."

"Grandmother—"

"Promise me! Give me your word that you will stay away from the earl."

"I promise."

Even all these years later Sebastian could still recall how flat his voice was as he had made that vow, could easily remember how hollow he had felt inside. He had given his word, and though it had been difficult and painful, he had kept it these many years.

But now his grandmother was dead and as far as he was concerned the promise she extracted from him was also gone, buried along with her in the cold, dark ground. Perhaps the only good thing to come of her passing was the freedom to pursue a course of action that would bring him peace and put to rest the event that defined his childhood, that shaped his adulthood.

At long last, Sebastian was going to take his fitting revenge against George Collins, the Earl of Hetfield.

Chapter 2

"It looks as if the worst of the rain will hold off until morning," Bianca Collins declared as she stared out the drawing room window. "Do you think Papa will arrive today, Eleanor?"

Eleanor drew her attention away from the sewing she held in her lap, raised her head, and smiled fondly at her younger sister. At eighteen years old, Bianca had fully come into her looks. She was breathtakingly beautiful, her features delicate and refined, her skin flawless and creamy white. Her hair was long and lush, the color of burnt autumn leaves, her eyes clear and sparkling and as green as the meadow grass in summer.

Yet Eleanor knew it was the sweetness of her personality, the goodness of her heart, and her optimistic outlook on life that gave Bianca her true beauty.

"'Tis impossible to predict what the earl will do," Eleanor said as she pushed her needle through the delicate muslin fabric on the hem of the gown she was sewing. "I fear our illustrious sire is rather like the weather."

"I've been so filled with curiosity that I've barely slept these last few nights," Bianca admitted. "Though I feel it deep down in my bones that Papa will have something wonderful to tell us."

"Hmm." The noncommittal murmur was all Eleanor could manage. She too had been sleeping poorly, anticipating the earl's visit. But while her tenderhearted sister had been struggling to contain her excitement, Eleanor was trying to tamp down her feelings of dread.

The message from the earl saying that he would shortly be in residence had come over two weeks ago. The brief, terse note had not been sent to his daughters, but rather to his butler, in order to ensure that all would be made ready for him. In Eleanor's mind that did not bode well for the visit, but she did not have the heart to point that out to her sister.

Bianca lived for these moments, these sparse times when their father remembered their existence and made a rare appearance in their lives. Spending but a few hours with the earl was all Bianca needed to make her feel as if she mattered to him, as if she were an important part of his life.

For Eleanor it was not as simple. She was very aware that the earl had long ago abandoned them. His various pursuits of personal pleasure, his travels abroad, and his social life in London all held far more interest for him than his two motherless children.

Eleanor had been raised by a succession of governesses, but at least she had experienced the gift of a mother's love for the first eight years of her life. Poor Bianca had never known their mother—she had died a few days after Bianca's birth. Perhaps that was the reason Bianca felt such unconditional love toward the earl; he was the only parent she had ever known.

The distracted, infrequent interest he demonstrated, the occasional affection he bestowed, seemed to be enough for Bianca. Not so for Eleanor. She wanted the impossible—she wanted her father to love her. Yet in her experience the earl had proven time and again that the only person he had ever loved was himself.

Eleanor knew she was not the ideal daughter. She was not blindly obedient, meek, or subservient. At times she had been too outspoken with her criticism of the earl's parental neglect. But her worst crime of all was her inability to make a good marriage.

The earl had grudgingly given her one Season in Town and she had failed to make her mark, had failed to dazzle society, had failed to capture a husband. She had not brought wealth, property, or connections to the family and at nearly six and twenty, she was now too old. 'Twas not surprising he had little use for her.

"I am hoping Papa will stay at least a few days once he does arrive." Bianca's face brightened. "There might even be time for him to meet Mr. Smyth. He has told me on more than one occasion that he would feel privileged indeed to make Papa's acquaintance."

No doubt. Mr. Smyth had recently taken up residence in their rural community. Claiming a distant relationship to Squire Williams had opened a few doors for the young man and he had taken full advantage of it, seeking to establish himself as a gentleman of means and culture. As far as Eleanor could tell, Mr. Smyth possessed neither in any significant quantities.

"The earl never mixes with the local society unless he has no other choice," Eleanor said.

"I know." Bianca sighed. "Still, I am anxious to hear his opinion of Mr. Smyth, though he is so much like Papa I am certain they will get along famously."

"Hmm." In Eleanor's opinion, being like their father was hardly an admirable qualification. Yet Bianca's remark was telling—and truthful. Eleanor realized that was another reason she disliked Mr. Smyth. He did possess the same controlling, domineering personality as the earl, traits Eleanor feared Bianca mistook for strength of character.

She also feared that Mr. Smyth had set his sights on Bianca not because he held her in any genuine regard, but rather because he thought the younger daughter of an earl would be a most fortuitous bride. If Eleanor believed he had true affection for Bianca she would have encouraged the budding romance, but she was highly suspicious of Mr. Smyth's motives.

Eleanor wanted the very best for her sister. The magic of love, the promise of happiness, the respect of a husband who truly believed Bianca was a gift to treasure.

Of course, she had wanted that for herself too, but the opportunity had come and gone many years ago. When she was too young and too naive to understand its value. When she foolishly let it slip beyond her grasp.

No, that wasn't entirely true. In order to achieve her heart's desire she would have had to leave her father's house and in doing so would have left behind a vulnerable, unprotected nine-year-old Bianca. The very idea had struck a nerve of guilt so deep and wide it still hurt to think of it.

Falling in love with a groom was such a cliché. The nobleman's daughter and the servant. Yet she had loved John Tanner with all of her seventeen-year-old heart, and he had returned that love unconditionally.

They knew their relationship was an impossibility. The only way they could be together was if they started fresh where no one knew of their past. It had taken months of plotting to formulate a plan of escape. They would first travel to Scotland to be married and then make their way to the coast, where John would find work.

It was fairly easy to slip out of the manor house the night that they had planned to run away, yet telling John that she was not coming with him had been the most difficult thing Eleanor had ever done. Though she had wanted him with every fiber of her being, Eleanor knew she had to embrace the responsibility of caring for and protecting her sister or forever regret her choice.

It was not a part of her nature to dwell on the past, to think of what might have been. Yet in the subsequent years there were moments when she wondered how her life would have been if she had been free to take a risk, to follow her heart.

Eleanor pulled the white thread slowly through

the delicate fabric, careful not to mar the lovely material of the gown she was remaking for Bianca. The dress had originally been Eleanor's, a remnant of her disastrous debut Season. It was long out of fashion, but the quality of the material was timeless and with a bit of clever needlework it was a serviceable gown. More than serviceable, really, since anything Bianca wore looked elegant and refined.

The earl was not overly generous when it came to his daughters' upkeep. By necessity, Eleanor had perfected her sewing skills, remaking many older gowns for herself and her sister. These days she spent far less time on her own garments, for she was determined that Bianca always appear in fresh, fashionable clothes.

Eleanor was debating whether to embroider a floral design at the base of the gown's bodice when she heard the sound of heavy-booted feet stomping down the hall. Her hands stilled as she strained her ears, listening for the deep, booming voice that would certainly accompany them. It came all too soon, shouting at one of the footmen to open the drawing room door. *Father.*

Eleanor swallowed hard, hoping to calm the sudden pain in her stomach. Before she had a chance to fully compose herself, the door swung open and the Earl of Hetfield stalked inside.

Though well into his sixtieth year, the earl was still a handsome man. Tall, commanding, with a head of silver hair and a pair of piercing dark eyes, he dominated any room.

"Papa! You've come home." Bianca rushed forward to embrace him.

Eleanor stayed seated. He was not the sort of

parent who liked to show affection, though he tolerated Bianca's attention without too much protest. As for herself, well, Eleanor could not recall an instance when her father had eagerly bestowed a hug to either of his daughters.

"Careful there, girl, or you'll crush my coat," the earl grumbled.

Eleanor's shoulders stiffened at the callous remark, but Bianca laughed and hugged the earl tighter. For an instant she envied her sister's naïveté. It protected her from hurt.

"I'm sure there is not a wrinkle to be found anywhere on your illustrious person, my lord," Eleanor said, eyeing his pristine white cravat and polished black boots. "Your valet would never allow it."

The earl tipped back his head and glanced at her, his brows drawing into a frown of puzzlement. *Good Lord, does he not even know who I am?* Her mouth dry, Eleanor forced her eyes to meet his, a shaky smile forming on her lips.

"I need a drink," the earl declared abruptly. "The roads from Town were a disaster."

"Let me get it for you, Papa," Bianca offered.

Without waiting for his answer, Bianca skipped over to the sideboard. Her lower lip curled under in confusion as she contemplated the trio of crystal decanters and variously shaped glasses.

"Brandy," Eleanor said, pointing to the tallest decanter. "And use the snifter."

"I'm surprised you remembered," the earl remarked as he swirled the generous portion of amber liquid in the glass Bianca handed him.

"I have an excellent memory," Eleanor said, wishing she had the nerve to ask for a drink for herself.

She rarely drank spirits, except for an occasional glass of wine with dinner. Yet she had a sinking feeling that this afternoon she was in need of a dose of false courage.

"Memory is a most unappealing trait," the earl said as he sat down. "Especially in a woman of your years, Eleanor." Raising the glass to his mouth, the earl downed the contents in a single swallow.

"You haven't journeyed all this way for a drink," Eleanor snapped, angry at the sting of hurt his words produced. Despite her best efforts, he still possessed the power to wound her. "Is there something specific you wanted?"

"I have come to take Bianca to Town," the earl announced. "'Tis high time she was properly presented to society."

Bianca gasped with delight, clasping her hands together in glee. "London? Truly?"

Eleanor frowned in puzzlement. "The Season has already begun."

"No matter," the earl replied. "Things always start off slowly. All the truly important balls and soirees are yet to come."

"It will take weeks to get ready," Eleanor said. "Bianca needs clothes, as well as instruction in deportment, etiquette, and dancing."

The earl waved his hand dismissively. "She needs only a single outfit to travel to London. We shall commission a wardrobe once we reach Town. As for the rest of it, I assume that you have taught her proper behavior. Are you now saying that you have neglected her all these years?"

Eleanor bristled at the unfair criticism. "I have

done my best, given my limited knowledge. You might recall my time in society was rather limited."

The earl favored her with a wry glare as if he needed no reminder of it. Eleanor felt herself start to shrink into her seat. John Tanner had left the estate two weeks before she went to London to embark on her disastrous Season. Heartbroken, she had gone through the motions, not caring that her plain looks and subdued personality had rendered her nearly invisible.

With a shake of her head, Eleanor pulled herself upright. She refused to apologize for the past.

"Fortunately, Bianca possesses both beauty and wit," the earl said. "She will be a smashing success, I am certain."

What was this all about? Apprehension churned in Eleanor's stomach, along with a healthy dose of fear. If their father's honest intention was to introduce Bianca into society, why had he waited so long to let them know of his plans? Why had they not been given time to prepare? Even under the best of circumstances, it would be difficult for the provincial Bianca to make a success of it.

"I am sure Bianca will enchant everyone," Eleanor said cautiously. "Though her success would be guaranteed if she were allowed the proper time to prepare. Why not present her next Season?"

"And miss out on this year's splendid crop of eligible bachelors?" The earl walked to the sideboard, poured himself another generous dose of brandy, then sat on an upholstered chair. "No, I've made up my mind. She will go now."

Eleanor felt another jolt of fear. The reason for the earl's haste was clear—he wanted, nay, he needed, to find a husband for his youngest daughter. As soon as possible.

That must mean his finances were in worse shape than usual. Eleanor was well aware of the two outstanding mortgages on the estate, the back pay owed to many of the servants, the accounts to various merchants that went unpaid. Normally the earl juggled his funds in such a way that each was paid just enough to keep the more aggressive creditors at bay.

Something must have changed. Eleanor wished she had the nerve to ask him what had happened. Yet even knowing why the need for funds so suddenly arose would not alter the earl's plans.

He was going to arrange a marriage for Bianca to whomever he could make the best deal with, the deal that most benefited himself. He most certainly would not allow anything as petty as his daughter's personal feelings toward her future husband to deter his decision.

Poor Bianca. A chill feeling of dread crawled up Eleanor's spine. Bianca's sweet innocence was no match for the manipulating earl. Eleanor turned toward her sister and the dread escalated. Bianca was smiling with delight, completely unaware of her fate.

"We shall have the best time," Bianca exclaimed. "Aren't you excited, Eleanor? It's been many years since you've been to Town."

"Eleanor?" The earl turned a disparaging eye upon his oldest daughter. "Bianca, I have come to bring you to Town, not your sister."

"Not Eleanor?" Bianca's face crumbled with disappointment. "Why won't she be coming with us?"

"She is not needed," the earl said dismissively.

Eleanor bit the inside of her lip, trying to remain as outwardly serene as possible. The earl did not engage in arguments with his daughters. He dictated and they obeyed. Yet with the proper approach, he could be persuaded.

"But of course Eleanor must come," Bianca declared, her voice shaking with emotion. "I shall be lost without her. Please, Papa?"

The earl briefly glanced at Eleanor. She forced herself to lift her head and stare at his stiff shoulders, refusing to be reduced to an insignificant afterthought. Bianca needed her and therefore Eleanor wanted very badly to go to London. But she would not beg.

Yet with each passing moment of silence, her fear heightened. What would become of her sweet sister if she were not there to oversee things? What manner of man would the earl choose for his youngest daughter? Eleanor shuddered. She had no confidence in their father's judgment or motivation.

"If you bring me, I can serve as both companion and chaperone," Eleanor said quietly.

"Please say yes, Papa," Bianca implored, hurrying across the room. She sank gracefully to her knees in front of the earl's chair. "I cannot manage without her."

Though it pained her to watch her sister subjugate herself in such a manner, Eleanor kept silent. Finally the earl raised one eyebrow and leveled a haughty, disapproving look at his eldest daughter.

"If it pleases you, Bianca, then of course your

sister may come along," he declared in a cool, languid voice. "Provided she makes herself useful."

Peter Dawson's fingers moved with elegant ease as he deftly shuffled the deck, then cheerfully dealt the cards. Sebastian, seated across from his friend, disciplined himself to appear calm and relaxed. After all, this was merely a friendly game of cards among gentlemen. Suspicions would surely arise if he appeared too anxious or agitated.

The Duke of Warren's ballroom was crowded and stuffy, making the card room a haven for the gentlemen needing a respite from the dancing and conversation. There were five of them seated around the table, but only one man truly interested Sebastian—the Earl of Hetfield. *His prey.*

It had taken Sebastian two weeks of careful planning to reach this point. He had returned to Town a few days after his grandmother's funeral bent on revenge, only to discover the earl was not in Town. Frustrated, Sebastian had spent his days waiting anxiously for the earl to return, honing his already impressive sword skills and perfecting his keen shot.

Then finally some good news. The earl had returned to Town four days ago. Assuming he would soon be out in society, Sebastian had visited three different events tonight in search of him. It was somewhat of a surprise to locate Hetfield at the duke's party, for it was far and above the most respectable entertainment of the night.

"Cards, gentlemen?" Dawson asked.

Sir Charles declined, Lord Faber took one. The earl took two, then drew on the stub of a cheroot.

He looked younger than Sebastian had imagined, and to be fair, far less sinister. Though he had known for years the identity of his mother's lover, Sebastian's promise to his grandmother had rendered him powerless to confront the man. He had therefore avoided meeting Hetfield, worried he would be unable to restrain himself.

Yet as he now gazed at the man who had driven his mother to suicide and forever changed his life, Sebastian was surprised at how calm he felt. Perhaps it was because his plan for revenge was so simple?

Sebastian knew the course he must take had to be an honorable one. Hence a duel would be fought between himself and the earl.

The practice of dueling had been employed for centuries by gentlemen throughout the world as a means to appease honor and exact justice. Though frowned upon by society, it occurred nevertheless and in far greater numbers than many believed.

Sebastian knew he had the grounds to accuse the earl of causing his mother's untimely demise, but he would not reveal the truth and sully her memory. Amazingly, his grandmother had managed to keep her daughter-in-law's suicide a secret. There had never been a whisper of scandal attached to his mother's name either before or after her death and Sebastian was determined to keep it that way. As far as society knew, this duel would be fought for a completely different reason.

It would be fought for something foolish and ridiculous and false—an accusation of cheating at cards. The ironic justice of it all sat well with both Sebastian's conscience and macabre sense of humor.

It would actually be fairly simple to call the earl's

honor into question. After Hetfield had won an especially large pot, Sebastian would accuse him of cheating, demand satisfaction, set the duel, and thoroughly disgrace the man. Either swords or pistols would serve nicely, since Sebastian was an expert at both.

"Benton?" With a practiced gesture, Dawson held out the deck. "Will you draw?"

Sebastian gave his cards a cursory glance, declined any new ones, then tossed a coin in the center of the table. The key to winning at *vingt-et-un* was an awareness of what cards had already been played, coupled with the ability to calculate the odds as to which cards would next appear. It was something Sebastian excelled at doing.

He watched closely as the earl lifted the edge of one card and stared down at it, contemplating his next move. Sebastian's adversary was a strong player, his moves bold and decisive. Of all the gentlemen at the table he was clearly the most skilled. Except for Sebastian, who was deliberately tossing away most of his winning hands.

At Dawson's signal the players turned their cards face up. "Twenty-one," Dawson said. "Lord Hetfield wins."

"Damn, Lady Luck is certainly smiling upon you tonight, Hetfield," Lord Faber grumbled. "That's three times in a row you've won."

"Perhaps you would prefer to switch to hazard, Lord Faber?" the earl asked with a smile.

"Ha! Hazard's a game for young fools," Lord Faber replied. "Makes no sense at all to throw away good coin on a pair of dice."

Play continued. The earl won the majority of the

next dozen hands, his pile of winning coins nearly double the size of any of the other players. Dawson was his usual congenial self, dealing the cards with good humor as he tried to keep the game light-hearted and friendly. Sir Charles continued drinking at a steady pace while Lord Faber pressed his luck with mediocre hands, inching the play to a higher pitch as he tried to recoup some of his losses.

Nerves on edge, Sebastian pushed his whiskey glass out of easy reach, not wanting to tempt himself. For this plan to work he needed to be sober and clearheaded. Accusations hurled by a man too deep in his cups were never taken seriously.

Sebastian would have preferred to confront the earl in a gaming hell, where the clientele was seedy and desperate, but that could have easily put his plan in jeopardy. Accusations of cheating in the hells were a common occurrence. With the rare exception, the recipients of these charges were less concerned about their honor and more focused on being allowed to continue in the game. Things rarely escalated to a duel.

"The bet is to you, Hetfield," Dawson said.

The earl had a six and five displayed and a third card turned facedown. He hesitated. Sebastian marveled at his outward calm, for he knew the concealed card made the earl's hand unbeatable.

Taking a deep breath, Sebastian smiled at the earl with the most serene expression he could muster. Hetfield returned the grin and tossed in another coin. *Excellent.*

"Another twenty-one?" Lord Faber exclaimed bitterly when the hands were revealed. "You really do have the devil's own luck tonight, Hetfield."

Finally! Lord Faber's annoyance could not have been timed more perfectly. Emotions raging, Sebastian cleared his throat.

"Strange, the last time I checked there were four kings in a deck. How is it exactly that you were able to play a fifth, Lord Hetfield?" Sebastian asked, his tone carrying an edge of accusation.

"A fifth?" Sir Charles spoke in a slow, slurred voice. "Are you sure?"

"I am," Sebastian replied forcefully, knowing it was indeed the truth, since he had been the one to maneuver the card into the earl's hand.

"That's preposterous!" the earl cried.

"No, wait, I think Benton might be on to something," Sir Charles said. "I believe I did see the king of spades earlier in the game too."

"Hell, Charles, you're too foxed to see much of anything!" the earl exclaimed.

"Rubbish!"

Sebastian held his smile. Sir Charles's exclamation of indignity would have been a bit more effective if he hadn't followed it by downing the rest of the brandy in his glass. Still, that was one player on his side. Two more to go.

"Did you notice anything amiss, my lord?" Sebastian asked, turning to the gentleman on his left.

Lord Faber coughed nervously, his thick, stubby fingers pressed against his mouth. "Now that you mention it, I might have seen the king of spades in the first round of play."

"You did," Sebastian insisted.

"What are you suggesting, Benton?" the earl asked, his voice sharp.

"I am suggesting nothing," Sebastian drawled. "I

am simply stating a fact. 'Tis impossible for you to have played that particular card *legitimately.*"

A gasp was heard, followed quickly by the low, muttering drone of voices. It spread through the card room like wildfire. *Good. Let them all talk.* An accusation of cheating was never lightly dismissed, even among the most hardened gamesters.

The tension in the room grew palpable and a remarkable stillness settled over everything. Play ceased at the nearest tables as the occupants turned their attention to the drama unfolding. Though it set him further on edge, Sebastian welcomed their interest. The more men who saw the exchange, the harder it would be for Hetfield to walk away.

"There is of course only one way for a *true* gentleman to settle the matter." Sebastian set his hands on the table, then pushed himself to his feet. "Name your second, Hetfield."

"What?" The earl jerked awkwardly to his feet, toppling his chair.

"I believe I have made myself perfectly clear. Are you going to defend yourself or not?"

A faint hint of emotion flashed in the earl's eyes. Fear? Recognition? Had he finally figured out that Sebastian was Evangeline's son, the woman he had scorned so cruelly all those years ago? The woman who had taken her own life because of the earl's disgraceful behavior.

Two spots of red burned in the earl's cheeks, yet his voice was calm when he spoke. "This is simply preposterous. You are, of course, mistaken, Lord Benton. I refuse to dignify this ludicrous bit of nonsense with a response."

"Yes, quite right, my lord." Dawson stuck his index

finger inside the top of his cravat and tugged nervously on it. "I am certain there was only one king of spades. This was all a misunderstanding that's best forgotten by everyone. No harm done, eh, Benton?"

Sebastian whirled upon his friend, seized by a strong impulse to grab him by the throat and shake him until his teeth rattled. "Stay out of it, Dawson," he ground out between clenched lips. "This is between me and the earl."

But his friend would not be silenced. Dawson moved closer and set his fingertips against Sebastian's chest as if trying to keep him from lunging at the earl. "Christ's blood, Benton, let it go," he whispered. "I doubt the earl was cheating, but even if he was, what does it matter? The wagers were not overly extravagant. Only Faber has lost a significant amount of coin and I am certain if you drop the matter he will follow your lead. Damn it all, if you keep pressing like this, things will turn very ugly, indeed."

Sebastian cast a dark glower at his friend. It had been a selfish mistake to allow Dawson to play. The man had too much integrity and common sense. Sebastian had wanted the security of having an ally at his back, but he had miscalculated badly. He had not told Dawson he intended to draw the earl into a duel, because he knew his friend would object to such a blatant act.

But he had reasoned that Dawson would take his side if something did occur. Integrity was so damn inconvenient! Sebastian tensed, the blood pumping furiously through his veins. Friend or no, he would not allow anyone to deny him his revenge.

"Either stand with me or stand aside," Sebastian said forcefully.

Dawson's head jerked back in surprise, his eyes filling with a curious mixture of confusion and hurt. "I swear, Benton, if I didn't know you better I'd think you were trying to provoke Hetfield into a duel."

Sebastian shrugged off that all too true comment and faced Lord Faber and Sir Charles. The two glanced uneasily around the card room. "Perhaps it would be best to let the matter go," Sir Charles suggested.

Struggling, Sebastian dredged up what little restraint he possessed. "I believe that question should be posed to Hetfield. 'Tis his honor that has been tainted."

All eyes turned expectantly to the older man. Panic lit his face, but he regained his composure. Sebastian saw the fine sheen of sweat on the earl's face. It was going to be very difficult for him to simply walk away at this stage. His honesty, and honor, had been called into question. He would have to accept the challenge to save both. *I've got you now, you damn bastard.*

"I still insist that no cheating occurred, but if there was something amiss with the cards, it must have been my error," Dawson interjected. "After all, I dealt the cards. Any blame must fall on me, not Hetfield."

"But you barely won any of the hands," Lord Faber insisted. "Unless you and Hetfield are in this scheme together?"

"Don't be an idiot," Sebastian said with a sneer.

"Dawson is the most honest, honorable gentleman I know. He would never cheat."

The response was instinctive. Sebastian did not even realize he had uttered the words until he saw the relief on the earl's face. *Shit.*

"Your confidence in me is most humbling, Benton. Thank you." Though he spoke congenially, Dawson's brow was furrowed as if he were trying to decipher a perplexing puzzle.

"All right then," Lord Faber said. "We all agree the accusation has no validity."

"The matter is closed." The earl's voice was urgent and curt. "We shall speak of it no more."

Sebastian barely heard the muttering of agreement from Sir Charles and Lord Faber. The earl turned and strode away. *No!* Sebastian felt the bile rise in his throat as he stared after Hetfield knowing he was powerless to stop him. A coldness welled up inside him, so strong and deep it stole his voice.

How had this happened? He had been so close, so near. It had all been going according to plan. That is, until Dawson stuck his nose into the mix. 'Twas like having a fish on the line, tugging and fighting. Inch by inch, yard by yard, reeling the prize closer, closer, and then, just as the fish was pulled from the water, it slipped from its hook and swam to safety.

Beside him, Sebastian heard Dawson exhale with relief. At the sound, his control snapped. A primitive part of Sebastian's brain shouted at him to pummel his friend until Dawson's face was bruised. If he could not taste the earl's blood, the blood he craved, he would settle for whoever blocked his path.

Fearing he would succumb to his rage, Sebastian

rudely turned away. Shoving aside a dandy standing in the doorway, he practically ran from the room. With each angry step he couldn't stop thinking that if Dawson had not intervened and smoothed it all over, this dilemma would have finally had a resolution.

Come morning he would have been facing the earl over crossed swords or pistols. By afternoon, the earl would have been disgraced, wounded, and in the most just circumstances of all, fighting for his life.

Chapter 3

Sebastian hurried down the hallway, paying scant attention to his surroundings. He passed beneath a gilded archway, then cursed under his breath when he realized he was standing in the duke's ballroom, surrounded by a sea of grandly dressed people.

It seemed as if no one had declined the invitation for this party. The large room was overflowing with guests. Which was hardly surprising, since the duke was related to many of the most influential and wealthy families in England. Anyone who was anyone clamored to be a part of tonight's festivities.

Sebastian's initial hope that the distraction of the crowd would ease his black mood was quickly dashed. His face felt tight, his eyes hard. Slowly, he unclenched his fist. He could feel himself trembling inside, shaking with rage and disappointment.

I must control myself! A pair of French doors leading to the gardens was close. Without hesitation, Sebastian stalked outside, snatching a glass of champagne from a passing footman. Never breaking stride, he downed the liquid in one long gulp, hoping the action might help calm him.

Alas, it did not. Sebastian's anger felt like a raging river, swollen to the edge of its banks with nowhere to go. He needed to leave, to go somewhere private, where he could be alone to release this scalding rage that threatened to consume him. Where he could drink until he was beyond feeling, beyond sense.

Vengeance is for God to decide. That was what his grandmother had repeated to him time and again when she had made him promise to leave the earl alone, to forgo any revenge. Had she been right? Should he turn the other cheek and forget?

For years he had taken his need for revenge and buried it deep inside himself. Could he do it again? Could he bury it so far, so deep that he never needed to face it? A vision of his mother's lifeless body invaded his head. Sebastian felt a tightness growing in his stomach as he struggled to close his mind to the memory.

Oh God, Mother, why did you do it? Was your pain truly so unbearable? Did you not realize how much I loved you, how much I needed you, how much I would suffer with your death?

Sebastian felt wetness on his face and realized it was tears. *Christ!* He was blubbering like an infant. He wiped them away irritably with a shaking hand, then began walking again, consumed by his need to get away. Though he was outside, the air felt as if it were closing in on him. His evening shoes were grinding against the crushed stone pathway as he hastened to the garden wall, searching for an exit. But there was none to be found.

Sebastian grimaced and glared at the solid brick wall in front of him. Tipping his head, his eyes scanned and assessed the imposing stone that apparently enclosed the entire garden. It easily stood ten feet tall, with decorative ironwork adorning the top. *Damnation!* It was too high to scale in his tight-fitting evening clothes, and even if he somehow reached the summit, those sharp, lethal-looking iron points would surely do irreparable damage to his clothing. Or his manhood.

Would that not be the perfect ending to this disastrous night? Walking through the duke's ballroom with a tear down the middle of his breeches and his arse hanging out for all to see?

Sebastian turned, took a few steps, then paused. Pivoting on his heel, he hurled his empty champagne goblet at the wall. The sound of shattering glass brought him a fleeting moment of satisfaction, yet did nothing to solve his dilemma. He was still trapped. In more ways than one.

With a grunt of frustration, Sebastian eyed the brick again, debating whether he should take a chance. But for once, common sense ruled. There was no help for it. He'd have to go back inside the house and through the ballroom in order to take his leave.

The duke's servants had lit torches in strategic points throughout the garden and lanterns were scattered in the higher trees. They twinkled like stars and enhanced the romantic mood. Sebastian could hear snatches of muted conversations as he wound his way down the various stone pathways. Fortunately he did not stumble upon any romantic trysts.

He had no sooner stepped back inside the crowded ballroom when he was waylaid by Lady Agatha and the Dowager Countess of Ashland. If not for the friendship the two older women had shared with his grandmother, he would have snarled at the pair and sent them on their way. Yet even with his temper still simmering, he found he could not be so rude.

"I see that you are not dancing, my lord," Lady Agatha said. "In deference to your recently departed grandmother, I am sure. 'Tis such a heartfelt and respectful gesture. You do her memory proud."

"Indeed." The dowager countess bobbed her head enthusiastically in agreement. "However, as I recall, her greatest wish was to see you married to a suitable lady. It might be a more fitting honor if you set yourself to accomplishing that task by seeking out the company of a few of the eligible debutantes in attendance this evening."

Lady Agatha pounced on the suggestion. "It might. The countess and I would be pleased to assist you."

"Oh, yes. Truly. We know all the girls from the very best families."

"We most certainly do. Mark my words, we could find you a suitable bride in a fortnight. Tell me, Lord Benton, do you prefer a lady with light or dark hair?"

Sebastian felt a tightening in his gut. The urge to reach out with both hands and place them around Lady Agatha's wrinkled neck was almost overpowering. But that would leave the countess free to continue talking. Perhaps he could bang their heads together?

"'Tis a most generous offer, ladies," Sebastian replied. "Having someone else procure a woman to please and entertain is something men fantasize over. I will most definitely call upon you if there is ever a time when I feel incapable of accomplishing the task on my own. Or if I lack the sufficient coin to pay for the pleasure."

Knowing he had gone too far, Sebastian forced himself to smile in order to leave the impression he was joking. Too bad he wasn't.

Still, his scandalous, improper remarks produced the desired effect. Lady Agatha and the countess went mute. Sebastian hastily bowed, then made his escape.

He was forced to take a meandering path through the crowd as he headed toward the exit. He did not pause to speak with anyone, though several people attempted to engage him in conversation. One particular set of ladies approached him with open, encouraging smiles, but the expression on his face must have conveyed his turbulent frame of mind, for they gave him a wide berth.

Yet as they passed him one woman snapped open her fan, then raised it to her lips to hide her comments. Disparaging remarks, judging by her frowning brows. About him, Sebastian was certain. *God Almighty, would this evening never end?*

He continued to move through the crush, his spirits rising slightly when he caught sight of the large, open archway leading out of the ballroom. At least he could finally see his way out. But the crowd seemed to be growing and he quickly found himself pressed close behind two chattering females, one in a gown of vivid green, and the other in an ensemble of subtle blue.

"Who is that insipid-looking redhead over there near the potted fronds?" Green Dress asked. "I'm sure I've never seen her before."

Blue Dress tugged at the dangling ribbon around her wrist, raised the attached quizzing glass up to her eye, and peered through the lens. "Oh, I met her earlier. 'Tis the Earl of Hetfield's daughter. Straight from the country, by the look of that outfit."

The Earl of Hetfield's daughter! Sebastian's head whirled so quickly he felt a wrenching pain shoot through his neck.

"My heavens, it is such a dreadful gown. Does she not own a looking glass? Truly, one would expect more from Lord Hetfield. How can he allow her to be seen in public? 'Tis an embarrassment." Green Dress shuddered, moving her hand over the silk of her own skirt, as if to assure herself that she was in a superiorly fashionable garment.

"She has a pretty sort of face, I suppose, but honestly, what was the earl thinking bringing her to Town after the Season has begun?" Blue Dress asked. "All the competent, fashionable dressmakers have been booked for weeks working on their clients' wardrobe. My maid told me that Madame Claudette nearly doubled the price of each garment when the earl insisted the gowns he ordered be ready as soon as possible."

"Did he pay it?"

"Judging by the dress his daughter is currently wearing, one must assume he did not."

There was a catty giggle, followed by a tsking

sound of disapproval. What a pair of harridans! Sebastian could almost pity the poor girl, but her connection to the earl made that an impossibility. She was the daughter of his enemy.

"Who is that dowdy female standing beside her?" Blue Dress asked. "Though a bit long in the tooth, she still looks too young to be a chaperone."

Sebastian did not bother waiting to hear Green Dress's reply. The Earl of Hetfield's daughter, eh? He had not known the earl had a daughter. His heart started to race. Anxiously he crossed the crowded ballroom floor, eager for a better look. Merely out of curiosity, he assured himself.

His eyes moved to the potted fronds. *Bloody hell.* A pretty sort of face? The young woman standing in the soft candlelight took his breath away. Her hair was a cascade of amber curls artfully swept up to bare her neck, her skin the color of rich cream. Her features were perfectly formed, perfectly proportioned. She had the ethereal, classic feminine beauty that transcended time, the kind of beauty that poets wrote of, that drove sane men to rash acts.

She appeared fresh and innocent and slightly nervous. He could detect her nerves by the way her head was constantly turning every which way as she took in the scene around her. Every few moments she would turn toward the woman standing beside her and say something. The subsequent answers given invariably made her smile. *Interesting.*

Sebastian was surprised she was not surrounded by a bevy of eager young bucks, each clamoring for her attention. Fashionably dressed or not, she was easily one of the most attractive females in the room.

The Earl of Hetfield approached and Sebastian's mood turned sour. The young beauty turned, smiled, then affectionately patted the earl's arm. He leaned close and whispered something in her ear. Her smile widened further.

A haze fell over Sebastian's vision. The picture of a doting father with his daughter tore at something deep inside him. Here was the earl, free to indulge himself in parental affection while Sebastian's mother was forever denied that joy.

Noting again with bitterness the apparent affection between the pair, a devious thought suddenly struck Sebastian. This lovely, innocent, virginal girl could hold the key to his revenge. The earl might not wish to defend his honor over a pair of cards, but he most certainly would risk all to save his daughter from ruin.

Sebastian was pricked by his elusive conscience, but only for a brief instant. This female was a means to an end and if it was the only way to achieve his revenge, then so be it.

His experience with females was almost legendary, yet Sebastian prided himself on the fact that he had always behaved like a gentleman. The various mistresses he had kept over the years had been amply rewarded financially and always treated with dignity.

The numerous affairs he had engaged in had always been with willing society women of experience who knew fully the consequences of their actions. They knew he would not marry them; indeed, often they were already married.

There had been several widows who had campaigned to be his viscountess, but he had made his views on matrimony very clear—he planned to stay single until he was at least forty. Even the constant badgering from his grandmother to take a wife had not altered this stand.

He had never outwardly lied to a lady, nor made promises he had no intention of keeping. And he most definitely had never seduced an innocent girl and then cast her aside.

There's always a first time.

Many a duel had been fought to preserve or restore a daughter's honor. Especially a young, innocent daughter. Sebastian grimaced.

Seducing the redheaded beauty would not be easy, since he would need to keep it a secret from the earl. After the incident this evening in the card room, Hetfield would naturally be suspicious of him. However, if he succeeded in ruining the girl in the eyes of society—and Sebastian was highly confident he would succeed—the earl would have no choice but to defend his family's honor.

Sebastian gazed again at his pretty young victim. Something jabbed inside him at the thought of what she would suffer. The censure of many, the relentless whispers of the gossipmongers, a scandal that would forever plague her. Yet beautiful women, he reasoned, always seemed to find their bearing and achieve their goals. Some man would eventually marry her, despite her tarnished reputation, and count himself lucky to have such a lovely wife.

At least she would escape with her life, which was far more than his poor mother. For a split second he worried that rationalization was solely to ease his conscience, but just as quickly, Sebastian tossed it out of his mind.

The earl laughed loudly at something his daughter said. Sebastian's lips also quirked upward, though his smile held no humor. His grandmother had been wrong. Vengeance was not for the Lord, but rather man's work. Sebastian knew the only hope he had to bring some measure of peace to his life was to strike back at the man who had caused his pain.

And now he had found a way to do it.

Eleanor became aware of the intense stare of the man across the room as the third waltz of the evening was played. He strolled the perimeter of the ballroom, yet his eyes never wavered. There was a determined, methodic edge to his scrutiny that was slightly alarming, for it seemed to go deeper than polite interest.

Naturally, this attention was not directed at her, but rather at Bianca. No one ever noticed the moon when the sun was shining so brightly. Normally, interest in Bianca from a handsome man would be welcome, but Eleanor had not been impressed by any of the gentlemen who had pressed forward for an introduction this evening.

The majority had been older, some as old as their father. A few had a desperate air about them, two greeted her with a lascivious smile, another openly leered at Bianca as he held her hand too long. This would most certainly not have happened if the earl had been there to offer Bianca support and protection, but he abandoned them soon after they arrived. He had briefly returned to check on them and just as swiftly removed himself outside for a smoke.

Eleanor shuddered to think how Bianca would have managed without her. As it was, it felt like her lovely, innocent sister was a lamb thrown to the wolves.

Though she did not voice any distress, Eleanor could see that Bianca was very nervous. Not so much for herself, Bianca had confided as they entered the ballroom, but her younger sister was mostly concerned about disappointing or displeasing their father. She was anxious that she would inadvertently make a misstep or appear awkward.

It angered Eleanor to see how much her sister cared, especially when contrasted with how little concern their father showed in return. Eleanor sighed, trying to control her anger, knowing it would only serve to distress Bianca. Attempting to distract it, she looked about the room. And realized the same gentleman was still staring at Bianca.

His eyes had a predatory look of a hunter on the scent of fresh meat. That hungry gaze of interest set the alarm bells clanging loudly in Eleanor's head.

She shifted her position to stand protectively in front of her sister and for a brief instant his eyes met Eleanor's across the room. An unexpected wave of heat flushed through her body. An odd reaction, surely, for though he was a handsome man, there were others in attendance possessing greater physical beauty.

He was tall, taller than most men she knew, with broad shoulders, muscular legs, and not an ounce of extra fat on his lean torso. His hair was dark and thick, his eyes the color of a stormy gray sky. The serene smile on his sensuous mouth softened the strong, bold lines of his face and enhanced his natural charm.

He was dressed in a black evening coat with black satin knee breeches, a gold embroidered waistcoat, a white shirt, and an intricately tied white cravat. He wore his clothes with a casual elegance that proclaimed him a man of great self-confidence and pride.

Eleanor scrunched her brows into a scowl, hoping to chase away his scrutiny, then realized his gaze was no longer on them. His eyes were darting about the crowded ballroom. Perhaps looking for his partner for the next dance?

A laughing group of guests stepped in front of him, and her view of him was gone. Shaking her head at her foolishness, Eleanor turned to her sister.

"Are you getting hungry? 'Tis nearly time for the supper dance. If I remember correctly that means the food has already been placed in the dining room. If we go now we can avoid the crush."

Bianca slowly shook her head. "I know you told me at these affairs the food is plentiful and lavish, but honestly, Eleanor, I couldn't swallow a bite."

"I understand."

Eleanor patted her sister's arm soothingly before noticing out of the corner of her eye that the handsome stranger was coming toward them. And he was not alone. Perched on his arm was a matronly woman dressed all in black. She was frowning in confusion as she took two quick steps to each of the mystery man's one. Eleanor decided she had to be a relative. What other woman would tolerate such manhandling?

The pair was heading directly toward them. Eleanor opened her fan and waved it absently before her face, hoping Bianca had not noticed these two. She was already a bundle of nerves. The attention of this arresting gentleman might push her over the edge.

"Ladies, I am sorry to interrupt, but the viscount is most insistent that I make an introduction."

Eleanor watched the older woman's bosom expand mightily as she sought to control her rapid breathing. The delay caused the gentleman's impatience to rise and he pressed himself forward.

"I am Benton," he said, fixing Bianca with a steady look as he bowed.

"Such impertinence, Lord Benton!" the older woman beside him exclaimed, pressing a hand over her still-heaving bosom. "Have your manners gone totally missing? You hauled me all the way over here so quickly one would think we were fleeing a fire. The very least you can do is allow me to make the introductions. Properly."

Lord Benton's eyes flashed hard and dangerous, then settled into a contrite gleam. "My apologies, Lady Agatha."

Lady Agatha harrumphed rather loudly. Eleanor would not have been surprised to see the older woman storm off in a huff, but then she noticed Lord Benton's hand clutching Lady Agatha's arm, preventing her escape.

With all eyes on her, Lady Agatha rose grandly to the occasion. "Now then, ladies, I would like to present Sebastian Dodd, Viscount Benton. These two enchanting creatures are the daughters of the Earl of Hetfield. Lady Eleanor and Lady Bianca."

Eleanor and Bianca curtsied, the viscount bowed.

Eleanor found herself gazing at his face, her eyes drawn to the strong line of his jaw, the firm, sensuous shape of his mouth. He had such marvelously appealing lips. She wondered what it would feel like to be kissed by him, to squeeze those broad, muscular shoulders as his lips brushed hers.

"Lady Eleanor?"

Blinking in embarrassment, Eleanor inhaled a shaky breath. What was wrong with her? The viscount clearly had no interest in her. Besides, such improper, risqué thoughts about a virtual stranger were ridiculous—and very much out of her character. "I beg your pardon, Lady Agatha. I did not hear your question."

Though Eleanor could have sworn it had been a female voice that was talking, it was the viscount who spoke.

"Lady Agatha and I were wondering why we have not seen either of you in Town."

"Bianca and I usually reside at our home in the country," she answered. "We have only recently arrived."

"How fortunate. Your presence adds the beauty we were missing and will serve to elevate the Season to a spectacular level," he said grandly.

Eleanor nearly rolled her eyes at the flowery sentiment. "London hardly lacks for beautiful women, my lord."

"Pretty, perhaps. Yet none quite as lovely as the two of you." He spoke the words to her, since she had answered him, but it was plain to all that he meant them for Bianca. "I believe there are many gentlemen who will take umbrage with the earl for delaying your arrival in Town."

"I have a suspicion that the earl is the type of man who keeps his most precious things hidden away, out of sight," Lady Agatha interjected with a superior smirk.

Bianca lowered her head modestly. Eleanor smiled dimly, relieved that a female's vapid smile was usually taken as a sign of agreement. Precious things! How preposterous. Why, if they knew the truth about the earl's treatment of his daughters they would be appalled.

So tell them. A devilish urge of honesty was something that plagued Eleanor at the most inconvenient times. As much as she would have liked to dispel this myth about their father, it would hurt and embarrass her sister. Not to mention enlightening any of these people as to her father's true character would be social suicide.

"Now that we have been properly introduced, I shall shamelessly beg for the honor of a dance," Lord Benton said. "Lady Bianca?"

Bianca looked down at the viscount's extended hand, then over at Eleanor. Heart fluttering with worry, Eleanor eyed the viscount suspiciously. The faint lines at the corners of his eyes told her he was too old for her gentle sister, the arrogance in his sensual smile bespoke of a sophistication way beyond Bianca's comprehension.

But Bianca's eyes were pleading with her to agree. She had promised herself she would be vigilant, yet not unreasonable with the men who paid court to her sister. So Eleanor nodded her head in permission.

Bianca's face broke into a smile. "I shall be delighted to dance with you, my lord."

In silence, Eleanor and Lady Agatha watched the pair walk away. "What can you tell me about the viscount?" Eleanor asked the moment the couple took their place in line for the quadrille.

The older woman nodded in understanding. "A handsome devil, is he not? And more than charming, especially when the mood suits him."

"Unmarried?"

"Of course. I would not have made the introduction if he were a married man." Lady Agatha lifted her chin and let out an offended sniff. "He has an old and distinguished title. The Dodds were royalists who fought beside King Charles and were rewarded handsomely for their loyalty when the throne was reclaimed. On his mother's side he can trace his ancestry back to the Conqueror, though there is rumored to be some Welsh blood mixed in several generations ago."

Lady Agatha's tone implied that was not a desirable connection, but Eleanor dismissed it as insignificant. "I do not want a list of his pedigree, Lady Agatha. What of his character? Is he a good man?"

"Good? Why, he is good at many things. An excellent rider, a keen shot, a fashionable dresser, as you can plainly see. He runs with a bit of a fast crowd, though that part of his life is clearly changing. His close friend the Marquess of Atwood married last year and has settled well into domesticity."

Eleanor had difficulty picturing Lord Benton doing the same. Still, it could happen. She digested the information thoughtfully. "So you believe it is

Viscount Benton's intention to follow his friend's lead and marry?"

Lady Agatha shifted uncomfortably from one foot to the other. "I have heard nothing specific about Benton actively seeking a bride this Season. But a man of his years must be thinking about settling down and setting up his nursery. I know it was his grandmother's fondest wish. What better way to honor her recent passing than to marry a suitable young woman?"

It was a skillful, yet evasive answer. What exactly was Lady Agatha trying to hide? Knowing she had only a limited amount of time to question the older woman, Eleanor considered the best way to get to the heart of the matter. "Tell me, Lady Agatha, would you encourage your granddaughter to set her cap for the viscount?"

The look of horror on Lady Agatha's face was all the answer Eleanor needed. "Goodness me, Emily is such a sheltered, timid girl. I'm certain Benton would not look twice at her."

"Bianca is equally young and naive," Eleanor replied tartly. "I thank you for your honesty, Lady Agatha."

"Good heavens, Lady Eleanor, I fear you have misunderstood my remarks," Lady Agatha began, but she was silenced by the arrival of Bianca and the viscount.

They were all smiles, clearly having enjoyed their time together. Eleanor waited, curious to see what the viscount would do next. It would be exceedingly forward if he asked Bianca to dance with him a second time.

For one wild, impulsive moment she wondered whether he would solicit her for the next dance. Eleanor's hand tightened on her fan. The very idea gave her a flash of excitement and she felt embarrassed for being so foolish.

"I usually ride in the park at the fashionable afternoon hour," the viscount said. "I do hope if we chance to meet, you will take pity on me and spare me more than a moment of your delightful company, Lady Bianca."

Bianca cast confused eyes toward Eleanor, clearly at a loss how to reply. Though they had been in Town for several days, Bianca's lack of a fashionable wardrobe had kept them virtual prisoners inside their rented townhome. They had not ventured much beyond the few blocks surrounding the residence, coming reluctantly to this evening's ball only at the earl's insistence.

"I am uncertain as to what my plans will be tomorrow," Bianca finally answered.

"Just say you will be there."

Bianca lowered her chin and blushed, her nod of acceptance barely perceptible.

The viscount smiled. "I look forward with great anticipation to seeing you again, Lady Bianca. And you also, Lady Eleanor," he added hastily, casting a consolatory glance in Eleanor's direction.

Her spine stiffened. She had no need of his pity.

Eleanor extended her hand in farewell, fascinated by the sudden tingling that shot through her when she ever-so-briefly touched the viscount's palm. Eleanor felt her cheeks warm at her schoolgirl reaction. She was far too mature to be so easily thrown into confusion by such a simple gesture.

"How was your dance?" Eleanor asked her sister the moment they were alone.

"Wonderful." The smile of delight reached Bianca's eyes, making them sparkle. "Lord Benton is very skillful. And when I accidentally missed a step, he apologized and said it was his fault, when it so obviously was mine. He is a true gentleman."

Two charming dimples appeared in Bianca's cheeks as her grin deepened. Seeing them made Eleanor's heart turn over.

"You liked the viscount?"

"Very much indeed."

"You don't think he is a bit old for you?"

"Old? Not at all. He's probably only a few years older than you. Surely you noticed all the other gentlemen who danced with me are as old as Papa." Bianca wrinkled her nose. "Or older."

"Yes, I had noticed." Eleanor bit her lower lip and sternly admonished herself to calm down. In her opinion, the viscount's age and reputation made him unsuitable for Bianca, but she was not going to say anything just yet.

Her sister had met very few appealing men tonight. Once her wardrobe was completed and they entered society fully there would be plenty of handsome, suitable men vying for her sister's affection. It stood to reason that the exposure to other young gentlemen would make the viscount less engaging.

Eleanor knew she couldn't count on their father to protect Bianca—that job would fall to her. And she fully intended to remain vigilant. This was Bianca's chance to make a good match and Eleanor would not allow it to be squandered. She was determined to do all that she could to ensure her sister achieved the happiness she so richly deserved.

A happiness that Eleanor was certain would not be found with a rogue like Lord Benton.

Chapter 4

The crowds in Hyde Park were particularly large the following afternoon. Sebastian frowned as he gazed out at the sea of open carriages, horseback riders, and pedestrians clogging the footpath. The sunny day and pleasant temperatures had brought them out in droves and not a single person appeared to be in a hurry.

He cursed softly beneath his breath, knowing it might take hours to find Lady Bianca. If she was even in the park. His one consolation was that he had come on horseback, which allowed him to weave his way around the carriages, instead of walking among them.

Yet after twenty frustrating minutes of that, Sebastian remembered why he seldom went to the park at this fashionable hour. It was bedlam.

Life would be so much easier if he could simply call upon Bianca at home, but by doing so he would run the risk of encountering the earl. And that might very well put an end to the relationship before it even began, effectively thwarting Sebastian's chance for revenge.

No, for the plan to have any chance of success, the *courting* needed to be conducted in a clever, calculating manner. He would meet the girl out in the open, in public places and at society events, never obviously stating his interest to anyone but her. This way, when the blow of her ruination was struck, the earl would be caught completely unawares.

"The sun must be blinding me, Dorothea," a cheerful female voice declared. "I swear I see Lord Benton."

"Benton? Impossible," the beautiful woman beside her replied. "He never rides in the park."

"Ladies." Sebastian touched his whip to the brim of his hat in greeting and smiled at the trio of women walking directly in front of him. "'Tis a rare treat to see all three Ellingham sisters together."

The women gathered around his horse and gazed up at him, a variety of expressions on their lovely faces. Of the three, he knew the youngest of the sisters, Emma, the best. Dorothea, the middle sister, was the wife of his closest friend, the Marquess of Atwood, so he had often been in her company this past year. Gwendolyn, the eldest, was a more recent acquaintance. He found her to be a levelheaded female with good instincts and a sharp wit.

She was regarding him now with keen interest and he squirmed slightly under her scrutiny. Though she lacked the ravishing beauty of Dorothea and the fresh, animated demeanor that made Emma such a pretty girl, Gwendolyn was a handsome woman in her own right. And she clearly possessed other more salient characteristics since she was married to Jason Barrington. Sebastian had to admire a woman with the mettle to tame one of the most notorious rakes on the *ton*. Or rather, former rakes.

"Come now, Benton, you have not told us what you are doing here today," Dorothea probed.

"I assume it would be obvious, Lady Dorothea. I am exercising my horse and taking the air."

"Pish-posh, my lord, we are not so easily fooled. The crowds are so thick your horse can barely move along the path," Gwendolyn said.

Emma clicked her tongue and gave him a saucy wink. "I agree, something must be afoot. Why else would Benton be here, immaculately attired, looking so handsome, so dashing, so virile?"

He looked down at Emma's teasing expression and raised his eyebrows. "You wound me, Emma. As you very well know, that is my natural state."

"Handsome, virile, and dashing?"

"Don't forget immaculate," Dorothea added.

"He is that too. Plus, sitting so tall and graceful in the saddle shows his well-muscled legs to the best advantage," Emma commented, turning to her sisters. "Don't you agree?"

They nodded and smiled.

"I might be sitting above you, ladies, but the sound of your dainty tones travels far. I can hear every word you are saying," Sebastian said tartly.

The women laughed. Sebastian tried to hold a stern expression but failed. Their good-natured teasing was well-deserved, since he took every opportunity to return it in kind.

With a sigh of resignation, Sebastian swung off his horse. He shifted the reins into his left hand, then insinuated himself into the middle of the group. The women closed ranks around him and they began walking, Sebastian's horse following sedately behind.

It was difficult traveling four abreast. A boisterous group of youngsters pushed their way forward, nearly knocking Lady Dorothea down. Sebastian's arm shot out instinctively and he grabbed her around the waist to keep her from falling.

"Goodness! Dorothea, are you all right?" Gwendolyn exclaimed.

"I'm fine," Dorothea replied, her voice breathless. "Thanks to Benton's quick reflexes."

"I am ever at the ready to take a stunning beauty into my arms," Sebastian quipped as he steadied Lady Dorothea firmly back on her feet. "Though we need to find a path less crowded. Atwood will have my head if anything happens to you, especially in your delicate condition."

A flush of red appeared on her cheeks. "You are not supposed to mention that in public."

Sebastian smiled. "Why ever not? Your husband speaks constantly of his impending fatherhood to all his friends. 'Tis as though he expects us to honor him with a round of applause or toss him a shilling as a reward for being such a clever fellow."

"Carter is rather pleased at the news." Dorothea lowered her head and blushed charmingly. Sebastian marveled at how her delicate blond features were enhanced by her pregnant condition. It seemed the old adage that a woman glowed while carrying a child was correct in Lady Dorothea's case.

"Atwood is over the moon," Sebastian clarified, linking his arm through hers. "Though I do believe his father is even more excited. I've never in all my life seen the duke so animated. I swear, he would do anything to please you, move heaven and earth if you merely hinted it would bring you happiness. My advice is expand your imagination and ask for something truly extraordinary. Like a private island. Or your own country. He can easily afford it."

"Her own country?" Emma giggled.

Dorothea also laughed. "Such nonsense, my lord. I believe you are attempting to distract us and avoid answering our questions regarding your appearance in the park today. Indeed, I can think of no logical reason for it. Unless . . ." Her voice trailed off suggestively.

"Don't tell me 'tis a lady who has brought you out into the sunshine, my lord?" Gwendolyn asked, looking over at him with amazed eyes.

"Viscount Benton brought low by a mere female? I cannot believe it." Emma pressed the back of her wrist to her forehead and sighed theatrically.

"I fear your normally keen minds have been affected by the sun," he said with a grin, though inwardly he was worried at how close the women had come to the truth. He did not want his interest in the earl's daughter to be known so quickly. Besides, it felt sordid to have these three women touched in any way by the scandal he intended to create.

Trying to elude their inquisitive gaze, Sebastian turned his head to the right, searching for a less crowded pathway. He found one that intersected ahead and led them all in that direction.

Majestic oak trees provided a bit of welcome shade and fewer people made the walking more pleasant, but it was the sight of two women coming their way that set Sebastian's heart pounding in an irregular rhythm.

Though they were still some distance away, Sebastian recognized them. It was the Earl of Hetfield's daughters. Lady Bianca, the shorter of the two, was twirling a lacy pink parasol above her head that matched her walking dress. He concluded her wardrobe must have arrived, for the ensemble was of the latest fashion.

Alas, Lady Eleanor's clothes had not been made ready. She was wearing a heavy gown of russet brown more suited for a colder day and a country environment. It was such a sharp contrast to the light, spring dress her sister wore, one had to feel some sympathy for her. It must not be pleasant to always be cast in the shadow of a younger, far prettier sibling.

Though he would have preferred to be alone, this was the opportunity he had been waiting for, the reason he had come to the park in the first place. Sebastian lifted the hand holding his horse's reins and waved. Lady Bianca returned the wave with an enthusiastic one of her own. He saw Lady Eleanor's back stiffen at the gesture and she closed her eyes briefly. He had not realized he had made such a strong impression on the sister. A strong, *negative* impression, judging by the grim set of her lips.

Damn! Apparently tongues had started wagging and his reputation had preceded him. A fact he confirmed a few minutes later when they met on the pathway.

There was not even the faintest suggestion of a smile on Lady Eleanor's lips when she greeted him, though she did relax her frown when he introduced her to the Ellingham sisters. Lady Bianca was all smiles and enthusiasm, while Lady Eleanor remained polite but not overly friendly. And she continued to look at him as if he were the last person on earth she wanted to see.

It was an odd feeling to be brought low by a plain-looking woman perilously close to becoming an old maid. Sebastian hastily reminded himself it didn't matter. Bianca was his target.

"Will you stroll with me, Lady Bianca?" Sebastian asked, deliberately ignoring the startled looks of the Ellingham sisters and the severe disapproval of Lady Eleanor.

He offered his arm to her and with a shy smile she took it. They broke away from the pack and moved ahead, though Sebastian was careful to keep a respectable distance. He pulled his horse to the left so the animal walked on the grass, sparing the four women behind them the direct sight of the stallion's hindquarters.

"Isn't it a lovely day?" Sebastian asked.

"Yes, splendid. I was told it rains often in Town, but the weather has been quite nice since our arrival."

"Are you finding the amusements of London to your liking?" he inquired.

"We have seen little of Town, but it has all been very grand."

"And what of the activities? Was there a particular soiree or party that you will claim as your favorite?"

"They were all equally enjoyable."

Sebastian waited, an encouraging smile on his

face. Lady Bianca shyly returned the smile, yet offered nothing else. That was it? That was all she was going to say? God help him, it was like pulling teeth.

They walked for several minutes without saying anything, the topic of the weather and how she was enjoying Town life already exhausted. In Sebastian's experience, prattling women were the norm—which he occasionally found amusing, yet more often an annoyance. It was, however, something he dealt with skillfully. Quiet was far more complicated.

"Do you enjoy riding?" he asked, casting about for a topic many country girls longed to extol upon.

"I do." She looked at him inquiringly. "And you, my lord? Are you a keen rider?"

Finally. Sebastian launched into a story about learning to ride when he was a youngster, embellishing parts with a self-deprecating humor that women always found irresistible. In no time at all Lady Bianca was clutching his arm reflexively as she giggled.

The viscount was very pleased.

"Your dress is lovely," he purred in a velvety soft tone. "That particular shade of pink adds a rosy hue to your complexion."

"Thank you, my lord."

He turned his head to look fully at her and discovered she was already gazing at him. She bit her bottom lip nervously as their eyes met and he could not miss the genuine admiration that washed over her face. A thrilling sense of victory shot through him.

This was almost too easy. A few honeyed words of flattery, a sultry glance, a seductive kiss and the girl would follow him anywhere. She would easily be led down the path to ruin, assuring Sebastian of his duel. And his revenge.

The conversation continued and before long Sebastian came to a realization that Lady Bianca was precisely as she appeared—a young woman barely past girlhood. At first impression one might think she was a tad frivolous and empty-headed, but he decided she was not a simpleton. She was a simple girl, unspoiled, sweet, and innocent to a fault. After their dance last night he had assumed she was a country lass merely in the need of some Town bronze, but he could now see that she was completely guileless.

A small breeze swirled through the air and he watched the way an amber-hued strand of hair teased her cheek. Yet instead of the familiar male stirring, Sebastian felt an odd sort of pang. She was so young. It somehow seemed wrong, almost depraved, to have any physical desire for her.

They stopped to greet an acquaintance of his. The rest of the women used the opportunity to join them and Sebastian made the introductions. Walter Brommer was a pleasant enough fellow, an urbane, witty sort that females took to immediately. He was also an outrageous flirt and soon had all the women smiling at his over-the-top compliments.

Sebastian glanced at the circle of females. Lady Bianca stood beside Emma and he could not help but compare the two. Lady Bianca was a year older than Emma, yet so much more unworldly.

He reasoned the difference might be attributed to the fact that Emma had older sisters. But Lady Bianca had an older sister. Or perhaps being raised in the country was the cause, yet Emma had also grown up in a rural village, raised with her sisters by an aunt and uncle after her parents had died.

It must be Emma's artist's eye that gave her a maturity beyond her years. That and her wicked sense of humor. Her clever tongue could keep any situation from becoming too dull.

Sebastian continued to study Lady Bianca. Her beauty was without question, but her overt innocence was a distraction. He had never understood the appeal of an untutored, inexperienced female. The idea of trying to coax a kiss from her rosy, plump lips made him feel like a lecher of the worst kind. Yet he would have to at least kiss her in order to create the scandal.

"Might I beg a moment of your time, my lord?"

Sebastian glanced down at the gloved hand resting on his forearm, then up into the face of Lady Eleanor. Her features were void of any specific emotion, yet Sebastian sensed an undercurrent of anxiety. It made him wary, yet it would have been impossibly rude to refuse. They set themselves off to the side, away from the boisterous group.

"Are you enjoying the afternoon, Lady Eleanor? Walking in the park, breathing in the fresh, crisp air? Or is it the society that interests you more than the grass and the trees?"

Her expression grew wooden. Lady Eleanor, it appeared, was not a woman who appreciated small talk.

"I am interested in you, my lord," she said. "Or more specifically I am interested in discovering why a man of your years, reputation, and experience is being so attentive to my sister."

"Isn't it obvious?"

"Not to me."

Sebastian frowned. "You do your sister a disservice with that remark," he said, with a tad more fervor than he intended. "Lady Bianca is a unique, remarkable young woman. A man would be a blind fool if he wasted the chance to win her heart."

She flashed him a cool look. "Do you mean to tell me that you have conceived a genuine affection for my sister after a single dance?"

He smiled charmingly, yet avoided her eyes. "You are forgetting the walk she and I just took. That makes it two meetings."

"I'm sure there are many who find your sarcastic wit a great delight." She lifted her chin, her manner, remarkably, even stiffer than before. "I, however, do not."

Well, that certainly put him in his place. Sebastian considered her quietly. He knew deception was essential to his plan, but whenever possible he hoped to avoid a direct lie. "No one can prevent a man's heart from going where it chooses."

She went very still. "How can a heart choose something it does not know?"

Her steady gaze made him want to twist and squirm. There was no way to answer her question without sounding like a besotted young fool. "The mysteries of the heart have confounded people through the ages," he said solemnly. "I fear I am at a loss to explain it."

"Well, this is all very sudden, very unexpected." She turned her face away abruptly, taking in a sharp breath. "I want only the best for Bianca. Her happiness is the most important thing to me and I will do all within my power to see her achieve it."

Sebastian frowned. Lady Eleanor's loyalty to her sister was commendable, yet her tenacity worrisome. This proper, virtuous chaperone could be a serious obstacle to his plan.

"Forgive me, Lady Eleanor, but how can you possibly know what will make your sister happy?"

"I know what will make her unhappy, Lord Benton." She turned her face to his. "A known womanizer with no sense of propriety, faithfulness, or restraint."

"And what does that have to do with me?" he asked softly.

She had the grace to blush, but she did not lower her gaze. "From what I have been hearing, that appears to be the essence of you, my lord."

Her insulting remarks should have incited his anger, but he found himself unable to dispute her claim. And admiring her for having the courage to confront him.

"I'll own that my reputation is not untarnished. I've hardly lived like a monk, but neither am I the villain you seem determined to make me," Sebastian said. "'Tis often said that a rake has no chance at redemption unless he has the love and guidance of a good woman to keep him from falling into infamy. Would you deny me that chance?"

"A man's redemption seems a monumental task for any female and even more so for a young, impressionable lady," she replied.

"Yet well worth the effort."

"You will forgive me if I hold my judgment on that opinion." She continued gazing at him, her expression unyielding. "After all, not every man can be saved."

"True." Sebastian felt his lips starting to curl into a smile. "Nor should they be."

She tilted her head, a hint of suspicion forming in the depths of her eyes. "Are you mocking me, my lord?"

"Quite the contrary, Lady Eleanor. I applaud your honesty. A trait I despair is sorely lacking in most women."

Though he suspected she was trying to prevent it, he saw the hint of a smile tugging at the corners of her mouth. It scarcely made her beautiful, but the softening of her expression showed him that she was, surprisingly, an attractive woman. Not stunning like her sister, but a decent-looking female.

She was tall, possessing the womanly curves he preferred in a woman. Her features were plain, yet soft. Her hair was a rich shade of brown, her eyes a twinkling hazel, with long, dark, lush lashes.

She was the type of female who looked best in vibrant colors, deep shades in jewel tones that set off the richness of her complexion and the sparkle in her eyes. Unfortunately, she did not choose to wear the colors that would enhance her appearance, but instead elected to dress herself in dull grays and serviceable browns. He wondered why.

"If your intentions are serious, Lord Benton, then I expect you to call upon us like a proper suitor. And if they are not . . ."

Sebastian gave her a startled look. "Surely you are not questioning my intentions?"

"I do not know you, my lord, but I know my sister. She is a sweet and kindhearted young lady who has led a very sheltered life. Though possessing a keen intelligence, Bianca is incapable of realizing when a man is trying to take advantage of her." Her prim voice grew even more forceful. "After all, 'tis a well-known fact you have an aversion to marriage."

He raised his brow.

"A fear of marriage?" she amended.

"Indeed?" Sebastian felt his muscles draw up tight. "My reputation isn't all that impressive, based mostly on my wild-oat-sowing youth. I daresay it makes a gentleman a more dashing, attractive catch."

"For whom? An impressionable young girl who doesn't understand the importance of character?"

Ouch. That stung. 'Twas bad enough to have his motives questioned, but her unerring quest for the truth was even more disconcerting. "Is that why you have never married?" Sebastian asked, hoping to divert her attention by changing the focus of the conversation. "Was true character lacking in your beaus?"

"No." For the first time she flushed. "He was noble in character, though not in birth, and proved his mettle by understanding the difficult choice I had to make."

Willpower alone kept the surprise from Sebastian's face. He had made the remark to throw her off balance, never imagining there actually had been a serious relationship in her past. How very interesting. Perhaps there was a way to use this to his advantage?

"What happened?"

She sent him a sideways glare and he expected her to tell him it was none of his business. Instead she shrugged and said quietly, "The social and financial chasm between us was too vast to breach without taking drastic measures. Sadly, I was not free to make them."

"Yet he was a man of good character? A man you admired?"

"Yes, very much." For an instant Lady Eleanor's eyes clouded with emotion. "And loved."

"You do not think Lady Bianca could love me the same way?"

Lady Eleanor blinked her eyes rapidly, coming back to herself with admirable speed. "I do not know my sister's heart, nor will I try to unduly influence it. But I will diligently seek to find a man for her who is eminently trustworthy and dependable. An honorable man who is steady and predictable."

"Dull."

"I beg your pardon?"

"You left out dull." Sebastian had to press his mouth firmly together to hold back his laughter. "Everything you said implies a dull fellow."

"You are wrong. Stability and respectability are not dull traits." Her brows furrowed for a moment. "Not always."

He sighed. "I seem to be hearing a great deal about what you want in a man for Lady Bianca. What of her wishes? Are they to be taken into consideration also?"

Sebastian fixed her with a stare that others found intimidating, yet Lady Eleanor's eyes never wavered from his.

"I have taken charge of my sister's welfare since she was a young child. 'Tis a natural, protective instinct, not easily dismissed."

Sebastian pursed his lips. Lady Eleanor was proving

herself to be a royal pain in his arse, though try as he might, he could not help but respect her. Even like her a bit. It was obvious that as the elder sister she had been the dependable, steady one. Possibly even a substitute parent.

"I don't know what I can say to ease your mind," he finally answered.

"That's even more troubling," she said grimly, before straightening her spine. "I acknowledge it is not my place to order Bianca's life, but I feel the need to protect her."

"Understandable. You are determined to protect her from disaster. Namely, me."

She closed her eyes briefly. He wondered whether she was embarrassed or trying to maintain her patience.

"My sister has a rather modest dowry," Lady Eleanor said. She opened her eyes and turned them fully upon him. "If your expectations were of a vast fortune, I am afraid you will be sorely disappointed."

Ah, so now she thought him a fortune hunter, in addition to an unscrupulous rake. No wonder she was trying to scare him off. "My estates are amazingly sound. I say amazingly since I can claim no credit for their solvency beyond hiring an honest, competent steward. That's not to say that I have piles of money to burn, but I am far from impoverished. Does that ease your mind at all, Lady Eleanor?"

Her mouth twisted, but before she could reply they were interrupted.

"Our carriage approaches," Gwendolyn announced in a loud voice. "Time for afternoon calls."

Sebastian set his fingers to his temples, grateful for the interruption. His conversation with Lady Eleanor had gone in so many directions his head was fairly spinning. Additionally, her interference had taken time away from his pursuit of Lady Bianca, but worse, he feared her continued diligence was going to make it difficult to manipulate young Bianca into a compromising position.

"May we give anyone a lift?" Dorothea asked. "Mr. Brommer? Ladies?"

Brommer declined the offer. So did Lady Eleanor, explaining their carriage was also in view. After a general farewell that encompassed everyone, she took up a position beside her sister, a protective expression on her face.

Ignoring the warning, Sebastian pushed himself forward. Singling Lady Bianca out, he boldly took her hand, delighted to see her color heighten.

"I had a most enjoyable afternoon," he said. "I look forward to seeing you again very soon."

"That is my hope also, my lord." Lady Bianca's smile was sweet and genuine.

A breeze fluttered across Sebastian's neck, but the chill of the air was nothing compared to the skeptical scowl he received from Lady Eleanor. *Hell, she was a suspicious sort.*

With the earl's daughters gone, Sebastian walked the Ellingham sisters to their waiting carriage. He braced himself for their merciless questions and teasing, but they were strangely silent. Deciding it was merely pure chance or dumb luck if he correctly predicted a woman's mood, Sebastian took advantage of the quiet.

Bowing low, he kissed each sister's hand before

assisting them into the coach. He waved as the vehicle rumbled away. Mounting his horse, Sebastian began the slow trek out of the park, once again weaving his way through the crowds.

This time, the delay barely bothered him. He replayed the conversations he had with Hetfield's daughters in his mind, concluding that caution was essential, especially where Lady Eleanor was concerned. Still, all in all, it had been a most enlightening and productive afternoon.

Chapter 5

Bianca chattered with breathless excitement on the carriage ride home from the park. Her delight was so great that she barely noticed when Eleanor did not join the conversation. By the time they walked through the front door of their townhome, a dull ache behind Eleanor's eyes had begun. She had not wanted to squash her sister's enthusiasm at this point by raising any objections to the viscount and the effort had resulted in physical discomfort.

Bianca excused herself and hurried upstairs, explaining she was anxious to remove her new ensemble to prevent it from getting soiled. Eleanor watched her go with an indulgent feeling of affection.

"The post arrived while you were out," the butler, Harrison, informed Eleanor as he took her cloak. "I have left it on the front table, as you requested."

"Thank you." Eleanor nodded cordially but did not smile.

She did not care much for Harrison. He was a stiff, formal man in his late fifties who seemed ridiculously impressed with himself. Eleanor had a vague recollection of hearing that Town servants usually felt superior to their rural counterparts and Harrison had proved that statement correct. It was yet another reason she missed the quiet, uncomplicated country life.

She shifted her attention to the aforementioned mail and her heart sank when she saw the woefully small number of invitations waiting for them. The earl was doing little to launch Bianca in society and his lack of interest was taking a toll. Given half a chance, Eleanor knew her lovely, kindhearted sister would be a great success, yet she worried that the chance would not materialize.

Eleanor crossed the hall to the drawing room. The scent of beeswax and lemon assaulted her nostrils, a welcome change from the smells they endured on the afternoon of their arrival. The house the earl had secured for his daughters had been run-down and neglected. The furnishings were hardly new or fashionable. Several chairs were missing from the dining room, sections of the carpets were worn in places, the fabric on the armchairs was stained and faded.

Eleanor would not have minded the tired atmosphere half as much if it had been clean. Everything seemed to be weighed down by a layer of dust and grime. It had taken the grumbling servants a full week of dusting, washing, and polishing to bring the place to Eleanor's standards, but the results had been worth the effort.

They could sit comfortably in the drawing room without sneezing from the dust, feel the warmth from the fireplace without breathing in sooty smoke, and see the outside world through the now clear window glass. And as she did just that, Eleanor noticed with some surprise that a carriage passing along the street drew to a halt directly in front of their door.

Visitors? It was late, yet still within the proper time frame for making afternoon calls. But the earl was away from home. Who could be calling on them?

Eleanor's questions were answered soon enough when the trio of sisters Viscount Benton introduced them to earlier in the day were brought into the drawing room.

"Do forgive our boldness, Lady Eleanor," Mrs. Gwendolyn Barrington said as she extended her hand in greeting. "We barely had an opportunity to converse with you and your sister at Hyde Park and were vastly disappointed that we did not have the chance to get to know you better."

"Yes, you were far too busy with Viscount Benton to bother with any of us," Miss Emma interjected in a sour tone.

"Emma!" Mrs. Barrington let out a nervous laugh. "This is no time for your sarcastic sense of humor. We barely know Lady Eleanor. She will think you abominably rude."

"I beg your pardon," Miss Emma replied. "I meant no offense."

Eleanor glanced over at the youngest sister, expecting her to look embarrassed or even chastised and was surprised to see the edge of hostility reflected in her gaze.

"Well, there is no denying that Benton does command everyone's attention when he is around,"

Lady Dorothea said with a forced smile. "Except of course when my husband is in the room."

"Now, Dorothea, I take exception to that remark," Mrs. Barrington said with a teasing grin. "'Tis usually my Jason who has the ladies all aflutter."

The women laughed and the tension eased slightly. They settled into the chairs Eleanor indicated. She was debating whether to ring for tea and worried that Cook would have nothing appropriate ready. Visitors were not a common occurrence, indeed, this was the first time anyone had come to call.

Deciding it was safer to forgo refreshments, Eleanor instructed Harrison to summon her sister. A smiling Bianca arrived and they were soon discussing the upcoming events of the Season.

Eleanor deliberately contributed little to the conversation, wanting instead for Bianca to take the lead. She was a bit hesitant and awkward at first, yet thanks to the friendly, open manner of their guests Bianca tackled the challenge admirably.

Eleanor was surprised to learn that the ladies were all fairly recent arrivals in London and even more shocked to hear they had been raised in the country. They had no noble connections to speak of, being granddaughters of a baronet. Yet somehow Mrs. Barrington had managed to marry into the family of an earl and Lady Dorothea, already a marchioness, would someday assume the title of Duchess of Hansborough.

Eleanor studied the two older sisters covertly as they talked. These country girls had risen far in the world. More important, they seemed happy. Their smiling, teasing references to their husbands bespoke of stable, loving relationships.

Thanks to her sisters' connections, the youngest, Emma, would have her pick of any gentleman when she decided to marry. Eleanor felt a deep pang of envy at her good fortune. Dear Bianca would not have such an easy time.

A social friendship with these women would be advantageous. But Eleanor's hopes that Bianca might form a genuine friendship with Emma, who was closest to her in age, were soon dashed. Beyond the absence of any additional rude outbursts, Emma's manner was not in the least approachable.

She sat silently, a decidedly prudish expression on her pretty face. Eleanor was unsure what they might have done to offend this young woman. Was she jealous of Bianca's beauty? Or was it something else entirely that had put her out of sorts?

Whatever the reason, Eleanor thought it poor manners to act so peevishly when among company. And it seemed rather strange that while the two older sisters were trying hard to be agreeable, the younger one was not especially easy to like.

The clock struck the hour and the visitors stood. "Thank you for a lovely visit," Lady Dorothea said as she tugged on her gloves. "I know the invitation is rather last minute, but my husband and I are hosting a small dinner party on Thursday evening. Nothing elaborate or fancy, just some family and close friends. If by any chance you are free, we would like you to join us."

"I am unsure if my father has any specific plans on Thursday evening," Eleanor replied.

"Gracious, forgive my rudeness," Lady Dorothea muttered. "Of course the earl is included in the invitation."

Eleanor smiled noncommittally. She could not fault Lady Dorothea for not knowing the inclusion of the earl hardly sweetened the invitation.

"Oh, do say you will come," Mrs. Barrington pressed. "After all, country girls must stick together."

"I will consult our social calendar and let you know," Eleanor said.

She and Bianca remained in the drawing room after their guests had departed, just in case any other callers arrived.

"You will accept Lady Dorothea's dinner invitation, won't you?" Bianca asked as they waited. "I'd really like to attend."

"Would you? I didn't realize you'd taken such a shine to Lady Dorothea. Or was it Mrs. Barrington?"

"How unkind of you to tease me," Bianca said with an airy laugh. "Tell me truthfully, do you think Viscount Benton will be there?"

Eleanor let out an inelegant snort. "I imagine it is possible. He claims a close friendship with the family."

"I know you won't believe me, but I would like to go even if he is not in attendance." Bianca twirled the end of the satin ribbon twisted through her hair, her expression thoughtful. "Of course, if the viscount does come, well, all the better for me."

Oh, Bianca. Eleanor's heart tripped with worry. Having Benton in attendance was the reason Eleanor had been reluctant to accept the invitation in the first place.

"The earl might have already made plans for you on Thursday evening," Eleanor said, wondering if that would be even worse.

Bianca's face fell. "No matter. If we cannot attend, I feel certain I shall see Lord Benton again somewhere else."

For Bianca's sake, Eleanor tried to smile, but she couldn't. With the roguish viscount and his unclear intentions looming on the horizon, it seemed that this trip to Town was going to be far more of an ordeal than Eleanor had originally anticipated.

For Sebastian, distractions had always been the essential element to leading a peaceful existence. Keeping busy with the daily nonsense of life helped one avoid facing its true difficulties. Yet ever since he set his course of revenge against the earl, distractions were harder to find.

A morning with his tailor or bootmaker, an afternoon looking over the latest crop of horses at Tattersall's or boxing at Jackson's Salon, an early evening spent lounging about his club or playing cards were no longer comfortable, easy ways to pass the time. The notion of revenge consumed his waking hours, making everything else seem trite. And he feared it would not be long before it also affected his sleep.

It seemed rather peculiar that having a strong purpose and direction in his life left him feeling restless and edgy, but that was the result. Truthfully, he had never felt quite so off balance.

The solution, he decided, was to break his usual routine. To that end he made his way from his bachelor apartments across town to the fashionable section of Mayfair and the new townhome of the Marquess of Atwood.

His intention was not to visit his friend, though he'd be pleased to have a chat with him. Rather, the purpose of the visit was to see Emma. Though their conversations were always spirited, Emma's presence usually had a calming effect on him, something he needed now more than ever.

Sebastian dressed with his usual care, ignoring his valet's fussy comments, ate a hearty breakfast, and called for his horse. Even though the day was cloudy, he set off at a leisurely pace. His mood improved with each block until Sebastian turned his mount down Atwood's street and caught sight of a familiar residence. A sudden knot clutched in his stomach.

The stately white-stone mansion with the distinct royal blue shutters had belonged to his grandmother. It was now his property, the most substantial asset of her modest estate, fittingly bequeathed to him, her only grandchild. Yet he had not moved into the home upon returning to Town. His name might be on the deed of ownership, but in his mind it was still his grandmother's house, a place where he had always been a welcome visitor.

Whether it was to hear the latest gossip or to give him a scathing lecture on a whole host of subjects, Sebastian's weekly visits were something that went beyond familial duty. They might not have always been pleasant, but they offered an odd sense of security.

'Twas astonishing really to think how much he missed those visits. How much he missed her.

As he rode by the house, he slowed his mount. The house appeared to be in good condition. The ornamental shrubs were neatly trimmed, the windows shining clean, the front steps newly washed. Yet the absence of the brass knocker on the front door indicating the family was not in residence rattled him.

It was a stark reminder of the permanency of death and the changes it wrought. A reminder Sebastian hardly needed at the moment. He looked away and spurred his horse to a quicker pace.

"Good morning, Hawkins," Sebastian said cordially when Atwood's butler answered the door.

"Lord Benton." The butler bowed respectfully but did not move aside to allow Sebastian into the house. "I regret to inform you that the marquess is not at home."

Sebastian raised his brow. It was the standard response given to callers when the family did not wish to be disturbed. But he was not a typical caller. In fact, he had never been turned away, unless no one truly was in the house.

Sebastian glanced through the open door at the ornate clock majestically positioned in the marble foyer, confirming the time. Eleven o'clock. Far too early for Atwood to be out. Far too early also for callers.

"Is Lord Atwood really away?" Sebastian asked.

"The marquess is not at home," the butler repeated in a low voice.

Sebastian frowned in puzzlement, staring back at the stoic servant. His face remained impassive. "But Atwood is never away at this hour," Sebastian pondered out loud, until suddenly the truth dawned. "Is that a blush, Hawkins?" he asked with a teasing smile.

The servant's eyes widened in horror, confirming

Sebastian's theory. Atwood was still abed, more than likely with his lovely wife beside him. Or under him.

"The marquess—"

"Yes, yes, is not at home," Sebastian interrupted. "Well, no matter. I'm here to see Miss Emma."

"She is painting," the butler replied, a small sigh of relief escaping. He opened the door wider and Sebastian sauntered over the threshold. Hawkins signaled discreetly with his left hand and a footman materialized. "Show Lord Benton to Miss Emma's studio."

Sebastian knew precisely where Emma did her painting, having been there numerous times. But he did not belay the command, deciding he'd already embarrassed the butler enough for one day.

Emma gave him a friendly, albeit distracted greeting when he entered her studio. She was facing the door, positioned in front of an easel that held a large canvas. The paintbrush in her hand was moving at a frantic rate. Sebastian was disappointed he could not view the canvas from where he stood, curious to see what had so inspired her passion.

"Obviously I'm disturbing you, but I'd like to stay anyway," he said. "May I?"

"Can you be quiet for ten minutes?"

"I can," he replied.

She nodded and he settled himself in an over-stuffed chair, one of only two pieces of furniture in the room. Silence descended, except for the sound of brush against canvas. It was a relaxed, undemanding noise.

Sebastian closed his eyes, concentrating on smells of the room, evoking pleasant memories of the hours he had spent in the studio posing for his portrait. The portrait his grandmother had commissioned from Emma a few months before her death. The portrait he had not yet seen.

After ten minutes or so, Emma heaved a sigh. Sebastian opened his eyes. Emma slowly lowered her brush. She gazed at the painting for a long moment. Finally, she removed it from the easel and gently propped it against the wall, facing inward.

Sebastian glanced curiously at the back of the canvas. Emma had always generously shared her work with him. What was it about this particular painting that made her so secretive?

"Is it finished?" Sebastian asked. "Can I see it?"

"No!" Emma blushed and took a protective step back, almost as if she were guarding the painting. "To both questions." She hastily lifted an unfinished canvas from the stack behind her and placed it on her easel.

Sebastian felt strangely hurt by her actions. "Hell, Emma, when did you become so temperamental?"

"An artist's privilege," she answered saucily. "And if I were truly temperamental, I would bar you from my studio and take great offense at your language."

"Point taken."

Slightly mollified, Sebastian asked her about the rest of the family. They chatted pleasantly for a while, discussing each member in turn, then moved on to mutual friends and acquaintances and the newest round of society entertainments.

"Are you coming to dinner tomorrow night?" Emma asked. "I was helping Dorothea write out the placards earlier and noticed a question mark by your name."

Sebastian frowned. An intimate, comfortable dinner

among friends sounded delightful, but he needed to be out in society, on the hunt for Lady Bianca. "I doubt I'll make it to dinner," he said. "There's the Wilfords' ball and Lady Georginia's soiree."

"Instead of spending the evening with us, you prefer listening to Lady Georginia's bucktooth nieces massacre a Bach concerto on their violins?" Emma shuddered.

"Maybe they won't play their violins," he replied wistfully, knowing Emma was right. The valiant effort put forth by Lady Georginia's nieces unfortunately did not make up for their lack of talent. Or their aunt's tone-deaf musical ear.

"Hmm, yes, perhaps they will choose to sing this year." Emma smiled and Sebastian groaned. "Pity about dinner, though. You'll be missed, but I shall make a point of giving Lady Bianca your warmest regards."

Bianca? Sebastian's heart picked up speed. He straightened in his chair and gave Emma a long look. "Lady Bianca? Since when is she a part of your sister's inner circle of dear friends?"

Emma shrugged. "I don't believe she has reached that place of honor quite yet. Rather, Dorothea felt sorry for her and Lady Eleanor. They seem to have made little impression on society. I think Dorothea was merely being kind by extending the invitation."

"They are coming?"

"Indeed."

"With their father, the earl?"

Emma's head tipped to the side. "No, I don't recall seeing his name on the list."

Abruptly, Sebastian grinned. "Then Lady Geor-

ginia's nieces can torture some other poor souls.
I'll be here enjoying dinner."

"Because of Lady Bianca?"

Sebastian's grin widened. "Her and others."

Emma tossed her head and muttered beneath
her breath. Sebastian's brow raised. "Pardon?"

"You surprise me, Sebastian."

"You are surprised by my interest in a woman? I
believe I should feel insulted."

"For heaven's sake, of course I know you like
women. Honestly, Sebastian, what sort of silly goose
do you take me for?" Emma slammed her paintbrush on the small table beside her easel, then
picked up another brush. "It's just that I assumed
your relationships were with older, more experienced females."

"Maybe I felt it was time for a change."

"And you have chosen Lady Bianca?" Emma rolled
her eyes. "She is nothing more than a pretty face, an
empty-headed creature incapable of deep feeling."

"That's rather harsh." Sebastian adjusted his position on the chair. "If I had been so quick to rush
to judgment when I met you, we might never have
become friends."

Emma's paintbrush paused in midair and she
looked sharply at him. "I am nothing like Lady
Bianca."

"I never said that you were."

"You were paying a great deal of attention to her
at the park the other day. Pray, tell me what is it that
makes her so special?" Emma asked as she slashed
her paintbrush across the canvas.

"She's different," he replied noncommittally.

"Are you planning on marrying her?"

Christ! Leave it to Emma to get to the heart of the matter without mincing words. He opened his mouth, then closed it without saying anything. The room grew quiet.

"Is that a *none-of-my-business* glare, Sebastian?" Emma ceased painting entirely, resting her hand against her waist, the brush dangling between her fingers. "Or are you unable to come up with an honest reply?"

"Neither," he said evenly. "'Tis a *we-are-going-to-change-the-subject* expression. What are you working on these days? Something extraordinary, I imagine."

She gave him a long, impenetrable stare before answering. "'Tis a landscape. My instructor insists I broaden my skills."

"Sound advice."

"I am a portrait painter, Sebastian. I find little inspiration in grass and trees." Emma sighed. "I've made a few sketches of Gwendolyn's twins, but they are too young to sit for a proper portrait."

"Then find someone else."

Her shoulders sank. "I promised Atwood I would not accept any commissions from outsiders. Your grandmother was the only one who was able to persuade him to do otherwise and allow me to paint you."

"I haven't seen the finished portrait yet," he mused.

"No, you have not."

The hurt in her voice was clear, stabbing at his heart. "I'm sorry. 'Tis just that—"

"I understand. 'Tis a painful reminder of your grandmother."

Sebastian felt grateful for her quick understanding

and acceptance. She was remarkably insightful for such a young woman. "Why don't you paint the duke?"

"He grumbles too much to sit quietly. I fear I would paint him with his mouth open and a scowl upon his noble brow. And that portrait would not endear me to my brother-in-law."

Sebastian laughed. "Atwood knows better than you or I how cantankerous his father can be. Don't fret. I will help you find someone." He stood and walked to her side. "I'll speak to Atwood myself, if necessary."

Her gaze darted to his, then shifted away. "You are very good to me, Sebastian."

"That's because I adore you, Emma," he replied, with a smile.

Reaching out, he placed his hand on her back, rubbing it reassuringly in a slow, circling motion. She heaved a large sigh and swayed toward him. Sebastian increased the pressure, trying to ease the tension from her body, missing entirely the spark of yearning in her eyes.

By Thursday, the weather had turned dismal. The lovely warm sunshine of the previous afternoons gave way to cool gray skies. Eleanor stood at her bedchamber window gazing out at the grim, damp day and sighed. Bad weather would dictate indoor activities, which meant the earl might stay at home.

Eleanor shuddered. It was never pleasant spending time in her father's company. He always managed to make her feel like an unwanted intrusion. It was better when Bianca was present, but lately she had begun to feel anxious whenever she saw her father and sister together.

The earl treated his youngest daughter in a condescending manner that grated on Eleanor's nerves. Bianca was so starved for attention she allowed it, and that was hurtful to witness. But it was her eager, anxious attitude to please their father that upset Eleanor the most.

The earl's behavior toward Bianca remained a deep puzzlement. Eleanor had been certain he had brought Bianca to London expressly for the purpose of finding her a rich husband. Yet aside from providing her with a fashionable wardrobe, he had done little to advance his daughter in society.

Eleanor had envisioned him escorting them to numerous social events where he would press Bianca on the men of his choosing, but that had not occurred. *Yet.* Of course it was preferable not to have him involved in their lives, but this neglect worried Eleanor.

More than once in the past week she had caught the earl eyeing Bianca with a calculated look, almost as if he were assessing her worth. It made Eleanor very nervous to think what their father might be planning.

She worried he might have already selected someone to be Bianca's husband. Perhaps he had already struck a marriage bargain with this person and was waiting for the right time to make the introduction to his daughter. Or announce the marriage, regardless of Bianca's opinion of the matter.

Eleanor knew money was the driving force behind it all. She knew her father gambled—most gentlemen did. But until coming to Town, she had not realized the amount of time he spent at the tables. Most likely it was an attempt to supplement his income, however, the fickle turn of a card could hardly be counted upon in times of need. No doubt the earl lost as much as he earned.

Having formed a friendship with their steward, Eleanor was aware of exactly how much profit the estate produced each year. She was also aware that the earl's investments had steadily declined in value over the past few years, but she saw no signs of personal economic restraint.

The earl liked the finer things in life: expensive wines, fashionable garments, prime horseflesh. He appeared to deny himself nothing, for these were items easily obtained on credit. But creditors could not be put off indefinitely. Eleanor's deepest worry remained that Bianca would be the one to pay for their father's excesses, that her happiness and future would be sacrificed to keep him in the style that he felt he deserved.

She sighed, then shook off her gloomy thoughts. The reason she had journeyed to Town was to protect Bianca from their father's plans. If she remained vigilant and determined, it did not have to turn out so badly.

Chin up, Eleanor told herself sternly as she strode down the hallway to the sitting room. She settled herself in a worn, yet comfortable armchair before the roaring fire, her needlework in her lap. She always thought better when moving her hands and the pile of garments that needed mending was never ending.

Eleanor knew the earl would be annoyed if he saw her engaged in such a menial task. *Servants* mended, *ladies* embroidered. But old habits died hard and the familiarity of this task calmed her nerves.

For a moment she longed for the peace of the country, the quiet, dull life where her biggest worry had been how to stretch the meager household budget to ensure the servants were paid each month.

"There you are!" Bianca exclaimed as she barged into the room. "I've been looking all over the house for you. The rest of my gowns were just delivered and I can't decide what to wear to Lady Atwood's dinner party tonight. Please, Eleanor, help me."

"Such drama, Bianca," Eleanor said with a smile as she glanced up from her sewing. "What has gotten into you? 'Tis not such a dastardly fate, my dear, having too many dresses from which to choose."

"Don't tease, Eleanor. I am truly in a quandary."

"Goodness, we can't have that, now can we?" Eleanor replied, repressing a smile. Obligingly, she put down her sewing and allowed herself to be dragged off to Bianca's bedchamber.

As she crossed the threshold of her sister's room, Eleanor could not contain her gasp of surprise. Never before had she seen such a large assortment of elegant garments. The normally neat chamber was totally transformed, nearly bursting with everything a fashionable lady could ever need, from dancing slippers to bonnets. In the center of it all was a sea of color, with gowns too numerous to count, placed carefully, almost reverently, upon the high four-poster bed.

Bianca fairly danced into the room, heading

directly for the bed. She lifted a gown from the top of the pile and turned toward Eleanor.

"What do you think of this one?" Bianca held up a pale green satin gown with a square-cut bodice that was heavily embroidered in gold thread. The color set off the green in her eyes and the gold brought out the lighter highlights in her amber hair.

"It's lovely." Eleanor stepped forward and lifted the hem. It felt soft and silky between her fingers. "Will you wear it tonight?"

"Should I? I mean, it's very pretty, but I thought it might make me look too young. How about the yellow?"

Bianca lifted another dress. It had a similar shape, but a round neckline and less embroidery. "That's also very pretty. But I like the green better. It reflects the color of your eyes."

Bianca bit her bottom lip. "You are certain?"

"I am. You will look ravishing."

Bianca smiled, but the smile seemed forced.

"Why are you so worried about your appearance tonight?" Eleanor asked, fearing she already knew the answer. "Lady Dorothea assured us it was going to be a casual dinner party."

"Oh, Eleanor, you know why." Bianca glanced away.

"Viscount Benton?"

Bianca nodded enthusiastically. "I'm a bundle of nerves thinking I might see him again. He's already singled me out. At the Duke of Warren's ball and again at the park the other day. I shiver thinking about what might happen the next time we are to-gether."

Inwardly Eleanor cringed. She too had thought a

great deal about her sister and the viscount, and it never once had a happy ending. "Bianca, dearest, you must not get your hopes raised too high. For a man like Benton, flirtation comes as naturally as breathing."

Bianca sank down on the edge of the bed, miraculously finding the one small spot not covered by one of her new gowns. "I've heard the gossip about his reputation and I've told myself quite sternly that his attention is nothing special, nothing I should take too seriously."

"I'm glad to hear it."

Bianca leapt from the bed, hugging her arms tightly around her waist. "Oh, but he is so dashing and sophisticated. I feel so different when I am in his company. I am excited and happy, yet nervous too. My breath quickens, my palms become damp. I vow my heart flutters and my stomach rumbles every time I am near him. What do you think that means?"

"He gives you indigestion?"

Bianca groaned. "I am serious, Eleanor."

"I know."

"Do you? Really?" Bianca leaned forward and grabbed Eleanor's hand. "There is something indefinable about the viscount, something compelling, something that goes far deeper than his handsome face and devilish smile."

Eleanor bit her bottom lip. It was even worse than she had feared. Bianca was feeling a dangerously strong attraction to the viscount, something that Eleanor felt very certain would lead to heartache. "'Tis natural for a woman to be attracted to such a handsome man."

"Is it? But, Eleanor, what does he see in me?"

A new conquest? Eleanor was tempted to give her brutally honest opinion, yet she could not bring herself to be so cruelly blunt. Especially when she had no specific proof. Only an uneasy feeling about the viscount's intentions.

"You are a beautiful girl with a warm, tender heart and a pleasing disposition," Eleanor replied, squeezing her hand.

Bianca pulled her hand away. "The viscount can hardly *see* my disposition. I'm worried that he might think I have a large dowry." Bianca reached down and smoothed her skirt. "Papa has never said, but I know that funds are tight."

"Not really, we have—"

"Stop, Eleanor, please." Bianca's mouth tightened. "You scrimp and save on everything. At home you juggle the tradesmen, trying to make sure everyone receives some payment, though I know the bills are never paid in full. And this house, well, 'tis nice enough, I suppose, but not in the best condition."

Eleanor's heart plummeted. She thought she had been so clever hiding the truth from her sister. "I don't know the true state of our financial affairs. Perhaps the earl has just been frugal with regard to our care."

"I should like to think that is the case. Now that we are in Town he has been more generous. With me." Bianca studied her with a probing gaze. "Oh, Eleanor, I feel awful. Papa has spent lavishly for my wardrobe but spared barely a shilling for you."

The comment struck a painful nerve and Eleanor struggled to keep her expression impassive. "This is your coming-out Season, not mine. I do not need a bunch of fancy clothes."

"It's been ages since you had a new dress. Ordering at least a gown or two would have been the decent thing for Papa to do. I was going to speak with him—"

"No!" Eleanor shot forward. "There is no need. Promise me you will let the matter drop."

Bianca smiled mischievously. "You did not let me finish. What I was trying to say was that I was going to speak with him, but then worried what I would do if he refused. I feared a terrific row, which I might very well lose. So instead I commissioned a few gowns from Madame Claudette with your measurements."

"Bianca!" Eleanor was shocked. Deception was not a part of her sister's personality.

Bianca turned and rummaged through the pile of gowns on the bed. Triumphantly she pulled out a gown and presented it proudly to Eleanor.

Tears threatened, but Eleanor blinked them away. The dress was truly lovely, simple without being severe, plain, yet elegant. Fashioned of deep blue silk, with rounded half sleeves and a low sweetheart neckline, it was a style that would flatter and enhance her figure. Instead of embroidery, there was a sheer white tulle overskirt gathered under the bust, trimmed with a matching blue ribbon to lend sophistication to the garment.

"I chose it from a drawing, but it seemed so right for you," Bianca said with an anxious smile. "Do you like it?"

"Very much, indeed. I could not have done better

if I selected it myself." Bianca smiled again and Eleanor tried to lighten her own heart.

"'Tis settled. I will wear the green and you shall wear the blue silk." Bianca walked across the chamber carrying both garments in her arms. "I have some matching slippers you can borrow and Anne will do our hair. She is a wonder with the curling tongs."

Bianca's excitement was nearly contagious, but Eleanor forced herself to be practical. "I agree to wear my new gown on the condition that you promise to be careful around Lord Benton," she bargained.

Bianca's brows furrowed together and Eleanor swore she could see her sister's inner struggles. "Very well," she finally replied. "I shall endeavor to be sensible about him."

It was not precisely the answer Eleanor sought, but she knew for now it would have to suffice.

Chapter 6

Eleanor drew in an inaudible breath as she crossed the threshold of Lord and Lady Atwood's home, the wind and rain swirling behind her. Two liveried footmen hurried forward to wrestle the door shut, while a third bent down to towel dry the floor.

The outside facade of the house was classic and understated, the interior fashionably elegant with a black and white marble-floored entry, a sweeping staircase, and a fresco painting of the heavens adorning the domed ceiling.

Beside her she felt Bianca tuck her hand against her hip to stop its trembling. Eleanor couldn't tell whether her sister was shivering from the damp weather, intimidated by the sumptuous, refined surroundings, or anxious at the prospect of seeing Lord Benton. Perhaps a combination of all three.

Eleanor could feel Bianca's trembling increase when they entered the drawing room. Trimmed in shades of gold, the decor was opulent and lavish, but Eleanor had little time to appreciate it. Lord Benton, starkly handsome in black evening clothes with a silver embroidered waistcoat and a flawlessly tied white cravat, descended upon them.

Eleanor braced herself, but before the viscount reached them, Lady Dorothea appeared, a tall, handsome gentleman by her side.

"'Tis delightful to see you both," Lady Dorothea said, her lovely features alighting with pleasure. "It's been raining so hard tonight I was afraid not all of the guests would be able to come."

"Thankfully the ones who matter most made it safely," Lord Benton interrupted as his white, even teeth flashed in a wicked grin. "Good evening, Lady Bianca. Lady Eleanor."

He bowed sharply, then reached for Bianca's hand and held it tightly. Eleanor watched in dismay as her sister stared into his eyes, swaying ever so slightly toward him. Panicking, she cleared her throat. Loudly. Bianca jumped, a charming blush flowering in her cheeks as she pulled her hand away.

"Stop accosting my guests, Benton," the other man said softly, "or else I'll banish you to the kitchens to eat with the staff."

"Oh dear, that will never do," Lady Dorothea remarked with a smile. "The maids will be swooning into their supper plates with Benton at the table. Better to send him out into the storm if he misbehaves."

"Yes, he can dine in the doghouse." Lines of puzzlement suddenly appeared in the other gentleman's face. "We did have the builder put up a doghouse, did we not, my love?"

"We did, though I'm embarrassed to admit Lancelot has never once set foot inside it. And I am even more embarrassed at our unforgivable rudeness, for I have not yet introduced you to our guests. Lady Eleanor, Lady Bianca, I am pleased to present my husband, Carter Grayson, Marquess of Atwood."

Eleanor and Bianca swept into a curtsy while the marquess bowed. The Marquess of Atwood was a classic example of a tall, dark, and handsome man. He possessed an inbred aristocratic manner of absolute authority that would have been exceedingly off-putting if not for his charming smile. Eleanor was favorably impressed.

His father, the Duke of Hansborough, whom they were introduced to next, was another matter entirely. In Eleanor's opinion, the older man embodied every cliché about the aristocracy in one neat package. Cold, arrogant, and superior, he was a truly intimidating figure.

He fixed his gaze steadily on her as she made her curtsy, his expression undisguised curiosity. "So you're Hetfield's eldest girl?"

Eleanor nodded.

"I knew your mother. A charming, fine-looking woman. Very graceful on the dance floor, as I recall." The duke lifted his brow as he made a sympathetic murmur. "You don't favor her much in looks."

Eleanor bit down hard on her lower lip to muffle her gasp of indignation. "My sister inherited our mother's coloring," she said through tight lips.

"And Lady Eleanor inherited her grace and charm," a masculine voice added.

Eleanor turned, uncertain who else was near

enough to have heard the duke's insulting remark. She suspected it was Lord Atwood, but instead Lord Benton stared back at her.

"The old man's testing your mettle," the viscount whispered. "As far as I know, the duke doesn't bite." The corners of Lord Benton's mouth turned up. "Very often."

"I am not worried, my lord," Eleanor hissed back. "I have faced down far worse in my day then a temperamental, insensitive duke. I imagine he will be vastly disappointed if I don't quiver and crumble."

"He will."

"Then I shall take great delight in disappointing him." Eleanor smiled pleasantly as the duke turned to speak with another guest. "Though I don't understand why he would take a particular interest in me."

"He's very protective of his daughter-in-law," Benton answered. "He wants to know everything about the people who become her friends."

Become her friend? An unexpected wave of melancholy swept over Eleanor. Her time in London would be brief. Even if she did form a friendship with Lady Dorothea, there was a very small chance that she would see her again after the Season was over.

Swallowing the sudden rush of self-pity, Eleanor turned her attention to the conversation swirling around her. Emma had joined their circle and she and the duke were engaged in a lively exchange.

"I for one am not disappointed he can't be here tonight. Lord Sullivan is a buffoon," the duke grumbled. "Thinks he's an expert on everything under the sun and takes great pleasure in spouting his nonsensical opinions."

"When asked or not," Lord Benton muttered under his breath. Eleanor dipped her chin to hide her smile.

"Lord Sullivan might be a bore, Your Grace," Emma said. "But at least he refrains from discussing his ailments, a topic that most older people seem to embrace with fanatical enthusiasm."

The duke stared at her, his silver eyebrows rising. "You had better not be lumping me into that category, young lady, or else I'll be forced to box your ears."

"I said *older people,* Your Grace," Emma replied with a saucy grin. "That could not possibly include you."

"Ha!" The duke smiled in appreciation, then turned to his son. "You had better watch this one carefully, Carter. She's going to lead some hapless fellow on a merry chase."

"I know that all too well, sir." The marquess grinned at his sister-in-law. "But eventually a clever man will catch her and then she shall be his problem."

"Carter!" Lady Dorothea wrinkled her nose at her husband. "I do not appreciate you referring to Emma as a problem."

"Come now, Lady Dorothea, you know Atwood was merely jesting," Lord Benton interjected. "Indeed, every man with an ounce of intelligence knows the only wives worth having are the problem kind."

"Benton's talking about having a wife?" Creases

formed on the duke's forehead. "He must be royally foxed."

A hearty laugh rumbled from the viscount's chest. "I was referring to other men's wives, Your Grace. Not one of my own."

"I have talked myself blue in the face over the joys of matrimony, yet sadly for him, Benton is still not convinced of the benefits of a wife." Atwood looked at Lord Benton, one eyebrow cocked in affection. Clearly he was very fond of the viscount.

"Nevertheless, it's deuced bad form to scare an old man like that, Benton," the duke said. "You know my heart could give out at any time."

"Surely you jest, Your Grace," Eleanor interjected smoothly. "I imagine your heart can withstand a great deal."

There was a slight pause. Then, with an irritable expression, the duke turned his full attention on Eleanor. "You sound surprised to hear that I have a heart."

"Not at all. However, if that particular thought ever crossed my mind, I would never be so rude as to express it out loud," Eleanor replied. "Especially when others are near enough to overhear such an unflattering remark."

Her lips curved. It was a clever set-down, one Eleanor was proud to have delivered. She had rebuked the duke's earlier discourtesy in a subtle, yet pointed manner.

"Benton," the duke said, his eyes still squarely on Eleanor. "If you were ever of a mind to get yourself a bride, you'd be wise to look no further."

"Indeed, Your Grace. Lady Eleanor has much to

recommend her. Alas, I worry that she also possesses the good sense to refuse me."

"She *is* a smart woman," Lord Atwood joked and everyone laughed.

Eleanor felt the heat of a blush rise in her cheeks. Her and Lord Benton? Whatever was the duke thinking? She examined the conversation in her mind, deciding the duke had surely been jesting. True, she was closer in age to him than her sister, but honestly what man would be interested in her when Bianca was available?

That was of course assuming the viscount was interested in acquiring a wife. Based on all that she had heard, including the good-natured barbs this evening from those who knew him best, it seemed unlikely.

A footman holding a silver tray laden with filled glasses approached. Conversation ceased as everyone shifted about and made their selections. Eleanor picked a glass of ratafia for herself and was about to offer Bianca a tumbler of lemonade when she noticed her sister walking away, Lord Benton at her side.

Eleanor opened her mouth to call her back, but the command faded on her lips. Try as she might, she could not control Bianca's every move. But she could, and would, keep a close eye on the viscount.

Settling herself on the end of an unoccupied couch, Eleanor slowly sipped her drink as she watched Lord Benton and her sister. Judging by Bianca's frequent smiles, blushing cheeks, and lowered eyes, Eleanor concluded the viscount was flirting outrageously, but she surmised even he could not behave with too much impropriety when in plain view.

Eleanor was soon aware that she was not the only one who had noticed the pair. Emma was positively mesmerized by them.

"They make a rather striking couple, my sister and the viscount," Eleanor remarked casually.

For a heartbeat Emma hesitated, a fleeting look of concern on her face. Then she leaned toward Eleanor. "Benton is trouble," Emma insisted, her voice pitched low. "You must not allow your sister to be deceived by his quick-witted charm and striking good looks."

"Strange, I thought you liked him."

Emma's eyes sparkled. "I do. He is marvelously entertaining. But I am not blind to his faults. Nor am I naive. He is a handsome, titled man in his early thirties who is known for charming women into his bed and has vowed not to marry until he is at least forty."

"One would have to question why you keep company with such a man," Eleanor replied, wondering at Emma's lack of restraint. Close friends tried to shield each other's reputations, not taint them. "Indeed, why would your entire family embrace him so completely if he is such an unscrupulous rake?"

Emma shrugged, her sharp gaze giving no quarter. "The friendship between my brother-in-law and Lord Benton is of long standing. They were schoolmates as boys, along with Mr. Dawson. The marquess would never stoop so low as to abandon his friends, no matter how tarnished their reputation. He has, however, expressly forbid me to be alone in Benton's company."

"Sound, prudent advice for any young girl." Eleanor's smile was wry. "I hope you take it."

"I know all about proper, acceptable society behavior," Emma answered. "Yet I am uncertain if the same can be said of your sister."

Eleanor's hackles rose automatically at the slight. Sister of the hostess be damned, she was about to deliver a scathing retort when she noticed Emma's fingers curling into a tight fist. *Goodness, the girl was twisted in knots. Over Benton?*

Perhaps. Still, the slight could not go completely unchallenged. Eleanor reached out and patted Emma's knuckles. "'Tis a great relief then, is it not, that Bianca is my concern and not yours."

Emma gave her a long, level look. But then her demeanor changed instantly, her face almost glowing as if lit from within. Eleanor turned her head and noticed Lord Benton walking across the drawing room toward them. He was alone. Bianca had remained on the other side of the room, talking with the marquess and two other young women whose names Eleanor did not recall.

As he drew closer, Eleanor saw the truth revealed in Emma's eyes. She was in love with the viscount. Eleanor glanced about the room to see if anyone had noticed, but no one thought anything unusual. It appeared what was so blatantly in front of them was too obvious to see.

For one brief moment Eleanor almost felt sorry for Emma. While it was clear that Lord Benton held her in great affection, he treated her as a younger sibling, not a possible wife.

Then again, the viscount was a close friend of her brother-in-law's. He might well marry her in the end, for men were ever practical when selecting a mate.

Eleanor pondered what this might mean for Bianca as the Atwoods' butler signaled supper was served. The guests strolled informally to the dining room and Eleanor's breath hitched.

It was a stunning room, boasting three chandeliers and easily seating the forty invited guests. It was a number Eleanor herself would never have assigned to a small dinner party, of course, she moved little in society and had never actually presided over one.

Her nerves eased as the meal progressed. Peter Dawson, seated on her left, was an interesting dinner companion. He soon had her laughing over tales of his boyhood antics with Lord Atwood and Lord Benton. She kept a close eye on Bianca but for long stretches allowed herself to relax and enjoy the delicious meal and witty conversation.

It was amazing how a glass of wine could mellow her nerves. Eleanor drained the first goblet by the time the meat course was served. She glanced down the table to where Bianca was speaking to two women, her face wreathed in a smile, then checked to see where Lord Benton was seated.

Relief swamped her when she saw the viscount was on the opposite side, several chairs away from her sister.

"More wine, Lady Eleanor?"

Mr. Dawson smiled at her while the liveried footman holding the bottle waited for her to answer. "Perhaps just a half glass," she replied, deciding it couldn't hurt.

The situation with Bianca and the viscount seemed

under control for the moment. It would be foolish indeed not to take advantage of this rare opportunity and enjoy herself.

As the dessert course was being served, Sebastian was surprised to find himself having a good time. Dinner parties at the Atwoods' were always lively affairs and tonight was no exception. The food was delicious, though he thought the fricassee of veal a tad overspiced, the conversation stimulating, if one avoided the duke's barbs, the company congenial, except for the occasional suspicious stares from Lady Eleanor.

Though seated several chairs away, he had been near enough to Lady Bianca to flirt with her intermittently during the meal, her shy smiles and warm blushes a sure sign of her interest. Sebastian's luck held as the gentlemen left the dining room after their port and cigars had been enjoyed and joined the ladies. The wicked weather had calmed considerably, from torrential rains to a lighter spring drizzle and now to a balmy mist.

Several of the guests used the opportunity to stroll in the garden and Sebastian promptly placed himself at Lady Bianca's side. She bestowed a welcoming smile upon her lips when he joined her, the moonlight casting a golden shadow over her delicate features.

Tucking her hand into his arm, Sebastian smoothly maneuvered down a secluded path, away from the others. *Like a lamb to the slaughter.* Damn, it was so much easier dealing with a female who didn't have a suspicious bone in her body.

They strolled leisurely down the garden path past formal flower beds in neat symmetrical shapes to a section where the shrubs grew denser in a wild, untamed manner. Torches had been lit in anticipation of the guests going outside, so it was easy to find their way.

Bianca chatted in a breathless manner that revealed her nerves. Sebastian listened only enough to make an encouraging murmur or pose a question to keep her talking, all the while plotting his next move, searching for the perfect spot to steal a kiss.

And after the kiss—what then? Be discovered? It truly wasn't all that shocking for a man of his reputation to be spied kissing a woman. The incident might stain Bianca's reputation but it would not ruin it.

No, he needed a grander gesture to facilitate her ruin. And anyway, he refused to do anything so crass as to create a scandal in the home of his closest friend. No, instead he would use this opportunity to ensnare her, to tempt her with a single private kiss followed by the promise of more. He would earn her trust, then skillfully plant the seeds that would lead to her reckless abandon, and that in turn would cause her father to defend her honor.

They reached a stone bench set in a small alcove. The scent of fresh rain and spring flowers filled the air, lending a touch of mystery and romance.

"Allow me." With a sultry smile, Sebastian gallantly removed his linen handkerchief from his pocket and wiped away the droplets of moisture from the bench.

Bianca giggled before settling herself gracefully.

Then she tilted her head and gazed up at him with luminous eyes. Encouraged, Sebastian placed his foot beside her on the bench and leaned in, taking her right hand in both of his.

"You look very beautiful in the moonlight," he said in a silky tone. He raised her hand to his lips and kissed the inside of her wrist softly.

Her eyes twinkled brightly. "I could say the same of you, my lord. Though I believe men prefer to be called handsome."

He moved her hand, placing it gingerly on his bent knee, then slowly released his grip. She swallowed deeply, her expression slightly dazed, yet she kept her hand resting intimately where he had placed it. The gesture spoke volumes, but instead of delight, a fission of guilt raked through him. Stalling, he cleared his throat.

"The air is damp," he said. "Are you cold?"

She shook her head. Sebastian felt her fingers curl over his knee, their warm strength causing the tension inside him to rise. He gazed into her wide eyes and a flush of dread washed over him. He could see her innocence clearly on her face, sense her trembling excitement.

Kiss her. The voice in his head shouted at him, but he found himself strangely reluctant to listen. It would be so easy to lean down and press his lips against hers. She would not resist, nay she appeared curious, eager for his embrace.

Yet the idea of pressing his attention on her caused a tightness in his chest that made no sense. He had been seducing women since his voice had deepened, but something about kissing this sweet girl left him feeling like a lecher. For all his experience, he had never been a man who was comfortable toying with a woman's emotions, especially a girl as young and innocent as Bianca.

She was beautiful, yet he felt no desire for her. He was uncertain whether it was her age, or her innocence, or perhaps even her connection to the infamous Earl of Hetfield that brought on this feeling. Yet whatever the cause, the result was clear—he could not go through with it.

Abruptly he pulled away. This he had *not* expected. Turmoil raged in Sebastian's chest. For a long moment he stared out into the darkened garden, one hand resting on his hip, the other rubbing the pain that had formed at the base of his neck.

A torrent of emotion surged through Sebastian. Anger, frustration, disappointment. He had set the course for the perfect plan of revenge but now found it impossible to follow the track.

He could hear Bianca's rapid breathing, could sense her confusion, but it was nothing compared to the anger he was feeling. For a moment he held his breath, wishing he had never started this crazy scheme, more angry than he could fathom upon discovering he was unable to complete it.

"We should go inside, before we are missed," he said flatly.

She blinked her eyes in confusion. "Already?"

Sebastian uttered a curse beneath his breath and lowered his head to meet her gaze. He hadn't anticipated such a stricken look. Hell, he wasn't all that impressive a man. Still, a female as young and gullible as Bianca was bound to find him attractive.

"'Tis most improper for us to stay out here

unchaperoned for so long," he said, trying to keep his voice even and calm. "I'm sure your sister will be distressed by your absence."

Her cheeks brightened to a deep red, visible even in the moonlight, so strong he could practically feel the heat of her blush. "We haven't been gone that long," she replied tightly.

"Long enough." He drew himself up to his full height, clicking his heels. Hesitating only a moment, Sebastian stiffly held out his arm. She glanced down at it, then glanced away. She didn't move. "Are you coming, Lady Bianca? Or do you prefer to enjoy the night air in solitude?"

A peculiar look crossed her features. Sebastian wondered briefly if she was going to display a fit of temper and he almost wished for it, as it would give him a chance to vent his own frustration. But ever the lady, Bianca wordlessly rose from the bench, the only sign of her annoyance her refusal to take his arm.

Silently, Sebastian grabbed her elbow and guided her back toward the house, moving at such a rapid pace he was practically dragging her. They had crossed the terrace when suddenly he heard Bianca gasp. He glanced up and saw her sister framed in the doorway.

"Lady Eleanor!" Sebastian exclaimed. "Hellfire, you gave me a fright."

Her mouth tightened. "I apologize if my appearance is so alarming, my lord."

Sebastian stiffened his spine and forced a smile. "I was not alarmed, ma'am, merely startled."

She let out a sigh. "I was wondering what happened to Bianca."

"I was walking with the viscount, Eleanor." Lady Bianca lowered her lashes as another blush of pink crept along her cheeks. "But the chill of the damp air brought us back."

"Lady Dorothea was just starting to serve tea," Lady Eleanor said. "I'm sure a cup will warm you."

The words had barely fallen from her sister's lips before Lady Bianca lifted the hem of her skirt and scurried inside. Sebastian expected Lady Eleanor to follow her sister, but instead she remained on the terrace.

Not wanting his hackles to rise any further, Sebastian took himself off to a corner of the terrace. Better to be rude than boorish. Removing a thin silver case from his pocket, he extracted a cheroot and placed it between his teeth. Rooting through his other pockets, he located his flint box, then lit the end.

Coaxing the cheroot to life, Sebastian pulled in a lungful of tobacco, then slowly exhaled. The sight of the curling gray smoke calmed his nerves, as did the sound of the trickling water from the nearby fountain. It was a monstrous piece, designed by an overeager, romantic young sculptor Lady Dorothea had taken pity upon. Atwood had vowed to take a hammer to it as soon as his wife took an interest in another artist. Sebastian thought that a wise move.

"If you'll excuse me, my lord, I will rejoin the—"

Lady Eleanor's face contorted into surprise as her voice fell silent.

"Is something wrong?" he asked.

"It's a fountain," she remarked stupidly.

"Indeed." His brows knit together in puzzlement and then he barked out a short laugh. "I must assume by your expression that your dinner companion, Mr. Dawson, has been telling tales out of school. Do you expect me to begin pulling off my clothing and splashing inside it?"

She drew in a shuddering breath. "I admit to never knowing what to expect from you, Lord Benton."

"Ah, you wound me, Lady Eleanor. Clearly you were not paying close attention to the tales. I have jumped into many a fountain, yet I am always deep in my cups at the time of my swim."

"And that makes everything all right?"

He shrugged. "I suppose it hardly makes it acceptable." He blew out another puff of smoke and waited for her lecture.

Her shoulders started moving and it took him a moment to realize she was not going to scold. Instead, she was trying to hold back her laughter. "You must be a sight to behold. Mr. Dawson said one time you dove onto your coat as it floated on the surface, then came up spewing water after you sank to the bottom," she said before breaking into a deep, throaty giggle.

At the sound, every sense inside him sharpened. The vaguely sickening feeling that churned in his stomach each time he contemplated kissing Bianca abruptly disappeared. For whatever reason, Sebastian admitted he could not bring himself to engage in a dalliance with Bianca and thus gain his revenge against the Earl of Hetfield.

But Lady Eleanor was another matter entirely.

For the briefest instant Eleanor's breath seized. Lord Benton's gaze was distinctly unsettling. Why, he almost looked as if he wanted to draw her into an embrace. Impossible! It had to be a trick of the moonlight or a distortion of the smoke from his cheroot.

Or perhaps he was insulted by the way she had laughed at him—well, not at him, but at his antics? Of course, he had laughed first, but a man's pride was a strange and precarious thing.

He said nothing else to her, yet unnervingly did not take his eyes from her face. Eleanor felt herself begin to fidget as her discomfort rose. Deciding it was probably best to leave the viscount alone with his odd mood, she excused herself. The moment she reentered the drawing room she headed directly toward Bianca, who was sitting alone on a love seat, an untouched cup of tea set in front of her.

"You look a little pale." Eleanor pressed her hand to Bianca's forehead. "Are you feeling all right?"

"I'm fine." Bianca glanced away. "Just a little tired, perhaps."

"Should we leave?"

"Soon, I think." Her eyes grew cautious. "I'd rather not be the first, though, if you don't mind."

"Of course." Worried by her sister's bland expression, she enfolded Bianca's hand tightly within her own. "Did you enjoy your stroll in the garden with Lord Benton?"

"'Twas fine. A bit chilled, as I said."

"The weather or the viscount?" Eleanor murmured with a smile, but it withered quickly at the sight of Bianca's tense, dour face. "Are you all right? Did something happen?"

"I'm fine." Bianca reached for her tea. Lifting the silver spoon resting on the saucer, she placed it inside the cup and began to stir. Around and around and around.

Eleanor's hand shot out to cease the movement. Bianca took her tea with no milk or sugar; there was no reason to stir the brew once, let alone ten times. "What happened out there?"

"Nothing!" Bianca's voice was low, yet vehement. "I thought he was going to kiss me. Truth be told, I hoped he would. But he didn't. He almost seemed, I don't know, angry at me. Why, I have no idea."

Bianca hitched her shoulders as if to shrug it off, but Eleanor could tell her sister was distressed. "I'm sorry."

"No, I'm glad it happened." Bianca's hand crept to her chest and she took in a deep breath. "It made me realize that you were right to caution me and I was foolish for ignoring you. The viscount is not the right man for me. He's far too old, for one thing, and no doubt set in his ways. Better to discover that now, for it gives me a chance to be more receptive when meeting other gentlemen."

Eleanor nodded approvingly. The thought of Bianca and Lord Benton had always made her queasy in a way she could never quite articulate. Yet the sight of her sister's sad face left Eleanor with a tight knot of guilt, worrying that her interference was the real reason the viscount had backed away from his courtship.

Chapter 7

Eleanor hastily tugged on her gloves as she descended the staircase. They were going to be much more than fashionably late to Lady Ashfield's garden party and it was all her fault. She had spent too much time this morning on household matters, barely leaving enough time to get ready.

The earl did not employ a social secretary, so the task of writing thank-you notes to various hostesses had fallen to Eleanor. And the growing feud between the cook and housekeeper could not be allowed to escalate any further. It simply had to be addressed immediately and with skillful diplomacy, since both individuals were essential employees.

"Is that what you're wearing?" Bianca asked when Eleanor reached the landing. "I thought we agreed you would wear one of my new gowns. I hung the lavender muslin in your wardrobe two days ago."

"I didn't have time to make the necessary alterations," Eleanor replied.

"Surely you could have found something else?"

Bianca asked. "Honestly, Eleanor, there are times I think you deliberately make yourself look older."

Eleanor pursed her lips, hurt by the edge of annoyance in her sister's tone. "Are you ashamed to be seen with me?"

Bianca's face crumpled. "Of course not! How can you even imagine such a dreadful thing?"

Eleanor lowered her chin, embarrassed by her comment. It was hardly Bianca's fault that she was dressed in a dull, serviceable gray gown, suitable for governesses and chaperones and spinsters. Truly, all that was missing was a frilly lace cap.

"Thank you for the gift," Eleanor said. "I promise to wear the gown as soon as I can alter it to fit me properly."

Bianca's expression lightened. "At least wear one of my new bonnets. Please?"

Not knowing what else to do, Eleanor nodded. Bianca smiled, then scurried up the stairs. She returned quickly, a frothy, feathery concoction in her hand.

Eleanor stood in front of the hall mirror and switched hats. She could feel a blush rising up her throat as she adjusted the whimsical creation on her head. It was youthful and frivolous and Eleanor felt like a fraud wearing it, for she was neither of those things.

"Father said he might stop by the party this afternoon," Bianca said as they stepped into the carriage. "There are a few people he'd like us to meet."

Eleanor stiffened at the remark, knowing she had been naive to think the earl would ignore them forever. He'd brought Bianca to Town to find her a husband, a rich one, Eleanor was certain. It stood to reason that he would eventually get around to accomplishing that task.

As the carriage pulled away, Eleanor concentrated on calming her nerves. She always suspected the worst when it came to the earl, but there had to be at least a dozen wealthy gentlemen in society whom her sister would happily accept as a husband. And as long as the settlement was large enough, the earl most likely would not object either. Or so Eleanor hoped.

It took nearly an hour to arrive at their destination, and Eleanor was glad to have the time to collect herself. After greeting their hosts, Eleanor and Bianca mingled through the crowd, searching for familiar, friendly faces. There were a large number of guests milling about on the Ashfields' terrace and lawns, partaking of the various refreshments. It was a glorious day filled with bright sunshine and blue skies and everyone seemed to be having a lovely time.

The gardens were simply spectacular. Blooms of all shapes and sizes in more colors than one could count were set in neat rows among the landscape, while other sections boasted tall flowering fruit trees. Eleanor wondered idly whether there would be any beestings, since the sweet floral scents were so abundant and irresistible.

"Oh, look, there's Father." Bianca waved merrily.

Eleanor could not contain her groan as the earl stepped on the edge of a flower bed, crushing several delicate blooms, and strode purposefully toward them. Elegantly dressed in a dark green coat, buff breeches, and shiny Hessian boots, he looked like a young dandy, though up close one could see the lines fanning out from the corners of his eyes.

"You're late," he grumbled.

"Not so very much," Bianca said with a smile.

"'Tis my fault," Eleanor added. "There were several household matters that needed my immediate attention."

"Then you should have stayed behind." The earl pursed his lips as he looked down at her. "Good God, didn't you glance in a mirror before you left, Eleanor? You look positively ridiculous in that bonnet," he commented in an exasperated tone before taking Bianca's arm possessively and leading her away.

"'Tis lovely to see you too, sir," Eleanor muttered. She gingerly touched the edge of her bonnet, then lowered her head and doggedly followed.

Stopping to greet a group gathered beneath a bower of willows, the earl bowed low. "Ladies, gentlemen, I'd like you to meet my daughter, Bianca," he said. "My dear, allow me to present Lady Audrey, Mrs. Hartgrove, her son, Mr. Jasper Hartgrove, Viscount Ogden, Sir Lucian Whitney, and Miss Everly."

Bianca executed a graceful curtsy. There was a chorus of greetings as everyone acknowledged the introduction and the usual inconsequential social conversation began. Eleanor stood awkwardly behind her sister for a few moments, trying to decide which would attract less attention—to stay or go.

Digging deep to rally her courage, Eleanor was preparing to quietly slip away when Lady Audrey abruptly ceased talking in the middle of a sentence and stared pointedly at Eleanor. "And you are . . . ?"

Everyone turned to stare. Eleanor felt her face begin to heat, but she smiled brightly, trying to brazen it out. The earl cast a lazy eye in her direction, then turned away.

"Oh, that's my older daughter," he said dismissively. "Eleanor."

"*Lady* Eleanor," she said defensively. His rudeness stung more than she would have thought, as did this public exposure to his disregard. "'Tis lovely to meet you all. And I must say, your bonnet is especially fetching, Lady Audrey. Wherever did you acquire it?"

Lady Audrey's puzzled eyes moved between Eleanor and the earl, but she recovered nicely. She told Eleanor of the milliner on Bond Street she frequented, then mentioned a dressmaker. Eleanor smiled encouragingly and feigned interest, all the while seething inside.

Fortunately, the earl did not linger. He spirited Mrs. Hartgrove toward the refreshment table when she mentioned how parched her throat felt. Sir Lucian also excused himself and Lord Waverly took his place. This time Eleanor was included in the introductions, since Lady Audrey made them.

There was a good deal of smiles and laughter peppered in with the conversation and Eleanor was glad to see Bianca relaxed and happy. Yet when the group decided to move to a sunny spot, Eleanor used the opportunity to go off on her own. Though she vowed not to show it, the earlier unpleasantness with the earl left her feeling shaken. A bit of solitude was needed in order to collect herself.

Spying a splendid rose arbor, Eleanor walked away from the crowd. When she reached the arbor, the heady fragrance engulfed her, along with an odd sense of peace. Though she had never been in this particular garden before, the familiar, welcome scent of the roses provided the serenity she craved.

Her solitude, however, was short-lived. Within minutes she heard the steady crunch of footfalls approaching. Glancing over her shoulder, she was more than surprised to see Viscount Benton striding along the shell-strewn path, his eyes fixed steadily on her.

"Lady Eleanor! I am delighted to see you again." He took her hand, his strong fingers wrapping possessively around hers. With a devilish smile he lifted it, pressing his lips suggestively against her wrist, somehow finding the small section not covered by her glove. "The hour was growing so late I feared you might not make an appearance."

A coy woman would have blushed and stammered and cast him a demure smile. Instead, Eleanor's mouth gaped open in surprise. "Me? You were waiting to see me?"

"Who else?"

Who else indeed? Eleanor could not believe he was being sincere. She studied him closely, but his gray eyes were unreadable. "Why are you so eager to see me, my lord? Are you angry at my interference between you and my sister, perchance?" Eleanor asked, hitting upon what she believed the only logical explanation.

"Do I look angry, Lady Eleanor?"

Heavens, no. He looked divine. His navy breeches hugged his muscular thighs in a most provocative manner, the matching jacket stretched the breadth of his wide shoulders. On another man the outfit would have appeared somber, almost dour, but Lord Benton had such a strong sense of style he easily carried it off.

"It would be understandable if you did hold some resentment toward me," she continued, still convinced he must be annoyed with her. Bianca was a beautiful woman. Any man would be upset to have lost her.

"I hate to disillusion you, ma'am, but your objections had no influence on my actions." His head dipped closer to hers, then his eyelids dropped a fraction over his eyes, giving him an almost dangerous appearance. "When I set my mind toward getting something I truly want, nothing, and I do mean nothing, stands in my way."

Eleanor had difficulty looking away. She forced her breath to come at a more even pace, willed her erratic heartbeat to slow. She had no doubt he spoke the truth about getting what he wanted and for one wild moment the intensity in his eyes seemed to say he wanted *her*.

It was ridiculous, of course. Laughable, really. Eleanor shook off her outrageous assumptions, convinced she was mistaken. Or wistful? Abruptly she pulled away. "If it was not my doing, then what caused such a sudden change in your attitude? Previously you were quite deliberate in your pursuit of Bianca."

"Yes, initially." The color in his eyes intensified.

"And then?" she prompted.

I noticed you. The words were not spoken. She believed she read them in his gaze, then instantly chastised herself for being a fool. Those sentiments were in her head, or rather buried deep inside herself, in a long-forgotten place where loneliness dwelled.

"I am significantly older than your sister," he said. "Even you remarked upon it."

"I might have briefly mentioned the difference in your ages," Eleanor acknowledged.

"You spoke of me as if I were practically in my dotage, my right foot poised above the grave."

"I never said such a thing."

"You implied it, but I am a gentleman and therefore refuse to call a lady a liar. However, the age difference was but one of the obstacles. After spending time with Bianca I quickly realized that though delightful, she is a girl. And I very much prefer a woman." He smiled fully at her. "I assume your sister suffered no permanent distress from the encounter?"

Eleanor's nostrils flared. "Are you certain? Perhaps after spending time with you, Bianca is ruined for all other men."

"Ruined?" He gave her a startled, strange look. "Neither one of us believe that, Lady Eleanor."

"Hmm." Her nostrils flared again and she stared at him reproachfully.

"What exactly does that stare mean? Are you now saying that you approve of a romance between me and your sister? Honestly, Lady Eleanor, you need to make up your mind. 'Tis no wonder women are lauded as fickle creatures when even a sensible one such as yourself behaves so irrationally."

Sensible? Had he just called her sensible? "Of course I don't approve of a match between you and my sister."

"Splendid, then we are in agreement." Lowering

his head, Lord Benton gave her a wicked grin. "Shall we stroll through the trees? The path is well marked and shaded in several areas."

Eleanor blinked rapidly. His mercurial moods were keeping her off balance. If she didn't know better, she would have sworn he was flirting with her. Which was completely absurd.

Her first instinct was to refuse to walk with him, yet she hesitated. She had come this way with the express intent of escaping from the party. What was the harm in accepting his escort?

Gingerly, she set her arm on his sleeve. "Are you familiar with this section of the property?" Eleanor asked.

"Not at all," he responded cheerfully. "But I am not so much of a Town fellow that I cannot follow a well-marked path. Have no fear, Lady Eleanor. I shall not lead you astray."

He laughed quietly, as though it were a private joke. Eleanor wondered if he had been drinking, but she smelled no spirits on his breath. Deciding she was being far too rigid, she told herself to dismiss the viscount's odd behavior and enjoy the surroundings.

They crossed an expansive lawn onto a path that led into the orchard. Apples, Eleanor realized, when she saw the white buds. The trees soon gave way to thicker woods, sloping upward. The viscount solicitously held her arm as they climbed, the incline growing steeper every few steps.

They walked in silence except for the sound of their breathing. Or rather her breathing. The steepness of the hill and the rapid pace of their steps left her winded, a problem the viscount apparently did not share.

"Ah, there is a lake," he muttered when they gained the summit. "Or rather a large pond. Shall we investigate?"

"All right." Eleanor gripped his arm tighter as they descended the slope, fearful of losing her footing and tumbling to the ground.

"You are exceedingly agreeable this afternoon, Lady Eleanor." His brow arched. "I like it."

She opened her mouth to rebuke him for teasing her, but the words did not come. His face was cast in the shadow of the towering trees and there was something in the strength of his profile, the line of his jaw, that made her pulse race.

What was wrong with her today? It seemed that all Lord Benton need do was glance her way and her wits scrambled. Shaking off her peculiar mood, Eleanor concentrated on the uneven path beneath her feet, though she remained very aware of the man beside her.

They reached level ground. Eleanor knew it was no longer necessary to hold his arm so tightly, yet she found herself strangely reluctant to let go of him. Almost as if sensing her dilemma, the viscount pulled the arm she held closer to his body, effectively trapping her hand.

Eleanor said nothing.

The pond was surrounded on one side by magnificent old trees, their branches swooping down to touch the edge of the water. Wildflowers dotted the landscape, the bright splashes of color a pleasing sight. Eleanor was tempted to pick a few and she smiled when she thought of how appalled her father would be if she returned to the party with a bouquet in her hand, a gesture that would surely scream unsophistication.

As they drew near the water, Eleanor quickly realized they were not alone. A young boy, whom Eleanor judged to be four or five, scampered along the shore on the opposite side, while a woman, most likely his nurse, stood nearby.

"I didn't realize the Ashfields have such young children," Eleanor remarked.

"They have quite a brood, if I recall. The eldest is nearly as old as me. This lad must be their youngest."

"Or perhaps he is a grandchild?" Eleanor suggested.

Before the viscount could reply, the youngster began shouting. They glanced over and saw the nurse was attempting to hold him back from the water's edge.

"He seems to have lost his boat, poor lad," Eleanor remarked, gesturing toward the miniature sailing vessel floating aimlessly in the center of the pond.

"Indeed," the viscount agreed. "By the sounds of his cries, I'd wager it's a prized possession."

The wails of distress grew louder as they approached and then suddenly ceased.

"I do beg your pardon for all the noise." The woman bobbed a curtsy. "Alexander's boat has broken from its rope and drifted away. I told him he shouldn't bring it out here today, but he was most insistent."

"Do you see what happens when we refuse to listen to the women in our life, young man?" Lord Benton asked.

"Yes, sir." The child sniffled as he tried to compose himself.

The viscount gazed out at the water. "I'm afraid with no wind to speak of, the boat will most certainly remain where it is now."

"I know." Tears once again filled the child's eyes. He wiped his nose with the sleeve of his jacket and hung his head dejectedly. Though she agreed the child should have obeyed his nurse, his despondent air tugged at Eleanor's heartstrings.

"Chin up, Alexander," the viscount commanded, patting the child on the shoulder. "'Tis clear we need to plan a rescue at sea."

"A rescue?"

"Yes. That looks like a very fine boat. We cannot simply abandon it." The viscount shrugged out of his jacket and handed it to Eleanor.

"Whatever are you doing?" she asked in alarm.

He grinned. "It's not a fountain, but you might remember I have an affinity for water."

"Good heavens, I hope you don't plan on taking off anything besides your jacket this afternoon, my lord."

Lord Benton merely widened his grin as he continued to remove his clothing. Once his embroidered waistcoat was off, he loosened his cravat, then rolled up the sleeves of his white linen shirt. Eleanor could not help but notice how his forearms were sleek, hard muscle, dusted with soft, dark hair. Her head began to swim at the sight.

"My goodness, the sun is hot," Eleanor exclaimed as she vigorously fanned her hand in front of her face.

"Perhaps you should sit in the shade, my lady," the nurse suggested. "Your face is rather flushed."

Embarrassed, Eleanor moved her hand faster, hoping the viscount had not overheard the remark. Relieved, she realized he most likely had not, since he stood at the water's edge, his torso bent low, engaged in earnest conversation with the boy.

Having settled on some sort of plan, Lord Benton walked to the shoreline, then gingerly took a step forward. Eleanor winced as his beautifully polished black leather boots sunk into the muck, well above the ankles.

He made a face but continued forward until the water licked the top of his knee-high boots. Eleanor watched his body sway back and forth and for a moment she thought he was going to topple into the pond.

Her breath hitched in suspense, but she soon surmised that he was trying to plant his feet on the bottom. Which explained why he had not removed his boots. When he at last got himself set, the viscount leaned forward and reached into the pond. Cupping both hands, he pushed them through the surface of the water, then stroked back in a wide motion. He continued at a steady, even pace, creating a small current.

It took a few minutes for the newly created waves to reach the boat. The moment they did, the toy began bobbing merrily and then, a minute later, gradually started moving toward the shoreline.

"It's working!" Alexander cried. Hopping from one foot to the other, the child ran to intercept his boat.

"Steady, lad," Lord Benton replied, sounding almost as excited as the boy. "You must have patience and wait for the vessel to come to you. If you tumble into the water, Nurse will be cross with both of us."

The boy giggled, yet obeyed the command. It took a fair amount of time for the boat to move close enough to be plucked from the water. Eleanor's arms ached just watching the viscount steadily stroking, the muscles in his back and shoulders rippling with every move.

"I've got it!" Alexander shrieked as he held the dripping boat above his head.

"Well done, Benton!" Lord Atwood's deep voice carried down from the top of the hill.

Eleanor turned to see the marquess, his wife clinging to his arm, as they descended the slope. Several other couples followed close behind. Eleanor squinted into the sunlight and caught sight of Bianca, Lord Waverly, Mr. Dawson, and Emma.

"A wise man never passes up the opportunity to play the hero," the viscount responded as he waded out of the pond. "You taught me that, Atwood."

"So I did." Laughing, the men slapped each other on the back.

"And this time you even managed to keep the majority of your clothing on when you went into the water," Mr. Dawson added. "Bravo!"

"Stop looking so surprised. I can act civilized when the occasion warrants," the viscount said, as he rolled down his sleeves.

Self-consciously, Eleanor handed Lord Benton his waistcoat and jacket, certain everyone must be wondering how she and the viscount came to be out here together.

"He rescued my boat!" Alexander exclaimed,

inserting himself into the middle of the crowd. "Isn't that grand?"

"Manners, young man," the nurse admonished, scurrying after him. "Oh, I do apologize to you all. My charge can be rather headstrong at times, especially when he is excited."

"No harm done," the viscount replied. He reached down and ruffled the boy's hair. "Though Nurse is right. Proper introductions are in order."

Alexander did his nurse proud, bowing to the ladies and shaking hands with the gentlemen as Lord Benton introduced everyone. The child then thanked the viscount repeatedly before being led away by his nurse.

"What a darling little boy," Lady Dorothea said wistfully.

"He's a little devil," the viscount said with a smile. "But I'm glad it all worked out in the end. He was quite fond of that boat."

"However did you get it out of the lake without getting your clothing wet?" Lord Waverly asked.

The viscount launched into a witty, exaggerated account of the rescue that soon had everyone laughing. As they paired off and started the walk back to the party, Eleanor was especially pleased to note that Bianca was relaxed and smiling, apparently suffering no lasting effects from her former infatuation with Lord Benton.

In fact, she seemed rather intent on Lord Waverly, who was solicitously helping her over the tree roots that sporadically marred the woodland path. Waverly seemed a congenial sort, a fine-looking young gentleman only a few years older than Bianca. It would be necessary to make inquiries about him, of course, but perhaps he would be a good match for her sister.

"Who would have thought our little jaunt in the woods would lead to such an adventure, Lady Eleanor," Lord Benton remarked as they converged on the refreshment table.

"I confess to being glad that you were there," Eleanor replied. She daintily bit into a sweet pastry, not realizing how hungry she felt. "I would have been little help to Alexander on my own."

The viscount leaned over so that his lips were inches from her ear. "I refuse to believe that you would have left the poor lad without offering any assistance."

"I'm afraid I don't share your delight for the water, my lord," Eleanor responded, pulling away so she could look into his eyes.

"Pity." He flashed her another of his devastating grins. Her lips twitched as she slowly smiled back, all the while wondering if she had been fair in her assessment of him.

It was unlike her to be so quick to demonize someone, to judge so harshly. Roguish reputation aside, the viscount was not all bad. He shared a genuine friendship with the marquess and Mr. Dawson, and unlike other men of his rank, did not take himself, or his position, too seriously. And it went without saying that few men would have ruined a perfectly good pair of boots to gain a child's smile of appreciation.

Lord Benton turned away to speak with Lady Dorothea. Eleanor studied him thoughtfully as she finished her pastry, her interest piqued. Apparently there was more to the viscount than his charming, handsome facade.

Sebastian leaned casually against a towering oak tree and watched Eleanor climb into her carriage. Bianca soon followed and he was struck anew at the startling differences between the two women. Eleanor could hardly compete with her sister's ethereal beauty, yet the lines of Eleanor's figure were vastly appealing, the grace of her movement strangely sensual. If one peeled away the unfashionable clothes and tossed away that ridiculous bonnet, it was clear Eleanor was an attractive woman, one he found surprisingly desirable.

He had come to the party with the specific intent of seeking her out and was pleased with the outcome. He had made a good start this afternoon, though he knew he would have to take care. Eleanor was not a naive young girl. She was intelligent and insightful. He could tell from her speculative glances and puzzled frowns she was suspicious of him and the attention he had so unexpectedly bestowed upon her.

Yet he had also seen something else, something that gave him encouragement. A spark of interest, a flare of excitement. Though she fought hard against it, she was attracted to him. And he fully intended to use that attraction to get past her barriers and win her trust. Once he accomplished that, it would be child's play to lead her precisely where he wanted.

The one obstacle that had most concerned him was her sister. Eleanor's loyalty toward Bianca was wholehearted and tenacious; she would avoid him completely if she felt it would upset her sister. He had blundered badly by first setting his sights on Bianca, but fortunately, she seemed to suffer no ill effects from his brief courtship. Indeed, her interest in Lord Waverly seemed genuine.

Ah, the fickle heart of a young woman.

He wondered if Eleanor's heart was equally as fickle, then quickly dismissed the notion. It didn't matter. He wasn't interested in her heart. He was intent on leading her down a path of seduction, just far enough to cause her ruin. Far enough to provoke her father into a duel and gain the revenge that ate at him.

Considering his next move, Sebastian strode toward the refreshment table, deciding he had earned a drink. A fitting reward for an afternoon of good work.

Chapter 8

The following morning as Eleanor embroidered and Bianca read, bouquets of flowers were delivered. Hothouse roses, long-stem lilies, along with nosegays of violets and daffodils. The colors enlivened the entire drawing room, the perfumed scent seeping into every corner. The servants were kept busy searching for vases while Eleanor and Bianca arranged the floral bounty.

"The violets are from Mr. Hartgrove. The daffodils from Sir Whitney. Viscount Ogden sent the lilies. Are they not lovely, Eleanor?" Bianca's face was beaming with excitement. "Oh, and look, these beautiful roses are from Lord Waverly."

"Red roses from Lord Waverly. That's rather forward." Eleanor arched her brow in a teasing manner. "Yet you don't seem very surprised."

"But I am. Ouch! That thorn is sharp." Bianca pressed her finger against her mouth to stop the small prick of blood. "Lord Waverly was charming and attentive yesterday, but I learned my lesson with

Viscount Benton. I intend to wait until a gentleman shows *true* interest before I reciprocate."

"'Tis about time some flowers were delivered," the earl said from the doorway. "I don't understand why it has taken so long for the single gentlemen to take notice of you, Bianca."

Startled, Eleanor whirled around. The earl was the last person she expected to see, since he was never up at this hour of the morning. Belatedly, she wondered how much of the conversation he had heard. "Bianca has made a most favorable impression on several gentlemen," Eleanor said.

"I can see," the earl replied. "The room looks like a hothouse. Well done, my girl."

Without asking, he reached out and took the cards from Bianca's hand. His expression remained stoic as he read each one and Eleanor wondered if he was searching for a particular name.

Giving no clue to his true feelings, the earl turned. As he was leaving, a footman entered. In his arms was the largest bouquet of all, a glorious arrangement of three dozen long-stem white roses. But when he plucked the card from the center of the blooms, the earl's brows drew together in a heavy scowl.

"Believe it or not, these are for Eleanor."

For me? Eleanor's hand shot to her mouth to stifle her gasp. She refused to give the earl the satisfaction of seeing her surprise. He handed her the sealed card without comment, then continued on his way.

A stab of hurt pierced her at his obvious disinterest, but she shook it away.

"Gracious, Eleanor, open the card already,"

Bianca pleaded, an edge of curious excitement in her voice.

Despite her attempts to prevent it, Eleanor's heart skipped a beat as she broke the seal. *"With thanks for an adventurous afternoon. Your most ardent admirer,"* Eleanor read aloud. Puzzled, she turned the card over, but there was no signature.

"Let me see." Bianca impatiently grabbed the missive. "The handwriting is bold and distinctive. No doubt the gentleman wrote the card himself."

"The only person I spent any significant time with yesterday afternoon was Viscount Benton. . . ." Eleanor's voice trailed off in confusion.

Bianca's eyes widened. "Do you think he sent them?"

"I can't imagine why."

"Perhaps he admires you," Bianca suggested. "He might be a rake, but he isn't a fool."

Eleanor let out a disbelieving snort. "'Tis more likely a joke."

"Eleanor, don't," Bianca scolded. "It pains me to hear you underestimate yourself. You have a great deal to recommend you. You are pretty and smart, loyal and witty. A gentleman would be lucky indeed to gain your affection."

Eleanor stared at the card. The bold, dark strokes demonstrated the strength and determination of the writer. That most certainly defined Lord Benton. Was it he? If so, why did he not sign his name? Glancing up, she met her sister's gaze. "Though I again say 'tis highly unlikely, I need to ask, would it distress you if the flowers were from Lord Benton?"

Bianca was silent for a moment. "No, not one

bit," she replied, taking Eleanor's hands. "There is no reason to think ill of him on my account. Though as a good and loyal sister I feel it my duty to warn you about him. He's a rogue. And fickle to boot."

Bianca smiled and the knot of worry inside Eleanor eased. If by some insane circumstance the viscount was showing an interest, she would be free to explore it. If she wanted. Did she? Eleanor honestly didn't know.

No sooner had the flowers been sorted out and placed around the room, the invitations began arriving. The pitifully small trickle that had marred their first week in Town had overnight turned into a tidal wave. Eleanor knew it was Lady Dorothea's stamp of approval that had opened so many doors for them and she was grateful for the support.

There were the usual balls, soirees, and theatre party invites, along with a more select number of concerts, dinners, and picnics.

"Goodness, it will take us a week to open all of these," Eleanor said with satisfaction.

"There are no less than three invitations for this evening," Bianca said with awe. "How will we ever decide which to attend?"

"We have already committed to a theatre outing organized by Lady Dorothea," Eleanor reminded Bianca. "Her father-in-law had graciously offered the use of his private box. It would be monstrously rude to cancel so late."

"I thought that was tomorrow night. I don't know where my head has gotten to these days." Bianca picked up the vase containing Lord Waverly's red roses and buried her face in the fragrant bouquet.

Her dreamy expression let Eleanor know precisely where her sister's mind had gone. "'Tis the opening-night performance of *A Midsummer Night's Dream*. Society will be out in full force. I'm certain we'll encounter many of our new acquaintances."

Bianca smiled softly. "You don't have to talk me into going, Eleanor. I am looking forward to it, actually."

"As am I," Eleanor agreed, looking behind her sister to the vase of carefully arranged white roses. "Shakespeare's plays are always so riveting."

Eleanor had only been to the Drury Lane Theatre once, many years ago during her forgettable London Season. She had been included in a party more as an afterthought, a warm female body to even out the numbers. It had begun pleasantly enough, but ten minutes into the performance she noted a striking resemblance between the actor playing the lead role of Hamlet and her estranged love, John Tanner.

The sight had rattled her completely, the stab of pain coursing through her heart swift and sharp, an aching reminder of what she had lost. Of the life she would never know, the love she would never share, of the future forever gone.

She had struggled to hold in her grief, allowing herself the release of a few tears during the more emotional moments of the performance, thankful there was so much misery in this particular Shakespeare tragedy. Her reaction, however, had been noticed and the incident caused her to be labeled an overly sensitive female, putting yet another nail in her socially unacceptable coffin.

With a firm force of will, Eleanor pushed the incident to the back of her mind as she entered the theatre this evening. As expected, the arrival of their large, boisterous party caused a bit of a sensation. She could hear the increase in the volume of conversation as they gathered inside the duke's box, shifting to and fro while selecting their seats.

Eleanor took a chair at the rear of the box, encouraging Bianca to move to the front. She wanted her sister to be able to see everything as she took in this unique experience, but she also wanted Bianca to be *seen*, especially by the single gentlemen down in the pit.

The duke sat in the front with Emma flanking him on his right and Bianca to his left, leaving an empty chair beside each girl. Directly behind him were the Atwoods, Lady Dorothea's sister Gwendolyn and her husband, Mr. Jason Barrington. Eleanor gladly occupied the third row, taking the end seat and leaving a pair of chairs beside her unoccupied.

Though at the rear, the view was excellent and Eleanor took her time as she slowly surveyed the crowd. The nobility were out in full force, easy to distinguish in their silks and satins and glittering jewels. She recognized many of them, though in so public a venue there were many new faces as well. Her attention occupied by her surroundings, Eleanor sensed rather than saw someone ease into the chair next to her.

"Sorry I'm late. The traffic was impossible. Have I missed anything of interest?" inquired the deep, masculine voice beside her.

A shiver tingled over her flesh. Eleanor turned

sharply and found herself glancing into a pair of smiling eyes.

"Lord Benton!"

"Is something wrong?" he asked.

"No." Straightening, Eleanor stiffened her spine and folded her arms self-consciously around her waist. "I'm just surprised. I was unaware that you'd be included in the theatre party this evening."

"Beg pardon. Should I have sent a note 'round preparing you?"

"*Warning* me would have been the courteous thing to do."

He let out a sharp laugh. Several heads turned in their direction. Eleanor attempted a smile to distract from her blush, yet feared it only made it worse.

The viscount winked at her, then turned his attention to the occupants of the box, greeting each lady, including Bianca, with a charming smile. Eleanor swallowed hard.

She had a chance to study him as he spoke with the others, noticing how the ends of his dark hair curled attractively at his collar. Though his jaw looked smoothly shaved, there was a faint shadow of whiskers on his face. Instead of distracting from his polished looks, the rugged appearance was a handsome addition.

"The duke is in a fine humor tonight," Lord Benton commented. "Seated between two lovely young women, like a thorn amongst the roses."

"I believe the correct expression is a rose amongst the thorns."

"I know, but that metaphor hardly applies to the duke. He is far more a thorn than a rose."

Clearing her throat, Eleanor cast him a sidelong look. "Funny that you should mention roses, my lord. I received a lovely bouquet of them this morning."

"Not surprising." The viscount shifted in his chair, then glanced down at the playbill in his hand.

She paused, gauging him. "The flowers were very beautiful and I should like to thank the sender. But the accompanying card was somewhat cryptic and merely signed 'your most ardent admirer.'"

His head lifted. "Are you trying to make me jealous, Lady Eleanor? A standard feminine ploy that rarely works as it is intended." Eleanor felt her face tighten, yet before she could say anything the viscount added, "What color were the roses?"

"White."

His lips curled. "Hmm, if I am not mistaken, white roses are often associated with marriage."

"Forgive me for being so foolishly mistaken," she said. "Naturally they could not have come from you."

Leaning toward her, he lowered his voice. "Are you certain?"

She gave him a severe stare, which only produced a devilish grin. Fortunately for Eleanor, at that moment the lights dimmed, the curtain rose, and the performance began.

She turned her attention diligently toward the stage, but alas the Bard's lyrical words could not capture her thoughts. She was restless and distracted and soon became aware of that strange, indescribable sensation of being watched. Eleanor could feel the tiny beads of sweat beginning to form on her upper lip as she struggled to keep her gaze focused straight ahead.

She knew without looking that it was Lord Benton's eyes that were trained so intently upon her and she flatly refused to give him the satisfaction of acknowledging it.

He was playing some sort of game with her. A game that intrigued her, frustrated her, excited her, puzzled her. A game whose rules she did not understand, which made the consequences all the more dangerous.

After what felt like an eternity, the theatre lights came back up and the audience started rustling about. Eleanor nearly slumped forward in her chair, so great was her sense of relief.

"Are you enjoying the performance?" Lord Benton asked. "Lysander is doing a splendid job, but I thought the actor playing Puck too old for the part."

"'Tis all quite extraordinary," she replied, realizing she had no real idea of what she had just seen, having been too distracted by the viscount to pay proper attention.

Eleanor turned away deliberately to speak with Lady Dorothea, gratefully accepting Lord Atwood's offer to bring her a glass of lemonade. Belatedly she realized it might have been wiser to accompany the couple, since it would have provided an opportunity to escape the close confines of the box and clear her head.

Almost as if sensing her desire to escape him, Lord Benton moved his chair closer. "Now that the lights are up, we must survey the crowd and relate the latest *on-dits* to each other."

Eleanor squinted at him. "Why is everyone so interested in what others are doing?"

"Because their own lives lack interest and meaning?" He tilted his head and let out a wistful sigh. "You aren't going to be offended by this, are you?"

Eleanor knew she should be. Truly, what business of hers was it when it involved the activities of other people? "I will listen, my lord. But I will not repeat any of it, not one single word. To anyone."

"Ah, a virtuous gossipmonger. Now that puts me firmly in my place, does it not?"

She raised her brow and assumed a haughty expression, but he was looking ahead and smiling and missed her reaction. Yet it soon became clear that the viscount was intent on having some fun.

"Pity you don't have a pair of opera glasses to magnify the view inside the private boxes," Eleanor said. "Heaven only knows what you could discover."

"Only amateurs and dowagers with failing eyesight use glasses." He took her hand and set it on his sleeve, allowing him to lean in very close. Her eyelids nearly fluttered closed as she caught a whiff of his clean, male scent. "There is an art to this that you must learn and learn quickly. Now, glance casually about the theatre, acting as though you are searching for someone. Quickly take in all that you survey, never allowing your eyes to linger too long on any one particular individual."

"Is this truly how the nobility spend their time?" she asked. "'Tis no wonder the House of Lords is in shambles."

"Knowing the best gossip always gives one an advantage. Prinny is the worst of the lot, by far. If you wish to survive, you must learn the art. Go ahead, try it."

Eleanor knew he was jesting, but she couldn't

resist the dare. Dutifully she turned her head and quickly scanned the crowd. "How was that?"

"Passable. For a first time." His voice lowered to a conspiring whisper. "Did you notice the couple one tier below directly to our left?"

"Which couple, my lord? Honestly, you must give me more of a clue."

"The lady is dressed in yellow and wearing the most godawful headdress man or woman ever created."

Eleanor tipped her chin and casually turned her head. Her eyes widened involuntarily when she caught sight of the group. "I believe I have found them."

"They are causing quite a sensation this evening."

"Because the lady lacks any fashion sense?"

"The lady's lack of taste should be an unpardonable offense, but that is not what has those who know abuzz." The viscount paused. "The man on her right is her husband. The one on her left, her lover."

Eleanor raised her brows and Lord Benton shrugged. She risked another glance at this group, wondering what sort of woman had the audacity to appear in public with her husband and lover. The husband suddenly looked up and caught Eleanor staring at him. He gave her a wide, knowing smile.

Eleanor gasped. "Oh my. I've been caught."

"Made a conquest too. Bravo, Lady Eleanor."

She felt a spurt of merriment. "I can't believe I'm finding this amusing."

A rueful gleam came into his eyes. "It passes the time when things get dull. I figure I have provided more than my share of fodder for the gossip mill. I should be entitled to some indulgence."

"Your drink, Lady Eleanor."

"Thank you, Lord Atwood." Eleanor accepted the glass gratefully, surprised to realize how parched her throat felt.

Mrs. Barrington, sipping a glass of wine, turned in her chair and they exchanged impressions of the play and the performances. The men discussed some political news, their views seemingly in accordance. There was no gossip shared and before long the play resumed.

Throughout the next act, it was Eleanor who kept glancing over at Lord Benton. His eyes were always on the stage, though she noted he drummed his fingers lightly on his knee.

At the next interval, the viscount stood and offered to escort Emma outside for some fresh air before the final act began. Watching them leave, a sliver of regret jabbed at Eleanor. She snapped open her fan, trying to chase away the heat of disappointment spreading up her neck to her face. It would have been great fun strolling the hallways, her arm on Lord Benton's.

No sooner had the emotion surfaced, Eleanor firmly scolded herself for such foolish thoughts. Her attraction to the viscount was both misplaced and foolish. By all accounts, there were numerous women already infatuated with him. Younger, prettier, far more interesting women. He did not need Eleanor to be added to the list.

At least Bianca had gotten over her interest in him. There had been a steady stream of young men paying calls during the intermissions, Lord Waverly among them. Eleanor could plainly see her sister laughing and flirting with them, encouraged by, of all people, the duke.

Since she had been so distracted by Lord Benton during the performance, the final act failed to hold Eleanor's interest. A sigh rushed past her lips when the play ended, but Eleanor was unsure whether it was relief or disappointment. Perhaps she just wasn't the type of person who enjoyed the theatre.

The duke declared himself too tired to join them for a late-night supper, but everyone else seemed eager for the evening to continue. The ceaseless rain once again fell upon them when they left the theatre and there was a bit of confusion as everyone scrambled to get inside their carriages.

Rushing forward, Eleanor gratefully accepted the helping hand of a liveried footman as she stepped into the marquess's coach-and-four. Believing that Bianca was following behind her, Eleanor relaxed against the plush velvet squabs, shaking the rain-drops off her cloak.

The carriage door remained open and she gazed out the window through the steady rain, waiting for Bianca. But instead of her sister, a gentleman entered, his face cast in the shadows. He sat directly across from her, then lifted his head. Amusement lit his face.

Lord Benton! Eleanor blinked, for a moment too stunned to react. "I am waiting for my sister," she said finally, breaking the silence.

"I saw Lady Bianca enter Atwood's coach, which is just ahead of us. I believe Lady Dorothea, Emma, and the duke were also with them."

"This isn't the marquess's coach?"

"No. It's mine."

"Oh, I do beg your pardon." Face flushed with embarrassment, Eleanor started to rise, but the viscount held out his hand.

"No need to leave. 'Tis a short carriage ride and we are all going to the same place."

It sounded perfectly reasonable. Indeed, it would seem ridiculously churlish to remove herself since it was, as he said, only a short carriage ride, and the rain was coming down even harder. Yet why did her stomach tingle with a sense of forbidden emotion as if somehow knowing being alone with him was unwise?

"Thank you. I shall accept your kind offer, my lord," she said a trifle nervously.

He nodded. "I do, however, have a small request. I can't ride with my back to the driver. The swaying of the carriage does disgraceful things to my stomach. Would you mind if we switched seats?"

"Of course. We would not want you to disgrace yourself." Eleanor smiled.

He frowned. "Do you find my discomfort amusing, Lady Eleanor?"

"Not at all. I was just thinking how much fun you must be on a long journey."

He grimaced. "A carriage is necessary for certain Town events, but I travel almost exclusively on my horse and avoid the inside of a coach whenever possible."

Eleanor glanced around the luxurious interior. "Then why own such a well-turned-out vehicle?"

"The coach is part of an inheritance from my grandmother's estate."

"Oh. I am sorry for your loss. Was it recent?"

"Last month." He cleared his throat. "I miss her very much."

The vulnerable emotion in his voice twisted her heart. It was never easy losing someone you loved. She wished she could say something to ease his sadness, to cushion his pain, but she knew words would offer little relief.

Eleanor stood, crouching inside the coach. She moved to her right, in order to allow the viscount room to maneuver as they exchanged places. He quickly scrambled to the other side. Eleanor waited until he was settled before attempting to sit down herself, but the coach suddenly lurched forward.

She screeched in alarm, thrusting her hand blindly forward. It landed directly above the viscount's head and she braced herself there, trying desperately to stay on her feet.

His hands moved up immediately, clasping her firmly around her waist. "Are you all right?" he asked.

"I . . . uhm . . ." Eleanor struggled to let the words out. The feel of his strong fingers holding her so possessively sent a delicious, disturbing tingle throughout her body.

He drew her closer and her hand slipped, landing squarely on the center of his chest. She looked down and found him watching her. Their gazes locked, their faces close enough for her to see the dark spikes of his lashes. Surprisingly long, full lashes that framed the most intense eyes she had ever seen. Eyes that were gazing very directly into her own.

The air drained from Eleanor's lungs. She always thought him a handsome man. He was all sleek, strong male, the embodiment of every wicked dream she had ever had. Yet it was more than his physical beauty that touched her, called to her. It was that unspoken promise, the sleepy sensuality in his eyes, the hint of a wicked, knowing grin that told her in no uncertain terms he would willingly fulfill her secret dreams of forbidden sensual delight.

For a split second Eleanor felt gloriously alive. She allowed the heat of his gaze to invade her senses, allowed the sharp excitement churning deep inside to spiral upward. It was as though everything else around her had fallen away and there were only the two of them trapped together in this moment.

They remained perfectly still for one additional instant and then she came back to herself, back to the reality of who she was, and more important, who *he* was and the utter ridiculousness of the situation.

He was a handsome rake, doing what men of his ilk always did, even with plain creatures like herself. Abruptly she pushed away, leveraging herself against his solid chest. He released an *oomph* of surprise and let go of her waist.

Legs trembling, Eleanor scrambled backward and fell haphazardly into her seat. The strength of her attraction left her feeling flustered and confused. "There, is that better, my lord?"

His brow furrowed into a frown. "Better than what?"

"Better than tossing up your accounts in the coach. Or rather all over me." She smiled brightly, willing herself not to reveal any of her inner turmoil, knowing she must look the fool, yet not caring. An awkward conversation was far preferable to what had just happened.

He stared at her, his eyes sharp with awareness. The light from the street lamps illuminated one side of his face, giving him an almost otherworldly appearance. The sight made her mind grow hazy. She shivered, uncertain why.

They rode the short distance to the supper party in silence and Eleanor was glad. The quiet gave her time to compose herself, time to push aside her ridiculous thoughts. Lord Benton was an accomplished rake; his sensual stares meant nothing. For him, it was as natural as breathing.

Time and again Eleanor had cautioned Bianca against losing her head when she was around him. With a wry smile, Eleanor admitted she would be wise indeed to heed her own very good advice.

Chapter 9

Two nights later Eleanor stood on the edge of the Hartgroves' dance floor and scanned the crowded ballroom. As with so many other balls, the space was packed so tightly it was difficult to see who was here. Suddenly Bianca whirled by, a bright smile on her face. She was partnered by Sir Reginald Black, a pleasant-looking young man with an outwardly kind disposition.

He had been paying particular attention to Bianca all evening, to the consternation of Lord Waverly, who hovered nearby. Eleanor reminded herself she needed to learn more about Lord Waverly's, and now, Sir Reginald's, situations. She could not relax her vigilance until Bianca was safely married to a worthy man.

But at this moment it was not her sister Eleanor's eyes so diligently sought to locate. It was Viscount Benton.

Ever since their carriage ride from the theatre, Eleanor had not been able to keep him from her mind. She had been vastly disappointed when

Benton had not made an appearance at the card party last night and even more dejected that he was not riding in Hyde Park at the fashionable hour this afternoon.

No additional bouquets of flowers had been delivered, forcing her to wonder if her suspicion that the viscount had sent the white roses was incorrect. But if not him, then who?

Eleanor had taken extra care with her appearance tonight, wearing a daring gown of gold silk that showcased a fair portion of her bosom. Her hair was arranged in a fashionable upsweep, and pearl earrings and a matching pearl necklace that belonged to her mother adorned her ears and throat.

She had secretly been hoping to dance with the viscount this evening, perhaps even be so bold as to try a waltz. But her preparations and anticipation were all for naught. After searching the ballroom, the card room, the refreshment area, and the terrace, she was forced to a most disappointing conclusion. Lord Benton was not here.

Eleanor sighed, trying to shake off her foolishness. *I'm tired, and this exhaustion has brought on a wave of unfamiliar emotions. 'Tis past time I let go of this morbid fascination I've developed for him. His initial interest in Bianca is gone, along with any excuse I have for being in his company.*

After assuring herself that Bianca was contentedly occupied on the dance floor, Eleanor made her way out of the ballroom. She roamed aimlessly down a corridor, turned, then followed the next one to the end. Her mind was so preoccupied it took her a few moments to realize she had wandered far from the party. The sounds of the ballroom were barely audible as she turned another corner and paused, trying to get her bearings.

Knowing she needed to retrace her steps, Eleanor whirled around. She took a single step, then heard a noise from inside the room in front of her. The door was ajar. Curious, she leaned forward and peered into the room. The interior was all shadows, the only light a fire burning in the hearth.

It took a moment for her eyes to adjust to the dim interior. As she scanned the room, she saw the floor-to-ceiling oak shelves crammed with leather matched spines. Impressed by the sheer number of volumes in the library, Eleanor stepped through the doorway to further investigate and suddenly realized the room was occupied. Standing near the long windows was the lone figure of a gentleman.

"Lady Eleanor, is that you?"

Dear God, it was Benton! "Good evening, my lord."

A hint of a smile tugged at his lips. "You look positively shocked to see me. I can assure you that I am not a gate-crasher. I was invited to the ball."

Of course she was surprised to see him! She had been eagerly searching ever since she arrived, expecting him to be in the middle of all the festivities, not hiding out by himself. But she certainly couldn't admit that to him.

Eleanor's heart started fluttering. "'Tis a relief knowing I won't have to report you to our hosts as an unwelcome guest. But you must own I am owed a bit of shock at finding you here. This is, after all, a *library*."

He lifted an eyebrow. "Are you implying that I am illiterate?"

"Not at all, though I would hardly classify you as bookish. Truthfully, it boggles my mind to consider the sort of reading material you prefer."

"Ah, yes, wicked, scandalous tomes dominated by bawdy language and, uhm, mature situations." A lighthearted expression sketched over his face. "Though I do draw the line at pictures."

"Pictures?" she asked, strolling farther into the room. "Such as those put forth in a children's story?"

He leaned indolently against the wall, crossing his arms across his chest, a knowing smile upon his lips. "There is nothing at all childish about the illustrations to which I refer."

Eleanor's brow furrowed as she pondered what could be so risqué about an illustration. "I've never seen such a book."

"I'm not surprised."

Eleanor frowned, instinctively knowing he was referring to something scandalous, yet having no idea what he meant. Deliberately keeping her gaze from straying to him, she cast her eyes along the shelves.

"'Tis a most eclectic collection," she commented. "Everything from agriculture to classic tomes in numerous languages along with recent, popular novels. Very impressive."

He strode slowly toward her, tilting his head as he scanned the same shelf. "French, Latin, Greek. Are you saying you can read all three?"

She nodded. "Along with a smattering of Italian. I suppose in your eyes that qualifies me as a bluestocking," she said, referencing that derogatory term.

"I never liked that label. It's demeaning." He considered her, his stare assessing. "I have always found intelligent women far more interesting. And entertaining."

"Yet society tells us they must strive to hide the quickness of their minds."

"Oh, hang society." He stopped before her, only inches away. "An *intelligent* woman's point of view is always valuable. Not always agreed with, yet valuable nonetheless. 'Tis the mark of a dim-witted, insecure man who refuses to admit it."

She fell silent, marveling at his comment. "'Tis good to know that I need not censure my opinion with you."

"Egad, I hadn't realized you had been holding your tongue." His lips curled. "I fairly tremble wondering what you will say to me now that we have established such open communication."

Eleanor tried to hold back her blush. She had been brutally frank with him at times, especially regarding her sister. "I shall endeavor to be circumspect, my lord."

"Sebastian." He reached out and twirled a wisp of hair slowly around his finger. "I'd very much like for you to call me Sebastian. And I shall call you Eleanor."

He stood improperly close. She could feel the heat of his body, smell the faint scent of his pleasant cologne. "There is something quite indescribable about you, Eleanor. I find myself thinking of you at odd times of the day. Why is that, do you suppose?"

She lowered her head, warmed by the idea that she had also been on his mind. Warmed, yet not entirely convinced. Handsome rogues like him did not seek out plain, older spinsters like her. And yet, his breathing seemed as unsteady as hers.

Sebastian leaned toward her, placing one hand on her waist and drawing her against his chest. His other hand cradled the back of her head, forcing her chin up. Gazing into his eyes, she realized he was going to kiss her.

All her insides turned to mush.

She was not a young, inexperienced girl. She had shared many a passionate kiss with John Tanner. But this was different. This man did not have a deep affection for her. Yet there was no denying the spell he had woven over her, the pull of sensual delight she felt whenever he was near.

A torrent of conflicting emotions surged through Eleanor. Being in Sebastian's arms made her feel like someone she wasn't—daring, almost wicked.

And she liked it.

A half smile played on his full, sensual lips. "I am going to kiss you now, Eleanor."

Despite her curiosity, her first instinct was to pull away. The library was secluded, yet not impossible to find. Anyone could wander in, just as she had done. The repercussions of being caught bordered on scandal, yet more important, it would be a bad example to Bianca if she were discovered in such a compromising situation.

He must have sensed her reluctance. His fingers tightened in her hair to keep her in place at the same time his hand slid from her waist to the small of her back. Eleanor shivered with anticipation. It had been a very long time since she had felt the press of a man's lips against her own.

She felt her body tighten, her gaze roving over his face. His expression told her the truth—he was indeed about to kiss her. She went so still she briefly forgot to breathe. But then she allowed her proper, priggish objections to vanish, gave herself permission to enjoy whatever was to come. Her heart skipped in anticipation, certain that his kiss would be as possessive and hungry as the intense gleam darkening his eyes.

Yet when it finally came, the initial touch of his lips upon hers was sweet and tender. No grasping, no crushing, no plundering. She parted her lips at that sweetness, at the promise of something more than passion.

Feather light, he ran his tongue across the seam of her lips and teeth, then slipped it farther into her mouth. The heat of it radiated through her, taking her breath away, jolting her to her very core. Though they were indoors, the stars spun over her head as she clung to his warmth, savoring every taste, every touch.

"Eleanor." Her name fell from his lips in a liquid caress. He trailed his mouth across her cheek to the curve of her throat. The tender, whisper-soft kisses set her skin ablaze. Senses reeling, all thoughts of propriety disappeared like a wisp of smoke. She was aware of nothing but him and a need inside herself that was growing more intense by the minute.

His hand swept down to the swell of her hip and she instinctively pushed herself forward, giving her hunger free rein. His mouth tasted divine. Her arms tightened around his neck, and she felt the lower half of his body, large and stiff, pressing against her stomach.

Because of me? she thought in amazement. *I have the power to incite such a passionate reaction in a man so sophisticated, so worldly?*

She kissed him deeply one more time, then forced herself to break away, lift her head, and meet his gaze. There was molten fire in his eyes and she shuddered at the evidence of his desire for her. *Remarkable.*

The silence between them was charged with emotion and unspoken needs. Eleanor felt a flush of embarrassment. Not about the kiss, which had indeed been glorious, but because they now seemed unable to manage any conversation.

"That was highly improper," she whispered.

"'Twas only a kiss, Eleanor. And not, I believe, your first."

She blushed. He casually touched her cheek with the tips of his fingers, sending another shudder of desire through her still heated body. "True, it was not my first kiss, but unless you declare yourself to have honorable intentions, it should be the last one we share."

He took her hand and pressed it against his chest. She could feel the steady thump of his heart. "Why do you assume my intentions are not honorable?"

"I have heard far too many comments on your opinion of marriage," she answered.

His brow quirked. "That does not mean I shall never marry."

"True, yet the facts cannot be denied. Forty is the age I believe you have set for yourself to take a wife. Unless you have one secreted away at your country estate?"

He laughed. She liked the way his eyes crinkled at the corners, liked the way his face appeared more boyish and carefree. *Goodness, he was a handsome devil.*

"No, there is no wife," he said, his gaze sweeping pointedly over her. "Not yet, at least. Though it could certainly happen well before I reach forty, if I find the right woman."

A swift current of excitement raced through her, but Eleanor tamped down her delight. He could not possibly mean what he was implying.

"Ha! I vow the betting book at White's is filled with wagers as to the length of your bachelorhood."

"It is indeed. I confess to placing a few of them myself. Just to keep the lads guessing." Amusement danced in his eyes. "While it is true that I have not yet discovered a compelling reason to marry, that does not mean I never will."

"For your title and property?" she asked, citing the usual reasons. Reasons that inexplicably made her feel a sad stab of regret.

"I hardly find those reasons compelling. Really, Eleanor, shouldn't there be more to marriage?"

"Well, there are kisses," she said airily.

His eyes sensually moved down the length of her body. "Kisses are merely the beginning."

Eleanor felt her cheeks flush as a shudder of pure desire shot through her body. "Are you trying to seduce me?"

"Is that what you want?" His tone was light and teasing, yet she clearly heard the thread of determination beneath it. Why was he so interested in her? Was she merely a challenge to him? Or was there more involved?

"That is preposterous," she lied, knowing she should pull herself free from his arms and return to the ball, retreating as quickly as her feet could go.

He took her hands in his and the yearning in his

eyes made her catch her breath. "I promise you that knowing someone in the biblical sense is an extraordinary occurrence, yet a real relationship between a man and a woman encompasses far more."

"A rake who values a female for something more than her body?" Oh, how she wanted to believe him! She considered him closely. He gazed back at her, almost as if he knew she doubted his sincerity. "You are either a fraud or a very good liar," she declared.

"Or a sensual, experienced lover who wants more from a woman than physical pleasure. Are you bold enough to guess the truth?"

"I don't really have to guess, do I, Sebastian? Your actions speak of a man who understands the game of dalliance and seduction, yet I suspect you refuse to commit yourself fully. You refuse to risk your heart."

"I willingly admit that I don't know the first thing about love. Real love. Proper love, between a man and a woman. But that doesn't mean I can't learn." He smoothed back a stray wisp of her hair and softly kissed her temple.

The tenderness of his gesture brought forth a sigh. Eleanor marveled that his affectionate petting was almost as stimulating as his passion. "You are a closet romantic," she accused.

"A fact I shall deny to the bitter end." There was an irony to his tone that tugged at her, that told her this was his true essence. In that instant she felt as if she had caught a glimpse into his soul, into the yearning he kept hidden from the world. And then, a most bizarre truth struck her.

The viscount was lonely.

A ragged sigh escaped Eleanor's lips. He was watching her with something guarded, almost vulnerable resting in his eyes. And in that moment her heart began to soften.

Sebastian's corruption of the earl's daughter was not going precisely as he had planned. The romantic light flickering from the library's fireplace cast a golden glow over her entire body, from the top of her head to the tip of her dancing slippers. He knew logically that it was the shimmering silk threads of her gold gown that caused this illusion, yet he still found it enchanting.

It was not supposed to be happening this way. He had intended the seduction to be calculated and methodical, with revenge and lust being the only emotions driving him forward.

Sebastian knew seducing a female of Eleanor's intelligence would be no small feat. Simple compliments and insincere flattery would not be enough. She required more depth, more introspection. To be successful he would have to entice her mind as well as her body.

She had lived too long in the shadow of her sister's beauty to realize her own value, to believe she could easily entice a man. And therein lay perhaps the greatest irony of all. Bianca might be a diamond of the first water, but Sebastian felt no sexual pull toward her.

Eleanor, on the other hand, could bring his body swiftly to aching hardness. Her kisses had been stirring, dazzling almost, igniting a craving deep inside. When they had separated he felt bereft, awash in unfulfilled longing. Sebastian was an experienced enough lover to know this was not only due to the lack of sexual release.

She had touched a nerve that hit not just a physical need, but an emotional one. Their kisses left him feeling a bit uncontrolled and adrift, rather like the boat he had rescued at the garden party the other day for the young lad. Sebastian had set himself on this course with Eleanor, but the current of passion had pulled him in an entirely different direction.

Even when she elected to spar with him, as she did more often than not, he found her company stimulating. And he was shocked to realize how charmed he was by her. Her quick wit, her intelligent reflections, her open desire.

He was trying his best to ignore these emotions. She was the daughter of his enemy, a man who had caused his mother's death, he reminded himself sternly, yet he was finding that he needed to push himself to take advantage of her vulnerability. *Hellfire and damnation, this is not the time to be developing a conscience. There will be no second thoughts about what I am planning.*

"You should return to the ballroom before you are missed," Sebastian said with deceptive casualness. "We can continue this discussion tomorrow evening. Are you attending the Tauntons' ball?"

"I believe so," she said softly.

"Excellent. Their library is even more impressive than this one and located in a separate wing from the ballroom. Meet me there at eleven o'clock. Be discreet when you leave the party and be sure to allow yourself plenty of time to find it. The mansion is massive. If you get lost, ask a servant for directions."

Sebastian paused to observe the results of his dictate.

Eleanor's dreamy, well-kissed look was gone. The alert, wary expression was back on her face, but her eyes were not filled with their usual sensible determination. Instead she appeared to be considering his words carefully.

Deciding he needed to add a touch more enticement, Sebastian lowered his head for another kiss. Framing her face with his hands, he took possession of her lips with smoldering demand, sipping fully the honey sweetness.

It was difficult to pull away. Torturous, really. When he kissed her it was impossible not to want more, not to take more. But this wasn't the time or place. With one final dart of his tongue he broke away, the harsh, uneven breaths bellowing from his lungs echoing through the cavernous room.

Eleanor swayed unsteadily in his arms and he held her upright, but only until he felt certain she could stand on her own. He noted with satisfaction that the wide-eyed, slightly dazed expression was back on her face.

"Until tomorrow, Eleanor. Don't forget, eleven o'clock in the library. I'll be waiting for you."

Giving her no time to respond, Sebastian gently turned her around and nudged her out the door. The moment she cleared the doorway, he shut it quickly, lest he be tempted to pull her back inside.

* * *

I won't go. Of course I won't go. 'Tis inappropriate.
Scandalous. Foolish beyond measure.

Those thoughts repeated themselves over and
over in Eleanor's head throughout the day, growing
louder as she prepared to attend the Tauntons' ball.

"You've altered the neckline on the blue silk,"
Bianca commented when Eleanor descended the
staircase. "Very daring."

"Is it too provocative?" Eleanor asked, nervously
checking the hallway mirror. The bodice was tightly
fitted and far lower than any other garment she had
worn. The round tops of her bosom were prettily
exposed and the sophistication of the dress gave her
fledgling confidence a boost.

"Women of a certain age can dress however they
please, because no one notices," the earl said impatiently. "It only matters that Bianca look appropriately beautiful and innocent. And she does."

"Eleanor also looks lovely, Papa," Bianca said loy-
ally, but the earl had already donned his coat and
gone outside.

It was an unfortunate circumstance that the earl
had unexpectedly elected to escort them to the ball
this evening. His presence soured Eleanor's mood,
but her father's criticism was soon forgotten when
they arrived at the party.

Her eyes anxiously searched the crowds while she
chatted amicably with their hosts. Her mind scarcely
registered the conversation, for she was trying her
best not to appear as though she was waiting for Sebastian.

She found herself missing him today. Especially
during the afternoon social calls when Bianca had
been surrounded by her usual bevy of admirers. As

Eleanor observed these gentlemen, she realized that Sebastian probably knew most of them. His opinion of their character and circumstances would be invaluable. If only he were there to ask.

But alas, the viscount did not call. He had in fact never called. Visiting a lady one admired was the usual, socially acceptable way to conduct a courtship and the viscount's absence caused a few moments of worry for Eleanor. Worry that she quickly dismissed. Sebastian was not like other gentlemen; she should hardly be surprised he refused to act in a similar manner.

"By any happy circumstance are you free for this dance, Lady Eleanor?"

Eleanor turned sharply and met the smiling eyes of Peter Dawson. "How very kind of you to ask."

She took the hand he offered. It was solid and warm and she grasped it tightly as he led her toward the lines that were forming for the dance.

She smiled at him as they joined hands and began, starting a pleasant conversation that continued each time the patterns of the dance brought them together. Eleanor remembered he was a particular friend of the viscount and though she longed to ask about Sebastian, she restrained herself.

Mr. Dawson was an excellent dancer. He was light on his feet, careful of her toes, and possessed a natural rhythm that made it easy for her to follow. Somehow she managed to chat and laugh, though she would have enjoyed herself far more if she had not been so preoccupied.

Mr. Dawson escorted her off the dance floor when the set ended and remained to continue their conversation. A uniform gasp of delight was heard when the orchestra began the notes for the first waltz of the evening. Eleanor turned her head to glance at the couples gathering on the dance floor when she spied Sebastian standing near the French doors, talking to Lord Atwood.

Gracious! Eleanor's heart sped up and she struggled to control her expression. She waited for him to turn and see her, and when he did his smile was so broad and welcoming her knees felt weak. Willpower alone kept her from rushing across the room to greet him.

"Punch?"

"Pardon?" She broke away from Sebastian's hypnotic stare and turned back to Mr. Dawson.

"You seem rather flushed, Lady Eleanor. I was wondering if you would like some punch to cool down."

"Yes, thank you. That would be delightful."

"Good evening, Lady Eleanor."

Oh my! Eleanor nearly jumped out of her skin she was so startled. *How had he managed to walk all the way across the room without her noticing?* "My lord." She curtsied.

"Sebastian," he reminded her with a wicked grin.

"Only when we are in private together," she hissed.

"May I say you look exceptionally fetching this evening. Blue is your color, ma'am."

"Thank you." Pink stole into her cheeks as she felt certain he was staring at her cleavage.

"Benton, good to see you." Mr. Dawson handed Eleanor her glass of punch and shook hands with the viscount. She expected one of the two men to leave but they settled in for a comfortable chat, making any private word with Sebastian impossible.

"Tell me, have you read any good books lately, Lady Eleanor?" Sebastian asked innocently. "I was recently in a library and several volumes caught my eye."

She met his gaze straight on in silent warning, yet his grin never faltered. "As a matter of fact I just finished *Ivanhoe,* by Sir Walter Scott," she answered. "It was highly entertaining, though one of my favorite historical pieces is *Le Morte d'Arthur.*"

"Sir Thomas Malory's tome?" Sebastian inquired. "Do you know it?"

"Very well. Contrary to popular opinion, I don't spend all my waking hours drinking, gambling, chasing women, and generally being a disgraceful rake."

"That's news to me," Mr. Dawson interjected with a teasing smile. "Oh, and you left out swimming naked in fountains."

Sebastian gave his friend a withering stare. "Legends are indeed a fascinating subject for a novel and none more so than the rise and fall of a powerful kingdom. Yet I cannot fully embrace a story that ends with the death of the king, the queen in a nunnery, and the hero knight a monk."

"I confess to liking the violence and bloodshed," Mr. Dawson admitted sheepishly. "'Tis a darn good adventure."

"True, but there is so much more than adventure. Arthur and his knights continually try to live up to their chivalric codes," Eleanor said. "Even though they usually fail."

"I shall venture a guess that Sir Lancelot Du Lac is your favorite character, Lady Eleanor," Sebastian remarked with a faint smile.

"Well, he is Arthur's most revered knight," Eleanor defended. "He assists damsels in distress and provides mercy for knights he has defeated in battle."

"But he is a flawed knight," Sebastian exclaimed. "His devotion to Guinevere shifts from courtly love to adultery, which leads to his ultimate ruin and Arthur's death."

"Guinevere is so contemptible it is difficult to understand Lancelot's reason for loving her." Eleanor shook her head. "Still, he wanted what he couldn't have, what was just beyond his reach. Is that not human nature?"

"The very essence of it, I believe. Don't you agree, Dawson?"

"I do. And with that said, I must go. I've promised this dance to Miss Hamilton. I had best go and find her. Excuse me. Lady Eleanor. Benton."

And then he was gone.

"Regretfully, I too have a partner for this set," Sebastian said.

Who? Eleanor nearly asked, biting her tongue to keep the question from escaping. "Pray, don't let me keep you, my lord."

He chuckled softly, the wicked gleam back in his eyes. "Sebastian," he whispered. "Eleven o'clock. Don't keep me waiting too long. I'm not a particularly patient man, Eleanor."

And then he too was gone.

As he walked away Eleanor felt a pang of jealousy.

He hadn't asked *her* to dance. But then she saw the viscount escort a woman twice his age onto the dance floor and a breath of relief shuddered through her.

Eleanor strolled along the edge of the ballroom, carefully avoiding making further eye contact with Sebastian. She also avoided the earl, who instead of heading toward the card room as he usually did, took to the dance floor with various young women.

The hours moved with painful slowness. Eleanor kept a chaperone's eye on Bianca, conversed with the other guests, partook of a few refreshments, all the while telling herself she could not possibly be so brazen as to keep this assignation.

Yet when the clock reached the appropriate hour, Eleanor found herself wandering through the labyrinth of hallways, following the complicated directions to the library given to her by a young footman.

By necessity, her relationship with John Tanner had been clandestine. The chasm of their social class, not to mention the fact that he was employed by her father, dictated that circumstance.

Yet this time, Eleanor told herself, she was not dealing with a young man caught in the throes of love. She was dealing with a practiced rake, an artisan of seduction. That fact alone should have deterred her from keeping this rendezvous, should have touched the practical, sensible side of her nature. Truly, her actions defied all rational thought.

Eleanor stood before the door for a full minute. It would not do for the viscount to see her so eager and harried. She needed to maintain some degree of self-respect.

She patted a stray curl, laughing nervously at her own ridiculous notion. Then, taking a deep breath, she reached for the brass knob and slowly opened the library door.

Chapter 10

The room was empty.

Eleanor blinked, taking in every corner of the vast room. Sebastian had not exaggerated. The Tauntons' library was twice the size of any other she had ever seen, with bookshelves from floor to ceiling. She had to stretch her neck as far back as it would go to see the top shelves.

In one corner of the room was a spiral staircase. Made of decorative wrought iron, it twisted upward seven feet, leading to a narrow walkway, also made of wrought iron. Eleanor realized that was the only way one would have access to the books shelved on the very top rows.

It was an ingenious design that would have fascinated her under different circumstances. She walked farther into the room, her pulse leaping as she confirmed she was alone, with only the crackling fire and a few burning candles to keep her company.

A fluttering panic erupted inside her, leaving a

sick feeling in her stomach. Why hadn't he come? Was he teasing her? Jesting with her?

Lightheaded and trembling, Eleanor sank down on a leather wingback chair. *What am I doing here?*

The door suddenly opened. Eleanor's head jerked up and her stomach bottomed out. Every nerve in her body prickled with awareness. He had come!

"Damn, I'm late." Sebastian hurried forward. "Forgive me. Lady Agatha was slightly out of breath at the end of our dance. It was necessary to find a chair for her to sit upon and rest and then locate someone to watch over her before I could leave."

"You should have greater care when selecting your partners," Eleanor replied, relieved to hear her voice sounded much calmer than she felt.

"Limiting my dancing to women under sixty is sage advice, yet they so enjoy the attention. I fear there would be many hurt feelings if I suddenly stopped." He smiled and extended his hand toward her.

Eleanor hesitated for a fraction of a second before taking it. At the touch of his warm fingers, a sensation unfurled deep inside her. He pulled her to her feet abruptly, catching and holding her within the circle of his arms.

"Hello there," he said in a deep, measured voice.

His eyes were blazing with fire. It should have been stilted, awkward, but instead it felt easy, comfortable.

"Are you enjoying the party, Sebastian?" she asked breathlessly.

"I am now, Eleanor."

Cradling her head, he leaned down and captured

her mouth in a kiss that drove any doubts from her mind.

His lips were warm and firm. She parted her own and he slipped his tongue in to teasingly stroke hers. Sighing deeply, Eleanor returned the kiss passionately, one hand going around his neck, her fingers curling through the soft hair at the nape.

He clutched her closer, making a guttural sound in his throat, groaning into the kiss. The taste and texture of him filled every sense and all she was conscious of was him. The feel of his hard, strong body pressing so intimately against hers, the clean, heady taste of his tongue and mouth, the intoxicating scent of cologne mixed with his own unique masculine scent.

She had come here tonight for these kisses. For the chance to ease her loneliness, her sense of isolation. For the chance to allow herself to *feel* so intensely, to *want* so desperately. Her growing regard for him was unexpected, as was her growing affection. Was that what made his kisses so overwhelming? Or had she simply been denied physical male affection for too long?

She closed her eyes and held back a moan. She had a wicked urge to thrust herself forward, too excited to be cautious, too swept up in the pleasure to think beyond the joy of his embrace. Sebastian broke the kiss, then rested his forehead against hers. Their warm breaths mingled, a strangely intimate occurrence. He shifted slightly, flicking his tongue against her earlobe. Pleasure rippled through her.

"Oh, Sebastian," she whispered against his mouth. "You make me feel so . . ."

"Yes," he prompted.

"Alive," she cried.

Lifting her chin, she sought his lips once again. He murmured her name, then delved inside her mouth, stroking her with his tongue. She clung to him, surrendering as he kissed her with undeniable passion and need.

His muscular thighs trapped her in place. Eleanor moved her hips reflexively, feeling the heat of his body even through the barrier of their clothes, becoming conscious of his erection pressing against the juncture of her thighs.

"I have never enjoyed kissing much," he whispered. "Until now."

His lips traced the shell of her ear slowly. Eleanor shivered, turning her head and invitingly offering her bare neck. He swooped down, pressing a line of warm, moist kisses from her throat to her shoulders. With tongue and teeth he continued to kiss her bare flesh, while his fingers took the lead, working their way inside the top of her bodice.

Eleanor's breaths grew deeper, her breasts rising and falling so rapidly she wondered if they would pop right out of her dress. Somehow the gown remained intact, but that did not deter the viscount. His hand moved deeper into her bodice until he cupped her breast. Sebastian brushed his thumb over her throbbing nipple, then gently rolled it between two fingers. Passion spiraled through her and the dampness between her thighs grew.

"Ahh," she moaned, her fingers digging into the hard muscles of his shoulders.

"Does it feel good, my sweet?" he rasped. "Do you want more?"

"Yes," she whispered, stunned at the sound of her breathy, anxious voice. Eleanor didn't know who that woman was, could barely believe she possessed such wanton abandon.

Her eyelids fell closed as he pulled the material of her bodice down, exposing her top half completely. The cool air caressed her heated breasts. It was insane. Reckless. Glorious.

Her breasts felt full, her loins throbbed. He nuzzled her nipples, his warm breath teasing. Moaning, Eleanor arched up against him, seeking release, fulfillment, knowing only he could give her what she craved most, needed most.

"You are so delicate," he whispered, an edge of awe in his voice. "So very lovely."

"Sebastian, please," she cried, running her hands over his chest.

"This," he whispered. "Is it this?"

He dragged his tongue roughly over her stiffened nipple. She cried out, a sob of passion, arching her back. She felt as if she were on fire. Lost to these maddening sensations, she was only vaguely aware of his hand reaching beneath her skirt.

His hand glided up her legs, weaving a path to her inner thigh until he reached soft curls. His fingers nestled there, rubbing lightly. Pure, strong pleasure shot through her. Eleanor could hear her breath coming in small, soft pants as she lifted her hips against his hand, seeking relief from the intense, demanding tension that was building inside her.

"Oh, Sebastian, I need, I want," she panted.

"Shh, I know. Let yourself go, Eleanor," he said in a throaty voice. "Come for me."

He angled her over his arm, lifting her closer, taking her nipple deep into his mouth. Eleanor whimpered, moving her legs restlessly. He suckled her breast as he fondled her, increasing the sensations to an irresistible urgency.

She could feel her body getting slicker, hotter as he stroked her, coaxing her flesh to quivering heights. The tension built and built until she thought she would go mad. Reading her body with acute accuracy, Sebastian pressed the palm of his hand flat against her core, then nudged two fingers inside her.

Eleanor could not keep still. There were no words to describe the feeling. Her body moved spasmodically as she jerked and wiggled beneath his touch. He seized her mouth in a fierce, heady kiss and she gave herself over to the mindless pleasure, wanting it to last forever.

But her passion was too overwhelming to be contained. A few more deft strokes of his clever fingers sent Eleanor quaking as the tension broke. Her body felt as if it were coming apart, exploding in a burst of intense pleasure.

A deep, keening cry filled the air. Hers? His? Dazed and drifting, she allowed her legs to buckle, trusting Sebastian to keep her upright, tightly held within his protective arms.

Gasping and straining, Sebastian tore his mouth from Eleanor's. He reached down, fumbling with the fall of his evening breeches. His erection was straining against the fabric so hard 'twas a miracle the buttons didn't break. He pressed her back against the brocade sofa that was but a foot away, following her down onto the couch, leaning on his left side so as not to crush her.

He could still feel Eleanor trembling, the aftershocks of her climax causing a few remaining spasms. It gave him no small measure of pride knowing he had given her such pleasure, had brought her to complete release, arousing his own passion significantly.

Sebastian hadn't come here tonight with the intention of taking Eleanor's seduction this far. He had just wanted to give her a taste, to pique her curiosity, to pull her deeper into his sensual web.

Yet he acknowledged that he was the one who had been caught. His desire raged within him, out of control. He was uncertain if she was a virgin. She had mentioned loving an unsuitable man when she was younger and it was clear she was not inexperienced. Yet there was such an honest element to her passion, a giving nature that bespoke of a limited knowledge.

Virgin or not, it hardly mattered. He reached for her arms and lifted them over her head. The movement caused her back to arch, exposing her naked breasts to his gaze. They were full and round, the dusky nipples peaked, ready and ripe for more kisses.

As he set his hand between her breasts, he could feel the beat of her heart beneath his palm. The dim, flickering blaze from the fireplace provided a small amount of illumination, bathing her in a shadowy light. Her eyes were closed, her face enraptured.

He wasn't certain why he found her so irresistible. True, it had been several months since he had engaged in carnal relations, but he had been deprived of robust sex for longer periods. She wasn't anything like the women he usually became involved with—perhaps that difference was what gave her such appeal?

As he bent to kiss her throat, an unexpectedly loud sound came from the other side of the room, near the doorway. Breaking away from Eleanor, Sebastian turned to investigate.

"Bloody hell!" he cursed, springing to his feet. With swiftness that astonished him, Sebastian fastened the top buttons of his breeches. Whirling around, he instinctively thrust Eleanor behind him, effectively hiding her from curious eyes.

"Is that you, Benton?" a slurred male voice asked. "I say, what do you have there, you sly dog? A tasty morsel, no doubt."

Sebastian's anger flared. How dare a worm like Arthur Peterson refer to a woman like Eleanor as a tasty morsel? Sebastian's fingers curled together in a tight fist and he envisioned himself planting that fist in the middle of the intruder's florid, laughing face.

"You are being unpardonably rude, Peterson," Sebastian declared in a low, threatening tone. "I demand that you leave at once."

"Without saying good evening to your companion? Now *that* would be rude."

The simmering anger surged like a firestorm inside Sebastian. "Be warned. If you take one step forward, I shall be forced to curve my hands around your neck and throttle you until you turn blue."

Behind him, Eleanor let out a small squeak. He

thrust his hand back to silence her. She grasped onto his arm, held tightly, then quieted.

Peterson's jovial expression turned wary. "No need to get yourself so riled, Benton. I was just having a bit of fun."

"Your fun is over. Now, get out," Sebastian growled, a murderous scowl knitting his brow.

Licking his lips nervously, Peterson started slowly backing toward the doorway, never once taking his eyes off Sebastian.

"Oh, and Peterson, if I start hearing vicious rumors about me, I will know the source. And I will be violently displeased. Do I make myself clear?"

There was a momentary flare of annoyance in Peterson's face, but then his expression changed. He nodded contritely, then followed Sebastian's dictate and hurried from the room, clicking the door loudly as he closed it.

"Do you think he saw me?" Eleanor's voice was soft, shaken.

Sebastian shrugged. His body was still taut with arousal, his blood fired with anger. Peterson's arrival could not have been more ill-timed, yet it unexpectedly provided Sebastian with the perfect opportunity. If she had been discovered, Eleanor would have been ruined. Utterly and completely.

The earl would have been outraged. He would have demanded that Sebastian do right by his eldest daughter, since marriage was the only way to redeem Eleanor's honor. And Sebastian would have refused, thus forcing the earl to defend his family name by the only other means available—a duel.

This had been Sebastian's plan from the beginning. Hell, it still was his plan. He truly had no idea why he had gone to such lengths to protect her just now. Was it because it was Arthur Peterson who had discovered them? A man with little to recommend him, a man who skirted the edge of polite society, existing on slander and gossip. Or was it something else?

Sebastian turned to look at Eleanor. She had pulled the bodice of her dress over the bare flesh of her breasts and was attempting to set her gown back in place. Shadows flickered over the soft curves of her body and face. Their eyes met.

Hers were luminous, yet somehow he knew not to expect hysterics or tears. Eleanor had more dignity, more strength of character. She would not collapse into a quivering heap of weeping.

"Is this a wager?" she whispered.

"I beg your pardon?"

"I asked if you have made a wager." She cleared her throat. "I know that sort of thing occurs among gentlemen. For amusement, I suspect, though I find nothing entertaining about it."

Sebastian felt his jaw drop. He had not expected an emotional collapse, but this accusation was a surprise. "You don't have a very high opinion of men, do you?"

Eleanor sighed. "I have a realistic view of men, whose faults equal those of women. Each can be cruel in their own way. The betting book wagers prevalent in gentlemen's clubs are notorious. Humiliating for the victims as their names are bandied about by the gentlemen of the *ton,* and assumptions are drawn about their character."

She said "gentlemen" very pointedly and he embarrassingly admitted she was right. Congregating men could act like perfect asses at times, he among them. "There is no wager, Eleanor. It distresses me that you would even speculate on the existence of one."

She sighed again and lifted her chin. It seemed to require an effort for her to hold his gaze. "A wager was as good an explanation as any when trying to understand your interest in me."

"I happen to like you. Very much." His stomach roiled with guilt, though he wasn't lying. He did like her, more than he realized, more than he should. Yet she must remain a means to an end or else his revenge would go unresolved. "Is it so impossible to believe I find you attractive?"

"Why me?"

"Why not?"

"Don't tease, Sebastian. I want to know. I need to know."

A muscle twitched in his jaw. "You are prickly and difficult, intelligent and loyal, and your kisses make me feel like a randy lad with his first love. Satisfied?"

She smiled and nodded her head. Sebastian slowly exhaled, not realizing he had been holding his breath.

"I like you too, Sebastian. I find your seductive charms quite irresistible."

"Ah, yes, seductive charms are the mark of any practiced rake worth his salt."

"You are worth far more than salt, sir," she said, a smile working across her mouth. Then abruptly her expression changed to serious regard. "I need to return to the ballroom. Your threat was most impressive, yet I worry how long Mr. Peterson will be able to hold his tongue. Finding you in such a compromising position is far too juicy a tidbit to keep silent. I vow he will reveal *something* to *someone* before the night has ended."

Sebastian grimaced. "I fear you are right. But you can't leave yet. Naturally we cannot be seen together, but Peterson's beady little eyes will be searching avidly for any unescorted females entering the ballroom, assuming one of those women was in here with me."

"Lord, I hadn't considered it." Her eyes grew worried. "What am I to do?"

"First, allow me to help you dress."

She nodded, then sat quietly as he restored her undergarments to their correct location, then fastened the buttons on the back of her gown.

"Thank you."

Sebastian fixed his gaze toward the darkened windows, wondering if he could help Eleanor out one and then take her through the terraced gardens around the side of the house. There were too many doors leading from the gardens into the ballroom for Peterson to be watching all of them.

"Can you climb out the window?" he asked.

"Now?" Eleanor looked toward the windows, then gave him a dubious glance. "'Tis very dark out there and rather a long drop. Aren't we on the second floor of the house?"

Sebastian shook his head. "You're right. 'Tis a foolish plan. We'll wait a few more minutes, then I'll leave without you. As soon as I find someone to help, I'll send them here. They can escort you back to the party."

"Someone?"

"Someone I trust. If you enter the ballroom with

another man, Peterson won't even consider you as a possibility for my *chère-amie*."

Eleanor nodded. "It seems a logical plan. The last thing I want is a scandal. 'Twould anger the earl and reflect badly upon my sister, hurting her chances to make a good match."

Pondering Eleanor's words, Sebastian removed a thin silver case from his inside pocket. The threat of scandal distressed her, yet her first thought was not for herself, but rather for her sister.

He extracted a thin cheroot. Holding it aloof, he asked, "May I?"

"Only if you let me try it." He raised his brow and she grinned. "I've always wanted to taste one."

He set the cheroot to his lips, lit it, then coaxed the tobacco to life. After exhaling a long stream of smoke, he handed it to Eleanor.

She examined it carefully before placing it between her own lips. *Lord above.* The sight of her eager mouth gently encircling the cheroot was one of the most sensual things he had ever seen. Sebastian hissed in a breath as his mind filled with erotic images of her taking him inside that lovely, wet mouth.

"Suck in a bit more," he instructed, the ache below growing harder.

"Oh." She wheezed, coughing hard and spewing out puffs of smoke. "'Tis dreadful. It tastes like ashes."

He took the cheroot from her hand, then produced a handkerchief so she could wipe her tearing eyes. "I suppose it requires time to develop an enjoyment for it," he speculated.

"Hmm," she muttered, before launching into

another fit of coughs. "I now understand why ladies are discouraged from smoking."

Smiling, he held out the burning ember, but she declined a second puff. Sebastian took in a few more lungfuls before tossing the rest of it into the fireplace, then turned to Eleanor. As much as he wanted to avoid it, he knew it was time to return to the ball. "You'll wait here, as I asked?"

Her head bowed in a faint nod.

The library was eerily quiet once he had gone. Eleanor paced restlessly, longing to leave, feeling trapped and alone. What if Mr. Peterson had already started blabbing about what he had seen? Surely that would bring one or two curious individuals to the library. And then everyone would know it was she who had been locked in an embrace with the viscount.

How would she possibly explain her behavior? To her sister? And her father?

A cold shiver of dread moved over Eleanor's spine. She could hardly imagine what the earl would do and say if she created a scandal. All she did know with certainty was that he would be furious and brutal toward her.

I must leave! Now! Eleanor scurried to the door, her hand reaching anxiously for the knob. She turned it, yanked the door open, then hesitated, her promise to Sebastian echoing in her head. She had heard the viscount was involved with scores of women, yet there had been no great scandal, no sordid disgrace for any of these females. Somehow, Sebastian had managed to protect them.

Slowly Eleanor pushed the door shut. She must put her faith in him. He said he would take care of things. While it was difficult for her to trust most men, she needed to believe that Sebastian would protect her too.

Sighing, she slowly circled the perimeter of the library. Locating a small sideboard, she noticed a decanter filled with amber liquid and glasses positioned by its side. Eleanor lifted the crystal stopper and took a whiff of the decanter contents. *Brandy.*

She poured a small amount into one of the crystal tumblers. It would be foolish indeed to return to the ballroom tipsy, but she needed something to calm her nerves. She tried to sip the drink, but her agitation got the better of her and she finished it off in three quick swallows.

The potent spirits spread through her body with a soothing warmth, relaxing away some of her tension. Some, but not all.

There was a knock on the door. Biting the inside of her lip, Eleanor straightened her shoulders and raised her chin, then watched in astonishment as the Duke of Hansborough entered the room.

"Lady Eleanor?" His eyebrow lifted sardonically as he cast her an appraising look.

"Your Grace." Words failed her. She sank into a graceful curtsy, her mind working furiously. What was he doing here? Had Peterson already told the tale of finding the viscount in the library? Was the duke here trying to discover if the story were true?

"I was asked to escort you back to the ball," the duke declared.

Eleanor looked at him hesitantly. "You seemed so surprised to see me, Your Grace. I wasn't certain if Seb . . . Lord Benton had sent you."

"Oh, he sent me all right. Arrogant cur."

"Did he tell you why?"

"No." The duke gave a humorless laugh. "Knowing Benton, 'tis something disgraceful, I'm sure, though I am shocked to discover it involves you. Thought you had more sense. For a woman."

"Well, I—"

The duke held up his hand, waving it insistently in front of her. "Cease. I don't want to know. Benton asked for my help and I'm providing it. Now take my arm and I'll see you safely back to the ballroom."

Eleanor's face flooded with heat. This was simply ghastly. She wanted very much to toss her head and refuse his help, but something in his gaze convinced her that would be very foolish indeed.

With as much dignity as she could muster, Eleanor placed her hand on the duke's outstretched arm. He grunted his approval and left the library. They walked the hallways silently, taking a different route than the way she had come. Eleanor speculated it was to avoid meeting any of the other guests, but she did not ask. It was simply too embarrassing.

After what felt like an eternity they arrived at the ballroom. Eleanor's heart thumped loudly in her breast, and her fingers tightened on the duke's arm.

"Chin up, eyes forward, cool, haughty glances at anyone who dares to level a curious look at you," the duke instructed as he nearly pulled her through the archway. "And for God's sake, try not to appear guilty."

Eleanor held her breath as she tried to follow the duke's advice. She braced herself, trying to prepare for anything, then gradually realized there was no need. No one gasped in sudden outrage, or twittered behind their fans, or pointed accusing fingers in her direction.

"Would you care to dance?" she asked the duke.

"An excellent idea."

They joined the last set as it formed. Eleanor tried to concentrate on the steps of the dance but could not prevent herself from looking about the room. She stumbled when she caught sight of Arthur Peterson, but he barely spared her a glance. The duke's arm shot out to steady her. He looked at her curiously and she gave him a withering stare.

"Good girl," he said.

Eleanor smiled openly, realizing disaster had been averted. She was safe from detection, thanks to Sebastian's plan.

She was feeling relaxed when the music drew to a close and ready to strike out on her own again. She linked her arm through the duke's as they left the floor, comfortable enough to be less formal with him.

"Thank you for your assistance, Your Grace. 'Tis much appreciated."

The duke hesitated. "I've no right to give you advice, but I'm going to anyway. I've known Benton since he was a young pup. He's managed to reform some of his wilder behavior these few months, but a leopard can never truly change its spots. As far as I know, he's never ruined a woman for the sheer pleasure of it, but anything is possible. Be very careful, Lady Eleanor, lest you get tangled up in some nasty business."

His lecture delivered, the duke bowed and left. Eleanor watched him disappear into the crowd with mixed feelings. A moment later she sensed someone coming up behind her. Eleanor turned and to her relief saw it was Bianca.

"I have just heard the most scandalous gossip about Viscount Benton," Bianca whispered.

"Really?" Nerves pounding, Eleanor tried to appear nonchalant.

Bianca glanced over her shoulder, making certain no one was near enough to overhear. "Apparently the viscount arranged a tryst in the library this evening and was caught in a most compromising position." She paused dramatically. "Both he and his female companion were discovered stark naked!"

"Oh my." Eleanor could feel the pulse beating rapidly in her neck. "Who was the woman?"

"No one is saying. 'Twas Arthur Peterson who found them, yet he refuses to divulge the lady's name, claiming he wishes to salvage her reputation. I asked Lord Waverly his opinion and he said that Peterson is one of the biggest gossips in London. The only reason he's not saying is because he probably doesn't know."

"Hmm, well, perhaps Mr. Peterson can't offer details because the incident never occurred?" Eleanor suggested.

"No, I'm sure there is something to the tale. Lord Waverly believes Peterson lacks the imagination to totally fabricate a story on his own. There must be some truth to it."

Eleanor forced a casual tone. "The details will most likely never be known, unless Lord Benton decides to defend himself against the malicious gossip and punish the person who started the rumors."

Bianca's eyes widened. "By calling out Mr. Peterson? Lord Waverly says Benton is a lethal shot and an excellent swordsman. I fear it would end very badly for Mr. Peterson."

"Oh, I doubt it will come to a duel," Eleanor said confidently, though she wondered precisely how the viscount would handle the situation. True, he had warned the man to keep silent, yet challenging Peterson directly could lend more credence to the story. Laughing it off as pure fiction might be the better route. "Lord Benton might be scandalous, but he is hardly bloodthirsty."

"Whatever he is, I am just glad that I followed your advice about him. By all accounts he is *not* a gentleman intent on settling down and being faithful to one woman."

Chapter 11

"You want me to do what?" Sebastian exclaimed, staring at Eleanor in astonishment.

"I want you to help me find a husband for Bianca," Eleanor repeated calmly.

"That's what I thought you said." His gray eyes widened. "I swear, I am speechless."

"Hmm." She took a dainty bite of her ice and regarded him seriously. This was the first time they had spoken privately since the Tauntons' ball, four days ago. The gossip about Sebastian and his infamous tryst was no longer a main topic of discussion among the *ton*, making it safe for them to appear together in public.

Mr. Peterson had been effectively silenced, by means Eleanor could only imagine, but it was the sudden elopement of Miss Allen and Lord Mortley that had taken center stage in the rumor mill. The bad blood between their two families was legendary, going back so many generations that no one could say with any certainty what started the original feud. Yet somehow these two individuals were able to look beyond their legacy and fall in love. Knowing the consent to marry would not be forthcoming from either family, the two lovers had elected to run away together.

Ladies were sighing over the details, gentlemen were convinced there was more to the story than had been told, and everyone was clamoring to know the truth of the matter. In her heart Eleanor wished the couple well, yet she was grateful their escapade had relegated the viscount's indiscretion inconsequential.

Coming to Gunter's this afternoon to enjoy an ice together was an inspired idea and Eleanor was pleased Sebastian had suggested it. This public setting was the perfect place to have a private moment.

There was a sizable crowd partaking of the delectable frozen concoctions. The temperature had been unseasonably warm, yet Eleanor believed the crowds still would have come if it were the middle of winter, for the frozen treat was unique and delicious.

Eleanor was aware of the speculative glances cast at their table. She was certain everyone was wondering why someone as handsome and sophisticated as Viscount Benton would choose to spend time with someone as plain and simple as herself. It was a natural question, one Eleanor had pondered herself.

Until that night in the Tauntons' library. Memories of his kisses, his caresses, remained crisp and clear in her mind. She might not understand why, but she was convinced that Sebastian's desire for her was genuine. And she gloried in it.

"I believe the cold ice has affected your brain," Sebastian finally replied. "You cannot seriously expect me to assist you in finding a husband for your sister."

"Oh, I am most serious." Eleanor shook off his objections and took another bite of her ice. The cool, sweet taste of lemon burst upon her tongue and slid down her throat with ease. Sighing, she closed her eyes and savored the moment. It was a most extraordinary sensory experience.

Opening her eyes, Eleanor lifted her spoon and noticed Sebastian was giving her a strange gaze. "Why are you staring at me? Have I spilled something on my face?" She hastily rubbed her chin with the linen handkerchief she had in her hand, but the cloth came away empty.

"Watching you eat your ice is nothing short of sensual torture," he admitted, gazing very directly into her eyes. "If you don't behave yourself, I shall have to dump a dish of it on my lap in order to stand without disgracing myself."

Eleanor slowly lowered her spoon. She was not *doing* anything. "I don't understand what you mean."

"I know." He shifted in his chair, wincing slightly. "That makes it even more maddening."

Her eyes narrowed. "Are you trying to change the subject?"

"My dearest Eleanor, I am attempting to save my dignity. This has nothing to do with your insane request regarding a husband for your sister."

Still not convinced, she leaned forward in her chair. Tilting her head, Eleanor glanced nonchalantly down at his lap. The bulge there was impressive and unmistakable, tenting the front of his breeches. He was unquestionably aroused. *At the sight of me eating an ice?*

"Oh my," she whispered.

"Oh my, indeed." He cleared his throat loudly and shifted once again. "Though I maintain your request for my assistance is illogical and bizarre, discussing matrimony will no doubt help to . . . uhm . . . deflate my current predicament."

She grinned shyly. It was foolish to feel flattered, yet Eleanor did. But she was also aware that she had waded into a situation quite out of her depth. Uncertain how to react in public to Sebastian's lingering looks, she picked up the thread of conversation.

"Lord Waverly has shown considerable interest in Bianca, but I was told he did the same last Season with another debutante, yet did not offer for the girl."

"I can't recall, but that's hardly surprising. Matrimonial gossip has never been a keen interest of mine." A ghost of a smile touched Sebastian's lips. "Waverly's a decent sort. Good family, though his older sister is a high-strung female with a grating voice. Can't count that against him, poor fellow. He holds his liquor, doesn't gamble too deep in the pockets, pays his debts on time. I suppose he'd make an adequate husband."

"Adequate?" Eleanor frowned. "I want to find someone for Bianca who is kind and of good character. Someone who will appreciate her not only for her physical beauty but for her tender heart. Someone who will protect and cherish her. A strong man who is not a bully, but who has the fortitude and courage to stand up to the earl."

Sebastian shrugged. "I don't know Waverly all that well. He could be a good choice."

"He could," Eleanor agreed. "If Bianca decides

she truly wants him. But it must be her choice. She's had so little exposure to gentlemen, I worry it won't be easy for her to make a decision." Eleanor frowned, remembering how enamored Bianca had been with the pompous Mr. Smyth back home.

"Bianca is a lovely girl," Sebastian said. "I'm sure there are scores of eligible bachelors beating a path to your doorstep."

"Thankfully, the numbers are growing. I believe your initial interest in her kept them pitifully small when we first arrived in Town."

Tiny frown lines appeared in Sebastian's brow. "Are you saying I scared them all away?"

"Stop looking so smug. I'm certain it was an unintentional result."

Sebastian's chest visibly inflated. Eleanor hid her smile. A man's pride was a powerful thing.

"So, will you help me?" she asked.

He fixed her with a look of speculative appraisal. "Honestly, it makes me shudder to even contemplate trapping some poor, unsuspecting gentleman in a parson's mousetrap. Most unsporting."

"Oh, for pity's sake, we are not trapping anyone," Eleanor protested, her cheeks turning pink. "Besides, I thought you were a secret romantic."

"Romantic perhaps, but I am not witless." Sebastian's teeth flashed a wicked grin. "What is my reward if I decide to offer you assistance?"

"The satisfaction of knowing you have done a good turn for someone," Eleanor answered promptly.

He sent her a narrow-eyed glare. "Try again."

"My sincerest gratitude?" she ventured.

He drummed his fingers rapidly on the table. "How sincere?"

Her eyes softened. "Let's just say you won't be disappointed."

"Promise?"

"My word of honor."

He thrust his hand out. "Agreed."

Eleanor rolled her eyes. He laughed and wiggled the fingers on his extended hand at her. Realizing he wasn't going to stop until she took it, she placed her right hand in his and shook, believing she had made a good bargain.

Eleanor was in desperate need of some insight to these men and she firmly believed Sebastian was the one to provide it. Strange how she had come to trust him in so short a time. Well, on certain matters.

"What do you know about Sir Reginald Black?" Eleanor asked, pulling her hand back.

Sebastian sobered. "Bit of a hellraiser. Very fond of cards, dice, and any other games of chance. He once placed a wager in the betting book at White's as to how many ladies would be wearing gowns of periwinkle blue at his sister's coming-out ball."

Eleanor's nostrils flared. "That *is* rather extreme."

Sebastian nodded. "Funny thing is, he won the bet. Took in over a hundred guineas from several grumbling gentlemen. Does that make it any better?"

"That he won? Goodness, no. He's off the list. The last thing Bianca needs to cope with is another gamester."

"Another?" Sebastian raised his brow.

Eleanor waved her hand dismissively, evading the question. She did not want to discuss her father.

"What about Sir Mark Frost? He's very handsome and seems to be a congenial type."

Sebastian groaned. "His conversation is hardly stimulating. All the man ever talks about is his horses and the crops he is growing on his estate. He has a peculiar obsession with yields, rotations, and the best soil for various plants. Rather frightening, really."

Eleanor sighed. "I hadn't realized. I thought my living in the country spurred that particular topic of conversation when we met last week. Pity, he's the right age for Bianca. And very good-looking."

Sebastian suddenly grew still. "You think he's handsome?"

"Devilishly so." Eleanor grinned saucily, liking the sound of jealousy in the viscount's tone. "Though he has more of an angelic look with all that curly blond hair."

"He's a bit soft for a man who spends so much of his time outdoors," Sebastian added, but Eleanor had already eliminated Sir Mark from the list.

"Who is that young man standing near the doorway?" she asked.

Sebastian obligingly turned toward the door. "That's Robert Bywater. He'll inherit a fortune one day, but I'm afraid that's really all there is to recommend him."

"Oh?" Eleanor's interest was certainly piqued upon hearing of his wealth. "He looks like a perfectly fine young gentleman."

Sebastian smiled. "He's a nice enough fellow, I suppose, but rather dim. No, exceedingly dim. If he married Bianca they would have beautiful children that alas would lack the wits to keep themselves out of their own way."

"You exaggerate."

"Most certainly not. Look for yourself; he's standing at the wrong end of the line."

She leaned to her left to see around the viscount and discovered Mr. Bywater was indeed in the incorrect position to place an order. Eleanor sighed. "Heavens, that won't do, now will it?"

"Face it, ma'am, you have landed the prime matrimonial catch of the season." Sebastian folded his arms across his chest and gave her a self-satisfied grin. "Me."

Eleanor swallowed hard. She was never exactly certain what to make of him when he uttered those kinds of comments. His sexual aggression toward her was obvious, yet he most certainly was not conducting a traditional courtship.

Though her heart quickened when she recalled the package delivered the morning after their sensual night in the Tauntons' library. A rare antique, leather-bound edition of *Le Morte d'Arthur* along with a single, perfect white rose. There was no note accompanying these romantic gifts, yet none was needed.

Sebastian flirted with her, cast her sensual stares, teased her, and did everything possible to make her laugh. He kissed her senseless at every opportunity but always stopped before their encounters went too far. He took pains to imply his interest in her was honorable, but he was equally honest about the truth of his roguish reputation.

He never spoke specifically of marriage, never stated firmly his intentions to make her his wife.

Eleanor truly had no notion of what he was thinking and she was practical enough to realize Sebastian might not have marriage on his mind.

He very well might have decided he wanted her for his mistress.

The very idea should have shocked her, insulted her. She was a virtuous woman, the daughter of an earl, a woman worthy of every regard and consideration. Dictates of society insisted that marriage was the only honorable course open to her if she wanted a physical relationship with a man.

Yet privately, she was not as inclined to follow society's rules as she once had been. Eleanor briefly closed her eyes and felt her world spin around her. Had she just talked herself into becoming Sebastian's mistress? When he hadn't even asked?

"Eleanor, where have you gone?" he whispered.

Her eyes flew open. Embarrassed, she glanced around, but no one seemed to have taken any notice. "Forgive me. My thoughts overtook my manners."

"Judging by your blush, they must have been very naughty. Were you thinking of me?" he asked, a hopeful look crossing his face.

She laughed nervously. "I was thinking of Bianca's future husband and imagining a happily ever after for her."

"What about your dreams? Your happiness?"

Eleanor hesitated. "I am far too practical to be waiting for my prince to come along."

Sebastian barked with laughter. "I should hope not. The Regent is possibly the most decadent man in all of Britain. He would never do as a husband for you."

Who would? You? Eleanor wished she had the nerve, and the confidence, to ask him. "We are not speaking of me. We are talking about my sister. I fear if I don't find her someone to marry, our father will."

His eyes searched hers. She tried to remain serene, not wanting to give too much away. The earl was her private demon.

"Don't you have confidence in your father's wisdom?"

"No." The word slipped out before she could silence herself. Irritated, Eleanor ate the last spoonful of her ice. "All finished," she announced, forcing a bright smile. She stood. Sebastian also rose.

"Would you care for another ice?" he asked.

She shook her head. "I would, however, like to stroll down by the Serpentine in the park. We can admire the swans and dissect the characters of the single gentlemen."

She sensed he wanted to protest, to probe deeper into her comment about the earl. Thankfully, her pleading expression persuaded him to drop the matter, for he grinned suddenly, offered her his arm, and said, "Whatever my lady desires."

Later that evening Sebastian entered his club. He was looking forward to reading the newspaper and eating a quiet supper before venturing out on his own for the night. Before leaving Eleanor this afternoon he discovered she would be attending the Wardsworths' dinner party, an invitation he had already declined.

After a moment's consideration, Sebastian determined it would be better if he didn't see her again tonight. He was walking a fine line but overall felt things were progressing nicely. Eleanor was becoming more and more infatuated with him, more relaxed, more eager for his company. He knew it was crucial that he not be too obvious in his pursuit, yet he needed to remain vigilant for any opportunities to advance his position.

Her comment about the earl intrigued him, but her tight-lipped expression told him in no uncertain terms it was a subject that was not to be broached. Pity, since that might have gained him insight to his enemy.

Sebastian had just placed his drink and supper order when he spied the Duke of Hansborough ensconced in a leather wingback chair near the fireplace, a newspaper opened in his lap. Striding over, he took the empty seat next to the older man, cleared his throat loudly, and waited to be acknowledged.

"Benton."

"Your Grace." Sebastian inclined his head. "I have not had the opportunity to thank you for your assistance at the ball the other night. I am grateful for your intervention."

The duke snorted and rustled his newspaper.

Sebastian cleared his throat again and continued. "The situation got quite out of control when—"

The duke held up his hand. "Please, spare me what I have no doubt is a fascinating, fictional tale. You asked for my help and I gave it, but I didn't do it entirely for your sake, Benton. I did it for the lady as well."

"Thank you nonetheless."

"She deserves better," the duke grumbled.

Sebastian grinned mockingly. "On that point we are in complete agreement."

The duke slowly lowered his paper, then fixed Sebastian with a steady look. "Lady Eleanor's falling in love with you and she's not the only one. Open your eyes and button your breeches. This sort of behavior might have been tolerable when you were a green lad, but you're a man now. 'Tis not only bad form, but cruel to leave a string of broken hearts in your wake."

Sebastian suddenly felt cold. *A string of broken hearts?* "I don't know what you are trying to say."

The duke tilted his head and met Sebastian's eyes squarely. "Think about it. You're not an imbecile, though you certainly play the part well at times."

Sebastian frowned, wanting to ask more, yet almost afraid of what he would hear. But apparently the duke had finished lecturing him. He picked up the newspaper and snapped it crisply in front of him, effectively dismissing Sebastian. Further words were an impossibility.

"Good evening, Your Grace."

Sebastian made his bow and left. Yet the duke's words haunted him as he ate his supper and Sebastian feared the grains of truth buried in the statement.

Late the following morning, Eleanor accompanied Bianca to the fan maker and after that, the dressmaker. Eleanor was hardly in the best of moods. Sebastian had not appeared at the dinner party last night and she missed him more than she could say. Without him, there had been no one of interest to converse with, no one to tease, flirt with, and laugh with her. It had been an exceedingly dull evening.

There were only two other customers when Eleanor and Bianca entered the dress shop. The proprietress, Madame Claudette, excused herself the moment they entered the establishment and hurried over, a welcoming smile upon her face.

"How may I be of assistance today, ladies?" she asked eagerly.

"We would like to commission two gowns—no, three new gowns for my sister," Bianca announced.

Eleanor dropped the length of green silk she had been admiring and turned toward her sister. "Bianca, no! The earl will have apoplexy when he receives the bill."

Bianca stubbornly shook her head. "I insist. I'm sure Madame Claudette knows exactly how to write the invoice so Papa won't question it. Isn't that right, Madame?"

The modiste nodded eagerly and Eleanor felt herself weakening. She had worn the two dresses Bianca had managed to secretly order when they first arrived in Town everywhere. It would be wonderful to have something new, but the earl's anger would be legendary if he discovered their ruse. Eleanor knew she should protest, but then her eyes returned to the emerald-green bolt of silk.

"Ahh, my lady has excellent taste." The modiste pulled the bolt from the pile and raised a length of cloth over Eleanor's shoulder.

"It's perfect for you!" Bianca exclaimed. "That shade highlights the gold in your hair and makes your eyes sparkle. We must have a dress made with it."

"I know the perfect style," Madame proclaimed. She rifled through a stack of papers on a nearby table and produced the latest copy of *La Belle Assemblée*. Flipping impatiently through the pages, she cried out in triumph when she located what she sought. "This one. It will flatter the lady's figure and showcase all of her assets."

Bianca made a noise far too similar to a squeal for Eleanor's liking. But she was reluctantly drawn to view the picture and then forced to agree Madame was right. The high-waisted style with its clever ruching beneath the bust and elegant long lines would give her a regal bearing.

"You'll need to take her measurements to ensure a perfect fit," Bianca said, nudging Eleanor toward the dressing room in the rear of the shop.

Giving in because it was easier, and because she really would like Sebastian to see her in such a glorious gown, Eleanor followed Madame's assistant. The dressing room was simply furnished, containing a row of hooks, a cushioned chair, and a small stool for customers to stand on when having their measurements taken.

Eleanor had just started to remove her gown when a short knock came at the door. Assuming it was either Bianca or the dressmaker, Eleanor called out, "Come in."

Sebastian leisurely strolled through the doorway. Her smile of welcome quickly turned to shock. Clutching her partially open gown to her bosom, she blinked rapidly, her eyes darting nervously behind him.

"Isn't this a charming surprise?" he asked, curling his fingers under her chin. "I noticed you through the shop window and simply had to come by to say hello."

Warmth stole into Eleanor's cheeks as she struggled to calm her breathing. "Are you out of your mind?" she hissed. "You cannot be in here with me! What if someone saw you?"

"Would that be a problem?" he asked casually.

"It would be a scandal," she hissed. "As you well know."

She tried to reach around him to open the door and push him out, but he blocked her way. "Calm down, Eleanor, I'm just having a bit of fun. There's no one else in the store. I wouldn't have come in here otherwise."

"This is a popular shop, Sebastian, frequented by most of the women in society," she replied frantically. "It won't remain empty for long."

"I beg to differ." He took a step closer. "A few coins slipped into Madame's palm has temporarily closed the store."

Her heart thumped inside her chest. Had he really done something so outrageous just to steal a few moments alone with her? She searched his face and his calm expression suggested that he was telling her the truth. *Oh my.*

Sebastian took another step closer, standing near enough that she could feel the heat of his body, could smell the woodsy tang of his cologne, a stark masculine scent in such a feminine domain. Eleanor tried to keep her eyes away from him, knowing her fading resistance would crumble if she gazed into his eyes. Determined, she veiled her emotions, taking deep breaths to steady herself.

Sebastian's hand reached out, his palm caressing

her back until she felt herself begin to relax. Then his head bent down, his lips moving over her neck, sending delightful shivers through her body.

"What are you doing?" she whispered.

"Saying hello properly."

She fought to keep her equilibrium, but his touch was too intoxicating. Sighing, Eleanor melted into him, reveling in the strength of his hard body. She didn't have to touch him to know he was aroused; his breathing was harsh and shallow, his hands faintly trembling as they caressed her body.

She savored the feeling of knowing he desired her. Savored it and allowed her own desire to take flight. Her mouth moved over his and she kissed him. Deeply, longingly. Sebastian groaned, his tongue meeting hers, mimicking the sexual mating they had not yet shared.

A tingling sensation skittered over her skin and Eleanor wished they truly were alone, with the time and privacy to explore this aching passion. But even though he had managed to have the shop closed, the staff was still there, as was Bianca.

Squashing her rising desire, Eleanor pulled away. "We must stop. Madame Claudette will be back any second to take my measurements."

"I'd like to assist her," he murmured. "Shall we remove your shift?"

"Sebastian!" Eleanor slapped away the hands that reached for her underclothes as she tried to get herself back into her gown.

He moved his hands to cradle her face. "We are finally alone, Eleanor. Let's not waste a moment of this precious time."

"What are you suggesting?" she asked warily.

"Let's be wicked, together, my dearest." He leaned down and murmured in her ear, "I'm remembering how it felt when I held you in my arms and you came for me. I need more memories like that, Eleanor."

He was holding her so tenderly, tears came to her eyes. Her mind told her this was reckless, foolish, but her heart refused to listen. Ah, foolish heart.

Sebastian drew in closer, brushing his lips against her temple, kissing her neck, moving his lips in a sensual line up to her ear. His lips tugged on the pearls of her dangling earbobs, nipping playfully. Eleanor's eyes fluttered closed as she allowed herself to be swept away on the passionate wave of desire.

A choked sigh escaped her. The fists tightly clutching her gown relaxed and opened, allowing the garment to slide silently to the floor. Restless with need, Eleanor moved her hands beneath the edge of Sebastian's jacket, aching to get closer, longing for the feel of his bare skin.

The silk of his waistcoat was cool beneath her fingers. Pressing harder, she could feel the rigid muscles beneath. Boldly, she ran her hands upward to the center of his chest. Sebastian hissed sharply and she felt a tremor run through him.

Knowing they could be caught at any moment added another wild, forbidden layer to their actions. "We shouldn't," she muttered weakly.

"I know," he agreed. "That's why we must."

A ragged laugh escaped Eleanor's lips. His kisses drugged her mind, his hands awakened her flesh, his heart touched her soul. He was the headiest of temptations. How could she possibly resist him?

Eleanor's wayward thoughts scattered as he untied the pink silk ribbon at the top of her chemise. Pulling the garment wide open, he bent and took her nipple into his mouth. She moaned and he suckled until she was hard, then shifted and claimed her other breast.

Trembling, she gripped his neck tightly, trying to hold on to her sanity. Desire was racing through her body, overtaking all other sensations. Eleanor closed her eyes, breathing in the heat he was creating. Her skin fairly burned, her fevered senses aroused to an almost painful pitch.

Eleanor sighed, cherishing the feelings that were racing inside her. The scent of him was all around her and she wanted this bold, thrilling, spellbinding connection between them to last forever. She ached to have his hands everywhere and the moment Sebastian caressed her between her legs, Eleanor's body started to convulse.

"Christ, you're already wet," he growled as he spread her legs open. "I have to taste you."

He knelt on the carpet in front of her. She had a vague idea of what he meant, yet the first touch of his mouth brought a yelp of shock from her.

"Sebastian, I'm not sure—"

"Shh, it's fine. Trust me, my dearest. Relax and enjoy. I know that I shall."

He reached up and drew her down beside him. Flipping her onto her back, he put his hands under her buttocks and lifted her. His tongue glided down her abdomen, his lips scorching hot. Embarrassed, she tried pulling her hips away, but his grip was too strong.

She felt herself tense as he dipped lower, and

then all thoughts of resistance fled. The pleasure of his wicked kiss was unimaginable. Feather-light and sensual, it reached inside her very soul. Her body began to open, allowing him to guide her on this extraordinary journey.

Undulating her hips forward, Eleanor shamelessly pressed herself against Sebastian's lips and tongue. That clever, clever tongue that knew precisely where to stroke, where to circle, where to tease. She felt herself falling, slipping away from reality, losing all sense of time and place.

The pressure was intense, almost painful as her hips continued to thrash against him fiercely. Her senses reeling, breathing in quick, hard pants, Eleanor dimly realized the whimpering sounds she heard were coming from her own throat.

Suddenly, with little warning, the pleasure crested as the climax rose within her. Eleanor cried out, and wave after wave of bliss rolled through her. Sebastian held her tenderly, staying with her until the final shudder, urging her to completion. He made her feel safe, beautiful, desirable.

Panting, Eleanor collapsed, every joint, every muscle going totally limp. She felt Sebastian move up beside her and she turned, sliding her arms around his neck, burying herself in the circle of his arms. Her entire being was encased in euphoria, sated from head to toe, yet there was also a tenderness inside her, a profound feeling she had never before experienced.

She lifted her chin and gazed into his eyes.

"Did you enjoy it?" he asked with a slight smile.

Her blush was her answer. "But what about you?"

she inquired, glancing down at the front of his breeches.

"'Tis not easy, but I can give without taking," he said between gritted teeth. "Besides, with no lock on the door we could be interrupted at any moment."

No lock! Panic assaulted her. She scrambled to her feet, searching for her gown, praying it wasn't a crumpled mess. Her movements were awkward as she jerked on her clothing, leaving hooks undone, ribbons untied.

Her hand went to her head, trying to smooth down the wisps of hair that were springing up everywhere. "I'm missing an earring," she announced in confusion.

"I think I might have swallowed it."

In spite of her panic, she laughed. "You, my lord, are simply too outrageous."

He grinned. "I believe you have the power to make me eat anything, my good lady. And relish every drop."

Eleanor blushed again, feeling suddenly embarrassed. "'Twas hardly my intention to have you chomping on my jewels, sir."

"To hell with the jewels. I shall replace them and buy you anything your heart desires."

"As a single lady it would not be proper to accept such an extravagant gift from a gentleman."

"As long as you accept my kisses, I am content." He reached inside her gown and fixed the fastenings on her chemise. "Best leave the gown open, so Madame can take your measurements."

Eleanor nodded, hoping the seamstress would not interrupt them soon. "Do you think she will know? About . . . this . . . ?"

Sebastian smiled as he adjusted his own clothing. "You are adorably flushed," he declared, setting his hat at a rakish angle. "Once she catches a glimpse of you, she will have her suspicions."

Eleanor groaned and he continued in a soothing tone. "Fortunately, this establishment has a back entrance, which I intend to make use of in a moment. Bianca shall be none the wiser." His eyes bored into her with a sensual heat that left Eleanor nearly breathless. "When will I see you again?"

Eleanor swallowed hard as she attempted to find her breath. "Tomorrow night, I suppose. I'll be at the Sinclairs' ball. Are you going?"

"I wasn't planning on it. But if you'll be there, then so will I." He leaned down and gave her a lingering kiss. "'Tis too long to wait until tomorrow evening. What about tonight?"

"We are going to a theatre party hosted by Lord Waverly."

Sebastian frowned. "Even if I come to the performance, I will barely see you. Can't you attend something else? The Reese-Joneses are having a musical soiree."

Eleanor shook her head emphatically. "Bianca is becoming serious with Waverly. I am, for all intents and purposes, her chaperone, even if my occasional lapse in judgment with you makes me a bad one. If I don't go with her, she can't attend."

Sebastian let out a long sigh. She was flattered at his frustration, yet the answer was so obvious. "We can be together again in a few hours, if you make an afternoon call. Why don't you ever pay a visit?"

His nostrils flared. Sebastian had never come to call, like a proper suitor. She wondered if she had touched a nerve with her question or discovered a truth. Not really wanting to know the answer, yet realizing it was important, Eleanor waited anxiously.

But the soft sound of a feminine gasp interrupted before he could reply. They both turned toward the door. Eleanor sighed with relief when she saw Madame Claudette standing in the doorway, her hand on the knob.

"I beg your pardon, my lady. I will return—"

"No, please, come in," the viscount interjected. "I was just leaving."

Sebastian's eyes met Eleanor's and she felt the full force of his regard. The emotion startled her so completely that she barely reacted when he bowed, then stepped out of the dressing room.

All without answering her question.

Chapter 12

The cloud of sensual delight surrounding Eleanor lingered throughout the day, into the night, and through the next morning, heightening when a single white rose was delivered. Concentration was nearly impossible. Time and again her mind drifted as she attempted to accomplish even the most mundane tasks only to discover she had done them incorrectly.

She gave Cook three different copies of the weekly menu, confusing the poor servant utterly. Eleanor sat diligently at her writing desk, staring blankly at the parchment for nearly an hour, trying to compose a simple thank-you note. She requested a footman bring her four vases while neglecting to ask for the flowers that would be placed inside them.

Daydreaming intermittently, she attended the theatre party hosted by Lord Waverly. It was a lively affair, comprising a group of people who were friendly and boisterous. That was, Eleanor decided, a good thing, since her thoughts were so consumed by Sebastian, she was incapable of even pretending an interest in conversation.

Try as she might, she couldn't help but close her eyes and relive those wicked, sensual moments they had shared in Madame Claudette's dressing room. The feel of Sebastian's hands and lips caressing her quivering flesh, the passionate intensity in his eyes. And each time she recalled those earth-shattering moments, she felt a rush of secret happiness.

She knew he was an accomplished rake, an experienced lover, yet she had never dreamed the erotic, exquisite sensations he evoked in her were possible. The incident had changed her, in a way that made her feel more womanly, more worldly.

Following Bianca down to the drawing room to await their afternoon callers, Eleanor caught a glimpse of herself in the mirror. These restless thoughts of Sebastian had brought a glow to her face revealing all her inner emotions, yet she almost didn't care. Almost.

These feelings were too new, too raw, too private to share. Fortunately, Bianca was so caught up in her own romance with Lord Waverly, she had little time to ponder the reason for Eleanor's distracted behavior.

Lord Waverly was, not surprisingly, their first visitor that afternoon. He was soon followed by several other gentlemen, the usual legion of Bianca's admirers, and several ladies. The men gathered around Bianca, while Lord Waverly stood protectively close and glowered at them. Bianca held court on one end of the room; Eleanor sat with the ladies on the other.

Eleanor hoped the afternoon callers would provide

some distraction and help the time pass more quickly. Eight more hours! Eight more hours until they left for the Sinclairs' ball, until she saw Sebastian again.

Heavens, how am I ever going to make it?

Eleanor stared down at her teacup, absently noting the cobalt blue of the pattern. Lifting her head, she realized there was an uncomfortable silence and she noticed Lady Mary and Mrs. Farnsworth exchange a curious glance. Apparently one of them had asked her a question.

"Perhaps," she said noncommittally, pouring more tea into her nearly full cup.

Mrs. Farnsworth looked a bit doubtful but was too polite to say anything. Eleanor wondered idly what she had been asked, then decided she didn't much care. The clock chimed on the half hour. *Oh goodness, still seven and a half more hours until I see Sebastian.*

Determined to occupy her mind with something else, Eleanor struggled to pull her wandering thoughts back to the moment. She tried valiantly to concentrate on Mrs. Farnsworth's comments, realizing she had to be careful or else she'd make a fool of herself.

Really, all that was required was that she murmur and nod and appear interested in what the women were saying. Even in her current distracted state of mind, she could manage it if she tried hard enough. Couldn't she?

Ten torturous minutes later Eleanor was congratulating herself on how well that was going when Harrison entered the room and announced, "Viscount Benton is calling, my lady."

"Who?"

"Viscount Benton."

"Now? He is here now?"

Harrison appeared startled and Eleanor realized how ridiculous she must have sounded. Of course he was here now; that's what the butler had said. *Now! He was here now!*

Eleanor's heart leapt into her throat, choking all sound. Sebastian never made afternoon calls; she had scolded him about that just the other day. Yet he was here. Her heart burst with a shot of happiness so strong she could barely speak. Eleanor turned a desperate eye toward her sister. Bianca bowed her head in acknowledgment, rose from her chair, and came to Eleanor's side.

"Viscount Benton has come to call? How perfectly charming. Please show him in," Bianca said regally.

Struggling to be calm, Eleanor set her tea aside. She turned a vapid smile on Lady Mary and Mrs. Farnsworth, trying to keep the emotions from showing on her face. She thought she succeeded rather well in maintaining an indifferent expression—that is, until Sebastian entered the room.

At the sight of him her mind flashed back to their illicit rendezvous and she felt the heat flooding her cheeks with color. He paused in the doorway, seeming surprised at the number of people in the room.

"Lady Eleanor, Lady Bianca," he said with an elegant bow. "'Tis a delight to see you both."

Though Eleanor had not extended it, he took her hand in his own. Her breath hitched. The touch of his lean, strong fingers nearly had her melting on the spot. All she could think of was how his hands had glided so skillfully over her flesh yesterday morning, how he had made her shiver and pulse with excitement.

Somehow she rallied, meeting his seductive gaze with a steady look. "What a lovely surprise. Welcome, Lord Benton."

"Thank you." He leaned closer to murmur in her ear. "I've recently been told that I don't make enough social calls and am determined to reform my ways."

His fingers closed tightly around hers and he squeezed her hand briefly. The intimate gesture pierced her heart and Eleanor dared not glance again into his eyes, certain she would lose all composure.

"My lord, may I introduce . . ." She glanced down at the two women seated on the settee and her mind blanked. What were their names?

Sebastian cleared his throat. "No introductions are necessary," he said smoothly. "Lady Mary, Mrs. Farnsworth, a pleasure."

The women acknowledged his greeting stiffly. There was a long, awkward pause. Eleanor searched her mind for an appropriate topic of discussion, yet found none.

"The weather is most fine this afternoon, is it not?" Bianca ventured.

"Yes, sunny, but not overly warm," Sebastian replied.

"I believe spring is my very favorite season," Bianca continued.

"Indeed." Sebastian glanced at Eleanor, then looked away.

Mrs. Farnsworth and Lady Mary said nothing.

There was another awkward pause. Eleanor reached for the teapot, gave it a small shake, then signaled for a footman. "The tea is nearly gone. Please bring a fresh pot."

Sebastian sat down in the chair closest to Eleanor. Bianca excused herself and returned to her bevy of admirers.

"That is a lovely frock, Lady Mary," Sebastian said. "Perchance is it one of Madame Claudette's designs?"

Eleanor nearly spewed out the lukewarm tea in her mouth.

"You are correct, Lord Benton. This gown is an original creation," Lady Mary replied with a superior sniff.

"Ah, she does have a talented eye. Yet dressing a woman with your charms is hardly difficult." Sebastian smiled, showing his white, even teeth. "I recently had the opportunity to visit her shop and found her items to be of the highest quality."

Mrs. Farnsworth's face lit with undisguised curiosity. "Whatever were you doing in a lady's dress shop, my lord?"

"Browsing the merchandise," he responded promptly. "Madame has some of the finest wares I have ever seen. Or felt."

Eleanor felt her skin flare with heat. She cast him a scolding sidelong glance. He winked in response. She pulled out her white linen handkerchief and discreetly pressed it against her neck. Goodness, it was warm. Perhaps instead of tea she should be serving cold lemonade?

Eleanor sneaked another look at Sebastian. He was chatting amicably with her callers, moving his

hands elegantly as he entertained them. The ladies'
disapproving manner had relaxed somewhat under
his charm, yet they were still a bit wary. She was certain they were wondering precisely why he was here.

A lock of his dark, silky hair suddenly fell over his
brow. He brushed it back, yet it stubbornly fell forward again. Eleanor's hand started twitching. She
wanted to reach over and touch it, to twine it sensually around her finger. She wanted to curl herself
into his lap, cuddling against his hard strength, to
press her lips to his lips, to—

"Isn't that correct, Lady Eleanor?" Sebastian
asked.

"Absolutely." She smiled broadly, struggling to
regain her dazed senses.

He gave her a knowing smile, then continued
with the story. Lady Mary and Mrs. Farnsworth were
on the edge of their seats, expressions intent. It was
not only the words he used to tell the tale, but the
deep, sensual inflection of his voice that had his audience enthralled.

Eleanor had just decided that she would never
grow tired of hearing his rich, deep baritone when
a discreet cough sounded next to her. She glanced
over and saw that her guests had risen to their feet.
Were they finally leaving?

"We shall bid you good day, Lady Eleanor, since
there are several other calls we need to make," Lady
Mary announced.

Eleanor rose. Sebastian did the same and for an
instant she panicked, thinking he was also going
to depart. Without thinking, she reached for him.
His eyes widened and he stepped deliberately in

front of her, concealing the telling gesture from the other women.

Finding her tongue at last, Eleanor croaked, "Thank you so much for coming. 'Twas lovely to see you both," she added, hoping the delight she felt at their leave-taking was not too obvious.

"I thought they would never go," Sebastian hissed the moment they were alone.

"It was horrid," Eleanor agreed. "I'm beginning to understand your aversion to these visits."

"Let's walk in the garden," Sebastian suggested.

Eleanor groaned. "I can't leave Bianca unchaperoned." As if to emphasize the point, a chorus of male laughter was heard from the other side of the room.

"Damn, there has to be somewhere in this house where we can steal a moment alone." Sebastian's brow lifted. "Is there a library?"

Eleanor laughed. He was incorrigible. "There's a bit of privacy to be found over there," she said, pointing to a small alcove.

"I'll go first. You follow in a moment," he dictated before turning on his heel.

Eleanor took but one step into the alcove before Sebastian yanked her hard against his side.

"This has been torture," he growled, taking her into his arms and kissing her fiercely.

She wrapped her arms around his neck, returning the kiss passionately as they shuffled farther into the concealed nook. Too soon, she pulled her lips away.

"We can only stay a moment," she warned.

"Eleanor." He framed her face with his palms and bent his head. The tenderness of his kiss was almost unbearable. She trembled, her heart swelling with longing. With love.

After one more kiss, they reluctantly broke apart. Silence fell between them, his gaze passing over her in a way that made her feel special, cherished.

She presented him with a smile, though what she really wanted were more kisses. His eyes twinkled, as if he understood her need, indeed, shared it. But alas, though they had been daring and unconventional previously, this was hardly the time or place to indulge their passions, and they both knew it.

"I'll see you tonight," she said.

"Most assuredly."

Eleanor kept herself concealed in the alcove until Sebastian departed. Finally collecting herself, she emerged, nearly colliding with her father as she stepped out into the room.

"Bloody hell, what are you doing hiding back there, Eleanor?" the earl exclaimed.

Eleanor bristled. Why must her father always be so sharp with her? Swallowing around the thickness in her throat, Eleanor glanced over his shoulder, then realized the room was empty. "Has everyone left?"

"Nearly. Bianca is having a private word with a gentleman in my study. I expect to hear some good news shortly."

Good news? Eleanor's mind worked quickly, the smug expression on the earl's face giving her a solid hint. Assessing his pleased demeanor, she surmised it had to be a marriage proposal and one that would assure him of a significant monetary gain.

Her heart leapt with gladness. At last! Lord Waverly had made his decision and was proposing to Bianca. His regard for her was obvious and she seemed to return it in equal measure. It was a good match for both of them, and thanks to Waverly's title and wealth, an acceptable marriage for the earl.

Restless with excitement, Eleanor waited for the happy couple to appear. Within minutes the door opened and Bianca entered the drawing room. But Lord Waverly was not with her. Instead Viscount Farley was by her side.

A hollowness weighted Eleanor's stomach as she watched them. She and Bianca had met Lord Farley only once and were not favorably impressed. He was an odious man with oily hair and a facial twitch that was both distracting and annoying.

Currently his face was flushed with excitement. He reached to take Bianca's arm and she turned away, releasing a long, shuddering sigh. A tingling premonition traveled up Eleanor's spine. She hurried to her sister.

"What's happened?" Eleanor asked.

Bianca's eyes were stricken, her face pale. "Lord Farley has proposed."

"Good God, he's older than Father."

Bianca glanced nervously from the earl to Lord Farley, as the two men gathered around the sideboard for a drink. "Actually, I think they are the same age," she whispered rigidly.

"Have you accepted him?"

Bianca flinched. "I asked for some time to consider his kind and generous offer."

"Have your wits gone missing? Why didn't you refuse him outright and be done with it?"

Bianca's eyes glistened. "I couldn't. Apparently

Papa owes him a great deal of money and he told me that I must accept this offer. Oh, Eleanor, what am I going to do? Lord Farley is simply dreadful. He held my hand as he proposed and it was all I could do to keep from screaming. He kept saying what an eminently suitable bride I was and how eager he was for the match."

Bianca's frightened voice shattered something inside Eleanor. How could she have been so foolish? This was precisely what she had feared, what she had worked to prevent. Eleanor thought she had been so careful, so clever. But clearly she had underestimated the earl's desperation and now Bianca would be the one to suffer.

"When do you have to give your answer?"

"By this evening. Papa wants to make the announcement at the Sinclairs' ball."

That gave them very little time. Eleanor gulped down the panic surging through her. "What about Lord Waverly? He appears to have a great affection for you."

"He said he loves me." Bianca's eyes filled with tears. "As I love him."

Eleanor stared into her sister's anxious face. "Chin up, Bianca. We are not going to sit idly by like a pair of half-wits and allow this to happen. If Waverly loves you as he should, he will move heaven and earth to prevent that announcement."

"How?" Bianca asked, laying a trembling hand upon Eleanor's arm.

Eleanor drew in a shaky breath and forced herself to think this through calmly. "You must write to Waverly at once. If he can match Farley's offer, the earl might be persuaded to let you refuse Farley and accept Waverly as your husband."

"Lord Waverly has not spoken of marriage yet." Faint color suffused Bianca's cheeks. "How can I possibly broach the subject with him? A lady cannot propose to a gentleman. It just isn't done."

Eleanor's eyes flashed fire. "Hellfire and damnation, Bianca, this is hardly a time to be considering the etiquette of the situation! If you do nothing, you most assuredly will end up as Farley's bride."

Bianca's mouth began to quiver. Eleanor felt a stab of regret for her harsh words, but there was no help for it. They had to act quickly and decisively to have any chance of thwarting the earl's marriage plans for his youngest daughter.

"Oh, Lord, I know you are right, Eleanor." Bianca lowered her voice. "Yet even if I could find the words to ask for Waverly's help, how will my letter reach him? He could be any number of places at this time of the day. I can't send one of the servants all over London looking for him."

On a long, shuddering breath, Eleanor turned to stare at her father and Lord Farley. Maybe she could reason with the earl and get him to postpone the announcement. If Lord Waverly's feelings were as strong as Bianca's he would not allow her to be taken from him. They just needed a little time.

Eleanor saw the earl lean in and whisper a few words into Lord Farley's ear. Farley nodded, then smiled broadly, showing several gaps where his teeth were missing. The earl looked up then and met Eleanor's eyes, his own glowing in triumph.

Eleanor's shoulders fell and a dark shroud of reality settled over her. The earl was not going to wait.

And even if Waverly could be reached, he'd have to offer a great deal more money than Farley to secure Bianca's hand in marriage.

Still, she refused to so willingly accept defeat.

Eleanor set a determined hand on her sister's arm. "Write the letter, Bianca. I know a way to ensure it will quickly reach Lord Waverly."

Sebastian had not expected to hear from Eleanor so soon after taking his leave of her, but the brief note her footman delivered was short and urgent.

I must see you. Meet me in my rose arbor as soon as you can. 'Tis imperative that you avoid detection by anyone except the servants. Please hurry.

Intrigued, Sebastian did as he was commanded, arriving within the hour. It was relatively simple to slip unnoticed through the back gate and locate the spot Eleanor had designated. She arrived a few minutes later, breathless.

As she drew near, Eleanor started to speak, but Sebastian slid his arm around her waist and covered her lips with his. She didn't kiss him back but instead pulled away. "For pity's sake, I have no time for this now."

Sebastian frowned. "I believe I've just been insulted."

A dark spot of color burned her cheek. "Your kisses are simply too distracting and the matter too urgent. I need you to find Lord Waverly as quickly as you can. Give him this letter and make certain he reads it immediately."

"Shall I quiz him afterward to make sure he understands its contents?" Sebastian asked, smiling to himself. Why was it that women always thought affairs of the heart were of the utmost urgency? Lifting the note Eleanor pressed into his hand toward the sunlight, Sebastian tried to peer inside. "What exactly does it say?"

"Sebastian, please!" She snatched the letter back, her bosom heaving. "This is not a joke."

"Apparently."

Eleanor's mouth narrowed in hesitation. "Forgive me. I know I'm acting—"

"Like a lunatic?" he offered.

"Oddly," she said at the same time.

Sebastian peered down at her. He had never seen her so rattled. "So, you have summoned me here not for my kisses, but rather to deliver a note to Waverly. From Bianca, I assume?"

"Yes. Her future happiness is in great peril." Eleanor's mouth tightened. "The earl is pressing her to marry Viscount Farley."

"That old goat? No wonder you're worried."

"Lord Waverly must be informed immediately. Bianca has explained it all in her note, along with what needs to be done to prevent this catastrophe." Eleanor's expression turned serious. "You are the only one I can turn to, the only one I can trust, Sebastian."

Good Lord, wasn't that a pitying thought? He waited to hear more, but her distress was so heightened it was clear she wasn't going to elaborate. Instead, her eyes were boring into his, pleading for help.

Strange, how he never hesitated, just wordlessly reached for the letter. "I am, as always, your devoted servant, Eleanor. I will not fail you."

Her features visibly relaxed. She hugged him briefly, then anxiously sent him on his way. Sebastian left the garden the same way he came, all the while wondering why this sudden, impulsive need to chivalrously come to her rescue made him feel so damn good.

Later that night, in the Sinclairs' crowded ballroom, Sebastian stood with one shoulder propped against the wall and watched the Earl of Hetfield announce the betrothal of his daughter, Lady Bianca, to Lord Waverly. The newly engaged Waverly made a heartfelt speech praising the many virtues of his future bride that had half the women in the room reaching for their handkerchiefs.

Sebastian would have felt better about his role in this affair if the outcome had angered the earl, but that clearly was not the case. Still, his actions had elevated his standing with Eleanor. The moment he got her alone he would discover exactly how high.

That opportunity arrived far sooner than he expected. Eleanor had been standing near her sister as the announcement was made, but when Lord Waverly finished his speech, Eleanor made her way through the crowd and slipped out to the terrace. Sebastian followed.

The light from the strategically placed torches illuminated his way. He waited until she stopped, then approached.

"So this is where you have hidden yourself. I'm surprised you are not huddled with the rest of the women, waxing elegant over the upcoming nuptials."

Eleanor smiled. "I suspect that is all we shall speak of until the deed is finally accomplished."

"Waverly seemed a bit dazed."

"A burst of female emotion can be unsettling for any man. Added to Bianca's excitement were Lord Waverly's two sisters and his mother, though I fear that dear lady has already taken charge of the wedding arrangements."

Sebastian's mouth curved. "Let me guess, she hopes for a grand wedding at St. George's in Hanover Square."

"Actually, you are wrong. They will be married at Lord Waverly's estate a month from now. 'Tis part of his lordship's family tradition, from what I understand."

"I imagine it will be a large crowd."

She gave a light shrug. "Probably."

"Dare I hope for an invitation?"

Eleanor made a face. "You courted the bride."

"Very briefly."

"I have a feeling Lord Waverly's mother will find that in bad taste. She is rather high in the instep." Eleanor's expression held a touch of skepticism. "I hope you won't be too disappointed if you aren't included."

"I shall endeavor to survive. However, I shall send an appropriately gaudy gift, just to tweak Lady Waverly's nose."

A glimmer of amusement entered Eleanor's eyes. "That's the spirit."

"I could never be married in front of a large crowd. I remember what a crush it was at Atwood's wedding, so many people it made your head spin."

He slanted a speculative glance at her. "I caught the bouquet, you know."

"Pardon?"

"The wedding bouquet. Lady Dorothea tossed it right at me. 'Twas her idea of a joke."

A teasing smile touched Eleanor's lips. "I'm sorry I missed it."

"It was comical," he admitted. "First Lady Atwood's bouquet and now playing Cupid for Waverly. It appears that my matrimonial roles are continually expanding. I confess, it makes me nervous."

She laughed softly. "Take heart, Sebastian. In aiding Lord Waverly you were not really Cupid, but rather more like Mercury, the winged messenger."

"Good point. And I was successful."

"Yes, it's turned out far better than I had hoped."

"I suppose now that Bianca is settled, it's your turn."

Her hazel eyes glittered in the moonlight. "To marry? How ridiculous. Who would want me?"

"I do."

It was frightening for Sebastian to realize that he spoke the truth. He truly did desire her, more than he ever expected, more than he could adequately express.

She was different from any woman he had ever known. He couldn't put a name to it, yet there was something unique and special that set her apart. Something that caused him to feel things he normally wouldn't. If she were anyone else's daughter, this might have a very different ending.

If wishes were horses, then beggars would ride.

Sebastian took Eleanor's hand in his, lacing their fingers together. He needed to convince her to run away with him in order to achieve her ruin and his revenge. Yet as he looked into her eyes it was the spark of hope that almost made him stop, that made his stomach roil in a wave of guilt.

It tore at his soul, but he ruthlessly pushed it aside. Instead, he pictured the anger on the earl's face, the shame when he learned of his daughter's disgrace. When he realized he would have no choice but to defend her honor.

"I share Waverly's desire to be married at home. The vicar who resides over my ancestral estate has said several times he would be deeply honored to perform the ceremony. But I would insist that it be done immediately and privately, without fanfare or family."

"That sounds ideal." Eleanor's tongue darted out nervously and she licked her lips. "However, one would need a special license to carry off such a feat."

Sebastian patted his coat pocket and held his breath.

The long silence that followed made him uneasy. He almost hoped she would refuse, but if she did, he knew he would merely have to devise another plan, one that would involve a more public disgrace.

Then suddenly she smiled and said in a quiet tone, "What are we waiting for, my lord?"

Chapter 13

The practice of not encountering her father for days at a time served Eleanor well for once, making it laughably easy to rendezvous with Sebastian. Two days after her engagement was announced, Bianca left for the Waverlys' estate very early in the morning, protesting mildly when Eleanor deemed it best that she not accompany her. This was the perfect time for Bianca to get to know her future in-laws. Besides, his lordship's mother and two sisters had experience planning a wedding at the estate. There was no need for Eleanor to tag along.

After seeing Bianca safely off, Eleanor packed a small overnight bag, hiding it in the back of her wardrobe. To avoid arousing any sort of suspicion, she kept to her usual routine for the next few hours. When the appointed hour arrived, Eleanor retrieved her bag and sauntered out the front door, informing Harrison she would not be back until late the following day. She noted an almost imperceptible raising of the butler's brow, but naturally he did not challenge her remark.

Eleanor made her way quickly to the secluded section of Hyde Park that Sebastian had designated as their rendezvous point. As he predicted, she saw no one she knew at that unfashionably early hour. Her anticipation grew with each step and she firmly tamped down any misgivings she had over these clandestine arrangements, telling herself that no matter what happened she was prepared to face the consequences.

She didn't see him, or the carriage, when she first arrived. Heart thundering in her chest, Eleanor anxiously searched the tree line. The small rim of her bonnet barely blocked the sun's rays, causing her to squint. Tension knotted her stomach and then suddenly she spotted Sebastian pacing behind a copse of oaks. The sunlight poured over him, surrounding him in a golden halo. Yet she was very aware he was no angel.

As if sensing her presence, Sebastian turned. He smiled at her, his face shining with such delight her heart skipped a beat. Eleanor worked to recover her poise as he approached, his stride long and sure. When he reached her, he tossed her small portmanteau to the ground, grasped both her hands, and brought them to his lips. "You came."

Eleanor let out a nervous laugh. "Were you worried?"

"Yes." He let out an oath under his breath and drew her into his arms. The palm of his hand flattened against her back, pulling her fully against him. Then he lowered his head and kissed her, capturing her mouth fully with his.

At the feel of his lips and tongue, a shudder rocked through Eleanor's body. He kissed her a second time, then pulled back. Their gazes locked, their short, rapid breaths mingling. "'Tis good to see you too," she whispered.

He groaned, tightening his hold on her. "Did you encounter any problems leaving the house?"

"None."

"No one will question your disappearance?"

She gave him a dubious look. "I haven't precisely disappeared. I informed the servants that I would be out until late tomorrow afternoon. No one is expecting to see me until then."

"And your father?"

Eleanor lowered her gaze. "The earl spends much of his time away from home. I doubt he will even be aware that I am gone."

Sebastian shifted restlessly. His concerned expression surprised and embarrassed her. She searched for a flippant, offhand remark, but her wits deserted her. How precisely did one explain that her father didn't give a tinker's damn about her?

Thankfully Sebastian let the matter pass. Arm in arm they walked to the waiting carriage. Eleanor lifted her foot to step into the carriage, then suddenly stopped.

"Second thoughts, dearest?" he whispered in her ear.

Dozens! Eleanor shook her head. "I'm remembering your queasy stomach and difficulties with a long coach ride. How will you manage?"

"By riding my horse." He sighed deeply. "'Tis nothing short of criminal letting all the privacy of a long carriage ride go to waste, yet I know there's no help for it. My stomach refuses to cooperate and allow me to take advantage of it."

"It's broad daylight," Eleanor exclaimed.

"And?" He raised his brow questionably and Eleanor blushed. But she also smiled.

"Are you certain you don't mind riding in the carriage alone?" he asked as he assisted her inside.

"I'll be fine. Safer it seems, considering your stomach problems. And amorous intentions."

"Saucy baggage." He leaned in and kissed the tip of her nose. "You unman me by speaking of such things."

Laughing, Eleanor leaned back against the brown velvet squabs. She saw Sebastian mount his horse. With a quick salute, he galloped out of view and she realized he was going to take a different route than the carriage out of Town. It was a wise move. Drawing the shade to maintain her anonymity, Eleanor tried to relax.

It was difficult. Her nerves resurfaced as the coach navigated the London streets and she questioned the rightness of her decision, concluding that running away with Sebastian was either going to be the most daring, marvelous moment of her life or the greatest disaster.

Fearing the long ride would leave too much time for reflection and doubt, Eleanor pulled out the book she had packed in her reticule. The poetry of Lord Byron provided a minor distraction, but true relaxation was impossible. Every time the carriage lurched to a halt in the traffic, she feared the door would be thrown open and she would be discovered.

Fortunately her nerves finally settled when they reached the outskirts of London. Sebastian reappeared outside her window, his reassuring presence an oasis of calm. The condition of the roads improved. The carriage was well-sprung and comfortable, the driver skilled and considerate.

Abandoning her book, Eleanor leaned her head back and closed her eyes. Before too long the carriage came to a stop. Shaking off her foggy countenance, Eleanor looked out the window, expecting to see they had arrived at an inn. Instead, she saw a large, looming structure of solid gray stone.

"Welcome to Chaswick Manor, my lady."

Eleanor took Sebastian's hand and stepped out of the coach. The late afternoon light was quickly fading, but she was able to take in the manor house and expansive grounds. Built centuries earlier, the main structure was a medieval castle that had been added to and modified over the years.

There was a somewhat modern columned portico in the center of the front facade with wide marble steps leading up to the front doors. Doors that were currently shut tight. Did the servants not know of their impending arrival?

Ignoring the fluttering in her stomach, Eleanor stretched her cramped muscles. "'Tis a very impressive residence," she commented. "Did you grow up here?"

"Yes." Sebastian smiled apologetically at his curt answer. "I've spent little time here as an adult. In fact, the last time I was here was several months ago for my grandmother's funeral."

Oh dear. She reached out to clasp his hand, but he turned away.

The front door opened and an elderly gentleman, presumably the butler, emerged. "Good day, Lord Benton."

"Ah, Higgins. See to the baggage, will you? And have my horse brought to the mews. He needs his dinner and a thorough brushing."

"Very good, my lord."

Eleanor smiled awkwardly as the butler bowed again. He walked respectfully behind her, keeping his eyes lowered, almost as if he didn't notice her. She thought it terribly rude of Sebastian not to introduce her and wondered if he was the type of aristocrat who didn't think his servants were worthy of basic human considerations.

Thoughts of the butler were soon forgotten as they entered the house, their footsteps echoing on the black and white marble floor. It was a cavernous hall, dominated by a grand staircase boasting elaborately carved balustrades and railings. Eleanor had never seen anything like it.

"The gargoyles on the newel posts were Grandmother's idea," Sebastian said. "She commissioned them when she came here as a young bride. Aren't they hideous?"

"Gothic architecture was very popular with her generation," Eleanor said, though she agreed completely.

The ghastly statues added a formality to the already cold atmosphere of the entryway, an area Eleanor always thought should be welcoming and inviting. She hoped the rest of the house would be different, but alas the grand, gloomy feeling continued as they made their way to the drawing room.

Eleanor could see that the furnishings were of good quality, but easily thirty years out of style. The interiors were done in dark colors, creating a dull, almost oppressive atmosphere. Though elegant, it lacked the comfort of a home and Eleanor could understand why Sebastian spent so little time at the estate.

The drawing room was slightly better. A newly lit fire blazed in the hearth, and thick Aubusson carpets in teal and ivory covered the floor. The coordinating draperies bracketing the windows were heavy velvet and overdone with fringe, but Eleanor caught a glimpse through them of a magnificent garden complete with graveled walks, perfectly trimmed box hedges, and beds of colorful flowers.

It was heartening to discover her future residence was at its core a fine property. A stirring of excitement rose inside her at the realization that she was soon to be mistress of this estate. It would not be too difficult to transform the place into a comfortable home for her and Sebastian. Furnishings could be rearranged, color schemes changed, vibrant carpets and artwork added.

Sebastian excused himself to arrange for refreshments, returning quickly. "I'm afraid I have some bad news," he said, sounding exasperated. "Apparently the vicar has been called away to Shropshire, to attend his sick mother. He isn't expected back until sometime later tomorrow."

The vicar was away? That meant they could not be married this evening, as they had planned. Cautioning herself not to overreact, Eleanor took a deep breath. "I am very sorry to hear of his dilemma. I shall pray for his mother's rapid recovery."

Sebastian grimaced. "We'll go into the village after tea. I'll send a servant ahead to secure a room for you at the local inn, then settle you there myself. 'Tis far from elegant, but it's clean. For appearances, one of the chambermaids will accompany you, and to ensure your safety I will also send James, my most trusted footman. He'll sleep outside your door."

"Goodness, you sound as if I am going into the heart of France in the middle of the war."

Sebastian puffed out a breath and ran his fingers through his hair. "You can't stay here without a proper chaperone."

Eleanor bit her bottom lip. "Who is to know?"

"The servants?"

"True, yet I'm sure they owe you some loyalty." He kept silent and she continued. "Well, at the very least they will hold their tongues for fear of losing their positions. Besides, once the vicar appears tomorrow, we shall be married by special license and this will no longer matter."

"We could elope to Gretna Green," Sebastian suggested unenthusiastically.

"I have no wish to travel on the Great North Road like a criminal fleeing the law," Eleanor declared. "We agreed to be married on your estate." She could sense he was starting to waver but was not yet convinced. Determined to persuade him, Eleanor reached up and laid a finger against his lips. "I want to stay here."

She realized when she spoke how true her words were. She had committed herself to this man and despite the impropriety of the situation she did not want to leave him. Even for one night.

"Are you sure?" His voice trailed away.

"I am."

Their eyes held for a moment until Sebastian broke the contact and glanced away. "I wish I could offer to sleep in the stables to ensure you are alone in the house," he said, his voice suddenly amused. "But hay makes me sneeze."

She smiled, trying to imagine him with a clogged head and a stuffy nose. The image was difficult to conjure, yet it made him appear more vulnerable in her mind, more human. He might be a sophisticated man with far more life experience, but in the end it was a comfort to realize he was still just a man.

Tea arrived. It was delivered by the housekeeper, the ring of keys around her waist jingling merrily. Eleanor lifted her chin and met the older woman's eye squarely, wondering what she must be thinking. Surely it had to be an unusual occurrence for the viscount to bring an unchaperoned female guest to the manor. What had he told the staff about her?

"Thank you, Mrs. Florid," Sebastian said to the servant. "Lady Eleanor and I will serve ourselves."

The housekeeper hesitated, eyeing Sebastian guardedly before nodding. She started to back out of the room, then stopped. "Beg your pardon, my lady. The staff and I would like to extend our felicitations to you and his lordship on your upcoming nuptials. We hope you'll be very happy."

Eleanor relaxed. Apparently Sebastian had informed the staff that she was his betrothed. Or he had told at least one individual, which in truth was all that was necessary. In Eleanor's experience, servants' gossip spread faster than wildfire.

"Thank you for your kind words, Mrs. Florid." Eleanor grinned. "I look forward to meeting the staff and working closely with you in the future."

Smiling broadly, the housekeeper dropped a hasty curtsy and quit the room. Eleanor reached for the silver teapot and poured a cup, handing it over to a scowling Sebastian.

"That was most unexpected," he declared, stirring milk into his tea. "I vow she was beaming at us like a doting grandmother."

Eleanor placed her hand on Sebastian's forearm. "Weddings cause females of all ages to act a bit giddy."

"Except you, thank heavens." He turned his arm and intertwined their hands, his thumb rubbing idly across her palm. "Mrs. Florid is at least sixty years old. One would hope a woman of her years is beyond acting giddy."

"I think it's sweet."

Sebastian huffed in disagreement. Eleanor poured herself a cup of tea, refusing to pick up the argument. This mundane, peaceful domestic scene put her in a contemplative frame of mind and she didn't want to spoil the mood.

They ate a few of the sandwiches from the tray and several of the cakes. Eleanor asked him questions about the estate and his boyhood years. He answered readily, spinning a few tall tales of his exploits as a young boy, making her laugh loudly when he detailed his attempt at being a highwayman at the age of five.

"Your neighbor actually handed over her emerald necklace?" Eleanor asked.

"Along with the matching earbobs." He smiled, his eyes twinkling brightly at the memory. "I was a very fierce thief, you know, passionate and determined."

"I believe it."

He laughed. "I can still recall how ecstatic I felt

with my success. Eager to show off my loot, I ran directly to my mother. She nearly fainted when I told her what I had done. Of course I was forced to return the jewels immediately.

"As punishment, my mother ordered my tutor to administer a sound paddling, then cried more than I did when it was over. My grandmother defended me staunchly, insisting that my mother should be proud to have such a high-spirited, imaginative son. And Lady Gately, my helpless victim, was also very kind. She insisted that no harm had been done and then confessed to having a soft spot for a fatherless boy."

"Were you very young when your father died?"

"Practically an infant. I have no memories of him at all." The regret in Sebastian's voice was subtle. It made Eleanor's heart ache to hear it.

"And your mother?"

Sebastian stiffened. "I was young, though unfortunately I remember her death with vivid, painful detail."

A lump caught in Eleanor's throat. She remembered well her own grief, for she too had lost her mother when she was a girl. Wordlessly Eleanor took Sebastian's hand in understanding, patting it gently until she felt his body finally relax.

"Tell me, what profession did you next attempt after failing to make a success of robbing the highways?"

Sebastian squeezed her hand. "Why, I prepared to become a pirate, of course. They work as a crew, therefore, the blame for these scurrilous acts are shared. I recruited several lads from the village to join my band and we plotted our first attack."

Eleanor's brows knit together. "The estate is land-locked."

He threw back his head and laughed. "Trifling details to a gang of boys intent on mischief."

She smiled and he told her several of his pirate tales. Eleanor was amazed at what he was able to get the other boys to do, then surmised that even at a young age his natural leadership had surfaced. Not until the ormolu clock on the mantelpiece chimed the hour did she realize how late it had gotten.

"I'll tell Mrs. Florid to push supper back an hour so there will be time for you to indulge in a bath," Sebastian announced, as he rose to his feet. "I'm sure you'd relish the chance to soak away the travel dust."

Only if you agree to join me. A rush of heat permeated her body at the sensual notion. Where had that thought emerged from? Eleanor wondered, but then one look at Sebastian's stormy gray eyes and she knew the answer.

Too shy to voice her wanton thoughts aloud, Eleanor reasoned there would be time enough for them to be together later tonight. The carnal ache she felt at the very idea of sharing his bed had her blushing like a schoolgirl. Fortunately, Sebastian seemed oblivious to her predicament.

Their feet made a scuffing noise on the marble steps as he led her up the grand curving stairs and along a narrow corridor, stopping at a door in the center. "This will be your bedchamber."

Eleanor raised her brow but said nothing. Of course it was necessary for her to have her own chamber, for appearance sake. But she had no intention of sleeping in it, unless Sebastian was there too.

"Where is your room?"

He pointed to the last door on the opposite side of the hall. "I sleep with my door locked. I recommend you do the same."

"Goodness, life is dangerous in Chaswick Manor. I never would have suspected. Back home the servants rarely lock the outside doors, let alone the interior ones."

Eleanor tried to smile, but his solemn expression stopped her. Sebastian was acting oddly. She felt as though he wanted to tell her something. Something relevant, something important, yet for some reason he couldn't.

"Danger comes in many forms, Eleanor. You would do well to remember it."

He reached out and smoothed a stray curl of her hair. The brush of his warm fingers on her cheek felt soothing, comforting. Eleanor closed her eyes and turned her face into his palm, rubbing against him like a contented kitten.

"But I feel safe with you, Sebastian."

His hand abruptly pulled away. Eleanor's eyes popped open. His face was a frozen mask of formality. *Goodness, what was wrong?*

"Supper will be served at eight," he said crisply. "I will fetch you myself and escort you to the dining room."

"I'll be ready," Eleanor replied, but he had already turned and walked away.

Sebastian kept his strides long and even, fearing if he did not get away soon he'd march right over to Eleanor and demand she leave. Fighting the urge and cursing himself mightily for the pang of conscience that was threatening to rip apart the very fabric of his carefully laid plans, Sebastian made his way to the stables.

Though the grooms had already brushed, fed, and watered his mount, he picked up a brush and started in on the horse's hind flank. Normally a soothing activity, the task did little to even out his mood.

Sebastian's gut churned. Eleanor was making this too easy for him. He'd half hoped she would take him up on the offer of a room at the village inn, but was not surprised when she refused. She trusted him. To keep his promise and marry her. To keep her safe.

He had played his part well, too well, really. She was besotted with him, so much so that her good sense had vanished. A sudden tightness in his chest accompanied a deep sense of guilt, because he knew that given the chance, he would in all likelihood do it again. Nothing would bring him any satisfaction until he exacted his revenge against the Earl of Hetfield.

Then why wasn't he savoring the sweetness of victory that was finally within his grasp?

Scowling, he switched the brush to his other hand and moved to the horse's left flank. The mount tossed his head and took a few steps away. With a sigh of disgust, Sebastian threw the brush into the corner of the stall. He paced the confines of the mews, wondering how he was going to survive the night with Eleanor under his roof, sleeping in a chamber a few doors away.

Sebastian's mood grew progressively grimmer as

the afternoon turned into evening. He was silent when fetching Eleanor for supper, the sight of her freshly scrubbed face and pretty green silk gown putting him on edge.

Their meal together was tense. The food was not elegant or fancy, but it was well prepared and plentiful, a credit to the staff considering they had no advance notice. Yet neither he nor Eleanor did it any justice.

Though she politely thanked the footman as each course was served and repeatedly conveyed her compliments to the cook, Sebastian noticed Eleanor ate very little. Mostly she pushed the items around on her plate, rearranging them in new patterns.

Sebastian did not even bother with that charade. He neglected his food entirely, electing instead to drink his dinner. After commanding the footman to leave the wine bottle by his side, he never let his glass become completely empty. Occasionally he took the initiative to top off her goblet, but Eleanor drank little.

Sebastian continued to wonder why her wits didn't return, why she didn't confront him and question the lack of a vicar to perform their marriage ceremony. She was a clever, intelligent woman—she should be suspicious of him.

"'Tis late. I'm certain you must be tired," he said as the dessert course sat untouched on their plates. "I'll have James escort you to your chamber."

"I'd rather wait for you."

Shit! She smiled sweetly, setting his blood pounding into a dangerous rhythm. Her open expression was a seductive invitation he was finding difficult to resist. Thank God they weren't alone or else he just might act on his desire, pull her onto his lap and kiss her senseless.

He wanted her naked in his bed, where he could enjoy her at his leisure, taking her again and again throughout the night. With a curse, he drained his glass. The frenzied image rendered him uncomfortably hard, requiring a few moments and another glass of wine before he could stand and leave the table. Surging to his feet, he sailed past Eleanor.

"Sebastian, wait!"

At her cry, the startled footman quickly pulled back the heavy, high-backed chair, assisting a surprised Eleanor to her feet. Sebastian wanted nothing more than to continue on his way, but good manners prevailed. He could not allow her to trail after him like a faithful hound.

Reluctantly he stopped, turned, and held out his arm. She gripped it tightly, leaning in so close he could see down the top of her low-cut gown. The creamy white globes of her breasts were a glorious sight, a temptation nearly impossible to resist. Yet he knew somehow he must.

Sebastian wrenched his eyes away, taking a few seconds to compose himself. Somehow he made his way up the staircase and down the hallway. Eleanor chatted softly as they walked, her voice a throaty hum of seduction.

Sebastian did his best to ignore it.

At last they reached her bedchamber door. He swayed slightly as he stood in front of it. *Hellfire and damnation, I shouldn't have had so much to drink.*

Knowing his judgment was never at its best when

clouded with alcohol, Sebastian tried to hurry Eleanor into her room. "Good night."

"Wait!" Her head came up, undisguised alarm leaping in her eyes. "Aren't you going to kiss me good night?"

Sebastian swore, cursing himself for not anticipating her request. Naturally she expected a sign of affection. She believed she was going to become his wife tomorrow. Breaking his resolve he stepped forward, tipped her head back, and kissed her lips, hard and fast.

"There! Now once again, good night, Eleanor."

She reached for him, but he avoided her grasp. "Shall I expect you in my bedchamber later?" she asked bluntly.

Bloody hell, she was killing him! He slowly shook his head. "We are not yet husband and wife."

"But we will be soon." Their gazes met, clashing. "Please stay with me tonight."

His mouth went dry, yet somehow he was able to snap, "I can't."

"Why?" She leaned closer and tipped her head invitingly.

Because I like you, I care about you. Because I harbor feelings for you that go beyond physical desire. Because you deserve far more than I am able to give you. Because I am using you to take my revenge against your father, perhaps even end his life.

It took a supreme act of willpower for Sebastian to keep his hands at his side. "We'll talk about things in the morning," he said gruffly. "Sleep well, Eleanor."

With that said, Sebastian turned and walked away. Noble acts were supposed to make you feel good, feel proud, feel strong, he thought. Pure rubbish. He felt awful. Frustrated, angry, even a bit depressed.

An acute sensation of regret formed in his chest, a feeling that he swiftly buried. He had brought Eleanor here to create a scandal, but he would not take advantage of her vulnerability. Staying in the house overnight, with only the servants as chaperones, was enough to ruin her. It would force the earl's hand and achieve the necessary result.

He might crave her desperately, with a fervor that bordered on irrationality, but he would not add insult by seducing her and taking her virginity.

He owed her at least that much.

Chapter 14

Eleanor felt as if she had just been slapped. She stared at Sebastian's retreating back, her mind a jumble of confusion. What was going on? Why had he left her? Did he no longer find her appealing, desirable? Or was it something about being back in his boyhood home that caused this puzzling behavior? Whatever the cause, the result was sheer disappointment.

Eleanor slowly opened the bedchamber door and went inside, shutting it with a resounding thud. Sinking onto the edge of a chair, she rubbed the bridge of her nose, trying to make sense of what was happening.

There was a sound at her chamber door, a soft knock. Eleanor's heart quickened. With a sigh of relief, she raced to the door and yanked it open. "I knew you had to be teasing—"

She quieted instantly when she found herself standing face to face with Mrs. Florid.

"Good evening, my lady." The servant dropped a hasty curtsy. "I was wondering if you required any assistance, seeing as how your maid isn't here and all."

"What happened to Lucy?" Eleanor asked, referencing the chambermaid who had assisted her earlier with her bath and dressing for dinner.

"She has too many duties below stairs," Mrs. Florid promptly replied. "But I can have her fetched if you would prefer."

"No, that won't be necessary. All I need is someone to unfasten the buttons at the back of my gown."

Mrs. Florid entered the chamber and closed the door behind her. Eleanor could tell the housekeeper wanted to chat but in deference to Eleanor's quiet mood restrained herself. She efficiently assisted Eleanor out of her evening gown, then soundlessly retreated at Eleanor's dismissive nod.

Clad in her underclothes, Eleanor sat at the dressing table, staring at her reflection in the mirror. This was not how she had pictured this night. She believed Sebastian would be the one removing her clothing, lovingly kissing each piece of flesh as it was revealed.

Instead she was alone, disappointment her only companion. Broodingly, she walked to the wardrobe, pulling it open. Divesting herself of her remaining garments, Eleanor wiggled into her nightgown, then returned to her dressing table to see how it looked. The new gown, borrowed from Bianca, was too snug at the bustline, pushing the tops of her breasts up and over the already low bodice.

The sensual garment should have made her feel desirable, but with no one to admire her in it, what was the point of even wearing it? Sighing, Eleanor began tugging the pins out of her hair, letting it fall to her waist. Lost in reflective thought, she untangled the strands with her fingers, then reached for her hairbrush.

Why had Sebastian left her alone tonight? For the past few weeks he had done everything humanly possible to catch her alone. Eleanor blushed at the memory of his ardent passion, his seemingly unquenchable thirst for her.

He had been clearly happy to see her this afternoon; his warm embrace and passionate kiss were sound proof of his ardor. So, what had changed? What was different?

Eleanor put down her brush and stared ruefully at her reflection. She could sit here until morning, questioning, pondering, speculating. Or she could discover the truth. She could ask him directly.

Sebastian's preference to be left alone could not be mistaken, but she couldn't let that dissuade her. Before giving herself a chance to reconsider her rash actions, Eleanor snatched the matching robe to her nightgown. Donning it purposefully, she tied the sash, then left her room. On bare feet she scampered down the corridor, stopping in front of Sebastian's bedchamber door.

Trembling slightly, her hand grasped the brass handle. She half expected it to be locked, for he had earlier claimed that he would do so, but when she turned the knob, the door opened wide. It creaked slightly on its hinges, the sound echoing loudly.

Barely able to see, Eleanor blinked several times as she stepped inside. There were no candles lit, the blaze from the hearth providing the only light. The flickering fire played over the dark tones in the spacious chamber, warming the cavernous space.

"What the hell are you doing here?"

Eleanor turned at the sound of his voice. He was on the opposite side of the room, sprawled in an oversized chair near the fire, his feet propped on a footstool. He had removed his evening coat, cravat, and waistcoat. His white linen shirt was open, the top buttons undone, allowing a glimpse of his muscular chest and the dark hair that dusted it. Her heart began to race.

"I asked what you were doing here," he repeated.

Eleanor took an involuntary step backward, her muscles tensing. He gazed at her with a clearly annoyed expression, his lean, handsome face conveying his displeasure. Eleanor thought he looked very much like a caged bear she had once seen at a country fair, angry and growling and ready to tear to shreds the first person who came near.

"You seemed a bit out of sorts when we said good night earlier," Eleanor said, walking slowly toward him. "I wanted to be certain everything was all right."

"Bullshit." Eleanor halted. His gaze looked past her and he swallowed hard, closing his eyes briefly. "I do beg your pardon. That was unforgivably rude."

"Yet totally honest, something I can appreciate despite the crudeness of the remark." She took a few more steps, which brought her directly in front of his footstool. Laying her hand gently on his knee, she added, "But you are correct. Checking on you is not the only reason I'm here. See, we can both be honest with each other. I think that's very important, Sebastian, don't you?"

He twitched as if she had stabbed him with the tip of a knife, then turned his face away. He stared down at the nearly empty glass in his hand, gripping the goblet tightly enough to turn his knuckles white. "Well, I think that is an exceedingly bad idea, sweetheart."

"Is it?"

He drank the last of the amber liquid swirling in his glass, then looked up at her. "All right, let's have it your way. You shouldn't be here, Eleanor. How's that for honesty?"

"Bullshit," she said softly, sinking down to her knees. She curled her arms around his bent legs, holding him tightly. "Being together tonight is what we both want, what we both need."

"No." He flinched and leaned forward. Grasping her wrists, he tried to push her hands away, but Eleanor refused to relinquish her grip.

The room became charged with emotions. Sebastian's belligerent gaze created goose bumps all over Eleanor's body, but she wouldn't back away. He was defensive and uncertain, as if something weighed heavily on his mind. Whatever it was seemed to be tearing him apart inside and she felt that she was the only one who could somehow make it right.

Eleanor tensed, awaiting his next move. He remained quiet and still for so long she grew uneasy. If only he would kiss her, then everything would fall into place. The tender press of his lips to her would ignite the passion he was holding so tightly in check, would release the desire they both craved.

Her attention moved to his mouth. He wasn't going to kiss her. She could read it in his eyes, could see it in the way he held himself so rigidly away from her. Well, there was only one remedy for that problem. Eleanor pushed herself forward and brought her lips to his.

She felt Sebastian's shock at her bold move reverberate through his body. He remained still and passive for a heartbeat and she panicked, thinking she had been terribly wrong, worried that he would reject her. Instead, his arms went around her, one hand palming her beneath her rear to pull her closer, into his lap.

His mouth plundered hers, making her feel vibrantly alive. Moving her hips, Eleanor felt the distinctive shape of his growing erection and her triumph was complete. Finally she was going to experience the closeness she had longed for, she was going to join her body, and soul, with the man she loved.

It was inevitable really that she would come to love him. He had taken notice of her when no one else had bothered, had showered her with masculine affection and attention, something she had received only once before in her life with John Tanner.

She had been a young girl all those years ago, unable to take what was within her grasp. Or perhaps it hadn't been her time and John hadn't really been the one. She had been naive, infatuated, yet too inexperienced to fully comprehend womanly love.

Though it was in many ways still a mystery, she knew the love she felt for Sebastian had enriched her life. It was a blessing really that her relationship with John had ended when it did, because that allowed Sebastian to enter her life at a time when she was mature enough to appreciate what a rare gift had been bestowed upon her.

The tenor of their kisses slowly began to change, becoming more restless, more urgent. Eleanor raked one hand upward through the thick strands of Sebastian's hair, kissing him deeply, trying to convey the depths of her feelings with her lips and tongue and hands. He returned her kisses, then muffling a curse, he suddenly tore his mouth from hers and held her at arm's length.

"You shouldn't be here," he growled, his harsh breathing slashing through the quiet, his hand tightening convulsively in her hair. "We shouldn't be doing this."

"So you have said." The agony on his face inspired a rush of emotion inside her. Gently she laid her hand against his cheek. "Honestly, Sebastian, you should know me well enough by now to understand that I seldom listen to anyone."

He gave her a distorted smile, easing away from her touch. "Drink?"

"Why not?"

She could see her answer surprised him. Nevertheless, he carefully set her off his lap, then lumbered to his feet. She noticed a half-full decanter on a small table. He produced a crystal glass and filled it, handing it silently to her. "Brandy," he explained.

"Lovely," she replied, taking a dainty sip, well aware of the liquor's potency.

She was pleased to note he did not pour another drink for himself. Instead he leaned against the fireplace mantel and folded his arms against his chest, his mouth turned down in a determined frown.

He looked dangerous and wicked. For a moment

Eleanor could imagine him as a pirate, a white, billowy shirt on his chest, black knee-high boots and tight buckskin breeches outlining his long muscular legs, a deadly cutlass clasped in his hand. There was such lethal appeal to his masculine beauty it almost took her breath away.

"Enjoying your drink?" he asked.

"Very much. 'Tis excellent brandy."

"You've consumed enough in your day to make a comparison, have you?" He shook his head and laughed, the sound stirring the sweet joy of desire deep inside her.

"Perhaps not, but I do know you well enough to surmise you would have the very best. Smuggled in from France, I'm certain."

"The embargo has been lifted. There's no need to smuggle French goods into England anymore."

"Well, gracious, where's the fun in having it legally?"

"God, you are a handful. I never realized it fully before."

"There's a great deal you haven't realized about me, Sebastian, but that's about to change." She twisted on the footstool, placing her glass on the floor, then tucking her feet beneath her. A pulse drummed insistently in the pit of her stomach as she struck what she hoped was an enticing pose. "Talk to me. Tell me what's wrong."

He said nothing. She waited. His gaze was somber as he stared at her, his face taut with longing. The sight brought all the tenderness and love she felt for him rushing into her heart, emotions that must have shown on her face, for he groaned and pushed away from the mantel, coming toward her.

"I won't take you to my bed. I can't. And I can't explain why," he said, his voice rough with urgency. "You need to leave, Eleanor. Please."

Sebastian's hunger was a raging storm. His cock was straining so hard and stiff it was painful to walk, his ballocks tightening to agony. All these weeks of sexual exploration and teasing with Eleanor without achieving his own completion had finally taken their toll. He was ready to explode, to fall upon her like some depraved, starving animal tearing into its first meal.

He had to get her out of his bedchamber! She was so tantalizing, so beguiling. Her charm was heating his blood, bringing his whole body alive with sensation. And he wasn't even touching her.

Cautiously he moved closer. The expression on her face made his breathing go shallow. She had let her robe hang open, tantalizing him with an unobstructed view of her sheer nightgown, of her white, creamy breasts. A bolt of need hit him full force.

"I can't leave yet, Sebastian. I see that you want me, feel that you need me." She lifted herself up to her knees, pressing the soft curves of her body against his hardness. "If you won't make love to me, at least let me ease you."

"Christ, Eleanor, what are you doing?" he moaned.

She pressed her palms flat against his chest and spread her hands over his pectorals. Sebastian inhaled a sharp breath and tilted himself forward as she began to wantonly explore him. She ran her hands sensually over his chest, over his ribs and down his abdomen, then back up again. Caressing his nipples through the fabric of his shirt, she leaned in, pressing a damp kiss in the hollow of his throat.

"You are magnificent," she purred. "So strong, so sleek, so muscular."

Something dark and tight twisted in Sebastian's chest. Something unrelated to the lust coursing through his body, something triggered by the wonder and honesty in her voice. In that moment he realized that his need for her was far greater than his resolve to resist her.

She wrestled with the cuff links on his sleeves, grinning triumphantly when she worked the silver links loose from their moorings. She next pushed off his shirt, baring his torso.

Sebastian stood there inert, allowing her questing fingers free rein, admitting to himself that he had lost the battle. The hot, fierce intensity of his arousal had taken control. He knew he was no match for it, especially when Eleanor was so determined to seduce him.

"Let's go to my bed," he whispered urgently, firmly pushing any other thoughts from his mind. She was going to hate him come morning, but tonight, ah tonight, she wanted to belong to him. And he wanted that too, more than anything.

Arm in arm they walked to the bed. Along the way Eleanor's robe disappeared, as did Sebastian's shoes. The mattress dipped with their weight as they settled in the middle of the bed. He reached for her the moment they were lying down, sliding his hands up to cup her breasts, which were nearly spilling over the top of her nightgown. She moaned and arched closer, and he couldn't resist taking one of the firm, rosy nipples into his mouth.

As he suckled her breast, Sebastian unfastened his breeches with an impatient hand, shoving the placket apart to free his stiff manhood. Groaning, he thrust almost blindly against her soft curves. He buried his nose in the soft mass of her tumbling hair and breathed deeply. God help him, even her scent was intoxicating.

"I want to touch you," she whispered wickedly. "Everywhere."

Her questing fingers combed through the trail of hair below his navel. Sebastian's hips twisted and he arched his back. Tenderly, she brushed the pad of her finger softly on the round head of his straining cock. He moaned. She thumbed the slit at the crown in a teasing circle, spreading the moisture slowly. He shuddered violently and she did it again.

"Eleanor," he panted, his fingers biting into her soft thighs. "You need to slow down, love, or else it's all going to end very soon."

She clutched his shoulder with her other hand, rubbing her face against his neck. "Please, Sebastian. I want to do this."

Christ Almighty! His hand reached out to cup her face. In the near darkness he could see her eyes shining brightly with desire. She'd never looked more lovely, more enticing. He leaned in and kissed her, touching his tongue to hers, sending shudders of pleasure through them both.

"Stroke me," he said with a choked groan. "Put your hand completely over me."

Obligingly, she wrapped her palm around the base of his erect penis and drew her fist up. He shuddered violently, bucking into her hand.

"Like this?" she asked, her voice straining with emotion.

"Grip me tighter," he gasped. "Faster."

She did as he commanded, finding the rhythm, stroking him until his hips were undulating off the bed. He felt himself on the edge of losing control completely, unable to gain a mastery over the situation.

"Sebastian?"

"Watch me," he growled, pushing the limits of her sensuality. "Watch what you are doing to me."

"I am," she muttered. "'Tis so beautiful. Come for me."

Then she dipped her head and her mouth closed in torturous bliss over his nipple. She pulled it into her mouth, sucking hard.

His hand went down between his legs and he closed his fist over her smaller hand, crying out loudly as he reached final completion. Sebastian could feel his hot seed spurting over their hands, gushing forth in a river of thick moisture.

He collapsed when it was over, his breathing still harsh and ragged. Eleanor stayed beside him for a few moments, then he felt her leave the bed. He wanted to call out to her to stay, but no part of his body seemed capable of movement, including his voice.

She soon returned with a damp towel, efficiently cleaning him off as he lay sprawled on the bed. Sebastian felt lightheaded and content, his mind too heavy with alcohol to sort out precisely how this had happened, his body too sated to care. When she was done, she laid down beside him.

"Are you all right?" he finally asked, somehow

finding the strength to raise himself on his elbow so he could look into her flushed, glowing face.

"I'm quite happy, thank you," she responded primly.

"That was simply . . . incredible. Thank you."

Color flooded her face and she ducked her head. He lifted the hand that was plucking nervously at the counterpane and slowly kissed each finger. "I never imagined you were such a bold, uninhibited woman. I find that very exciting."

"I'm glad." Her head turned on the pillow and she stared at the ceiling.

"But I'm ashamed of myself for treating a lady so shabbily."

"Ashamed?"

"A considerate gentleman does not leave his partner unsatisfied."

"I am hardly unsatisfied, sir."

"I beg to differ." He lifted himself higher and loomed above her. Lowering his head, he kissed her fiercely, plundering her sweet mouth. She responded eagerly, her tongue boldly mating with his. When they both came up for air, she was smiling. "Give me twenty minutes, love, and I'll show you precisely what I mean," he rasped.

"Twenty?"

"Ah, actually it appears as though fifteen will do the trick, if you kiss me like that again."

Fifteen minutes? Really? Eleanor glanced down at his groin and realized he wasn't exaggerating. With her eyes on him, his penis began to stiffen, rising through his opened breeches.

"That doesn't seem possible and yet . . ." Her voice trailed off in wonder.

"It isn't usually the case," he agreed, gazing at her with heavy-lidded eyes. "Though already satisfied once, I still want you, need you. With a passion that borders on madness."

"All hail miracles," she whispered, rubbing herself against his chest, pressing her stomach against his.

Laughing, he took hold of the sides of her nightgown and began sliding it upward over her body. Obligingly Eleanor raised her arms and Sebastian lifted it all the way off and tossed it to the floor.

She should have felt embarrassed to be so exposed, but all she could think about was seeing him naked too. Her hands reached for his breeches, but he was quicker, pulling the garment off his body himself, throwing it beside her discarded nightgown. The throb of her pulse quickened at the sight of him, his thighs sleek and muscular, his thick manhood jutting up proudly from a thatch of dark hair.

He was all hard planes and unleashed power, and the raw strength of him fascinated her, calling to her curiosity and simmering passion.

She reached for him the same moment he reached for her. Smiling, they touched each other's faces, then Sebastian gently moved her hand away. "It's my turn to pleasure you," he insisted, brushing his fingers lightly over the hardened peaks of her nipples.

She moaned with delight when he dipped his head and drew one nipple into his mouth, the piercing sweetness flowing through her. Eleanor shivered and gasped as he suckled her, cradling his head to her chest, her hands tightening in his hair.

Her breathing became quick and shallow as he slid his hand down her belly and between her thighs. She could feel herself becoming lusciously wet as he deepened his touch, stroking her back and forth with the tip of his fingers.

The hunger continued to build inside her and she moaned his name, moving her legs restlessly, her hands running frantically from his back to his buttocks, then back up again. "Please," she murmured, her voice a ragged sob. "Oh, please, Sebastian . . ."

"Tell me you want me, Eleanor," he whispered, as he moved above her. "Tell me, sweetheart."

"I crave you. Only you. I want you inside me, my love." Eleanor lifted her arms to embrace him, welcome him. His knee came between her thighs, pressing her legs wide apart. She could feel him position himself at her opening and then he eased the head of his penis into her wet moisture.

Gasping at the sensation, Eleanor clutched his back nervously as he pushed deeper. She felt stretched and filled and aching. Not precisely in pain, but the edge of her passion was inexplicably starting to recede.

"Sebastian?"

"I'm sorry, sweetheart. There's no help for it," he murmured.

She heard his words through the thunderous rushing of desire and confusion rumbling in her ears. He entered her fully, pushing deeper, harder. For an instant she couldn't breathe, her body tensing with anticipation of the unknown and then he thrust his hips forcefully.

She screamed at the sudden, sharp pain, but he was ready for it, his mouth dipping over hers, capturing the sound. Then he stayed perfectly still.

Eleanor opened her eyes. Sebastian was braced above her on his forearms, looking down into her face. His eyes were dark with passion and concern, the intensity searing her very soul.

"I'll wait a moment until you become accustomed to the feel of me," he promised, kissing the tip of her nose.

She smiled. "Sebastian, if we do this for the next fifty years, and I fervently hope that we shall, I will never feel *accustomed* to it."

With that said, Eleanor's body warmed, the tightness inside her relaxed. Tentatively she rocked her hips, relieved to find the pain was no longer as sharp, the pleasure still an unfulfilled promise. She heard him groan and he rested his head against her chest for a moment, clearly fighting for control.

"Are you trying to kill me, ma'am, or is that just an unfortunate side effect?" he groaned.

She laughed, moving her hips again, hardly believing the various emotions such an intimate act could produce. Pleasure, pain, laughter—it was all amazing, all glorious, all wonderful—because she shared them with Sebastian.

Feeling more confident, she curled her fingers into the lean muscles of his buttocks and lifted her lower body. It was all the encouragement he needed. He drew back, then deepened his next thrust. The movement filled her with such a sense of completion her eyes filled with tears.

He set a rhythm that she was quickly able to match, arching into the glorious hard strength of him, taking him deeper into her body, deeper into her heart. Heedless of her frantic panting, she savored each thrust, the friction it created pushing the building pleasure and tension. And then suddenly the pleasure broke, crashing over her in waves.

She cried out, her senses scattering utterly. Quaking and shivering, her body trembled as she clung to Sebastian. He continued to thrust, angling her hips to achieve the deepest penetration.

As the firestorm inside her began to cool, Eleanor realized Sebastian was still large and stiff inside her, having not yet achieved his satisfaction. Her eyes locked on his and she tightened her arms around his back, urging him on with nonsensical murmurings of love as he frantically plunged his hardness into her welcoming body.

Suddenly, he stilled, and then a violent shudder rocked him. Eleanor could feel his entire body shaking violently as the surge of his hot seed filled her. It seemed to go on forever, but then abruptly he collapsed against her, his cheek pressed to hers. Stroking his hair, she kissed his damp temple, savoring this extraordinary feeling.

He stayed on top of her for several long minutes, his weight pressing her into the mattress. Gradually she felt the final vestiges of tension leave his body. He made a sound, a cross between a sigh and a moan, then pressed a kiss to her mouth.

Murmuring her name, Sebastian rolled onto his back, pulling her with him. Eleanor rested her head against his shoulder and snuggled close. Her heartbeat eventually slowed and she felt an almost uncontrollable urge to talk, to verbalize and ana- lyze what they had just shared. To ask why he had been so hesitant to take her to his bed and make her his, and was he pleased now that he had?

But the sated lethargy of bliss was quickly overtak- ing her body. She could tell by Sebastian's even breaths that he had already fallen asleep. His warmth surrounded her, making her feel com- forted, protected. Heart bursting with emotion, she slowly closed her eyes and promptly joined him in a contented slumber.

Chapter 15

The opportunity for conversation never surfaced during the night. After a brief, dreamless sleep, Eleanor was awakened by the feel of a warm, damp cloth between her legs. She opened her eyes and found Sebastian standing at the bedside, gently administering to her. His face was so troubled at the sight of her virgin's blood, she felt an overwhelming need to comfort him.

"It only hurt for a moment," she said.

He flinched. "I'm sorry. I never meant for this to happen. Any of it."

"But I'm so happy that it did," she answered, sitting up to embrace him.

Their initial kiss and tender caress soon led to other things. Sebastian eased into the bed beside her, sliding close to take her in his arms. Before long he rolled onto his back and Eleanor found herself straddling him, her thighs suggestively stretched over his.

Trepidation, along with a hint of anticipation,

filled her. She had some idea of what he had in mind, yet wasn't precisely sure how it was going to work.

"Use your knees to lift your hips," he instructed, his voice gruff with strain.

She did as he bid, gasping when he grabbed her waist and pulled her forward. She felt the tip of his erection slowly start to ease inside her wetness, but then he stopped.

"Is something wrong?" she whispered.

He shuddered beneath her. His eyes were glazed with passion, his muscles rigid as he struggled for control. "I want this to be good for you, too."

He placed his hand low on her belly, working his fingers between their bodies. He stroked her gently and pleasure rocked through her. She lowered herself slightly, hovering over him. Sebastian inhaled a ragged breath and gripped her hips, then at his urging she slowly sank herself onto his jutting penis, savoring the hot, thick fullness.

She stared into his eyes, seeing the passion there, knowing it matched her own need, her own emotions. Bracing her hands on his broad shoulders, Eleanor clenched her inner muscles and started to ride him. Her movements were clumsy at first, almost hesitant, but he encouraged her, whispering wicked instructions in a sensual, throaty tone that made her shiver.

He seemed content to allow her to set the pace and rhythm. Eleanor found the pleasure and power of being in control of their lovemaking exhilarating. She tested his endurance, teasing him with sensual movements and then suddenly he growled and grasped her buttocks. Holding her tight, he jerked the lower half of his body, driving hard and fast, thrusting up into her until they both climaxed.

A few hours later it was the feel of Sebastian's wet mouth showering her body with kisses that brought Eleanor gradually out of a deep slumber. His gentle, clever kisses kindled the arousal tightening deep in her womb.

She made no protest when he turned her onto her stomach and moved her into a kneeling position. Grasping her hips firmly, he entered her from behind, stretching her to accept his thick length.

Then he started moving. Each thrust delivered a groan of pleasure to her heightened senses. The darkness engulfed her, the heat of his body surrounded her. Eleanor lifted her head, tossing her hair, crying out as he brushed the tip of his finger back and forth over the slickness between her thighs.

She tried to match his sensuous movements with her own, pushing back to meet his thrusts. His erection seemed to grow even harder and she was nearly weeping at the sensation of him filling her so completely.

He relentlessly drove them both farther and faster until the bliss tore through her and her body collapsed in ecstasy. His breathing was harsh and ragged against the back of her neck and through the haze she felt his body shudder and spasm. He let out a hoarse cry as he came inside her, shouting her name.

An incredible, overpowering happiness filled her. This was more, so much more than she had hoped it would be. Eleanor fell asleep in Sebastian's arms, his hands stroking her hair, his warmth soothing her, her heart irrevocably bound to him.

A bold streak of sunlight greeted Eleanor when she awoke in her own bed early the following afternoon. Alone. Her arms felt empty without Sebastian, her body cold. She hid her disappointment from Lucy when the young maid brought her hot chocolate, and chatted pleasantly as the servant helped her wash and dress.

Sebastian was already seated at the dining room table when Eleanor entered, a cold plate of uneaten food resting in front of him. Their eyes met and she somehow managed not to blush. He rose politely and dismissed the servants as she sat down. Eleanor's stomach gave a sharp squeeze at his worried, solemn expression.

"We need to talk," Sebastian declared.

She nodded in agreement, but they were interrupted by an apologetic Higgins. With great effort, Eleanor managed not to drop her teacup when the butler delivered his astonishing message.

Apparently the Earl of Hetfield had just arrived and was waiting in the drawing room.

"My father?" Eleanor's face paled. "What is he doing here?"

Sebastian abruptly stood, dismissing Higgins with a sharp wave of his hand. *Damn it all to bloody hell! I wanted to explain everything to Eleanor—well, try to explain—but now it is too late.* The thread of distress in her voice was unmistakable, yet Sebastian knew he had to ignore it. "I imagine the earl has come for you."

"How did he know where to find me?" she asked in a reedy voice.

"Before we left London, I arranged to have a letter delivered, informing him that you had come away with me."

Her eyes immediately filled with questions. Questions that Sebastian had no intention of answering.

"I wish you had asked me first," she admonished in an even tone.

"I apologize." He turned away. "I think it best if I meet with the earl in private. I'll send Higgins for you when we've settled everything."

He practically ran from the dining room. Eleanor's puzzlement tore at him, but he could not let it distract him. He needed all his wits about him to face the earl.

Upon hearing that Hetfield had arrived, the feelings of revenge that had started all this madness returned in full measure, so much so that the tightness in Sebastian's chest was nearly a burning rage by the time he reached the drawing room.

The earl glanced up the moment Sebastian came into the room. Dressed in fawn breeches, a tan waistcoat, and a dark green jacket, Hetfield was impeccably groomed, not a hair out of place. Clearly he had not rushed on his way to his daughter's rescue.

"Why have you summoned me here?" the older man asked. "Eleanor, what in the blazes is going on?"

Sebastian turned and looked over his shoulder. Damn! Would she never listen? He told her to wait in the dining room because he wanted to spare her this scene. Well, there was no help for it now. He had to play the hand he'd been dealt.

Feeling as if the earth was shifting beneath his feet, Sebastian moved to Eleanor's side, deliberately placing his arm intimately around her waist. "She's with me," he declared smugly.

The earl's eyes narrowed. He would have to be a simpleton to miss Sebastian's implication. "You spent the night here together, without a proper chaperone?"

"We did," Sebastian confirmed.

Eleanor stifled a groan. Her head lifted, her gaze shooting to Sebastian's, helpless, pleading. He looked away. "'Tis not as bad as it seems," she said defensively, turning to her father.

The earl's jaw tightened. "It *seems* perfectly scandalous," he replied. "If anyone finds out, Eleanor's reputation will be ruined. Since you've called me here to witness this scandal, Benton, I assume you plan to marry her. Immediately."

Sebastian shrugged, unimpressed with the earl's indignation. "Funny thing about assumptions, Hetfield. They are often wrong."

The older man's face hardened. "What are you saying?"

Releasing Eleanor, Sebastian gave a short, mirthless laugh and strolled to the fireplace. "I'm not going to marry your daughter, immediately or otherwise."

Eleanor made a wordless sound of shocked distress, then went quiet. Out of the corner of his eye Sebastian saw her cringe and wrap her arms around herself. She wasn't looking at him anymore. She was staring at the ceiling.

The earl stiffened. "Why would you dishonor her?"

"He did not—"

"Be silent!" the earl shouted at Eleanor, then turned to face Sebastian. "Your smug expression tells me clearly she spent the night in your bed, Benton. Was it a lark? Surely you cannot have found her attractive. I must therefore assume it's something else.

"First there was the card game at the Duke of Warren's ball where you falsely accused me of cheating, and now this mess. What's your game, man?"

"Revenge." Sebastian spat the word out with all the fiery loathing he felt deep down inside.

"For what? I don't know you," the earl protested.

"You knew my mother," Sebastian said harshly. "Or have you forgotten?"

A short silence fell. The earl's face twisted and a haunted look flashed through his eyes. "I remember the countess. You probably won't believe it, but I always regretted that things between us ended badly."

"Badly? Your heartless neglect brought about her unnecessary death. And for that you will at long last be held accountable."

The earl's mood abruptly shifted and he made a sound of confusion. "If you meant to challenge me to a duel, you would have done so years ago."

"Circumstances prevented it. Besides, I would never sully my mother's honorable reputation by revealing how you took advantage of her vulnerability."

The earl's eyes lit with dawning understanding. "Ah, so instead you have ruined my daughter's reputation, in order to force the issue. Clever."

Sebastian commanded himself not to react, not to betray his true emotions. Hearing it said so succinctly made him feel like an utter cad. *Christ, I am no better than Hetfield, toying with an innocent woman's feelings.* He risked another glance at Eleanor. The shock on her face, the anguish in her eyes cut him to the quick, but he ignored her and pressed on, the need for revenge supplanting all other emotions.

"Lady Eleanor's reputation is not yet sacrificed, since no one else is aware of this incident. Choose your weapons and name your seconds, Hetfield," Sebastian said, fixing the older man with a hard stare. "If we meet on Hampstead Heath tomorrow at dawn, I swear to never reveal what has happened. Your family's honor will be saved, no matter what the outcome of our duel."

Abruptly, the earl's casual air fell away. "You cannot be serious."

Sebastian cast him a look of disgust. "If not tomorrow, then the following day. That is the most time I will allow."

"And if I refuse to participate in this little melodrama you've so carefully concocted?"

A vein throbbed in Sebastian's forehead. "You already know what will happen."

"Oh, yes, you will tell everyone of your scandalous affair with my unmarried daughter." The earl tugged on the cuff of his jacket, then brushed a small piece of lint from the sleeve. "Go right ahead and make your announcement. Take an ad out in the *Times* if you'd like."

Sebastian's jaw dropped.

"I'm calling your bluff, Benton."

Sebastian's gut tightened with a hard twist. "I'm not bluffing."

"Perhaps. Perhaps not." The earl shrugged, his disinterest clear. "Either way, it matters very little to me. If you ruin Eleanor, I shall disown her, banishing her from my home and family. The scandal will barely graze me. If Waverly becomes squeamish about it and forsakes Bianca, she will marry Farley and I will receive a sizable settlement from him.

"If you say nothing, well, I have yet to decide on a suitable punishment for the witless Eleanor. Either way, I refuse to issue a challenge, refuse to engage in a duel with you for any reason, under any circumstance."

For an instant Eleanor's surroundings faded to nothing. Surely she had misheard. Of course she had. Sebastian would never have planned and plotted all of this in order to exact some sort of revenge against the earl. No, that couldn't possibly be correct.

Sebastian liked her. Her clever wit, her intelligent conversation, her staunch opinions. He cared for her. Considered her feelings, her wishes, her desires. He wanted to be with her. To cherish her, protect her, keep her safe. They were going to be married, by special license, here in his boyhood home, by the family vicar.

He had made love to her last night. Several times. And in the early morning too. Tenderly, reverently, with passion and love. It had been glorious, wonderful, more than she could ever have imagined, ever hoped.

It was all a lie. A cruel, vengeful lie.

Eleanor struggled to concentrate, to hear what else was being said, but a ringing began in her ears. Her knees felt weak and she realized if she continued to stand she was going to collapse. Hand over hand she clutched the end of the sideboard and slowly made her way to the brocade settee. Sinking down into its softness, she focused on remaining upright, trying to shake the numbness from her body.

The tension in the room was oppressive. Eleanor folded her arms tightly and ran her hands vigorously over her upper arms. She felt cold down to the marrow of her bones, ill with shock. Her body ached, but it was her heart, her bruised and broken heart, that pained her most.

Lies, it was all lies.

The man who had made love to her repeatedly last night, who had held her close, worshipped her body with his own, brought her such tremendous joy, had betrayed her. It had all been a deliberate manipulation, a deceit that would enable him to settle a score with her father.

Leave! Rise to your feet, turn toward the door, and walk away.

The command screamed silently in her head, yet she was paralyzed, rooted to the spot. Forced to endure the embarrassment and humiliation that was clawing at the final vestiges of her shattered pride.

What was the earl saying? Her dazed mind struggled to separate the words from the emotions, to listen and comprehend.

They were arguing. Over her. No, over their duel. A duel her father refused to accept. After all, her honor was worth nothing to him. She was worth nothing to him.

Eleanor pressed a fist to her mouth to keep from making any sound. The agony inside her was threatening to slice her in half. Battling back her tears, she clutched at her chest, pressing hard against the aching pain.

With Herculean effort she managed to stand. Harshly commanding herself to move, she managed to put one foot in front of the other and finally made her escape.

Neither Sebastian nor the earl attempted to stop her. Honestly, she doubted either of them even noticed she was gone.

Seething with anger and frustration, Sebastian watched Hetfield pull on his leather gloves with slow deliberation. The revenge he had so carefully planned, had so meticulously calculated, was crumbling to dust and there was nothing he could do to salvage it.

The anger inside him was quickly turning to helplessness. The earl was leaving. What now?

"Hetfield!"

The earl turned, his expression bored. The anger simmering inside Sebastian rekindled. White-hot anger. For the way the earl had so callously treated his mother, for the disregard he had showed Eleanor, for the injustice that would forever go unpunished.

"It's over, Benton. Take my advice. Be a gentleman and forget it."

The words, spoken in such a smug, cavalier tone broke Sebastian's temper. Rushing forward, he planted his fist in Hetfield's stomach. The earl let out a muffled sound, then doubled over as the air was knocked out of him. Waiting only until Hetfield had straightened, Sebastian jabbed with his right hand and smashed his fist into the earl's jaw.

The earl staggered backward and fell to the floor. The drawing room door burst open at the commotion. Two bewildered footmen entered, each staring in astonishment at the older man prone on the carpet, then at Sebastian.

"Lord Hetfield is leaving," Sebastian announced, flexing his fist. The knuckles were red and bruised. "Please escort him to his carriage."

The footmen ran to help the earl to his feet. Once standing, he shrugged the servants away, then reached up to wipe away a trickle of blood from his cheekbone. "Though I admit no wrongdoing of any kind, I shall allow that to pass."

"Pity. I was hoping you'd take a swing at me so I could lay you flat on your back again," Sebastian replied in an icy tone.

A muscle jumped in the earl's jaw, but he said nothing. Turning with a huff, he strode out of the drawing room, flanked on each side by a footman.

The moment he was alone, Sebastian sagged against a chair. Punching Hetfield had felt good, a momentary release of frustration and anger and pain, but it had faded quickly, leaving him with a hollow feeling of regret and a nagging sense of failure.

The earl was a malicious bastard, lacking both honor and conscience. His treatment of Sebastian's mother had been unforgivable, yet his treatment of his daughter was not much better. Learning how little regard her father had for her must have been devastating to hear, a pain she certainly did not deserve.

Oh, Eleanor! Mired in guilt, Sebastian turned to face her, then realized she was gone.

The clock ticked loudly, each second feeling like an hour. Eleanor sat quietly in the wingback chair of her bedchamber, her packed portmanteau resting at her feet. The sound of footsteps in the outside corridor momentarily roused her from her stupor and her heart skipped as the door opened.

Summoning her courage from the depths of her pain, Eleanor lifted her head, steeling herself. Sebastian stood in front of her, staring at her with deep emotion stark in his eyes, a combination of detachment and desolation.

Furiously, Eleanor blinked back her tears. There was no time to indulge them. She had to be on her guard for what was to come.

"I wasn't sure where you were," he said quietly.

She linked her hands together to stop them from trembling. "Is the earl gone?"

"Yes."

"Will there be a duel?"

"No. He refused."

Sebastian looked so defeated she might have felt an ounce of sympathy for him if her heart was not frozen with the pain of betrayal.

"I too will soon be gone, but I couldn't leave without asking you. Why?"

Thankfully he did not pretend to misunderstand. "The earl had an affair with my mother, I believe shortly after he became a widower. She found herself with child and he refused her any aid. In desperation she hung herself. I was the one who discovered her lifeless body."

Eleanor shuddered. It was even more heinous than she had suspected. "How old were you?"

"Twelve."

"Too young to exact your revenge. Yet why have you waited so long?"

"I promised my grandmother I would not confront the earl. When she died a few months ago I was at last free to pursue justice."

"Were you going to kill him?"

Sebastian shrugged. "The potential to inflict a fatal wound always exists with swords or pistols. I confess I would not have felt any remorse if I landed a mortal blow."

A part of her understood his bloodthirsty need, given what her father had done, but she could never condone his methods. "Unfortunately, the earl thwarted your clever plan rather neatly, did he not? I realize now Bianca was your original target. That was what you intended, wasn't it, to ruin my younger sister?"

Sebastian gave a curt nod and she continued.

"You know, it might have ended differently if you had used Bianca. I believe my father has a very marginal regard for her, but more important, she is of greater value to him. He brought her here to make a profitable marriage, and embroiling her in such a sordid scandal would have made that difficult.

"Then again, he might have thrown her to the wolves as he has done with me. If not Viscount Farley, he would have found someone willing to pay for the privilege of marrying an earl's daughter. You see, he is not bound by any rules except his own.

Nor does he possess a gentleman's code of honor. A trait you share with him."

She knew it would gall Sebastian to be compared to his enemy, but she could not resist saying it.

He glanced away. "I know my actions cannot be excused by explaining the past, but I am truly sorry for what I have done. I never meant to hurt you. I promise that I shall do everything in my power to protect and guard your reputation."

She let out a hollow laugh, clenching her fingers together so tightly it hurt. "'Tis a bit too late for that, my lord."

His mouth thinned. "Maybe not. Only you and I and the earl know that you stayed here last night."

Reputation be damned! It was her heart that was in ruins. Could he not see it?

"I don't care a fig about society's opinion of me," she stated emphatically, "except that my stupidity might harm Bianca. I would never forgive myself if she suffered because I'm such a gullible simpleton, easily duped by a bit of male attention and flattery. It must have been so amusing for you to watch the dull, plain spinster make a fool of herself, though Lord knows how you found the stomach to kiss me."

He winced. "On the contrary. Kissing you has always been the greatest of pleasures." He ran a hand through his already tousled hair. "I knew it was wrong, but I swear, Eleanor, you must believe me when I tell you that though I tried, I was unable to resist you."

A twinge of guilt cramped her stomach. She could not lay the blame entirely at his feet for their physical relationship. He had left her alone in her bedchamber last night—she was the one who had pressed the issue, had essentially seduced him.

"Yes, I made it impossible for you to turn me away," she admitted dully, the sorrow slicing through her like a cold, damp wind. "Coming to your chamber last night, behaving like a whore."

He visibly flinched. "My God, it wasn't like that, Eleanor."

Her heart stirred at the pain in his voice and she cursed herself for being twice a fool. "Wasn't it?"

"No, never. Making love to you was beautiful, perfect. A memory I shall long treasure, though I realize I haven't the right."

He sent her a look of such regret and tenderness she nearly lost the thin thread of her composure. Her bruised heart curled in wariness and she knew she couldn't let herself think or feel or else all would be lost.

Abruptly she stood. "I'm leaving."

"What are you going to do?"

"I'm not certain," she whispered, fear shimmering through her. She could not return to London. The country was a possible destination, but would she be able to live at the family manor with such uncertainty, knowing at any moment the earl might appear and toss her out?

At length, she drew a deep breath, then straightened her shoulders. "All I do know is that I refuse to wallow in self-pity and remorse for the rest of my days. You aren't worth it."

"On that point we most definitely agree."

She sent him a blistering glare, then stalked toward the door, picking up her luggage on the way. "Farewell, my lord."

"Wait!" His voice was raw. "Where are you going? How will you get there?"

Her back stiffened, taut as a wire, but then her head lowered until it rested against her chest. She felt so tired. "My great-aunt in Bath will offer me refuge."

"Are you certain? Shouldn't you send a message first and make sure you will be welcomed?"

Eleanor refused to even think about it. To be turned away was simply too unbearable a concept. "Aunt Jane is the sister of my maternal grandmother. She has never married, but is a progressive-minded female who has always disliked the earl. I have only met her twice, but we exchange letters several times a year. She will shelter me until I sort myself out."

Saying the words out loud gave Eleanor a confidence she did not entirely feel. But it helped enough to still the panic whirling inside her. She observed Sebastian fumbling in his pocket and had a sudden inkling of what he meant to do. "I swear by all that is holy, if you try to give me any money I will slap you."

His arms stilled, his hands slumped to his sides. "At least take my carriage. It is comfortable and safe. You can't possibly travel on a public coach without a proper lady's maid."

"Ah, yes, my precious reputation again."

"Eleanor, please. Be sensible."

Though she hated to admit it, he was right. Being contrary just to prove a point was foolish. It was like her Scottish housekeeper liked to say, *'Twas a foolish lass indeed who cut off her nose to spite her face.*

"I'll use your coach," she said grudgingly. "But I need to leave *now*."

He nodded. "It will only take a few minutes to have the team harnessed."

Reminding herself to breathe, Eleanor descended the staircase, Sebastian at her heels. Thankfully none of the servants were in view. It would have been too humiliating to see Mrs. Florid or Higgins. As it was, she could only imagine the talk that was going on below stairs.

Agitated, she paced the foyer while Sebastian made the arrangements. Though it felt like hours, it was only a few minutes until he returned. Her muscles drew up tightly as he approached. Either seeing or sensing her resistance, he did not offer his arm. In tense silence they walked out the front door, side by side.

Eleanor scrambled inelegantly inside the carriage without assistance, making certain there was no chance for a final good-bye. Her pride in shreds, she pulled the carriage door shut with a resounding thud. Her nerves were at the breaking point and she knew she could not endure another word or even a glance from him.

She heard Sebastian give the order to drive on. Eyes planted straight ahead, Eleanor refused to look out the window until they had turned off the drive and started on the main road.

It was then that she noticed how blue the sky was, how brightly the sun was shining, how warm and lovely the temperature. It was a beautiful day, picture perfect in nearly every way. The type of day she would have relished taking a leisurely stroll in the garden, or an afternoon reading under a shady elm.

Or best of all, a day joyfully spent in Sebastian's company, in Sebastian's arms.

No, that will never happen. Eleanor closed her eyes, fighting back the pain, trying to smother her sobs with her hand. But it was no use. Her heart was shattered, her dreams destroyed. The tears rolled down her face unchecked. She cried, not only for what she had lost, but for what she would never have—a partnership with a loving husband who understood and respected her, and children to raise and cherish.

Yet she sobbed hardest of all because she knew, despite everything, she would never cease to love Sebastian.

Chapter 16

The carriage ride to Bath was surprisingly un-eventful. The coach driver was skilled and knowledgeable, the two grooms efficient. They chose the cleanest, safest posting inns, making all the arrangements for meals, rooms, and fresh horses. They also paid for everything, though Eleanor never witnessed an exchange of coin.

She was treated with the utmost courtesy and respect. Even the weather cooperated, remaining sunny and rain-free for the duration. It had all the elements of a pleasant trip, but of course Eleanor could not shut down her mind, turn off her memories, or ignore the reason she was going to Bath in the first place.

Sebastian. How could you? Her thoughts and emotions in constant turmoil day and night, Eleanor struggled to get a grip on the situation and herself. Regret was a constant companion, accompanied by uncertainty and heartache. Yet it was anger that surfaced most often, anger at Sebastian for his callous treatment of her. Anger at herself for being such a naive fool. Anger at her father for his cruelty toward all the women in his life.

By the time she arrived at her aunt's townhome, numbness had set in and Eleanor knew she was functioning on sheer will alone. She allowed one of the grooms to guide her to the front stoop and knock on the door, making no protest when he informed the butler who she was and whom she wanted to see.

Great-Aunt Jane took one look at her beleaguered face and hastened her inside. Eleanor was profoundly grateful. She was shown to the best guest chamber in the house, a pretty, airy room done in lovely shades of yellow, appointed with delicate, feminine French furniture.

After a warm bath and a strong cup of tea, Eleanor climbed into the big four-poster bed, huddled under the pale yellow satin counterpane, and slipped into oblivion.

She stayed in bed for two days, forcing herself to eat a few bites of food from the trays the solemn-faced maid brought to her, telling herself that tomorrow the heavy-limbed fatigue she felt would lessen and she would rouse herself from the bed.

On the morning of the third day, Eleanor scolded herself severely, then literally dragged her weary body to the dressing table. She sat listless as the maid arranged her hair, then helped her dress in a simple, high-waisted day gown. Ready at last, Eleanor made her way to the dining room, still uncertain precisely what she was going to say to Aunt Jane.

"'Tis good to see you standing on your feet, Eleanor." Aunt Jane was a short, slender woman with silver hair and piercing, intelligent blue eyes. She smiled with closed lips, then released the lorgnette she had been using. It dangled from her neck at the end of a silver chain, resting comfortably against her flat chest. "Are you feeling any better?"

"Marginally."

Aunt Jane nodded. "Sit. Some hot food will put the color back in your cheeks."

Smiling her thanks at the footman who pulled out her chair, Eleanor did as she was commanded. Feeling no hunger, she stared listlessly down at the plate of food placed in front of her. Then realizing she was being ungrateful, Eleanor gingerly picked up a fork and attempted to eat.

"I've been reading yesterday's *Times*," Aunt Jane said as the footman refilled her coffee cup.

Eleanor's fork clattered noisily on the edge of her still-full plate. "Oh?"

"There is nothing in there about you." Aunt Jane rattled the newspaper as she folded it, gesturing for the servants to leave. "I think it's a good sign, don't you agree?"

"Yes," Eleanor whispered. "Though an item might yet appear. I think it only fair to warn you."

"I am a respectable woman, Eleanor, received in all of the best homes. If you'll pardon my boast, many consider me a pillar of our close-knit community. I am not, however, a prude." Aunt Jane reached across the table and patted Eleanor's hand. "I assume your father has forsaken you in your time of trouble?"

Eleanor struggled to swallow. "We are estranged, a breach that is in all likelihood permanent."

"A pity. For him." Aunt Jane pushed her empty plate away. "Not that I am surprised to hear of it. The earl always was a horse's arse."

Eleanor grimaced and Aunt Jane continued. "If you want to talk about what happened, I shall listen and give my opinion and advice."

"Forgive me, I . . . I . . . cannot as of yet."

"That is perfectly fine," Aunt Jane replied soothingly. "Thanks to the foresight of my mother, I am a woman of independent means. Since you are no longer under the earl's protection, you may make your home with me for as long as you wish."

Eleanor sagged visibly with relief. "I don't want to impose. If you do not employ one, perhaps you would consider me for the position of companion?"

Aunt Jane squinted harshly. "You are the daughter of an earl, Eleanor, a lady born and bred. Do not seek to lower your position by demeaning yourself with work."

"I am not used to being idle, Aunt. I will concede to your wishes, but I am determined to make myself useful to you."

Aunt Jane's features softened. "I am so glad you have come to me, Eleanor. For reasons he never explained, the earl deliberately kept you and your sister from me. I always wanted a closer relationship with the two of you, and regret mightily that I did not push harder to achieve it.

"Alas, women have little power in this world of men. We must not squander it, but use it wisely. Though I am sad for the circumstances, I am delighted to have the chance to help. Your letters have been much appreciated over the years, especially since I have no other family."

Eleanor cleared her throat. "I am more grateful than I can say, Aunt Jane. Without you, I truly do not know where I would have gone, what would have become of me."

Though she fought to keep herself composed, Eleanor's voice quavered on her final words.

"Chin up, Eleanor," Aunt Jane commanded. "'Tis far too early in the day to be so maudlin. Now, if you are finished pushing the food around on that plate, I'd like to show you the rest of *our* home."

Eleanor's throat tightened. She felt the tears burning behind her eyes and could not quiet the sob that escaped. Aunt Jane's expression remained calm, though her eyes became noticeably shiny. "Go on, dear girl. Have a good, hard cry. Then dry your eyes, hold up your head, and consign those who have put you through such misery to the devil."

Over the next two weeks, Eleanor's days took on a strange, routine pattern. Breakfast with Aunt Jane, accompanied by a lively discussion of the events reported in the newspaper. The remainder of the morning was devoted to correspondence, though Eleanor had only Bianca to write to and no reply was received. The lack of communication distressed Eleanor greatly, yet she was not surprised, for there was a strong possibility her letters were being intercepted by the earl.

Once their correspondence was attended to, Eleanor usually read or embroidered while Aunt Jane handled the household matters. After a light luncheon, there were calls to make, shops to visit, and weather permitting, a brisk walk in the park.

Evenings were occupied with supper parties, card parties, concerts, and the occasional assembly. Thanks to Aunt Jane's influence, Eleanor was easily accepted into the small circle of Bath society and if there was speculation as to her sudden appearance it was never repeated within Eleanor's hearing.

It was not the frantic pace of London during the Season, but there was plenty to do if one was of a mind to keep busy. The majority of Aunt Jane's friends and acquaintances were advanced in years, but Eleanor also met people nearer to her own age. She was always polite and distant among company, and unfailingly grateful she encountered no one she had previously met in London society.

It was the simple, uncomplicated life of a genteel noblewoman, confining in some ways, yet because they were a female household, 'twas liberating in others. Eleanor repeatedly told herself she would eventually adjust and come to accept that with the exception of a few variations, this was more than likely how the rest of her life would play out.

Considering all that had happened, Eleanor knew she was a very fortunate woman. Even if she didn't always feel like one.

Losing contact with Bianca was the worst part of her banishment. She missed her sister constantly and worried what the earl might have told his younger daughter about Eleanor's abrupt departure from Town. She was also very aware that Bianca's wedding was scheduled to take place in a few short weeks. When she expressed her concern to Aunt Jane, the older woman concurred with the need for caution, since Bianca still lived under the earl's protection and was subject to his whims.

Once Bianca was married, however, it should be much easier to reestablish a connection. As for the wedding, well, Aunt Jane decreed they would attend, invited or not.

Two weeks to the day that she arrived, Eleanor sat in the drawing room, a book in hand, while Aunt Jane reviewed the weekly menus. The quiet was soothing, the atmosphere pleasant. Like most older people, Aunt Jane was rather set in her ways, but Eleanor found they got along very well together.

Aunt Jane never questioned her when she appeared at the breakfast table listless and red-eyed after a difficult night, never pushed her to participate in social events if she asked to stay behind. Eleanor was more grateful than she could say for the kindness and understanding she had been shown. Without it, she feared she might have lost her sanity.

"There is a gentleman at the door, Madame," the butler announced as he shuffled into the drawing room, then held out the visitor's card on a silver tray.

"At this hour of the day? 'Tis far too early to be paying calls." Aunt Jane reached for the ever-present lorgnette dangling around her neck, lifted it to her eyes, and peered at the card. "Are you certain the gentleman asked for me, not Lady Eleanor?"

"He asked to see you, Madame," the butler confirmed.

Eleanor glanced up from her book and frowned. Aunt Jane's butler was an elderly man, with fading eyesight and rheumatic knees. His stiffness came from his physical limitations rather than his proper attitude. He was long past the age to be pensioned off, yet insisted working gave him purpose and thus Aunt Jane kept him on staff.

"Clearly the gentleman has come to the wrong establishment," Aunt Jane bristled. "I am not acquainted with him, nor any of his people."

A tingle of concern spread through Eleanor's fingers. "What is the gentleman's name, Aunt?"

Aunt Jane wrinkled her nose and peered again at the card. "Viscount Benton."

Eleanor's book fell to the carpet. She believed she had progressed beyond the sharp, stabbing feeling of pain, but knowing he was here, standing outside the door, brought it all to the surface, brutal and real.

The butler looked over at Eleanor, then back at Aunt Jane. "Shall I tell him that you are not at home?"

"Eleanor?"

"Send him away," she croaked, her stomach tied in a knot.

The butler bowed and shuffled off. Eleanor retrieved her book from the floor and settled it in her lap. Her heart was pounding with nervous dread, her mind racing. *Why is he here? What does he want?*

It didn't matter. There was nothing between them except deception and betrayal. She had no interest in seeing him again, no intention of listening to any more of his lies.

A few minutes later there was a gentle tapping on the drawing room door and the butler reentered. "Please forgive this second interruption, but the viscount has informed me in no uncertain terms that he will not leave the premises until he has spoken directly with you."

"Of all the nerve!" Aunt Jane rose to her feet.

"Call for Harry and George and instruct them to forcibly remove this man at once."

"Wait!" Eleanor cried. As much as she would love to see Sebastian tossed out on his ear, she knew her aunt's elderly servants were no physical match for him. "As you have no doubt realized by now, I am acquainted with the viscount. All things considered, I think 'tis best if we agree to see him. There's no telling what he might do if we continue to refuse."

"I will bow to your superior knowledge on the subject," Aunt Jane said. "Though I don't have to like it."

A few minutes later the butler returned, followed into the room by an imposing, familiar form. Eleanor just stared. He was far more somber than she remembered, no flashing smile, no twinkling charm. He was still as handsome and finely groomed, a noble specimen indeed, yet he looked different, changed in some way she couldn't articulate. Or maybe she was finally seeing him with clear eyes.

"Viscount Benton," the butler sniffed, revealing his annoyance.

"Ladies." Sebastian bowed.

"I have allowed you admittance because my niece thought it the only way to get rid of you," Aunt Jane announced, going on the attack before the viscount had a chance to rise from his bow. "But I do not like it. Not one bit. And I do not appreciate being threatened in my own home, my lord. One would think a peer of the realm possessed better manners."

"I regret that my high-handed methods have

caused you distress, ma'am," he answered. "Yet I was fully aware that Lady Eleanor would not receive me unless I insisted. My only other recourse would be to meet her in a public setting and I feared that might cause her greater distress."

"Don't try to paint yourself in an admirable light, sir," Eleanor said flatly. "We both know you never consider my feelings when plotting your actions."

She tilted her chin. For an instant their eyes locked and Eleanor swore it felt as though her heart stopped beating.

"Eleanor, please," he implored. "We need to talk."

"I have nothing to say to you."

Something flashed in his eyes and for the first time she realized he was nearly as agitated as she felt. "Then listen instead," he said.

"I don't know if I can," she whispered.

"Ten minutes," he begged.

Ten minutes! It seemed a lifetime. Could she manage? Could she be in his company for that long without breaking down, without completely losing her composure, her self-respect?

"Ten, and not a minute more," she agreed, refusing to meet his gaze. "Aunt, would you mind giving us some privacy?"

Aunt Jane's shoulders went rigid. "I will wait directly outside the drawing room doors. Along with several of my sturdiest footmen. A single shout will bring us inside in seconds."

As her aunt departed, Eleanor took a steadying breath, fighting to compose herself. Ten minutes. All she had to endure was ten minutes and Sebastian would be gone from her life forever. Then perhaps she would finally be able to put this nightmare behind her.

I shouldn't have come, yet how could I not?

When entering the drawing room, Sebastian had addressed the elderly aunt, but his eyes had gone instantly to Eleanor, seated on a sofa near the window. She looked prettier than he remembered, her skin porcelain smooth, her hair pinned with soft curls that shimmered in the morning sunlight.

She was so lovely, so delicate and forlorn, it almost hurt to look at her. Knowing she would not be happy to see him, he expected resentment, anger, hostility. He might have even done as she asked and walked away, if not for the glint of tears in her eyes.

The sight of them had shaken him, had squeezed something deep inside his chest, confirming in his heart what he feared to be true, yet had difficulty accepting.

It was going to be nigh impossible to bridge the wide and deep chasm that existed between them.

Still, he was determined to try.

"I have brought you a letter from Bianca," he said, reaching inside his breast coat pocket.

Eleanor extended her hand eagerly for the missive. "Does she know what has happened? What has the earl told her?"

Sebastian sat on the edge of the sofa, careful not to move too close. "Apparently your father has said nothing. I spoke with Waverly the moment I returned to London, reasoning he was the only way

I'd be able to get word to Bianca. She was quite beside herself when she discovered you were gone."

A line of worry furrowed Eleanor's brow. "I wrote immediately to allay her fears. The earl must be intercepting my letters."

"I believe that to be the case."

Her shoulders stiffened and she glanced away. "What did you say to Waverly? How did you explain it all?"

"I gave him no details, merely told him that it was my fault you were estranged from the earl and that you had gone to stay with your great-aunt in Bath until the dust settled."

A blush of pink shaded her cheeks. "Then they do not know the truth?"

"No one does. There has not been a breath of scandal attached to your name, or mine, for that matter. Your reputation has been saved, Eleanor."

"Ah, so I can go back to the way everything was before all of this happened?" Her gaze pierced his. "You will forgive me, sir, if I cannot bring myself to thank you for saving me from that final humiliation."

Her flat, detached tone struck him like a whip. He had caused it, along with the haggard look in her eyes, the deep pain on her face.

I'm sorry. The words stuck in his throat. Saying them felt like even more of an insult. She would never believe him anyway. He had lost the right to offer his compassion when he betrayed her.

He wanted to say something that would make everything all right, whisper words that would adequately explain, words that she could understand and accept. Words that would soothe and comfort.

Yet no words existed.

"There is something else I'd like you to read." He held out another piece of parchment. She gazed at it suspiciously, then tentatively pulled it from his grasp.

"What is it?"

"An announcement of our upcoming wedding. I will have it printed in the *Times* the moment you agree."

"To marry you?"

Her incredulous tone stung more than he wanted to admit. He knew that at one time she had harbored deep feelings of regard for him, perhaps even fancied herself in love with him. Apparently all that she felt for him now was loathing and disgust.

"Marriage is the sensible course for both of us and the only way I can possibly make amends to you."

She sucked in an astonished breath and he braced for the insults as she refused him. Instead, she pressed the back of her hand to her mouth, looking as if she might be ill. It was no more than he deserved. Yet so much worse than he ever imagined.

He heard her exhale slowly. A pronounced silence settled between them.

"It appears you believe I have not suffered enough, have not been punished enough for my father's sins," she finally said. "Or else your mind is still so consumed by your need for revenge that it has finally snapped."

He crossed his arms over his chest. "Though I know you have no cause to believe me, I make this offer in good faith. I am not as wealthy as some, but

I have a comfortable living. I will settle a generous allowance on you. As my wife you will have financial security, social position, and the freedom to do what you want."

Her eyes widened and he knew she realized he was being serious. "A wife is subject to her husband's will. There is no freedom in that kind of arrangement."

"Legal documents can be drawn up with your specifications to give you whatever rights you require. In addition to Chaswick Manor, I have a much smaller holding on the coast. We can visit the property before we marry, and if you like it, you may use it to set up your household."

Her face grew calm and even, lacking in all expression. "We wouldn't live together?"

He gave a sharp nod. "I want to live with you, to be your husband in every way, but I know it will take time before you are ready to accept it. I will wait. Our relationship will be as you dictate. Many aristocratic couples spend time apart. It would not seem so unusual if we start our marriage that way."

"You are proposing a marriage of convenience? One in which you would continue living your life basically as it is now?"

"There will be significant changes for me." Sebastian shifted uncomfortably on his seat. "I believe fully in the sanctity of the marriage vows, which is one reason why I have not taken a wife. If we marry, I will remain faithful to you."

He saw the glint of disbelief in her eyes and could not fault it. He was actually finding it an amazing promise himself, but one he was bound and determined to keep. If she would have him as her husband.

"You are not the sort of man who can remain celibate for the rest of your life," she said.

"True. That is why after we marry I reserve the right to try to persuade you into my bed, into my life." He felt a ray of hope as her pale cheeks suddenly flamed with color. "Whatever else has gone on between us, you cannot deny that we have a great passion for each other. It can offer us a beginning, a place to start."

She shook her head slowly. "You only pursued me to strike at the earl."

"My initial motive was revenge, but the feelings that I developed for you were very real, very true. My actions were immoral, unforgivably wrong, but my affection was never false, my desire never feigned. I cared deeply for you, Eleanor. I still do."

She gave him a long, impenetrable stare. "You cared for me to such an extent that you lied, manipulated, and preyed on my gullibility to get what you wanted?"

He cringed. She was right, of course. His actions had been reprehensible, but they did not negate the feelings he had for her. He struggled for a way to explain it, to make her understand, but it was all so jumbled in his heart and mind he could not find the words.

Sebastian drew in a measured breath. "Will you at least consider it?"

"I cannot. There is more, much more, to marriage than passion. Friendship, companionship, respect, trust. Things we cannot possibly hope to share. Perhaps you are being honest, perhaps you do have some feelings for me, but it doesn't matter. It's too late. Our relationship has been too severely damaged. 'Tis beyond repair." The disillusionment shimmered in her face. "Besides, you hate my father."

"So do you."

"That I shall not deny, but his blood runs through my veins. If we marry I firmly believe that one day you will come to resent that fact. And then . . . and then, oh, Lord, we shall truly be stuck in hell together."

"Eleanor, please, my feelings—"

"If you feel anything for me at all, 'tis obsession," she said angrily. "I am an extension of the earl. You cannot strike at him, so you will strike at me."

The shock reverberated through him. Was that truly what she believed? That he had no affection or regard for her, that he was that callous and cruel? "Oh God, Eleanor, what have I done?"

"You have broken me, my lord." She rose, tears glistening in her eyes. "But never fear, I will mend. Please go now. Your ten minutes are up."

Caught in a tangled web of disappointment and regret, Sebastian cast one final imploring look at her. "Take some time and think about what I have proposed," he pleaded. "If you change your mind, send word to me and I will come at once."

"I won't change my mind."

She meant it. He muttered an oath as something shifted inside his chest. He had hoped her capacity for forgiveness would extend far enough to give their future a chance, but he saw that he had wounded her too deeply. The kindest thing he could do now was leave her in peace.

In despair, Sebastian bowed, turned on his heel, and left. And as he walked slowly out into the late morning sunshine, he remembered why he had never wanted to care so completely for a woman.

It hurt too damn much.

Chapter 17

Sebastian returned to London, going directly to the elegant townhome he inherited from his grandmother. Once there he proceeded to get himself drunk. Utterly foxed, three sheets to the wind, completely in his cups. Miraculously, he was able to stay upright for two days and two nights, until finally on the morning of the third day he succumbed to the cumulative effects of too much brandy and too little food and passed out.

He awoke almost twenty-four hours later to a pounding in his head that nearly rendered him blind, wincing repeatedly as he opened his unfocused eyes. The pain certainly rendered him senseless, for as he glanced about the well-appointed room, with its gold silk draperies and rosewood furniture, he had no idea where he was sitting. Or rather lying, since he was stretched out on a gold damask sofa, the mud on his boots marring the lovely fabric, creating stains that no amount of washing would remove.

His mouth was dry, his tongue swollen, his limbs

cramped and aching. Scrubbing a hand through his tousled hair, Sebastian tried to piece together the events of the past few days, but the effort brought a heavy pounding inside his brain that would not cease. It took several minutes for him to realize the noise was actually someone knocking on the door.

"Enter!" he bellowed, the shout causing additional discomfort to his head, as well as his stomach.

Sebastian sat up gingerly, rubbing his temples, waiting for the room to cease its spinning. A servant walked in, then came to an abrupt halt as he surveyed the scene. Four empty crystal goblets and as many empty decanters were strewn on the floor, along with several pieces of Sebastian's clothing.

"I do beg your pardon for the interruption, my lord," the servant said in an overly loud voice. "You have a caller. A female caller."

Eleanor? The instant joy inside Sebastian died a swift, painful death as the memories of his visit to Bath swept through him. Eleanor hated him. She would not be calling here. Ever. Wherever the hell here was.

"Who are you?" Sebastian blurted out, squinting at the servant.

For a moment the man stared at him blankly. "I am Bennington, my lord. Butler to the late Countess of Marchdale. Your grandmother."

Sebastian eyed the room with a frown of concentration, finally recognizing his surroundings. Yes, that was right, he had decided on his way back to London that he needed to put the estrangement with Eleanor behind him; he needed to move forward with his life. And the first order of business was going to be taking charge of his grandmother's estate. As he took inventory of the drawing room, Sebastian decided that plan had apparently gotten off to a very poor start.

A chair was overturned, a painting removed from the wall and set to rest against the fireplace, which was unlit, and the ormolu clock had ceased ticking, due to the fact that its gilded arms had been broken off. They were standing upright in an antique vase looking for all the world like two barren stems of gold. Had he done all this? Sebastian wondered. He must have, yet he certainly didn't recall any of it.

"I require coffee, Bennington," Sebastian said hoarsely. "Pots and pots of strong, hot, black coffee."

"Only coffee, my lord?"

Sebastian's stomach dipped at the thought of food, the nausea rising to his throat. "Just coffee."

"And your caller?"

Sebastian hesitated a moment before reaching for the card on the butler's silver tray. *Miss Emma Ellingham.*

Emma. Dearest Emma. "Show her in at once. 'Tis never a good idea to keep a lady waiting, Bennington."

"Do you think that wise, my lord?" the butler asked, staring pointedly down at him.

Sebastian followed the servant's gaze, taking inventory of his own appearance. His jacket and cravat lay discarded on the carpet, his waistcoat hung open, and his shirt was unbuttoned halfway down his chest. A tentative touch of his jaw revealed a rough, heavy beard. "I'm not fit company for a lady, am I?"

"You need a bath, my lord. A shave, a fresh change of clothes, and a hearty meal."

"And coffee," Sebastian insisted, clutching his temples with the thumb and middle finger of his right hand.

"Very good, my lord. I shall tell the lady to call another day."

"No, wait. Tell her to return in an hour." Sebastian hauled himself to his feet, swaying slightly, his stomach lurching. "Two hours."

Bennington looked none too pleased at the order, but being a properly trained butler, he knew better than to question his employer. Making no attempt to tuck in his shirt or straighten his clothing, Sebastian took a few steps toward the door, trying to decide if he wanted his bath steaming hot to comfort his body aches, or icy cold to soothe his pounding head. Perhaps he could sit in a hot tub while plunging his head into a cold basin?

Weaving noticeably, Sebastian lifted a hand to grip the edge of the sofa. But the room continued to spin and he knew there was no help for it.

"My lord?" Bennington asked. "You don't look well. May I be of some assistance?"

"Stand clear," Sebastian growled, moving as fast as his feet would carry him to the other side of the room. He managed to grab the vase with the clock hands inside just as his stomach started heaving. With a disapproving Bennington as an audience to his humiliation, Sebastian cast up his accounts, though it was mostly liquid in his stomach that needed to be expelled.

"I shall tell the lady to return in *three* hours," Bennington pronounced, and then he departed.

Sebastian had neither the strength nor the nerve to challenge him.

Emma was waiting when Sebastian appeared in the morning room three hours later. A lovely smile broke out on her pretty face and she came to him swiftly, catching him in a tight embrace. "I didn't think I'd ever get past the gargoyles you have guarding the door. If I didn't know you better, I'd worry that you were avoiding me."

"Never," he proclaimed, hugging her tighter, reveling in the feel of her delicate form. She carried the scents of freshness and lemons in her hair, combined with a slight undertone of paint. Comforting, familiar smells. "I've just been busy, that's all."

"With your brandy."

He turned quickly, wincing as the pain shot through his head. "How did you know? Do I look that hung over?"

Reaching out, she caught hold of his hand. "Servants talk, Sebastian. I know you've been keeping company with your brandy decanters these past few days."

"It did take a fair number of them to achieve a suitable state of numbness," he admitted.

Emma's delicate brows drew together in a sharp arch. "Why was that necessary?"

"I couldn't possibly explain." Her face crumpled. He looked guiltily away, then back. "'Tis just silly male posturing."

Emma squeezed his hand. "You can tell me anything, Sebastian," she said calmly. "I'll never judge you. I'll never gossip about you. Or Lady Eleanor."

Sebastian eyed Emma anxiously. He thought he had been so careful. "What have you heard?"

"About Lady Eleanor? Nothing much. She was hardly noticed in society when she did appear, but my sister considered her a friendly acquaintance and has taken note of her absence. Dorothea went to call upon Lady Eleanor and was turned away without explanation. Naturally that gives cause for speculation over her sudden disappearance."

"She hasn't disappeared. She's gone to Bath, to assist an elderly aunt."

"How do you know?"

"I met Waverly at the club last week," Sebastian answered readily. "He told me." Though hazy, his brain, or at least part of it, was still functioning. Along with the strong need to protect Eleanor.

He saw the doubt creep into Emma's eyes and braced himself, uncertain what he would say if she pressed the matter.

"I hope you intend to move permanently into this house," Emma said. "I should very much like having you a few doors away, so I can visit at all hours of the day."

Sebastian appreciatively seized the new topic of conversation. They discussed the neighborhood, and a few of the neighbors, then spoke of Emma's sisters and their families. She told him a funny story about her brother-in-law Jason Barrington, then related a naughty tale about her sister Dorothea.

Yet although she was lighthearted and smiling, Sebastian sensed something was amiss with Emma. There was a slight hesitation before she spoke, an edge of nerves in her gestures, a restless quality to her conversation.

Tea was brought. Emma served, but both of their

cups remained full, the lovely cakes and sandwiches untouched.

"I can stand the suspense no longer, Sebastian," Emma said, rattling her teacup as she set it down. "What do you think of your portrait? Do you like it?"

Sebastian frowned, remembering the portrait his grandmother had commissioned from Emma just before she died. The portrait he had not yet seen.

"Let's view it together." He rose and held out his hand. Emma clasped it firmly, though he thought he felt a slight trembling.

Hand in hand they walked into the long gallery. Since this was not an ancestral home, landscapes and other scenes were intermingled among the portraits, Sebastian's favorite being a pair of spaniels from the era of Charles II. The dogs were perched beside a flowering hyacinth bush, their soulful brown eyes eager and happy.

They drew to a halt when they reached his portrait. Emma squeezed his hand tightly, then let go, taking a step back. Sebastian smiled inwardly at her artist's nerves and gazed upward at the painting.

Uneasiness stirred within him. He must still be suffering the effects of too much brandy, he reasoned. Or mayhap it was the bright sunshine that put the glow in the portrait?

Sebastian was not a vain man. He knew he was handsome, knew that women found him attractive. He also knew that the portrait Emma had created was beyond flattering. She had hidden every one of his flaws and in turn accentuated each of his attractive features, rendering him a vision of male perfection.

His eyes were not that dark or piercing, his

shoulders not half as broad, his jaw not nearly as firm. This was a portrait of an Adonis, a godlike man with no faults, no weaknesses. The artist had taken more than license with her subject, she had infused her emotions on the canvas.

Deep, heartfelt emotions. For him.

"I must tell Atwood he needs to buy you a good pair of spectacles," Sebastian said with difficulty, trying to absorb the impossibility of it all. Emma could *not* be in love with him.

"Glasses would make no difference," she joked, catching his eye, but there was no humor in her expression. "This is how I see you, Sebastian."

"Oh, Emma," he said in a strangled whisper.

Her spine stiffened. "Is it really so awful?"

"The portrait?"

"No. My love for you."

Bloody hell, she had gone and said it. Though in truth there was no hiding it, not after viewing the portrait. Her love was there for anyone to see, contained boldly within each brushstroke. How could he have been so careless? How could he have not known?

"You are far too young to be talking of love," he chided gently.

"I'm not a child, Sebastian," she replied with stilted dignity.

"You're not a woman either."

"Nearly," she said defiantly.

"Hardly," he insisted.

His comment was met with silence.

He reached out with extreme gentleness, his fingers caressing her damp cheek. "Oh, Emma, you must not cry. I'm not worth it."

Her lips trembled and she gave a brief shake of her head. "You are worth anything, everything to me, Sebastian. Don't you know it?"

Sebastian closed his eyes. Her feelings were real and genuine. 'Twould be beyond cruel to make light of them. "I love you too, Emma, but not in a romantic way. You are the sister I never had, the companion who is kind and funny and makes me laugh, who tells me the truth when I need to hear it, who accepts me for the fool I often am.

"You are so precious to me. The idea of hurting you makes me ill, yet I cannot perpetuate false hope. There will never be anything between us of a romantic nature."

"You don't mean it."

"I'm afraid that I do. In a few years' time, when you are older and ready for it, I know you are going to meet—"

"Don't!" she screeched, fierce anger flashing in her eyes. "Don't insult me with platitudes and meaningless drivel. I deserve better."

He felt like a monster. Her unhappiness and pain were eating him alive, yet the facts were unchangeable. What she wanted so desperately could never happen. "You're right. Those words are meant to make me feel better, not you. I'm sorry."

Reaching out, he enfolded her in his arms. She stiffened. Using the lightest of touches, he stroked her shoulder in what he hoped was a comforting, brotherly manner. They stayed that way for several minutes, the tension starting to escalate.

"I think I am going to hate you for a long time, Sebastian," she whispered, tears choking her voice.

He sighed. "I know, sweetheart. I will miss you more than I can ever say."

Wrenching free of him, Emma picked up her skirts and ran down the hallway, her sobs intermingled with the sounds of her rapid footsteps. His initial instinct was to chase after her, but he surmised that would only prolong her pain.

Hellfire and damnation, could this week get any worse?

Cursing again loudly, Sebastian slowly walked from the gallery, wondering how it could be that after all these years of chasing and bedding a variety of women, he knew next to nothing about the female mind and heart.

"I now pronounce you man and wife. What God hath joined together, let no man put asunder." The vicar smiled. "You may kiss your bride, milord."

There was a titter of laughter, then a rousing round of applause as Lord Waverly dipped his head and did precisely as the vicar suggested. Bianca's hands rested on her new husband's shoulders and he deepened the kiss, their mouths clinging together. Some of the young bucks crowding the family chapel started whistling and the couple broke apart.

Bianca looked angelic as her face reddened with embarrassment. Dressed in pale yellow, with her hair swept upward in soft waves and a matching yellow veil on her bonnet, she was the picture of a happy bride.

Handsome and elegant in his wedding finery, Lord Waverly was an impressive groom, sporting a telltale flush beneath his cheeks. Apparently the kiss had affected him too.

The chapel on Lord Waverly's estate was small, yet beautifully appointed, with gray stone walls, stained glass windows, and brass chandeliers. Colorful bouquets of spring flowers tied with white bows had been stuffed into every conceivable space and the glow of candlelight lent a romantic air to the ceremony.

Seated beside Aunt Jane in the second row, Eleanor's eyes shone with tears of happiness. At least something good had come of this disastrous London Season. Bianca was safely married to a man she loved, a peer who seemed to hold her in equal regard. Eleanor folded her hands and said a quick prayer, hoping they would have a long, happy life together.

Amid cheers and congratulations, the newly married couple walked down the aisle, the church bells pealing joyfully. Once outside, they climbed into an open carriage, its sides decorated with white bridal ribbons, flowers, and tulle. A crowd of well-wishers from Lord Waverly's estate, as well as residents of the local village, gathered to catch a glimpse of the bride and groom. To the delight of all, Lord Waverly stood, kissed his wife's hand, then tossed several fistfuls of coins into the air.

Shrieking and laughing, the children scrambled to fill their pockets with the bounty. The carriage pulled away, slowly making its way through the crowd. The congregation spilled out of the chapel and the invited guests strolled toward the manor house. Bianca glowed as she greeted everyone who passed through the receiving line, the smile never leaving her mouth or her eyes.

When it was her turn, Eleanor clutched her sister

tightly, then dutifully admired the diamond and sapphire wedding band gracing Bianca's finger. "We are going on an extended wedding trip through Europe," Bianca confided in an excited tone. "Italy, France, even Russia. But once we return you must come for a long visit."

"It would be my pleasure," Eleanor replied honestly. She had missed Bianca dreadfully these last few weeks and hoped being in her sister's company would help ease the dull pain that had become her constant companion.

Crystal flutes of chilled champagne were served and the guests took their seats for the elaborate wedding breakfast. They dined on ham and lobster patties, thin slices of beef, boiled quail eggs, flaky pastries with sweet almond cream, and hothouse strawberries.

There were toasts to the health and happiness of the newlyweds along with salutes to their good fortune at finding each other. As the champagne continued to flow and the rounds of toasting progressed, a few rowdy suggestions were made to the groom concerning the wedding night. Those remarks were met with raucous laughter and Eleanor was pleased to see Lord Waverly take it all in good-natured stride.

As breakfast wore on, Eleanor found herself in need of some fresh air. After informing Aunt Jane, Eleanor slipped away unnoticed, finding her way outside to a private terrace. Standing near the railing, she gazed out at the vast expanse of lawn and neatly clipped formal gardens, musing over the fact that Bianca was now mistress of this lovely estate, her future secure.

What of my future?

The question was unwelcome, an unfortunate reminder of the empty years that stretched before her. She knew she had been right to refuse Sebastian's marriage proposal, had been right to turn him away.

But here she was weeks later, still struggling to come to terms with her feelings of love for him. It seemed a ridiculous, idiotic emotion given how much he had hurt her, yet there it was, an ever-present reminder of what her life might have been.

She was in love with Sebastian and would no doubt feel that way for the rest of her life. A fine future, indeed.

The sound of footsteps broke into her brooding reflections. Eleanor turned, her eyes resting on a group of wedding guests gathering at the French doors on their way out to the terrace. She blinked in the sunlight, hoping she was mistaken, then realized she was right. Among their numbers was the Earl of Hetfield.

With careful diligence, she had avoided her father all day. Eleanor felt her shoulders sink in an attempt to melt into the background, but then her pride came to the forefront. There was no reason for her to feel so ashamed. The debacle with Sebastian had not been her fault. She had been a victim and as such deserved sympathy, not censure.

The sound of voices grew louder as the French doors opened. Eleanor's mouth went dry and her heart labored with heavy, slow thumps. She didn't want to see him or speak with him. Still, he was her father. There was no need to make a scene, no reason that they could not be civil to each other for a few minutes. This was, after all, Bianca's wedding day.

She approached him cautiously, her head high. The earl's gaze connected with hers and she saw a flash of recognition in his hard eyes. Then a shutter fell over his face and he turned his head very deliberately away from her. He continued moving forward, walking past her, acting as though she did not exist.

The cut direct. At first Eleanor stood motionless, too stunned to react. She had underestimated him. His cruelty ran deeper than she ever imagined, his anger at her behavior obviously unforgivable. Heat scored her cheeks. She was aware that the other members of his party must have seen his action, were no doubt wondering why the earl had deliberately shunned his eldest daughter.

A wave of mortification rolled over Eleanor and she admitted she had underestimated herself too. She believed she was free of the need for parental approval, parental support, especially given the fact that the earl had always been indifferent toward her, or at times outwardly disapproving.

All would not have been forgiven, or forgotten, had he acknowledged her, but it might have been a start. Instead he had chosen to publicly abandon her, destroying any chance of reconciliation.

She averted her eyes from the others in the group, then felt one of them move to her side.

"Was that your father?" Aunt Jane asked with protective concern.

"No, Aunt Jane, that was a stranger."

* * *

The return to Bath had all the earmarks of a homecoming. The servants smiled and bid Eleanor welcome, the close-knit society embraced her with eagerness and inclusion. Her bedchamber felt familiar and comfortable, affording a sense of security that any single woman forced out into the world on her own would appreciate.

Aunt Jane continued to be Eleanor's salvation, understanding and supportive, and she thanked God every day for placing the older woman in her life. Letters arrived from Bianca, cheerful missives detailing all the amazing places she and Waverly were visiting, the wondrous sights they had seen.

Life was pleasant, if a bit dull. As for the loneliness, well, Eleanor hoped it would lessen over time. Or that she would learn to manage it better.

Unfortunately, her tumultuous emotions began manifesting themselves physically. Initially there were slight changes to Eleanor's body, that gradually became more noticeable.

Her breasts were slightly swollen and tender at the slightest touch. There were afternoons when weariness overcame her so completely she needed to close her eyes for a short nap. At different times of the day her stomach would suddenly feel queasy and the smell of certain foods made her nauseous.

To combat this change Eleanor curtailed her evening activities, going to bed earlier each night and sleeping later each morning. She tried to eat a more sensible diet of plain food, eliminated all sweets, ate as many fresh vegetables as possible, drank no wine. Yet the symptoms persisted.

She did her best to hide the malaise from Aunt Jane, convinced she would feel better soon, hoping that time and the passing of the warm summer weather would return her to normal.

Then one morning while sitting in the drawing room, Eleanor rose from her chair and nearly fainted. The dizziness overtook her so quickly she needed to grab onto the chair back to keep herself from keeling over.

"I'm summoning a physician," Aunt Jane declared, her gray brows drawn tight with concern.

"Oh, Aunt Jane, I hardly think that is necessary," Eleanor protested. "'Tis just a bit of vertigo, nothing more."

But Aunt Jane would not be persuaded and Eleanor soon found herself lying upon her bed and being examined by a local doctor. He was a stern-faced, middle-age gentleman who kept his expression neutral each time she answered his embarrassing personal questions.

Eleanor had little experience with doctors, having been blessed with a healthy constitution as both a child and an adult. That, coupled with the doctor's unfathomable expression, made it impossible for her to determine if this was a serious situation or was, as she hoped, a result of her recent heartache.

To make matters worse, once the examination was completed, the doctor gathered his medical instruments, repacked them in his bag, and left without saying a word. Eleanor's imagination ran wild with concern, heightening considerably when Aunt Jane appeared at her bedside, her face somber.

"Has the doctor gone?" Eleanor asked, panic

rising. "He never said what he thought could be wrong. Tell me, Aunt Jane, is it very serious?"

"Given the circumstances he thought it best if I speak with you." Aunt Jane sat on the bed and took her hand. "It appears, Eleanor, that sometime early next year you are going to have a baby."

Chapter 18

Sebastian glanced ruefully down the dusty, deserted lane and wondered if his decision to press ahead had been the right one. For the past two hours he had seen no signs of life except for the occasional bird soaring through the sky or rabbit bounding through an open meadow. The lack of civilization in the area surprised him. He had thought by now he would have happened upon a farm or a cottage or some dwelling where the inhabitants could offer him assistance.

With a sigh he glanced up at the bright autumnal sky, trying to determine the time of day. In his haste to leave the posting inn this morning he had neglected to wind his watch and was forced to rely on the sun.

A smile tugged at Sebastian's lips as he surveyed a few puffy white clouds. He could no more determine the time by observing the sun's position than he could predict the weather. All he knew with certainty was that it was daytime and despite the crisp fall air he was warm. And thirsty.

No matter. He would continue walking his horse until he found help. A measured, logical reaction to the dilemma, something that would have no doubt eluded him a few months ago.

Failing to enact his revenge against the Earl of Hetfield and his subsequent betrayal of Eleanor had forced Sebastian to take stock of his life. And he had not liked what he saw. Change, he decided, was essential and to that end he at long last embraced the responsibilities of a peer of the realm.

The last few months had altered him. He no longer kept late hours, rarely gambled, drank nothing more potent than a glass of wine with supper. For the first time in his life he took a marked interest in his lands and the workings of his estates. He attended the session at the House of Lords with punctual regularity and was considering sponsorship of a bill demanding higher pensions for veterans of the Napoleonic wars. He even spoke of marriage, though his heart ached when he contemplated spending the rest of his life with a woman other than Eleanor.

His closest friends, Atwood and Dawson, joked that they hardly recognized him, and Sebastian had to agree. Hell, he barely recognized himself.

One of the most profound changes was something he never anticipated. His title. Thanks to the untimely demise of a distant cousin and the lack of male issue on that side of the family, Sebastian was now the Earl of Tinsdale. The title came with limited funds, but there was substantial land in the wilds of Yorkshire in the inheritance. Property that Sebastian was on his way to inspect. Until his horse came up lame.

A quick examination revealed a missing shoe on the animal's left rear leg. Figuring the last house he had ridden past was a good five miles behind him, Sebastian elected to press on ahead. He gathered the reins and began walking, the stallion following docilely behind. Without his added weight he hoped the horse could travel a good distance without sustaining a permanent injury.

The road curved to the right and Sebastian observed a large cat snoozing peacefully in a patch of sunshine on the top of a weathered stone gate. The sight buoyed his spirits. The feline was too hefty to be feral; therefore, the farm or cottage that supplied its meals must be near.

He passed through a copse of fairly dense trees. The setting reminded him of the walk he had taken with Eleanor at the Ashfields' garden party. Then again, nearly everything reminded him of Eleanor, and no matter how hard he tried he could not remove her from his mind. Or his heart.

He was a fool to have allowed his need for revenge to destroy their relationship. It had taken a few months, but Sebastian knew now that his grandmother had been right when she exacted that promise from him to forgo any acts of vengeance. Even if he had succeeded, it would not have changed the past. And worst of all, he still would have wounded Eleanor unjustly.

Countless times over the past few months he had reached for pen and paper, wanting to set things right between them. But he knew there was no way he could make up for the harm he had done Eleanor. At best he could hope that over time the memories of her would cease to haunt him.

As he climbed over the next hill he spied a sturdy two-story vine-covered cottage in the valley below, a puff of smoke curling from the chimney. Relieved that help was finally within reach, Sebastian quickened his pace.

A beefy man dressed in dusty workman's clothes greeted him with a friendly smile. "I can fetch the blacksmith from the village, sir," the man said after Sebastian explained his dilemma. "He'll have this stallion put to rights in no time."

"I appreciate your assistance," Sebastian replied. "As long as your employer doesn't object to you being taken away from your work."

"Mrs. Stewart won't mind helping out a gentleman in need," the servant responded confidently.

"Nevertheless, I insist you get permission first." Sebastian removed a small gold case from his inside breast coat pocket and extracted a calling card. "Give her this, please."

In no time at all the man returned. "Mrs. Stewart said she'd be pleased if you would take tea with her in the parlor while you wait."

After extracting a promise to be called before the blacksmith began his work, Sebastian complied. A maid-of-all-work met him at the front door, curtsying repeatedly when he crossed the threshold. Her wide-eyed stare and nervous demeanor demonstrated how rare it was for a titled individual to visit. He hoped Mrs. Stewart was not similarly awestruck. It would make waiting for his horse to be reshod rather vexing.

The interior of the cottage was of a modest size. It was tastefully furnished with a decidedly feminine hand, featuring floral prints, pastel colors, and delicate accent pieces. Some of the items were well-worn, while others appeared new. It was a prosperous household, with the appropriate trappings, the home of a gentleman.

He followed the servant to the parlor, but instead of announcing him the maid blushed, curtsied, and scurried away. Pausing before the open door, Sebastian scanned the interior, noting the presence of a lady near the window. Her back was toward him, but something about her seemed so familiar he felt a peculiar tingle slither down his spine.

He took a step forward, certain his eyes were playing tricks. He blinked several times. Had he been thinking of her so often and so hard that his brain conjured her likeness in another woman?

"Eleanor?"

At the sound of his voice, the woman turned. *Christ Almighty!* It was Eleanor, of that there could be no doubt. For a moment the two of them stared at each other blankly. Her face was pale, her eyes wide. Those beautiful eyes, intelligent and confident, now filled with surprise and something else. Fear? It wounded him to know she was afraid to meet him again.

She was wearing an amber-hued muslin gown, trimmed with brown silk ribbons. The high-waisted style emphasized her height and slender grace and when she moved, the folds of the muslin softly molded her figure. Sebastian blinked again.

Her shape was not at all as he remembered. Her breasts looked fuller, but it was her stomach that drew his attention. No longer flat, it now boasted a pronounced, protruding roundness. It took a moment before he realized what that meant.

"Bloody hell, you're pregnant," he said bluntly.

A panorama of emotions flickered across her features and then her hand reached down, covering her belly in a protective gesture. "I . . . uhm . . . well, yes, obviously I am increasing." Her cheeks flushed red and an awkward silence ensued.

She inhaled slowly and deeply, then sank down to the sofa. "What are you doing here?" She lifted the calling card she held in her hand. "The card Robert gave me says the *Earl of Tinsdale.*"

He felt his eyes narrow. "I recently inherited the title from a distant relation. I am on my way to Yorkshire to inspect the property and the manor house, which I was told had been badly neglected. My horse threw a shoe and I was forced to stop and ask for aid."

She looked at him in disbelief. "You came to be here purely by coincidence?" she asked.

"Apparently." He dragged his gaze from her troubled eyes, lowering it to her rounded midsection. "Or maybe it was fate."

Her breath hitched. For a moment she simply looked at him, as if she could not trust what she was seeing. "Damn fate," she muttered.

Sebastian's heart beat painfully in his chest. For months he had dreamed of seeing her again, of having a chance to seek forgiveness, to make amends. Now it was too late. She belonged to another man.

"Your husband must be very pleased about the child," Sebastian said. "Is he here? If you don't object, I would like the chance to meet him and offer my congratulations."

Her mouth dropped open. "My husband?"

"Mr. Stewart, isn't it? Your manservant referred to you as Mrs. Stewart."

For a moment she stared sightlessly across the room, her hands unmoving in her lap. Then she tilted her head and lifted her chin a touch higher. "There is no Mr. Stewart. There never has been," she said firmly, gazing at him with grim, sober resolve. "For obvious reasons I am claiming to be a widow."

The room suddenly felt airless. Sebastian stared at her rounded belly, emotion thickening his throat, astonishment and disbelief rippling over him. "What are you saying, Eleanor?"

The question hovered between them, crackling the air. "I'm roughly five months along," she finally answered. "The child will be born sometime next year, most likely in late February."

His body went still as he did the calculation, though it was hardly necessary. She had been a virgin when she came to his bed, and given her heartache when they parted, it was most unlikely she would have started a relationship with another man. The child was undoubtedly his.

Emotions, tumultuous and uneasy, churned in Sebastian's stomach. "Why didn't you send word to me?"

"I didn't think you would want to know."

His chest squeezed and he found himself unable to dispute her claim. His prior behavior toward her justified her thoughts, even if they were untrue. Sebastian crossed to the window on the opposite side of the room and looked out over the rolling hills to the horizon.

"I will purchase a special license in London and

return in a few days. We can be wed by the end of the week." Pronouncement delivered, he turned to see her reaction.

She rose, crossing her arms tightly beneath her breasts. "Goodness, after all this time you can still surprise me, Sebastian. I never thought you would offer marriage." She studied him for several long minutes. "I guess the long-dormant honor inside you occasionally escapes. Well, you have done your duty and offered to accept responsibility for the child. I suppose I should thank you for it, but frankly it is the least you can do."

He nodded, feeling duly chastised. "Where shall we marry? 'Twould be awkward to do so here, since everyone believes you are widowed. And very recently, given your condition."

"I never said I would marry you."

"But you must! You are carrying my child."

She turned her back to him. "Please, Sebastian, be reasonable. Our past makes marriage between us an impossibility."

"You have every right to despise me, Eleanor, but circumstances dictate change. We must marry for the sake of the child."

She shook her head slowly. "I have established myself as a respectable widow in this community and am slowly gaining acceptance. When the baby is born, it will not carry the sting of illegitimacy, nor will it suffer the cruelty of being a bastard. Aunt Jane is well situated financially and has been both kind and generous. The infant shall want for nothing."

"I want my child to have my name," Sebastian insisted stubbornly.

"I want my child to be raised in a household of love and respect," Eleanor countered.

He dragged in an unsteady breath. "You must do what is best for this baby. Luckily you have been able to pull off your little charade for now. But sooner or later someone will come along who knows the truth and then you will suffer for it. As will the child." Her face paled and he knew he had found her weakness. "The only solution is marriage. You know that, Eleanor."

She raised her eyes to the ceiling. "You have every right to be bitter about what the earl did to your mother, what he did to you. My baby is part of his bloodline. How will you look upon this child and not remember how much you despise the earl? How will you ever accept this innocent being into your life, into your heart?"

Conceding the point, Sebastian calmed his voice. "I admit it won't be easy, but that doesn't mean we should not try."

His child would be raised with all the advantages of wealth and privilege. Yet he could not guarantee his feelings, because he honestly didn't know if he could see beyond the fact that the earl was the child's grandfather. Eleanor started shaking her head and Sebastian's stomach knotted. He should have told her what she needed to hear, but he couldn't lie to her. Never again.

"I was raised by a man who disliked and neglected me," she said. "I will never allow my child to suffer a similar fate."

"While the earl is the very last person I would wish to be grandfather to my children, I can guarantee that I will never treat my offspring the way he has treated you," Sebastian countered hotly.

He saw the uncertainty in her eyes and it made him even more angry. If he couldn't convince her, then all would be lost. Unless he forced her into marriage. Could he do it? He knew her weakness, knew exactly what he could use as leverage.

"I can't marry you, Sebastian."

Her words crushed him. Knowing he now had no other choice, he moved closer, fixing his gaze intently on her eyes. "I suspect the warm reception you have received from the community will change abruptly when they discover you are not a widow, but instead an unwed mother-to-be."

"You wouldn't," she whispered, horrified.

"I wouldn't want to," he clarified. "That doesn't mean I would not do it. Please, don't force my hand, Eleanor."

Her breath came in shallow pants. Her stricken eyes cut into Sebastian's heart, but his options were few. Her reputation was the only bargaining chip he had and if forced, he would use it.

"You would label your child a bastard, to be shunned and ridiculed, forever burdened with shame?" she asked.

"More than anything I want to protect this baby. That's why we must marry," he replied, hoping his sincerity would mollify her enough to be reasonable.

"And you hope to achieve my compliance by threatening me?" She raised her brow. "A novel approach."

He smiled then. Her ire must be waning if her

sarcastic wit was emerging. He wondered if a kiss would change her mind and seal the arrangement?

Eleanor watched Sebastian's lips tighten and realized precisely where his thoughts were heading. He was going to kiss her, was he? Well, let him try.

She narrowed her eyes as tightly as she was able, but the dratted man only deepened his smile, his masculine presence overwhelming the room, dominating every corner of the feminine retreat she and Aunt Jane had created.

This was not happening! It had taken them weeks to locate this cottage and almost two months to establish themselves among the community as well-bred gentlewomen. And now Sebastian had threatened to expose her as an unwed expectant mother if she did not agree to marry him.

She tried to draw in a breath, but her lungs constricted. It exasperated her to be at his mercy, but her days of being a victim were over. If she decided to marry him it would be because she believed it to be best, not because he coerced her.

And she was considering it, even though she had just told him no. She assumed that his proposal was partially motivated by a sense of guilt, but that didn't overly concern her. She might not like it, but his argument had merit. There were practical reasons for accepting this offer that could not be dismissed out of hand.

Added to the practical were the emotional. After recovering from the initial shock of seeing Sebastian enter her parlor, Eleanor had felt a surprising rush of euphoria, followed by an overwhelming longing.

The deep, bruising ache of hurt and the blazing anger of betrayal she felt toward him were gone, no doubt mellowed by the passing of time and faded because she carried his child. She was wary and guarded, of course, but that was to be expected. Yet as she gazed into his eyes, the lure of what might be possible if she were willing to take a chance and marry him was a real temptation.

She still loved him. With an intensity that let her know for as long as she drew breath, logic would never play a role in her feelings for him. Love was not an emotion she could control. She must either reject or embrace it.

Did she dare surrender to the yearning deep inside? Would she be able to protect her unborn child from a father who might be uneasy around it, who might be emotionally distant?

Eleanor closed her eyes. These questions could not be duly weighed and considered while Sebastian stood in front of her, clouding her senses. And if he did kiss her, good heavens, her wits would truly scatter.

Her eyes popped open. "I will concede that your proposal deserves consideration. However, I will not be bullied by you or any man. I need time to contemplate your proposal and by God, I shall have it."

His gaze lingered on her lips for a heartbeat and then he nodded. "All right. If you promise that you will give my offer serious consideration, I will wait. But don't take too long, Eleanor. In order for the child to be legitimate we must marry before it is born."

* * *

Four days. For four days Sebastian cooled his heels at the local inn. Despite the comfortable accommodations, excellent service, and tasty food, he was miserable. Word had quickly spread that there was an earl staying at the inn and he had been besieged by the local gentry with invitations. He had politely refused them all, fearful of his reaction if he encountered Eleanor in a social situation.

Alas, his reclusive nature turned him into an even greater curiosity. He tried to keep to his rooms as much as possible, but eventually boredom set in and he would venture outside. Where he was immediately waylaid by virtual strangers, stared at and whispered over by nearly everyone he encountered. Ridiculous.

There had been no word from Eleanor and his notoriety made it impossible for him to visit or even write her, for he trusted no one to deliver the letters without announcing it to one and all. The lack of communication worried him and he feared she was ignoring him deliberately, simply waiting for him to leave so she could dismiss him from her life. The thought left him in a decidedly sour mood.

On the afternoon of his fifth day in what he now regarded as purgatory, Sebastian decided he had had enough. He would take out his mount for a long ride and make his way to Eleanor's cottage. He would strive to remain undetected, but if he were spotted, then so be it.

Plans made, he strode quickly to the public stables where his horse was being kept. As he hurried past the shops on the main street, he happened to glance inside one where he noticed a group of women clustered around a display table. Eleanor was among them.

The sight of her hit him with the force of a punch. She looked radiant, the swell of her abdomen barely visible beneath the folds of her cloak. The opportunity was too perfect to call it anything other than fate. True, he had promised her time to make her decision, but he had given her time.

He pushed the door open and strolled into the shop. Astonished silence greeted his arrival. "Good afternoon, ladies." He lifted his hat and gave them all a sweeping bow.

Eleanor's eyes grew round. Aunt Jane's lips thinned in disapproval. All the other women blushed, smiled, or did both. He noticed one fix her bonnet, another hastily pinch her cheeks to add color.

"Lord Tinsdale." A sharp-faced matron garbed in a hideous gown of deep orange answered his greeting, then swept into an awkward curtsy. The others quickly did the same, with the exception of Eleanor and Aunt Jane.

He smiled. "You will pardon the interruption, but when I spied all of you from the window I realized I could not go by without coming inside and greeting an old friend."

Several sets of eyebrows raised and a dull muttering was heard. Judging by the anxious glances the women were throwing at one another, it was clear they were taken aback by his statement.

"We were unaware that you counted someone among us as your friend," the matron admitted, casting a glare at the other women, obviously searching for the individual who had dared to with-hold such a juicy *on-dit.*

Sebastian flicked a glance at Eleanor. She remained silent, her grim scrutiny of him so intense it nearly burned a hole through the fabric of his jacket.

"How are you today, Mrs. Stewart?"

As expected, the resulting silence was deafening.

The matron's eyes narrowed with skepticism. "Mrs. Stewart? My goodness, whoever would have guessed? Why, you've been here these many days, my lord, and she has never once uttered a word about you to any of us. Pray, tell us, Mrs. Stewart, where did you meet his lordship?"

Eleanor visibly gritted her teeth before quietly muttering, "In London."

The matron flushed, the red in her face clashing markedly with the orange of her gown. "Aren't you the sly one, my dear. We had no idea you moved in such exalted social circles, did we, ladies?"

The women nodded fervently, their expressions accusatory. Eleanor's face drained of color. She looked helplessly from the group of women to him. Trembling, she opened her mouth to speak, then closed it, sighing in resignation.

Say it! Reveal her real name, her true rank, her lie. It's for her own good, as well as yours. Sebastian smiled softly, imagining Eleanor as his wife. Then he thought of the heartache and humiliation she would suffer when he told these women the truth. His smile slid away.

"'Twas actually Mr. Stewart with whom I was better acquainted," Sebastian said, laying a gentle hand on Eleanor's arm in an attempt to calm her trembling. "His untimely passing was a harsh blow to those of us who were privileged to know him, for he was an honorable man, one without equal, a man I was proud to call my friend."

"Indeed, Mr. Stewart was a man of unparalleled virtue," Aunt Jane broke in quickly, relief edging her voice. "It has been a sad and difficult time without him."

She tugged Eleanor away from Sebastian's grasp and after a hasty good-bye, hustled her out of the shop, leaving him behind to field the myriad of questions posed by a gossip-hungry group of women.

When he finally escaped, he could feel a headache starting behind his eyes. Thankfully, the fresh air offered some relief. Intending to get a great deal more of it, Sebastian headed purposefully toward the stables. He had just turned the corner when he heard his name being called.

His insides twisted at the sight of Eleanor rushing toward him. No doubt she was coming to thank him. And bid him farewell. 'Twas a bitter pill to swallow.

"You couldn't do it," she said breathlessly, her eyes shining. "You couldn't tell them the truth about me."

"No." He exhaled roughly, the bite of failure sharp in his chest. "But this does not mean I am going to abandon you and our child. I will send funds, make periodic visits to ensure—"

"I'll do it," she interrupted. "I'll marry you."

Sebastian paused, certain he had misheard. "Say that again."

"I'll marry you," she repeated, regarding him evenly.

"But your secret is safe, your position here as the widow Stewart even more secure now that the lie has been collaborated by me. An earl." He managed a wry smile and to his complete amazement she joined him.

"Yes, the ladies were most impressed. I had forgotten how darn charming you can be when you put your mind to it."

"So it was my charm that finally made you accept?" he asked lightly.

She shook her head. "The scene could not have been more perfect if it had been written in a play. Nearly every female of social importance gathered together in one place. It would have been so easy, effortless really, for you to have told them the truth. Yet you didn't expose me, Sebastian. You *couldn't* expose me." Her eyes softened. "And that gives me hope."

Chapter 19

They were wed three days later with a special license in a simple ceremony at a church en route to Yorkshire. A teary-eyed Aunt Jane and the vicar's wife served as witnesses. Eleanor wore a pale blue muslin gown made months ago in London by Madame Claudette, with the bust and seams let out to accommodate her fuller figure.

Her condition was noticeable, of course, but neither the vicar nor his wife made any comment or gave any indication that something was amiss. Eleanor decided they must have been paid very handsomely to effortlessly pull off such a warm, personal service on such short notice.

Throughout the ceremony Eleanor remained keenly aware of her handsome bridegroom, standing so still beside her. Many a woman would envy her good fortune at snagging such an impressive man for a husband, but Eleanor's feelings were decidedly mixed.

Sebastian's actions in the shop had renewed her faith in his character, had given her hope for the future, yet she knew well the risk she was taking. If she were wrong about him, she would be miserable, but it was her unborn child who would suffer the most.

The vicar paused, looking at her expectantly. *There is still time to back out.* Eleanor swallowed as a pang of fear twisted inside her. Was she making a horrible mistake?

Her nervous gaze swung to Sebastian. He tensed, sensing her conflict, probably wondering how he was going to explain things to the vicar if she turned on her heel and fled. Then Sebastian's warm hand closed gently over her cold one. She shuddered.

"'Tis your turn to recite the vows," he said, his voice low and steady.

Courage, Eleanor. She bit the inside of her cheek to calm herself, then carefully repeated the words, binding herself to him through this life, and the next, to a man she loved with all her heart. A man who made her uneasy.

Sebastian pushed the diamond-encrusted ring past her knuckle and settled it into place. It was done. They were married. Together they accepted congratulations from the vicar and his wife. Aunt Jane hugged her fiercely, then turned to Sebastian.

"I thought you a weasel of the first order the day you stormed into my drawing room, my lord," Aunt Jane proclaimed. "But my niece assures me there is more to your character. I must trust her judgment, yet only time will tell if my initial impression of you stands."

On that ominous note, they left the church, traveling to a nearby inn where Sebastian had arranged for a wedding supper to be served. Aunt

Jane accompanied them and Eleanor was glad of the company. She was not yet ready to be alone with her new husband.

Though the food was varied and well-prepared, Eleanor scarcely ate a bite during dinner. Sebastian did the same. She could not help but notice that he drank only one glass of wine. Aunt Jane finished the bottle and was snoring quietly in her chair by the time dessert was served.

"Our rooms have been made ready," Sebastian said after their uneaten dessert had been cleared. "You can retire whenever you wish."

"I think I'll go now," Eleanor replied. "It's been a long day."

She nudged Aunt Jane's shoulder. The older woman came awake slowly, frowning with momentary disorientation. The innkeeper's wife arrived to show Aunt Jane to her chamber, then returned to escort Eleanor.

"Our finest room," the innkeeper's wife announced proudly, taking Eleanor through a small sitting room into a spacious bedchamber.

Eleanor muttered her approval, trying to calm the butterflies rioting in her stomach and ignore the large bed occupying the majority of the space. Set against the wall, the tester bed rested on a pedestal, the blankets and sheets turned down for the night, the green velvet bed curtains untied and waiting to enclose the area.

With the help of her maid, Eleanor undressed, washed, and donned her usual nightclothes. In deference to it being her wedding night, she added a silk robe in a vivid shade of red, a gift from

Aunt Jane. By adjusting the folds of the garment she was able to cover her belly. Mostly.

Once alone, Eleanor sat in an armchair beside the window. She considered removing a book from her portmanteau but knew there was no way she could concentrate on the words or follow the story. Her nerves simply would not allow it.

Thinking about the day behind her and the night ahead were not options either. She struggled to fill her head with pleasant, inane images like a litter of puppies or the first buds of spring and had just succeeded in calming her nerves when the door opened.

Sebastian entered, wearing a dressing gown of sapphire blue. His chest was bare, but she could see the gray of his breeches peeking through when he walked. A faint quiver traveled through her.

He must have changed in the sitting room, but her thoughts had been so scattered, she hadn't heard him enter the suite. She watched silently as he shut and locked the door behind him, then went to the hearth. Grasping the poker, he stirred the flames.

"There's a distinct chill in the air this evening. Are you warm enough?" he asked.

Eleanor lowered her gaze. There was a time when he would have smiled at her with heavy-lidded eyes and made a suggestive remark about keeping her warm throughout the night no matter how cold it got. Self-consciously she tugged at her robe, adjusting it over her protruding middle and admitted that her wedding night nerves might very well be in vain.

Though he claimed his desire for her had not been feigned, she was very much aware of the reasons he had originally pursued her. Months ago perhaps she had been able to stir his blood in some small way, dressed in a fashionable gown and looking her best. But now?

Her pregnancy had brought many changes to her body. How could any man find her attractive, least of all someone with Sebastian's experience?

"The fire is fine," she said, finally answering his question, "the chamber comfortably warm."

He set the fireplace poker aside and crossed the room toward her, his expression shuttered, his eyes slightly narrowed. She scrambled to her feet, not wanting him to have the advantage of looking down at her. Her movements were hasty and clumsy, rendering her momentarily unsteady.

His arm shot out, grabbing her elbow. "I've got you," he said with a smile.

But do you want me? The words reverberated in her head and she sincerely hoped they did not show in her face. Her attraction to Sebastian was as strong as ever—it would be humiliating if he did not feel at least some desire for her.

His gaze moved down her body, pausing at her waist. When she stood, her silk robe had opened, revealing her nightgown and the roundness of her belly.

"I hadn't realized you were so big," he said, his voice tinged with awe. "It does not appear this pronounced beneath your clothes."

"Do you find me unsightly?" she asked nervously.

"No! I find all this strangely . . . intriguing." His hand moved down to her hip, resting there for a moment. Then he laid his palm over her belly, slowly tracing the shape. "It must have been a tremendous shock when you discovered your condition. How did you react? What did you feel?"

"Pure terror," she confessed. "If not for Aunt Jane's kindness and understanding I might have gone mad."

"Tell me," he said. "Tell me everything."

She almost refused, but something in his eyes compelled her to speak. She started slowly, but then the words fell over themselves as she opened her memories and relived the moments. She held back nothing, telling him of her fear and anger, worry and despair, and how those emotions had gradually turned to acceptance and then finally anticipation.

While she spoke, Sebastian's hand remained tightly splayed over her belly, almost as if he were trying to make a connection with the unborn child in her womb. It was an odd feeling, comforting, yet also erotically stimulating.

"I'm sorry I wasn't with you from the beginning," he said.

"That was my decision." She drew a quick breath. "Are you sorry about the baby?"

"Not precisely."

Hardly the most enthusiastic response, but at least it was honest. She wanted to probe deeper, to learn more about what he was thinking, feeling, but the baby suddenly shifted.

Sebastian's hand jerked away. "It moved!"

"Yes." Eleanor smiled. "That's been happening more and more frequently."

Sebastian's eyes widened. "Does it hurt?"

She shook her head. "It's reassuring. The doctor told me that a healthy, active fetus is a good sign."

"Hmm." Color crept up his neck.

"Don't tell me you are embarrassed?" Eleanor asked with a smile.

A peculiar expression flashed across his face. "If you must know, I'm feeling like a bit of a lecher."

"Why?"

"You're with child! In a delicate condition, a delicate state, and all I can think about is bedding you."

"Truly?"

He groaned. "Good God, Eleanor, my desire for you has never waned, never lessened. Not once in all the months we've been apart." To prove his words, Sebastian opened the front of his robe. Eleanor nearly blushed when she caught sight of his arousal, thick and heavy, straining against his breeches.

He hesitated and she realized he was waiting for her to let him know if she also desired him. Eleanor stared helplessly. She couldn't find her tongue, couldn't say what she wanted, since she honestly didn't know. On one hand it was a welcome relief to know he still found her appealing, yet was she ready to accept him as her lover? Was she ready to start trusting him?

Well, she had married him. *In for a penny, in for a pound.* "You once told me you would honor your marriage vows of fidelity," she said.

"I will."

"Even if we do not have carnal relations for a long, long time. Perhaps never."

His eyes flared. "I shall be faithful and cleave only to you. I have never forced a woman into my bed in my life. I most certainly do not intend to do so with my wife, a woman I respect above all others."

It was a good answer, delivered with a sincerity

that she believed. She lowered her guard, ever so slightly, allowing herself to remember how it felt to make love with him. The strength of his kisses, the pleasure of his touch, the power of his passion.

"My desire is not as obvious as yours, yet 'tis equally as strong. Force won't be necessary."

"Eleanor." Sebastian whispered her name throatily.

She went into his arms without thinking, her hunger for him like a storm, raging and passionate. They held each other for a long time, drawing strength from the embrace, tentatively reestablishing an emotional bond. She didn't want to think about the wrong he had done to her in the past or how vulnerable she would be if she opened her heart to him again. She wanted to believe in the good in him, in his vows of devotion, in his promise of fidelity.

Their lips met, and Eleanor clung to him, savoring the touch of his lips and wanting more. Time seemed to still as they shared long, heated kisses. Pleasure flowed through her veins. She could feel her breasts tighten and a restless heat settle between her legs. He stroked his fingers up and down her back and she leaned toward him, basking in the closeness.

Gently he pushed her robe and nightgown off her shoulders and slid the garments down over her breasts. Her nightclothes continued falling until they gathered at her ankles, leaving her naked, vulnerable.

"My darling Eleanor," he said in wonderment. "You are so very beautiful."

She blushed at his outrageous flattery, knowing she was at her core a plain-looking woman, yet in that moment she felt pretty, cherished. Relaxing further, she tingled with anticipation as Sebastian kissed his way along her jaw and throat, trailing kisses down to her breasts. With a groan he took a nipple into his mouth, nearly shattering her with the sensation.

He suckled and tasted until she was moaning, her fingers twined into his hair. She stretched on her toes, pushing herself closer to him as he lavished his loving attention on her, her breath heavy and uneven.

"We'd be far more comfortable in the bed," he muttered, lifting her in his arms.

She remained silent as he carried her there, setting her in the middle of the mattress. He removed his robe and trousers, then came down on top of her, keeping his weight on his elbows. The warmth of his naked flesh was an exquisite, erotic sensation and Eleanor heard herself whimper with need.

He began kissing her again, his knowing hands caressing her until she trembled. The blood quickening in her veins, Eleanor arched into the hard length of him, feeling his hot skin, his jutting arousal. He was hard as granite and she reached lovingly between their bodies to stroke him, then pulled him toward her, urging him to complete their joining.

"Please, Sebastian," she moaned. "I need you."

"Whatever the lady wants," he murmured against her lips.

He kissed her again, quick and hard, then gazed down into her eyes. Eleanor could feel his powerful thighs pressing her legs open and she forced herself to relax. He parted her with his fingers and eased into her. Gasping at the fullness, she bent her knees and twined her legs around his, pulling him in deeper.

He groaned loudly, a deep, male sound of satisfaction. A slow, deep rhythm began as he angled his body to give her the most pleasure, then drove into her, increasing the pulsing excitement between them until she screamed. The oncoming rush of completion overtook her, yet it was the unexpected opening of her heart that gave her the greatest pleasure.

He might have wounded her in the past, but when she was without him she had felt lost in emptiness, had retreated to the place inside herself where nothing could strike at her or hurt her. Joining with him again in this vulnerable, intimate act made her feel again, brought her back from the isolation.

Sebastian held her until she stopped shuddering, then started moving again, filling her with deep, penetrating strokes. She moaned in delight, gripping the sheet to stop herself from sliding up the bed.

She could feel his increasing urgency with each movement. His kisses grew rougher and she met him kiss for kiss. He was relentless, driving himself harder and faster and she welcomed it, hugging him tightly, straining her inner muscles to bring him release.

There was an instant of stillness before his entire body went rigid and a rush of his hot seed bathed her womb. Gradually his trembling stopped. He sighed, then slumped over her, his head coming to rest on her shoulder, his hair tickling her neck.

After a slight hesitation, she reached up and tightened her arms around him.

"Am I crushing you?" he asked in a sleepy voice.

"A little."

Muttering a curse, Sebastian lurched upward. "You should have said something sooner. Was I too rough? Are you hurt?"

She stared at him, one eyebrow lifted. "I'm fine, Sebastian. No need for such panic."

Sebastian scrutinized her closely, needing to assure himself that she had not suffered any ill effects from their rigorous lovemaking. Her expression was soft, not pained, her breathing calm, her eyes clear. Finally convinced she was indeed fine, Sebastian settled himself on the pillow next to her. There was a rustling of sheets and blankets as she reached for the covers, spreading them evenly over them.

"Sleep well," he said, hoping she would turn to him.

"You too."

He watched her adjust her position in the bed, a shot of disappointment piercing his heart when she turned onto her side to face away from him. Before long she dozed. Sebastian waited for several minutes, keen to any signs of her waking.

When he was convinced she was well and truly asleep, he moved himself into position and wrapped her in his arms. As the hours of night stretched on, he cradled her against him, a swell of possessiveness dominating all other emotions.

It felt so good to hold her again, to feel her warmth, to hear her deep, even breaths, to watch over her as she slept. His mind was no longer

tortured by worry and doubt, was no longer speculating about where she was, what she was doing.

Gradually, Sebastian began to relax, the misery
that had haunted him for the past few months
fading, a ray of hope replacing it. Here in the cocoon
of darkness without the past pressing in upon them,
anything seemed possible. Including a happy life together.

With a soft, gentle touch, Sebastian nuzzled his
cheek against hers, then pressed his lips to her
temple. "I love you, Eleanor," he whispered.

It was the first time he said the words aloud, and
although she did not hear them, it made him feel
whole expressing what was in his heart.

Whole and hopeful. Not a bad start, considering
their tumultuous past, a history that stood between
them so solidly they might never be able to overcome
it. Yet more than ever, Sebastian was determined
to try—and even more determined to succeed.

The next morning they began their journey
north, to Sebastian's new estate. Aunt Jane had
elected to return to Bath and Sebastian was relieved. It was awkward enough trying to establish a
relationship with Eleanor; having a critical audience
observing it all was a complication he neither welcomed nor wanted.

Due to his motion sickness, Sebastian was unable
to join Eleanor inside the coach he hired for the
journey, yet he purposely rode beside her window
whenever the width of the road allowed. Occasionally she would lower the glass and they would

exchange a few words, but the arrangement was hardly conducive to meaningful conversation.

There was an unmistakable underlying tension between them when they stopped for the night that gradually escalated as the evening progressed. Though his desire to make love to her never faltered, Sebastian felt it presumptuous to assume Eleanor would welcome him in her bed and made certain their accommodations included a sitting room.

Thankfully he did not need to use it. He spent his nights making love to his wife, striving to make a connection between them that at times felt so close, but continued to elude him. Though she was passionate and enthusiastic, Eleanor seemed to be holding herself away from him, keeping a part hidden that she refused to share.

Each night he waited until she fell into an exhausted, sated sleep before cradling her lovingly in his arms. Only then was he able to achieve his own slumber.

Sebastian kept telling himself it was not a bad beginning. They were civil to each other, polite and respectful. She smiled when he joked with her, appeared interested when he discussed his plans for the various properties he owned, expressed her thanks when he saw to her comfort and needs.

It was those pleasant moments that gave him pause and kept his spirits bolstered thinking that things with his new wife would improve, that the detachment she cultivated so carefully would end. And much of the time he actually believed it.

On the afternoon of the fourth day they arrived. Sebastian pulled his mount beside the carriage after

they pulled through the tall iron gates. He heard
Eleanor's gasp of surprise and followed her gaze to
the sprawling house up ahead. Built during the
time of Henry VIII, the mansion boasted numerous
chimneys and rooftops and more rooms than one
could count.

It was a charming, romantic stone facade, complete with battlements at the corners, yet as they
drew closer, the neglect of the property was evident
from the weed-choked drive to the dirt and grime
accumulated on the diamond-shaped glass panes.

"Did the staff know of our arrival?" Eleanor asked.

"Word was sent ahead so they would not be taken
unawares," Sebastian answered, a frown creasing his
brow. This was not how he wanted to welcome his
bride to their new home.

Things did not improve once the rented coach
rolled up to the front of the house, for there were
no servants to greet them. Sebastian dismounted
and handed his horse off to one of the outriders,
then assisted Eleanor out of the carriage. As Sebastian was wondering if they were going to have
to knock on the massive oak door to gain entrance, it opened and a petite gray-haired woman
stepped out.

"Good afternoon." Her gaze lit with curiosity and
speculation.

"Hello. Are you Mrs. Ellis, perchance?" Sebastian
asked, grateful to have recalled the housekeeper's
name. It was listed among the many notes sent to
him about the estate by his solicitor.

"I am Mrs. Ellis. And you must be the new earl,"
she answered, dropping a perfunctory curtsy. "I

regret to say I cannot provide much of a welcome, but I shall try my best."

"Are you here alone?" Sebastian asked.

"Nearly. We've been short-staffed for years. The earl always claimed it was a foolish waste of money paying servants when he wasn't in residence, though those who were hired were rarely paid a decent wage. As you can see, 'tis a very large house. I do my best, but without help . . ." Her voice trailed off and then she shrugged unapologetically.

"Your best is not very impressive, Mrs. Ellis," Sebastian stated dryly.

"But I feel confident it will improve with a trained staff behind you," Eleanor interjected, pressing herself forward. "'Tis good to meet you. I am Lady Tinsdale."

The housekeeper looked momentarily stunned. "I was not informed that the countess would be coming," she said stiffly. "The manor is barely fit for a gentleman to occupy. It certainly won't do for a lady, especially one in your delicate condition."

"No need to fret, Mrs. Ellis. I'm far hardier than I appear," Eleanor replied smoothly, linking her arm through Sebastian's. He smiled. It felt good to have Eleanor beside him.

Sebastian drew himself up. "We should like tea served in the drawing room at once and after that a tour of the house," he declared, his voice ringing with authority. "Please see to it, Mrs. Ellis."

As he walked through the massive oak door, Sebastian became aware of Eleanor's fingers digging into his arm.

"Brace yourself," she whispered. "Mrs. Ellis's

calculated expression makes me think she has planned your welcome very carefully."

The moment they entered the house, Sebastian knew Eleanor was right. The ancient entrance hall boasted ornate plasterwork that was covered in cobwebs. The paint was faded in sections, lighter in others, indicating the areas where paintings or tapestries had once hung. The shabbiness increased as they passed through several sparsely furnished rooms before reaching a drawing room with a decidedly musty odor.

There was evidence of a hurried cleaning, but the silver was unpolished, the worn carpet dirty at the edges, the fire unlit. Hoping to dissipate the unpleasant smell, Sebastian pushed open a set of velvet drapes. Choking dust flew through the air, the motes floating in the sunbeams streaming through the mullioned windows like tiny snowflakes.

Sebastian turned at the sound of Eleanor's sneezing, his expression grim. "Should we sack Mrs. Ellis the moment she returns?" he asked, handing her his handkerchief.

"No. Let's wait and see how quickly she can recover," Eleanor replied, wiping her watery eyes. "To be fair, I'm sure the earl was a neglectful, absentee employer. It is impossible to run a household of this size without an adequate, well-trained, well-paid staff. I'm sure this demonstration was intended to emphasize that point with you."

"It has succeeded," Sebastian acknowledged, the chair creaking as he sat down.

Tea arrived, brought by a young man with a nervous gap-tooth smile. The mundane, domestic task of having Eleanor pour and prepare a plate for him lightened Sebastian's mood. He was hungry after their journey, though he paused a moment before taking a bite of cake, afraid Mrs. Ellis might have taken her household crusade too far and done something to the food.

"The cakes and sandwiches are delicious," Eleanor commented. "Though I waited until you ate one before trying mine."

A laugh rumbled up from his chest. "You always were an intelligent woman."

"I thought the mismatched china a nice touch," Eleanor remarked as she poured them each a second cup of tea.

"Along with the frayed napkins," Sebastian said, tossing his linen on a low table.

He knew he should be infuriated by all of this, but Eleanor's calm presence tempered his mood. Besides, there were other far more important matters in his life than a shabby, ill-equipped estate. Like earning the trust and love of his wife.

Mrs. Ellis entered the room, her expression still sullen. "Do you wish a tour now, my lord?"

"No. I fear the dirt and grime will distress the countess and depress me," he replied, allowing a bit of the outrage he felt to infuse his tone. "We will view the house after you have had an opportunity to clean it thoroughly." Ignoring the housekeeper's muffled gasp, Sebastian continued. "Send to the village for however many servants are needed, but I expect the main rooms on the first floor to be thoroughly cleaned by tomorrow afternoon. Is that clear, Mrs. Ellis?"

"Yes, my lord."

"Excellent."

"Since I did not know Lady Tinsdale was coming, only the master's suite has been prepared," Mrs. Ellis said, her gaze sweeping the ground.

"No matter. The countess and I will share the chamber," Sebastian answered. "'Tis how we prefer it."

There was a squeak of surprise from the maid clearing away the tea tray. She hastened out the door, the housekeeper on her heels. There was a long moment of silence and then Eleanor started giggling.

"Perfect," she said, a smile still tugging at her lips. "Now you've scandalized the servants. All within the first hour of our arrival."

Sebastian lifted his brow mockingly. "A new record for me, I believe."

"Hmm. Let's hope there isn't a fountain on the property. The moment you take one of your infamous swims, your reputation will be sealed."

"Honestly, Eleanor, servants enjoy the eccentricities of their employers. It makes them feel superiorly moral."

"That might have been the case in your past, my lord, but you now need to be respectable."

"However will I manage?"

"It will be nigh impossible, I fear," she quipped as she broke into giggles.

Sebastian's heart melted. Impulsively he reached for her hand, gripping it tightly. "I adore hearing you laugh."

"It does feel good."

He lifted their clasped hands to his mouth and kissed her wrist. She smiled tenderly and his heart soared. "Come, let's go inspect the master's chambers, my dearest. Frankly, I cannot wait to see the surprises that await us."

Chapter 20

Life settled into a domestic pattern over the next few weeks that Eleanor found both comforting and surreal. Under the watchful eye of Mrs. Ellis, the manor house was thoroughly cleaned, then slowly put in order. Antique treasures were discovered in the attic rooms, along with mice-eaten tapestries and broken furniture.

Eleanor rescued the pieces she liked, gave away what she didn't, and threw out the rest. She hired local craftsmen and frequented all the village shops for the necessary materials, giving the local economy a much-needed boost. Though Sebastian explained it was necessary to set aside substantial funds for improvements to the tenant farms and estate acreage, he gave her a generous household budget. It felt wonderfully cathartic redoing the various rooms, creating a home that was uniquely hers.

By unspoken agreement she and Sebastian worked hard at being an exemplary couple. They spoke to each other in modulated, polite tones and were always civil in public and private. Eleanor consulted

Sebastian over all the major decisions she made in the house; he asked her opinion on the management of the estate. They entertained the local gentry and went to church on Sunday. She made visits to the tenant farms. He accompanied her.

He treated her with respect and kindness, encouraging her to speak her mind. They discussed art, music, and books, agreeing on the merits of some pieces and engaging in spirited debates on others. He complimented her appearance at least once a day, even as her mirror clearly demonstrated how round and plump her body was becoming.

Awaiting her each morning on her dressing table was a silver vase with a single white rose inside. Warmth blossomed in her chest every time she saw it, but the day she caught Sebastian placing the rose inside the vessel, her heart opened a little bit more.

They shared a bed every night, oftentimes making love. Sebastian never failed to satisfy her, and himself, exploring her newly discovered sensuality with passion and skill. His carnal desire helped to weaken her emotional defenses, yet despite all their efforts, there existed a barrier of caution between them and too often she felt unsure about the strength of their relationship.

Sighing, Eleanor drew out a fresh sheet of parchment and began writing suggestions for next week's menus. She was still debating whether they should have lamb or beef on Tuesday when she heard the sound of muffled voices coming from outside her window.

Curious, Eleanor left her writing desk to investigate. An unknown carriage had reached the front door, the occupants slowly disembarking.

Two gentlemen on horseback accompanied the carriage and then Sebastian rode into view.

Lean, tall, and broad-shouldered, he was coatless, dressed in a full-sleeved white shirt, snug black breeches, and knee-high boots. She could clearly see the muscles in his thighs as he swung effortlessly off his horse, then strode forward to greet the others.

Her heart began to pound. The sight of him made her breath catch in her throat, made her feel powerless to turn away. Why did he have this effect on her? How could the mere sight of him at times reduce her to a giggling schoolgirl?

Almost as if sensing her regard, Sebastian looked up at the window. She froze. Their eyes met and he smiled. A sensual heat flushed across her chest, striking at her heart. She sternly told herself to trust that emotion, to let it crush the tiny seeds of doubt lurking inside. To believe they could have a life together built on a foundation of love.

Was it possible? Preoccupied with these heady thoughts, and the sight of her handsome husband, Eleanor barely noticed the individuals who had climbed out of the coach.

Despite her ever expanding belly, her footsteps treaded lightly on the polished floors as she went down to greet the guests. She entered the drawing room unannounced, her eyes landing on a group of four people gathered near the fire, seeking the warmth to chase away the late autumn chill. She immediately identified the Reverend Chancellor and his wife, along with their nearest neighbor, Sir Thomas, but the other man was a stranger.

Or was he? Of medium height, with blond-streaked

hair and a strong, firm jaw, there was something about him. . . . Surprise rose in Eleanor's throat. *It wasn't possible, was it?* She stared almost rudely at the gentleman, cataloging the familiar features that were unchanged but for the maturity of age.

He surveyed her with equal intensity. "Lady Eleanor?"

It was him! Her lips parted in a disbelieving smile and her heart filled with genuine joy as she grasped his outstretched hand in greeting. "John Tanner. It's been a very long time since I've seen you," she said, gazing into the astonished eyes of the man she had loved so passionately when she was a young woman.

Standing near the doorway, Sebastian scowled as he watched the awestruck look of delight on Eleanor's face. Who was that man to her? Obviously someone she knew well.

Sebastian moved to speak with his neighbors, his eyes ever mindful of his wife sitting cozily next to this unknown Mr. Tanner.

"Tell me, Sir Thomas, is Tanner originally from this area?" Sebastian asked.

"No. I believe he was born and raised somewhere in the countryside not too far from London. He set out as a young man to make his fortune in the Colonies and has now returned with an eye toward acquiring property in the area."

Sebastian didn't like the sound of that plan. "Do you happen to know what line of work he was in before he left England?"

"As a matter of fact, I do. He was a groom. For an earl, I think, though I'm not sure which one. Tanner might have made his fortune in mining, but the man still has a way with horses."

Sir Thomas accepted a glass of whiskey from a footman, nodding his head in thanks. Sebastian refused a drink, a lump of jealousy forming in his chest. He knew only that the man Eleanor had loved as a girl was someone she classified as unsuitable. A groom would certainly qualify.

He wanted to ask more questions, but the reverend and his wife joined them.

"Isn't it an astonishing coincidence, my lord? Lady Eleanor and Mr. Tanner knew each other when they were younger." Mrs. Chancellor took a dainty sip of her Madeira, then smiled cheerfully. "I vow they have a great deal of catching up to do."

Sebastian grinned, feigning polite surprise and interest, all the while aware of the blood pounding through his veins and roaring in his ears. He had difficulty following the ensuing conversation, as his eyes kept straying to Eleanor. Her head was bent close to Tanner's as they spoke, the privacy and intensity of their discussion obvious.

Sebastian's first inclination was to stalk across the room, pull Tanner to his feet, and shove him out the door, but he somehow managed to hold his temper in check. He would not act boorishly and embarrass his wife in front of their guests no matter how extreme the emotions churning inside him.

After ten agonizing minutes, Sebastian gazed again at Eleanor, almost willing her to glance his way. Miraculously, she did. Relief soothed his pride when their eyes met. He smiled at her. She smiled vaguely back, then immediately turned her attention to the man beside her.

The pain burst inside his chest, slicing him to the marrow. Sebastian's jaw ached with the effort to hold back his emotions, but somehow he did, keeping his jealousy at a slow, steady simmer, controlled and contained beneath a congenial facade. At the conclusion of the visit, he even managed to walk the guests out to their carriage, bowing politely to Mrs. Chancellor and shaking hands firmly with the men.

The urge to crush Tanner's hand as he gripped it was childish and nearly all-consuming, but Sebastian forced his fingers to loosen before arousing the other man's suspicions. The rational side of his brain told him he was acting like a fool, but even after living together for weeks, Sebastian was no closer to knowing his wife's true feelings for him, and that uncertainty left him vulnerable.

Fingers curling into fists at his sides, Sebastian made his way back to the drawing room. Eleanor was still seated on the settee gazing out the window, her pensive gaze focused on the departing carriage. Daydreaming about her young lover?

"Tanner was the one, wasn't he?" Sebastian asked without preamble. "The young man of noble character you fell in love with when you were a girl?"

"Yes." Her whimsical smile tore at Sebastian's heart. "John was a groom in my father's household. Kind, considerate, always ready to listen to the hopes and dreams of a lonely girl. We were so foolish, yet so determined. I doubt there is anything in this world more impractical than young lovers."

Sebastian stiffened, but she seemed not to notice. "He appears to have made his mark in the American

Colonies. Sir Thomas said he possesses a sizable fortune."

"Yes, he's been remarkably successful."

Sebastian fidgeted with a silver button on the cuff of his shirt. "Was that what you were discussing for so long? His success?"

"That and other things. A lot has happened since we last saw each other."

"Is he married?"

"No. Though he hopes one day to settle down. John was always a man who valued family."

A true paragon. Sebastian gave an impolite snort. "Did you encourage him to buy land in the county? Sir Thomas said Tanner was looking for a property to purchase."

"John mentioned he wanted to find a good place to set down roots. I hope that he does stay here. I'm sure he would make an excellent neighbor." Her expression turned thoughtful. "Sebastian, whatever is the matter? You look positively thunderstruck."

Sebastian swallowed convulsively, looking into her lovely face. This was harder than he thought it would be. He wanted so much to be unselfish, to be able to make the noble choice and sacrifice his own happiness for hers, yet the very idea of losing her made him break out in a cold sweat.

"You deserve to be happy, Eleanor, and more than anything I want to be fair to you. 'Tis clear your affection for this man remains strong, yet I must insist that you stay well away from him. The consequences if you rekindle this relationship would be disastrous."

Her mouth dropped open. "Is that what you

think? That I am interested in a romance with John?"

"I know that he wants you."

"Oh, really? After being reacquainted for less than an hour. Not to mention that I am married and round with another man's child, yet John and I are going to begin an illicit love affair? I would be insulted by that remark if the very idea of it wasn't so ridiculous."

"What's wrong with your figure? 'Tis voluptuous. You are glowing, for Christ's sake. Of course he wants you. Any man who doesn't is a fool." Sebastian leaned in closer. "Tanner is still in love with you. 'Tis obvious in every glance he casts in your direction."

"I'm sure you are mistaken about John's feelings." Color swept into her cheeks. "Our relationship ended long ago."

"In affairs of the heart the passing of time matters little."

"You speak from experience, no doubt," she remarked.

"Actually, yes." He caught her hand. "My love for you has not wavered for months. In fact, it only grows stronger, which is why I cannot willingly let you go. Truth be told, I will fight to keep you."

"You love me that much?" she asked, going very still.

"With all of my heart, with all of my being. Surely you know that, Eleanor? I feel a rush of euphoria every time I set eyes on you, pleasure at the mere sound of your voice. My heart races when I hold you in my arms. When I wake early in the morning, I find that even in sleep I've reached for you, overwhelmed by the need to touch you, to connect with you.

"I know things are far from perfect between us, yet I also know I could not bear how hollow my life would be without you in it." He knelt before her. "Thanks to you I am learning to believe in myself, to believe that I can be a man worthy of your love. You can't expect me to forsake the dream that someday it will come to pass. 'Tis too cruel."

Her eyes grew enormous. "I'm not asking that of you, Sebastian."

His relief was so strong he nearly slumped forward. "Then there is still hope for us."

"Oh, dearest, there is far more than hope. There is love, too." Her face broadened into a wide smile. "You're jealous!"

"That pleases you?"

"That delights me! The scowl on your face, the passion in your voice. *'I will fight to keep you.'* You truly love me, don't you?"

"More than anything. And I fervently hope that someday soon you will return my love."

She slid her arms around his neck and leaned into him. "That day has arrived, Sebastian. I love you. With all of *my* heart and all of *my* being. It feels like it has always been that way. Even when I was angry and hurt, my love for you never waned, never faded. I was simply too afraid to trust in it, to believe in it. But no longer."

"Oh, Eleanor." Her words caught at his heart. He lifted his chin and brushed her lips, then pulled her closer for a deep, ardent kiss. She slid gently off the settee and he caught her in his lap, fitting her perfectly against his chest.

"Now, just to make certain, you have no strong feelings for Tanner?" Sebastian asked when the kiss was done.

"Heaven's no! I will always remember with great fondness the regard we shared all those years ago. But I was a girl at the time, and now that I am a woman, I know that I need a man," she said softly, her eyes shining with love. "And you, sir, are the only one that I want."

Eleanor and Sebastian spent the next few days in the master bedchamber ensconced in each other's arms, forgetting the world outside. In between bouts of sensual, creative lovemaking, they slept, ate sumptuous meals brought on trays by blushing servants, and talked. And it was in those days that they realized the peace and contentment they had each sought so diligently to uncover was to be found in the love they shared.

Spooned in Sebastian's arms among the rumpled bed linens, savoring the feel of his strong, hard body, Eleanor sighed with delight. Her body was warm and sated, her heart brimming with joy. Easing away slightly so she could gaze at her love while he slept, she turned her head. And met two mischievous gray eyes.

"Oh, good. You're awake." Sebastian dipped his chin and claimed her lips. For a long, sensual moment Eleanor yielded to his passionate invitation, opening herself fully to the sensations. Her breathing was rough and unsteady when she pulled away and then she heard him whisper, "I love you, Eleanor."

"Tell me again," she replied, touching her fingertips to his lips, adoring the desire she saw reflected in his face.

"Lady Tinsdale, despite your ridiculous new title—by the way, have I mentioned how much I dislike our new name? I much preferred being Benton—anyway, I wanted to say that I love you. And adore you. Your clever wit, your unmatched charm, your loyal heart, your honorable nature. I cherish you for the rare jewel of womanhood that you are and if you need to hear more, I shall continue singing your praises and proclaiming my love until I no longer have breath."

"I believe that will suffice for this afternoon, my lord." Eleanor smiled, moving her hand to his cheek, knowing she was without question the luckiest woman in the world. The doubts that had plagued her had melted away the moment she had witnessed Sebastian's jealousy, the moment she realized the love he carried so strongly in his heart was deep and true.

He found her mouth again, and she felt the tenderness, as well as the passion, in his touch. Things were just starting to get interesting when a loud knock sounded on their bedchamber door.

"My lord, I apologize for disturbing you," a male voice on the other side called out.

"Then don't," Sebastian shouted at their butler. "Go away."

There was a slight pause. "I will, naturally, do as you bid, but first I must know what to do with a delivery from London that has just arrived."

Sebastian looked down at Eleanor. "Did you order anything from Town?"

She thought for a moment, then shook her head. "Lady Tinsdale has not ordered anything from London. Whatever it is, send it back at once."

There was the distinct sound of feet scuffling, then a white folded sheet of parchment was shoved beneath the closed door. "This note accompanied the delivery. And might I add, my lord, 'tis a very large cart and a very, very large crate."

Grumbling with annoyance, Sebastian leapt from the bed. "Oh, for Christ's sake, must I do everything around here?" Eleanor turned on her side to admire the view as her naked husband retrieved the note, broke the seal, and began reading it. "It's from Atwood. Apparently he and Lady Dorothea have sent us a wedding gift."

Eleanor sat up in bed, clutching the sheet to her bare breasts. "And it required a cart to deliver it?"

"A very *large* cart, if our butler is to be believed," Sebastian emphasized. "I'd best go down and investigate or else we'll never get any peace."

"Wait, I'm coming too. After all, a wedding gift is meant for both parties."

Sebastian threw on a pair of breeches and a shirt while Eleanor hurried into a simple day gown. Sebastian obligingly assisted with the hooks at the back of her dress, though he insisted on pausing every few moments to press kisses on her neck and shoulders. Finally presentable, they descended the stairs together, Sebastian's warm hand on the small of her back guiding her through the foyer and out the front door.

Once outside the house, they didn't have far to

travel. There was indeed an enormous crate awaiting them, one that took five men to lift from the cart and set down in the middle of the drive. Eleanor watched with growing curiosity as the boards were pulled off and the straw packed around the item pulled away.

"Hellfire and damnation!" Sebastian yelled, before he broke into laughter.

Eleanor moved closer for a better look, tugging away more of the straw. "Isn't that the fountain from Lord Atwood's garden?" she asked.

"The very same," Sebastian replied. "And it's even more hideous than I remember."

Eleanor tilted her head to the side for a better view, trying to find something to compliment. But there were too many spouting statues, too many columns and shells and trailing vines, too much marble, too much of everything to appreciate the craftsmanship. "I had not realized it was so . . ."

"Ugly? Gaudy? Enormous?" Sebastian circled around it slowly, his face wreathed in amusement. "The first time I set eyes on this monstrosity, I knew Atwood would eventually find a way to get rid of it. But I never imagined this would be how he'd do it. He's a damn clever man."

"Well, we obviously have to keep it. Atwood is one of your closest friends. No doubt he and Lady Dorothea will come to visit one day. It would be horribly rude if their wedding gift was nowhere to be found."

"We could say it was broken on the journey," Sebastian suggested, taking a hammer from one of the footmen.

"No, wait!" Eleanor cried, as he swung his arm

upward. "Though I appreciate and value your newfound maturity and sense of responsibility, never let it be said that marriage has turned you into a priggish, stuffy man. I have heard a great deal about them from your friends, yet have not witnessed one of your infamous fountain swims."

"And you won't, at least not until the weather warms." Sebastian slowly lowered his arm. "Still, I fear your good taste will be soundly questioned if we prominently display the fountain."

A burst of laughter caught in Eleanor's throat. "This is a very large estate. Surely we can find a secluded spot somewhere. Then, when the mood strikes . . ." Her voice trailed off and she lifted her brow suggestively.

He smiled broadly, then slid an arm around her shoulders. "If I swim, you go with me," he whispered. "Without wearing a stitch of clothing."

She pulled back to eye him, her face warming at his sensual expression. Life with Sebastian was many things, but it was never dull. "Why, my love, I think that's a simply marvelous idea!"

Epilogue

An agony-filled scream pierced the late afternoon stillness. Sebastian cringed, the sound reverberating through his entire being. Swallowing hard, he adjusted the brush in his hand and resumed the rhythmic stroking of his horse. Standing just outside the stall, Lord Waverly paused, bit his bottom lip, then resumed his pacing.

Sebastian struggled to keep his mind blank, to ignore what was happening inside the manor house, in his own bed, knowing if he pictured Eleanor's suffering he would surely go mad. Twelve hours. For twelve hours she had been laboring to bring their child into the world and still no results.

Good God, how much more of this can she endure? Can I endure?

"I heard the Tories' plan to introduce an agricultural bill in this next session of Parliament. Do you think it's worth considering?" Waverly asked.

Sebastian scowled. Waverly was doing a heroic job trying to distract him, but there was nothing anyone could say that would ease his torment. And while he appreciated the effort, Sebastian had long since passed the time when he even bothered to reply.

He was, however, glad of the company and he knew Eleanor was grateful to have her sister by her side. She had initially protested when Bianca announced she would attend the birth. Though married, Bianca was not yet a mother and Eleanor expressed her worry at her delicate sister witnessing the still unknown mysteries of childbirth.

Lord Waverly had voiced a similar concern, especially after the couple revealed they had recently learned that Bianca was also expecting a child. Yet Bianca refused to budge on the matter and stubbornly insisted until she got her way. Apparently, the sweet, shy, accommodating Bianca was maturing into an opinionated, strong-willed woman.

Another cry, louder, longer, shriller than the others, sounded through the air. Sebastian felt his knees weaken. Enough! Not caring that he had been thrown out of the chamber three times already, Sebastian stormed from the stables, tossing the brush in the corner as he ran.

There were four women in the bedchamber—well, five including Eleanor. One maid, the midwife, Aunt Jane, and Bianca. He was turning soft if he couldn't manage his way past that group, even if the midwife's arms were thick and beefy.

"Wait!" Waverly shouted. The younger man grabbed his shoulders and hauled him back. "I was instructed to keep you away from the bedchamber. Bianca will have my head if I fail at my task."

Cursing, Sebastian turned, fists flying. "Damn it,

Waverly, what will you do when it's Bianca brought to bed in childbirth?"

Waverly paled, then slowly released his grip. "Will you at least tell her I tried to stop you?"

For the first time in many hours Sebastian smiled. "I'll say you nearly ripped my arm from its socket."

Waverly nodded. "Good luck."

Unencumbered, Sebastian stormed into the manor and bounded up the stairs, taking them two at a time. On the way he passed several servants, their faces lined with worry. *They love her too,* he realized, though in his heart he knew he should not be surprised. Eleanor was a kind, fair mistress who appreciated the good work they did. She had turned their Yorkshire estate into a home that made them all proud.

Throwing open their bedchamber door, Sebastian marched inside. Bianca turned the moment he entered, a wide smile upon her face. "Sebastian! We were just going to call you. Look, you have a son. Isn't he beautiful?"

She held the babe out proudly, but Sebastian barely glanced at her arms. Ignoring her, he strode forward, his gaze locked on Eleanor. She lay pale and motionless in the center of the large bed, a sheet drawn to her neck.

"Why is she so still?" he croaked, dropping to his knees beside his wife. Fingers trembling, he lifted Eleanor's hand and pressed it to his cheek.

"She's exhausted, my lord," the midwife said. "Birthing is hard work."

"She's sleeping?" he ventured as he smoothed the damp tendrils of hair off her forehead.

"Yes," Aunt Jane replied. "It has been a very long, hard ordeal for Eleanor. You need to let her rest."

Logically, Sebastian knew she was right. Yet he also knew there was no force on earth strong enough to wrench him away from his wife's side. He pressed a gentle kiss onto her palm. The steady beat of her pulse reassured him, yet he wished she would open her eyes.

Almost as if she were aware of his dilemma, Eleanor's eyelids fluttered, then slowly opened. "Sebastian, where's the baby? Where is our son?"

Her voice was hoarse, raw from hours of screaming. It pained him to hear it. He signaled to his sister-in-law and Bianca came forward, placing the small bundle she held in the crook of Eleanor's arm. Then she and the other women discreetly exited the room, leaving the new parents alone.

Eleanor stared down at the child while Sebastian continued to gaze at her. Her face was pale, nearly ashen, and there were dark circles beneath her eyes. He swallowed against the tightness in his throat, knowing he might have lost her, realizing it would have been impossible to go on without her.

"There are tufts of dark hair on his head," Eleanor muttered in awe. "And look, he has a strong brow and square chin."

With an audible swallow, Sebastian looked down at the child. There was something vaguely familiar about the infant's features, a likeness that caused Sebastian's memory to stir. The infant took a shuddering breath, then opened his eyes.

Sebastian gasped. The resemblance was unmistakable and nothing short of remarkable.

"Oh, Sebastian," Eleanor cried. "He looks just like—"

"Your father," Sebastian finished, his lips breaking into an ironic grin.

"Dear Lord." Eleanor shifted, clasping the babe closer to her breast, her protective mothering instincts emerging. Sebastian wondered at the fates that were so determined to test his measure, so intent on seeing him fall, and decided that retribution for past sins clearly came in many forms.

There was no way he could not respond to the wary plea in Eleanor's eyes. Taking a determined breath, he once again observed the child. Fuzzy and unfocused, the baby nevertheless managed to meet his eyes with unfailing accuracy. The initial shock started to fade and in its place Sebastian felt a warmth blossom inside his chest, softening his heart. The child was a miracle, rare and precious, someone to nurture, cherish, and protect.

"I believe I've just fallen in love for the second time in my life," Sebastian whispered, his voice choking with emotion.

Reaching out, he stroked his finger along Eleanor's brow, then gently touched the baby's cheek. The infant blinked in response and flailed his fists, nearly striking Sebastian on the chin.

"Manners, young man," Eleanor cooed. "You must be respectful of your papa."

Papa. Sebastian closed his eyes. He was a father! "I love you with all my heart, Eleanor. Thank you for my son. He is a beautiful baby."

"He is rather perfect, is he not?" Eleanor sniffed, a single tear falling down her cheek.

"He's damn brilliant," Sebastian insisted. "Oh, my love, don't cry."

"I'm so happy, Sebastian. And relieved."

Sebastian understood. Though he had tried not to show it these past few months, it had worried him also. How would he react when the baby was born? Would he truly be able to unselfishly love a child who carried the earl's blood?

"It doesn't matter that he looks like your father," Sebastian said calmly. "Honestly. He could look like my bloody horse and I'd still want him, still love him. Because you are his mother."

Eleanor gave him a watery smile. "Though I'm not thrilled at our son's resemblance to the earl, I am relieved he doesn't look like your horse." She kissed the top of the infant's head, nuzzling him close. "Aunt Jane told me that babies change a great deal as they grow. Perhaps the resemblance will diminish."

"It might. Either way, it doesn't matter." Sebastian's heart lightened and a rush of optimism flowed through his veins. "He's ours, Eleanor. All ours. We will share our love with him, teach him right from wrong, show him how to be strong and honorable. I have no doubts he will do his mother proud."

"And his father."

"Yes." Smiling broadly, Sebastian leaned forward and sealed that promise with a kiss, pouring all the joy and love he felt so keenly into it.